The Sisters of Siam

A novel of 19th-century Thailand

Caron Eastgate Dann

Second revised edition

First edition published as The Occidentals by Asia Books, Bangkok, 1999 (under the name Caron Eastgate James). Published in German as Das Erbe der Schwestern, by Nymphenburger, Munich, 2003 (hardback); by Knaur, Munich, 2005 (paperback); and by TechniSat, 2007 (audio).

Cover photo by: Caron Eastgate Dann

Contents

Prologue

The smell of cigar smoke lingered in the dark, silent house, and he shrank back toward the sash window he had climbed in by.

What if the man were still here? The last thing he wanted was to cause a disturbance—for he had come only to claim what was his. But then he recalled that, of course, she never allowed her gentleman callers to stay the night. Most of them were expected home, anyway.

It wasn't really stealing, he tried to convince himself. It was merely settling the score. He would certainly not be able to sell the thing here—and perhaps not anywhere—but if he could not have it, then he wanted to make sure she could not, either. He would rather bury it in his garden for someone else's eureka, perhaps a century hence. In any case, she would never know for sure that it had been him. Rogues abounded here, and it could be anyone who had stolen it. He would go home to Melbourne with it tomorrow. Home to his wife. He would figure out the rest later.

If only the woman had stuck to their deal—their 'gentleman's agreement', so to speak—their secret stake, in her name, its obtaining paid for by him, with profits to be shared between them. They had planned to escape together, and he would surely have lost everything else once his double life was discovered.

When he had made his lucky strike, he considered it a fortuitous sign, that he and the woman were meant to be together. But she soon became distant. She began making excuses that she had to be elsewhere. Business was brisk, she said, no time to dilly-dally. She was seldom at home when he called, and finally, in the saloon, she pretended not to know him at all. She was rich now, and planned to open an establishment of her own. Not here, she said, somewhere pleasant. Somewhere with a better class of clientele.

She drank heavily each night after work and he knew now that she would be unconscious and would not hear him creep into her bedchamber. In the moonlight, he saw three empty bottles of Wyndham's Shiraz on the living-room table. The wine was transported from New South Wales at great expense, an affectation of hers when everyone else drank brandy. Beside the bottles was a half-full glass. Another glass had overturned and the red wine formed a dark puddle around it and had dripped on to the wooden floor. He imagined her laughing drunkenly, not bothering to pick up the fallen glass. And the man, in his urgency to have her, grabbing her and half-carrying her upstairs. And she wouldn't have stopped laughing—at him, not with him. She despised men, thought them pathetic.

The smell of smoke became stronger as he climbed the stairs, but it was more acrid now than tobacco. He crept quickly along the narrow passage—the familiar way to her room—and saw the smoke curl out from under her door like Minerva's snakes. He flung it open but immediately stepped back, gagging. The room was alight and the flames had already engulfed the curtains round the four-poster bed. He called out her name, meaning to save her.

But as she suddenly reared up and coughed, wild-eyed, he saw the cotton sack on the low table at the end of the bed, and knew immediately what it must be. He stepped quickly into the room toward it.

When she saw him, she called out, choking, "Help me, for God's sake!"

Would he choose to save her, or the object he had come for? No one would ever know he had been there. On impulse, he reached out and grabbed the sack with the tin container inside, hauled it over his shoulder and rushed back to the door.

But then he hesitated and turned back to her. What was he thinking? Of course he had to do what he could for her. He put the sack down by the door and went back into the room, but the heat was too intense. The flames had already spread across the floorboards and had taken hold of the heavy velvet curtains over the windows.

She sank to her knees on the bed, her arms flailing desperately as the flames began to swallow her. In a moment, the fire would be upon him too, and they would both die.

He turned, picked up the bag once more, and hurried down the hallway. He descended the stairs, threw the sack out the window he had come in by and climbed out himself, pulling the sash down behind him. He felt consumed with guilt and cowardice, but nevertheless moved furtively down the lane. He looked back once, to see the top storey of the house completely alight, and felt consumed with guilt at his cowardice. He knew it would not be long before the neighbours in the sleepy town noticed the fire.

He moved more quickly now, away through the darkness with the bag over his shoulder. He heard distant shouts of alarm, but he kept walking and didn't look back again.

Part 1

February 1868—August 1869

Chapter 1

Gulf of Siam, February 1868

Edward Fairburn adjusted his stiff collar and wide necktie as another trickle of sweat worked its way down his back, soaking into his already damp shirt and waistcoat. The ship swayed and creaked, and he grabbed the railing once more, almost tripping over a sack of rice, one of scores that seemed to have been strewn at random about the deck.

He had discarded his heavy green jacket days ago, and he felt under-dressed without it, despite the cloying heat. But there, on a steamer in the Gulf of Siam, tossed by the waves and roasted relentlessly by the searing tropical sun, no one was concerned with the proprieties of dress. The other passengers were too busy themselves coping with the suffocating temperatures, poor food and cramped conditions on board.

His checked woollen trousers, thick long-sleeved white shirt and high-buttoned green velvet waistcoat were almost more than he could stand in the heat, and his fashionably long side whiskers itched him irritatingly. He envied the Chinese and Siamese sailors their bare chests and their colourful cotton panung—a sort of loose trouser that was wrapped round the waist then pulled through the legs and tied—but he could never have considered discarding his attire for theirs. He was an English gentleman and was obliged to appear as one at all times, regardless of circumstances. Besides, his pale English complexion could not have withstood the incessant burning rays of the equatorial sun for any length of time. He was glad of the protection provided by his felt bowler hat, although it, too, added to his sweltering discomfort.

It was the fifth day of the journey from Singapore to Bangkok, and for what seemed like the hundredth time since they had set sail on the grubby steamer *Chao Phya*, he wondered what had possessed him to make this journey to the mysterious Far East. He thought of his wife and daughter in Melbourne, and what they would make of this detour.

As always, he felt mostly guilt when he thought of Charlotte. She had suffered so much because of him. Would she be angry when she received his letter saying he was not returning to her by the most direct passage? He already knew the answer to that question.

If he had travelled on the Devitt & Moore Line's celebrated new vessel, *Sobraon*, he would have been back in Australia within eleven weeks, and as a first-class passenger, would have enjoyed every luxury along the way. Instead, he had sailed to Singapore, and had been obliged to wait ten days in that crowded, humid outpost—where he knew no one— until he could obtain passage on the erratic steamer service to Bangkok.

He was accustomed to travelling first class, but on the decrepit *Chao Phya*, he might well have been travelling steerage. The accommodation below deck was filthy, and the air so foul and stifling that most of the passengers, even the ladies, preferred to spend the nights of the journey uncomfortably on deck, clearing a space between the rice sacks, ropes and whatever else lay around, and sleeping as best they could. There was no provision for bathing or washing, and the food prepared by the Chinese cook was strange and unpalatable to any of the passengers not accustomed to Asian spices. How they longed for a good English side of beef, with roast potatoes, peas, and a thick, smooth gravy made from the drippings.

Unlike most of the other Europeans on board, Edward

wasn't seasick, nor did he suffer from any stomach ailment. Nevertheless, he would be delighted to bid farewell to the *Chao Phya*, although its master, Captain Orton, had been very obliging.

Most of all, Edward was concerned about how the humidity would affect his expensive new photographic equipment, despite the fact that his portable folding-bellows camera had been constructed of teak instead of the usual mahogany. Teak, the W. W. Roache company in England had assured him, was perfect for the tropics, being naturally adapted to resist heat, damp, and even insect infestation.

He wondered also how the chemicals necessary for photographic development would survive the rough voyage. Or were the bottles already smashed, leaving him with chests of leaking developer, collodion, cyanide, acetic acid, and the like? If any of it were damaged in any way, then he had made the trip for nothing, for the purpose of this Far East sojourn was to photograph the Kingdom of Siam and its inhabitants.

It was all very well to travel the world in relative comfort to such places as California and even to Victoria, Australia, but a journey to Siam was another matter entirely. It would establish him as an adventurer; a roving photographer in search of the world's most exotic subjects. One more miserable night on board and they would arrive at their destination, the captain had told him.

Here was Captain Orton now, sauntering toward him as if he were taking a Sunday stroll in the park, rather than negotiating the slippery hardwood decks of a rolling steamer.

"Do you see, Mr Fairburn?" he called out, pointing beyond the starboard bow. "We've sighted land. We're approaching Siam."

Edward squinted and placed a hand on his forehead to shade his eyes. In the blinding white light, he could barely make out the shadowy strip in the horizon. "Yes, indeed. And a welcome sight it is too, Captain, if you don't mind my saying. Should we be landing tonight then, sir?" he asked hopefully.

The captain laughed with a loud snort. "No such luck for you, Mr Fairburn. I'm afraid you're stuck on my humble vessel for at least another night."

"At least?"

"In order to reach Bangkok, we have to cross the bar into our namesake, the Chao Phya River. It depends on the tides."

"I see," Edward mumbled, resigning himself to the continuing discomfort. "Well, at least we're within sight of our destination, Captain."

The captain strolled on and Edward was alone once more. As alone, at least, as a person could be on a vessel which carried—as well as its cargo and eight other British passengers —some two hundred or more Asians of various nationalities, many of whom spent their time huddled in tight circles on deck, gambling and smoking opium.

From what he could discern, several games were popular. Some were played with large decks of long, narrow cards illustrated with Chinese portraits. Another involved a brass cup and a wooden cube which was painted half red and half white on one face. The 'banker' would place the cube on the deck, painted face up, without allowing anyone to see it, then cover it with the brass cup. The participants would then place wagers on which direction the white half faced. Those with money on the winning side appeared to be well rewarded, while those with stakes on the other three sides lost them to the 'banker'—for whom the game appeared to be a most profitable enterprise.

"At least it passes the time," a fellow passenger—a Mr Deakin—remarked to him as they stood watching the gambling. "Wouldn't mind joining them m'self, if they'd have us. Mind you, they'd probably fling up their arms in horror and jump overboard if we even approached them."

Edward laughed. "Can you blame them for thinking us strange, Mr Deakin? Besides, we'd look mighty unusual in our woollen suits, crouched among a group of men we couldn't communicate with. They'd have us, all right. We wouldn't stand a chance."

That night on deck, he was able to sleep soundly for the first time during the voyage, despite the incessant snoring of Mr Deakin nearby, and the continual, raucous gambling games. Perhaps it was the knowledge that he would soon he on land again, or perhaps his sleep was aided by a refreshing breeze that—for once—had lowered the temperature enough to leave him merely lightly perspiring.

He awoke early next morning, however, to find himself itching fiercely all over. "Damnation!" he swore as he leapt from his resting place, covered in biting red ants.

Sometime during the night, seeking a more comfortable position, he had moved his head to rest on a sack of sugar cane that had been invade by hordes of insects. Having had their fill of the sack's contents, some had ventured on to the next interesting prospect: Edward. Despite his close-fitting clothing, some had managed to work their way inside. He could feel the prickly sting of their bites all over him.

"God save me!" he gasped, beating his trousers and pulling off his ankle boots and stockings. The other passengers stared at him in bemusement, but he was desperate.

"For goodness' sake, man, what's got into you?" the captain exclaimed as he strode over to investigate the commotion. His passenger appeared to be performing a war dance on deck.

"Ants, Captain," he explained as he continued to beat his trousers. "The blighters besieged me while I slept. Never in all my life..."

Captain Orton tried not to smile. "Well then, you'd best go below and sort yourself out. My boy will bring you some water."

"Thank you, sir. Much obliged." Edward knew how precious fresh water was on the steamer and it was not generally wasted on trivialities such as washing.

"On your way, then. The laddie will be down directly."

As Edward disappeared below, Captain Orton suppressed another grin. That one wouldn't last long in Siam, he thought. The landed gentry, by the look of him—and too accustomed to the comforts of life. Despite Edward's claim that he had "roughed it" on the gold fields of California and Victoria, he certainly wouldn't be prepared for what awaited him in Bangkok. It would be interesting to observe what became of him in that stifling and alien environment, the captain mused.

∞∞∞

Melbourne, Australia, February 1868

There was a clatter on the porch, then an impatient tapping at the front door. Charlotte heard her daughter's high-pitched squeals of excitement behind it.

"Mummy, Mummy, come quickly, let me in. It's come at last. A letter from Father!"

The housekeeper, Mrs Bains, opened the door and Elizabeth almost tumbled through the entranceway and into the front room where her mother was sitting.

"Look, Mummy, it's finally come," she cried.

Charlotte set aside her needlework and took the letter. Elizabeth was right; it was his handwriting on the envelope.

To her daughter, the letter could mean only one thing: that her father was returning home to Melbourne soon, with chests full of gifts from England. To Charlotte, however, a letter from him no longer gave her a thrill of anticipation. She shivered, rather, with apprehension, for she could never know what scheme he would be planning next, or even if he would return home at all this time. They had not parted on the best of terms.

He had been gone for more than a year already, insisting

when he left that he must return to his parents' Yorkshire estate immediately. He cited family business concerning trust funds and properties left to himself and his brothers by their grandfather. Yet to her knowledge, he had had no recent epistle from Home.

"It's imperative, Charlotte, that I'm there," he had told her then. "I must ensure I receive my fair share. I wouldn't put it past my brothers to try to cut me out. You know we've never got on. To them, I'm the black sheep—the prodigal son who no longer deserves their consideration."

He had left directly, and she wasn't fooled. She was convinced the real reason was to escape the problems of their marriage, and the monotony of his studio photography work in Melbourne. True, he had just returned from the goldfields at Ballaarat, but he hadn't talked of it much. After an enthusiastic start, he seemed to have quickly lost interest.

Seven-year-old Elizabeth was restless as her mother turned the letter over in her hands. "Hurry, Mummy. Let's see what he says. Maybe he'll be on the next ship, do you think?"

"We shall see," she replied, taking a carved ivory letter opener from its tray on a side table and neatly slitting the top of the envelope. She withdrew a single page.

"What does he say? What does he say?" Elizabeth hopped from foot to foot.

"Elizabeth! Please do sit down and behave yourself like a young lady. I shall tell you Father's news when you allow me a chance to read his letter myself first."

Elizabeth did as she was told, jumping on to a large armchair next to the chesterfield where her mother was seated. Charlotte was slim and rather short, but the wide crinoline under her silk skirts made it impossible for her to fit into an armchair.

Elizabeth's eyes were bright with anticipation, but she clasped her hands tightly and tried to distract herself by looking round the room. She loved the front room, despite the fact that she wasn't allowed in there alone. It wasn't a proper parlour, since it was the only sitting room they had, and so was not used solely for visitors. But Elizabeth thought it very grand, with the gilt-framed mirror hanging over the marble mantel above the fireplace and the heavy gold drapes with elaborate grey tassels over the windows. What she liked most, though, was the rosewood cabinet with glass doors that stood in one corner. It was filled with souvenirs of their travels. Charlotte called it a "whatnot" and its treasures included ornamental elephants carved of ivory, a small rock with a thin streak of gold that her father had found on the Californian goldfields, and some exquisite pieces of heirloom china that had belonged to Grandmother Fairburn's mother. Charlotte always said that it was a miracle the china hadn't been smashed to pieces during their travels. She also said that one day, when they returned to England, Elizabeth would see what a really grand room looked like, because Grandmother Fairburn lived in a "mansion". Elizabeth turned back to her mother, who was still reading the letter.

Actually, Charlotte was perusing it for a second time to ensure she had read it correctly. She felt a hollow shock, yet at the same time was not really surprised he wasn't returning yet.

Friday, December 20th, 1867

Dearest Charlotte,

I am very sorry I have not written for so many months, but there has been that family business to attend to: successfully, I might add, but with no thanks to Theo or Albert. I made also a short trip to Paris, to see the wonderful Exhibition, which you may have seen reports of in the Melbourne Argus.

While in Paris, my dear, I saw an exhibit that greatly intrigued me. It was the Siamese section and it included the most unusual artefacts, rich silk materials, and, most interesting of all, a set of photographs of the Siamese King.

The next news I have for you, dearest, will come as something of a surprise, perhaps even as a shock. You know, Charlotte, how serious I am about my photography, and you know well how I love a new adventure. On my return journey, I have decided to make a detour to Siam and I hope to take similar photographs to those I saw in Paris, for a future exhibition of my own.

I shall sail first to Singapore, from whence Siam is apparently a pleasant six days' journey by steamer. By the time you read this, my dear, I shall probably be in Siam, or close to it, so please do not worry.

I shall write again soon, but I am not certain about the efficiency—or even the existence—of mail services from Siam, so do not be surprised if it is myself in person who arrives home before my next letter. Give my love to Elizabeth.

It was signed simply "Edward", with no endearment. She sank against the chesterfield with a sigh, and closed her eyes.

"Mummy, what's wrong? Father is all right, isn't he? He is coming back soon?"

She sat up again and forced a smile. "Yes, darling, of course. Your father will be back as soon as he can. He has a little more business to attend to, that's all."

"Something else in England?"

"No, not in England, Elizabeth."

"Then where? What do you mean, Mummy? Did he go back to California?"

She glanced back at the letter. "No, dear. To a place called Siam, he says."

"Si-am?" Elizabeth grappled with the unfamiliar word. "But where's that? Is it in Europe or America?"

"Neither, darling."

"Then where? Why don't you tell me, Mummy?"

Charlotte looked across at her daughter's imploring eyes and sighed again. "I have to admit, I've no idea. Let's go and look at the globe in your father's study, shall we?"

Chapter 2

"Farang! Farang! Farang!" Everywhere he went in Bangkok, he was followed by the excitedly-whispered Siamese word used to describe white foreigners. And there were giggles from men, women and children alike.

Westerners, especially those with fair hair and green or blue eyes, were ugly curiosities to the Siamese. These bizarre creatures with their long noses, huge ungainly bodies and in- sipid colouring were unhygienic, too. Sweat ran in streams down their red faces and damp patches appeared through the clothing on their backs and under their arms. It was no sur- prise, for they insisted at all times of the day on wearing their ridiculously heavy costumes that covered them from head to foot.

Neither did the farang make any attempt to see that their teeth were blackened with betel-nut juice. No self-re- specting Siamese—or Thai, as they referred to themselves— would allow his or her teeth to remain white. Some, particu- larly the wealthiest women, used a black pigment to colour any spots that were not perfectly darkened, for—as the old Siamese saying went—"any dog can have white teeth".

Clearly, these farang cared little for their appearance. Nevertheless, a passing European made for an interesting di- version, and sometimes became a source of humour and con- versation for days.

Edward found Bangkok and the Siamese people equally fascinating. He had never seen or imagined a city quite like this. Aside from the fact that Bangkok was traversed by a network of canals rather than roads, its most interesting feature, to him, was its markets. He was captivated by the great bazaar at the city's southern end. There were hundreds of stalls, as well as ponds full of fish, sharks, and eels which were sold live or killed on the spot so the buyers could be assured they were fresh. There were strange fruits he had never seen or heard of before: the red spiky rambutan, the smooth-skinned green or yellow mango, the huge jackfruit, and the foul-smelling but prized durian.

He was forced to hold his breath as he passed the displays of dried fish and squid, and there were piles of pork, chicken, and beef which were all left open to the stifling air and covered in grotesque flies that fed on, and laid eggs in, the flesh. No one paid them any mind, and the meat was simply brushed off before being sold or made into curry that was cooked with coconut milk and the fiery little chilli peppers that were sold everywhere. Spicy pastes were added to the curries, and a strong sauce called *nam plaa*—made from the fermented fish juice—was sprinkled over other types of food. And of course, there was rice, long-grain and the shorter-grain glutinous varieties, available by the sack-load, or in whatever quantity the buyer required.

Rice was becoming a less exotic ingredient in England, and Mrs Beeton had included 40 recipes in her *Book of Household Management* in 1861. On his most recent visit, Edward had noticed how the book had influenced the cook at his mother's house. She had served rice, not as a breakfast kedgeree, but in a soup at the main midday meal. When cross-examined by the mistress-of-the-house over its suitability, the unflappable woman merely said, 'If it's good enough for Mrs Beeton, it's good enough for me, ma'am."

There was little else familiar to a Western sense of sight, smell or taste. Edward was willing to try the food, but he wanted to discover the exact ingredients before he bought anything from the vendors, who cooked their dishes in clay pots over hot coals. However, his simply-worded questions were met only with stares or muffled giggles of embarrassment. How he expected them to understand him was something only he could know, they thought, and they became even more incredulous as he began to gesticulate when his words failed to communicate his meaning. They had heard that the Lord of Life, King Maha Mongkut, could converse fluently with the foreigners, who were now coming to Siam in their hundreds. But they were not certain they could believe the rumours. Why would the Lord of Life want to know the language of such inconsequential creatures?

Sometimes, he felt discouraged and lonely, and he would sit in the saloon of Falcks's hotel, where he had taken a dingy room, wondering if he had made the right decision. He needed an assistant for his photographic work and he had hoped, on his arrival, to employ a local boy who could understand English well enough to follow instructions and not get the developing chemicals mixed up. He now realised, after his experiences in the markets, that it would be impossible to find a suitable employee by himself. He resolved to ask at the British Consulate when he went there to introduce himself to Mr Knox, the consul.

* * *

Two days later, he sat with Mr Knox on the verandah of the consulate. Situated on the banks of the river between the Portuguese and French legations—but some distance from the American—the consulate was a large two-storey building raised from the ground and surrounded by narrow verandahs with intricately carved latticework on both levels. The grounds and the sweeping paths, bordered attractively with small rocks, were beautifully kept by several Siamese gardeners.

A light wind, cooled by the river, brought slight relief from the heat, and sweet-scented flowered trees swayed in the breeze. Strange birds flitted amid them—squabbling, pecking at grubs, catching insects—and Edward saw a large long-tailed lizard dash across the lawns as if he were late for an important appointment.

A servant soon brought out a tray and placed it on the cast-iron table in front of Mr Knox.

"And you say your ambition is to photograph the King, Mr Fairburn?"

Edward took a sip of his gin and tonic. "Indeed, Mr Knox. And as many of his subjects as will sit for me."

"Do you have some samples of your work? I'd be most interested to see more of this ... er ... 'art form', I'm tempted to call it. But I'm sure it'll never take the place of a good illustration, eh? Fascinating innovation, though. I understand the technological advances are astonishing."

"They are indeed," Edward confirmed, reaching for his leather portfolio which contained some of his recent work, and handing a selection of large prints to Mr Knox.

The consul took the photographs and turned them over one by one as Edward explained their subjects.

"I took these shortly before I left England, in some of the new factories in Yorkshire. This set is called 'The New Age' and I hope they'll eventually be part of an exhibition."

Mr Knox was perhaps more impressed by the obvious advancements in industry at home that the pictures revealed, than by the pictures themselves, but he nevertheless pronounced Edward a proficient photographer. "Is your family involved in the factories?" he asked.

"No, my father is Sir Theodore Fairburn, the banker. But one of his friends in the textile mills gave permission for me to take these pictures."

Mr Knox nodded and then seemed to retreat into thought for a moment. "Are you really set upon photographing His Majesty, Mr Fairburn?"

Edward suddenly felt doubtful at the consul's tone. "Why, yes, if it's at all possible, sir."

"Oh, I should think permission can be obtained. The King's actually quite taken with the idea of being photographed. He has sat for several portraits already. There are so few photographers in this part of the world though, so I think your chances are good. However ..." He paused, wondering exactly how to phrase his next comment.

"Yes, Mr Knox?"

"Well—are you married, Mr Fairburn?"

"Yes, indeed. My wife and daughter are in Melbourne, Australia. And awaiting my return, I might add."

"Ah, I see. Well, in that case, I'm afraid they may have a long wait. That is, if you wish to realise your photographic ambition."

The consul took another sip of his gin and then leaned across the table, as if to share a confidence with Edward. "You see, things do not happen quickly in Siam. In fact, I can honestly say they move at a snail's pace. The King has many pressing business and social matters to attend to, not to mention the demands of a huge household of wives and children. He may agree to be photographed this month, but then again, you may have to wait six months. One never can tell here. And, once you put in such a request, it would be the height of rudeness to withdraw it and leave. Once you ask to photograph the King, you have to wait until the King decides he wants to be photographed. Then again, you might arrive on the appointed day, only to be told he is unable to be present because of pressing business of state, and you might have to wait another six months." He looked directly at Mr Fairburn. "You see, then, how it is. He is an extremely busy man."

"Six months, or longer!" Edward exclaimed. "I hadn't imagined that."

"Well, we shall see." Mr Knox signalled to the servant to refill their glasses. "And by the way, a word of advice. You shouldn't expect ordinary Siamese to be thrilled at the prospect of being photographed. They believe such images steal a part of their soul from them. Nonsense, of course, but they're a superstitious lot and it doesn't do to offend them."

Edward's eyes widened. He hadn't expected this to be

nearly as complicated. "Indeed!" was his only comment.

"Where are you staying at present, Mr Fairburn?"

"At Falcks's Bowling Alley and Billiard Hall. Not the most salubrious of lodgings, I'm afraid."

"Nor the most wholesome of company, I'll warrant. And not the sort of accommodation you've been used to, I dare say."

"Well, I'm only too pleased my dear mother doesn't know of my cockroach-infested room."

"Why don't you rent a house? I know of a vacant property close to here that would be quite suitable. Who knows, you might decide to stay."

"I'll certainly consider it—the house that is," Edward replied uncertainly. "Meanwhile, Mr Knox, I'd be much obliged if you could mention me to the King's officers. Perhaps even an introduction in the right places, if I could be so bold to ask?"

"Well, you won't get an audience, of course," the consul was quick to inform him. "But I'll see what I can do about getting you invited to any parties or receptions the King is holding for foreigners. In fact, if you're still here in August, you may be able to join an expedition to the south. His Majesty's an accomplished astronomer by all accounts and has apparently calculated the exact time a total eclipse of the sun will occur on the eighteenth of that month."

Edward nodded enthusiastically. "That sounds very interesting indeed, Mr Knox. I'd be most grateful."

"I'll keep an eye out for a suitable assistant, also. You'll probably have to teach him English yourself. But don't worry, Siamese are fast learners, industrious and fastidious."

They talked more of the country and the other foreign residents and Edward eventually took his leave, with thanks to the consul for his promised assistance. He went down to the riverside and was promptly able to hire a small boat for the short distance along the Chao Phya to the pier nearest his lodgings. Fortunately, Falcks's was located near a well-known temple, so he needed only to give its name, Wat Kaeo Faa, and the boatman knew where to stop, despite Edward's poor intonation

As they slid through the greasy brown water, he gazed at the scene all round him, shaking his head in amazement at the variety of crafts and dwellings on the river. There were small, flat-bottomed vessels piled high with all manner of produce, mostly piloted by women or children who rowed from house to house selling their wares. There were large, squat barges loaded with rice that sat low in the water waiting to be disgorged. Similar vessels that had already been emptied of their cargoes began making the return journey upriver, with their crews—the families who lived on board—lolling about the decks. There were also thousands of floating houses and shops. Most were made of bamboo, with pointed, thatched roofs, but there were some of polished teak constructed in the same style. They were all open to the river and their residents seemed unconcerned about their complete lack of privacy.

Each houseboat was decorated with stylised carvings that rose into the air at each corner of the roof like curved, raised and pointed elephant trunks. Each one also accommodated a spirit house, a richly decorated miniature house in which the spirits of the site were said to reside. The Siamese believed that whenever they felled a tree to construct a house, the spirits who dwelled there must not be made homeless. Thus, they were provided with their own home placed prominently on a pedestal at the front of the main house, or in a position where its shadows would never fall upon the spirit house. Offerings of food and drink were regularly placed on the spirit house, and if the main house was improved, so was the spirit house—for if the spirits saw that the human residents lived more comfortably than they did, they would take up residence in the main house instead, which could have dire consequences for the human inhabitants. The beauty of the floating houses was that they were moored in such a way that if a family wanted to move elsewhere, they simply unhitched their home and floated away.

Almost everywhere along the river, temples and *chedi* —the circular spires that marked the burial site of a monk or prominent person—rose from the verdant banks and from amid the ramshackle wooden and bamboo houses. The *chedi* resembled glittering needles of gold rising into the sky, and the pointed temple roofs were decorated with green and orange tiles that shimmered like snake scales in the afternoon sun.

The most stunning of the riverside temples was Wat Arun, a 260-foot-tall pagoda-like structure which was entirely embellished with a mosaic of broken Chinese porcelain shards. Further upriver were the spires and *chedi* of the Grand Palace itself, where the King lived in sumptuous surroundings of gold, jewels and other treasures reputed to be more splendid than those any Western ruler had possessed.

Edward looked down at the river. It was decidedly murky, with all manner of discarded objects floating on its oily surface—household refuse was simply tipped directly into the water—although he saw plenty of fish jumping, too. He had heard that the King had issued an edict against "the inelegant practice of throwing dead animals into the waterways"—but if the number of dog carcasses floating in the river was any indicator, he concluded that even the Lord of Life's commands were not always heeded.

Bangkok was mesmerizing and he planned to begin his work as soon as an assistant could be found to help him carry the more than one hundred pounds' weight of equipment necessary to take photographs in the field. Finding someone suitable would not be an easy task.

Several days later, he received an invitation to attend a party at the British Consulate. He eagerly awaited his introduction to Bangkok's expatriate society and hoped it would provide the connections he sought.

Chapter 3

As he walked up the steps from the pier to Mr Knox's large brick house on the night of the party, he could hear the buzz of conversation and the tinkle of glasses. Several groups had gathered on the expansive verandah and were talking animatedly, or simply gazing through the flowering trees toward the river.

The scene that greeted him in the large ballroom was a welcome one indeed. Despite the heat, which had hardly dissipated in the night air, everyone had dressed in the correct formal attire for the occasion, as Edward himself had done. The ladies added sparkling flashes of colour to the room, with sweeping silk dresses in pastel hues of pink, mauve, buttercup, and light brown. Many of the gowns were fashionably low-necked or off-the-shoulder, with tiny puff sleeves. The men were more uniformly dressed, of course, most wearing white waistcoats, frilled shirt-fronts, black knee-length evening coats and tight-fitting black trousers.

Even after sunset, the temperature was at least eighty-five degrees, but no gentleman could be seen to take off his coat and appear in his shirt-sleeves. It would not have done at all and would have been tantamount almost to parading about in one's underwear. They never mentioned the heat, but from time to time the gentlemen used silk kerchiefs to mop their brows, while the ladies dabbed at their cheeks with lace-edged handkerchiefs, or used delicate fans to cool their faces. Several servants were charged with the laborious task of operating punkah fans, and many of the guests moved closer to the slight breeze they afforded. For the first time since he had arrived in the Far East, Edward felt entirely at ease. Here was European society transported, with all its rules intact.

Siamese serving girls carrying trays of drinks and hors d'oeuvres were present in great numbers. They wore traditional silk panung, but so as not to offend the foreigners, they also wore European-style blouses. Siamese women customarily wore only a wide sash draped across their chest, which did not necessarily cover the breasts—nor was it intended to do so. It was incomprehensible to them why these European women covered themselves completely at all times, to the extent of wearing heavy gowns to bed that concealed their bodies from neck to foot. Was it any wonder so many of their husbands looked elsewhere for pleasure?

Although she was Siamese herself, Mrs Knox always ensured her foreign guests were catered for with familiar food, and the consulate's supplies were regularly replenished by ships arriving from Europe and Singapore. As Edward had already heard, the consul had met his future wife, Prang Yen, when she was a lady-in-waiting at the court of his late friend, Wang Na ('Second King') Phra Pin Klao, a younger brother of King Mongkut. Mr and Mrs Knox had married in 1854 when she was 17, and they had three children—Fanny, 12, now in Europe at school, Caroline, 10, and Thomas, 7.

Knox had fought with the British Indian army in the China Wars and had arrived in Siam in 1851 at the request of Phra Pin Klao, a champion of all things western, who employed Knox to drill his troops. Knox joined the British Consulate as an interpreter, shortly after it was established in 1857, and he had done well enough to be promoted to head of the legation as consul-general in 1864 and had remained close friends with Phra Pin Klao until he died in 1866. He was also firm friends with Pin Klao's son, Prince Bovorn Vichaichan, who had been made a prince (but not Second King) of the front palace after Pin Klao's death. It was whispered that, although Knox had friends in high places in both Siam and England, he was a trouble-maker, and many of the Siamese did not like him.

Mr and Mrs Knox saw that Edward was offered a drink, then introduced him to a group they thought would interest him before they moved off to circulate among their other guests.

Among the clique was John Chandler, a long-time resident who—twenty years before—had become the first person to journey up the Chao Phya River by steamboat. He was the United States Consul from 1859 to 1865, then became the official interpreter for the Siamese Harbour Department. He had also established an English-language school and tutored Crown Prince Chulalongkorn at the palace. After twenty-five years in Siam, he was due this year to retire to the United States, with a generous cash award from the King.

In the group also was Captain John Bush, who had come to Siam in 1857 and was now harbour master and managing director of the Bangkok Dock Company. He was an old sailor with countless tales to tell of the seas he had traversed and the ships he had sailed.

There was also Joseph Shaw, a young Presbyterian missionary, who held a glass of tonic water and looked conspicuously uncomfortable at the turn the conversation was taking.

"Damned good idea, this pink ticket thing the wives have taken to, if you ask me," Captain Bush remarked. "Then no one has to fool anyone, do they?"

Edward noticed Mr Shaw's face redden, and he wondered what the captain meant.

"I can see your point, but I don't know if such an arrangement should be condoned," Mr Chandler added. "What about you, Mr Fairburn? What do you think about the pink tickets?"

"I'm afraid I haven't the faintest idea what you're referring to, Mr Chandler. Perhaps you might enlighten me."

Captain Bush guffawed and broke in to explain. "Well, it's not exactly the sort of thing one can elaborate on too much in mixed company." He lowered his voice and leaned closer to Edward. "It's simply an agreement the foreign wives have with their husbands."

Edward was intrigued, but still baffled. He glanced at both Mr Chandler and Mr Shaw, who now appeared even more uncomfortable.

"Sort of agree to turn a blind eye," Captain Bush continued quietly, 'to any extra goings-on, if you understand what I mean." His voice then became almost a whisper. "They think it's better to agree to their husband taking a ... second wife, shall we say, when he's away from home, or when the wife goes home on hiatus—or even a number of ... ah ... consorts."

"More like concubines," Mr Chandler commented wryly, and Captain Bush held a finger to his lips to shush the man.

Edward couldn't believe his ears. He glanced quickly round the room at the elegant women dressed in silks and adorned with pearls. "You mean to say that some of these ladies openly approve of their husbands committing adultery?"

"Well, I wouldn't say 'openly approve' exactly," Mr Chandler rejoined. "More 'discreetly agree to'—because if they didn't, it would happen anyway."

"That's quite extraordinary," Edward commented, shaking his head.

Mr Chandler noticed Mr Shaw's embarrassment. "Indeed, Mr Fairburn. But then, I don't suppose we should be talking about such things in front of the reverend here."

"Oh, I don't have the honour of being addressed as 'reverend'," Mr Shaw responded quickly, glad to change the subject. "I'm merely a teacher with a calling."

"And still a bachelor, too," Mr Chandler added for Edward's information. "No lucky young lady soon to become Mrs Shaw?"

"No, I'm afraid not. There's very little opportunity here to meet a suitable young lady who could help me in my work."

"Why don't you marry a Siamese woman, like I did?" Captain Bush suggested heartily. "They make the best wives in the world, though I will say, they rule the roost, make no bones about it."

Mr Shaw looked uncomfortable again. "Well, I'm not against marrying a Siamese woman. But she would have to be a Christian, of course."

"Now you're making things very difficult for yourself," the captain said. "You missionaries aren't having much success, are you?"

"Well, we pray and we continue our work. That's the best we can do."

"Excu' me, sir," a soft Siamese-accented voice beside Edward spoke.

He looked round to find a serving girl offering a tray of hors d'oeuvres. To his relief, all the food was English—or as close to it as possible. As he took a scotch egg from the tray and accepted a serviette from the girl, he could not help noticing how attractive she was. Her deep brown—almost black—almond-shaped eyes tilted at the corners, and as soon as their eyes made contact, she immediately looked down, aware of his scrutiny. She did not giggle shyly as so many of the others did, but turned and walked gracefully and soundlessly away. The Siamese almost always went barefoot—with the exception of the noblemen, who wore pointed slippers—and one rarely heard them coming or going.

The conversation resumed, picking up where it had left off about the missionaries' work among the Siamese. Edward, however, could no longer concentrate. He asked himself why he had not seen before how beautiful the Siamese women were. Had he been blind? At first, he had considered them strange, with their blackened teeth, bare feet, and tufted topknots. But he was growing more used to them the more he saw of them, and this young girl's sultry beauty had instantly captivated him. He began to look—as discreetly as he could —at the other serving girls round the room, and he was now very much aware of their satiny skin, their petite bodies, their delicate faces, their lack of pretension, and most of all, their beguiling eyes. He could see "his" girl going about her business, offering trays of elegant titbits to various guests. He wondered if she worked at the consulate, and he wanted to know her name. It would, of course, have been quite impossible for him to ask.

In the servery, Kesri prepared another tray of food for the guests. There were no punkah fans out here, and it was stifling. She would rather have been cooking over searing flames because at least then she could have worked in the outdoor kitchen. She loathed serving these ungrateful, ugly farang, despite the fact that her friends considered her fortunate to work at the consul's house whenever there was a party. She saw the foreigners at close quarters, they reasoned, was well reimbursed for her services, and wore a beautiful uniform—though they weren't impressed by the restrictive farang chest covering she had to wear. But still she saw no dignity in it. Even though she was a paid servant now, and no longer a possession, it wasn't enough for her. When she returned to the ballroom, she circled with the tray of food close to the group the new man was with.

By the end of the evening, Edward had received invitations to dine at several homes, and had made some useful contacts for photographic commissions. He had also spoken to a number of the ladies present. Although greatly intrigued by the revelations made earlier in the evening, he made no reference, of course, to the alleged pink tickets. He was, however, fascinated by the women's adjustment to the conditions in Siam. Despite the heat, the swarms of mosquitoes and the unavailability of many things taken for granted at home as part of civilised living, they seemed, generally, to be happy here. He noticed a few trying very hard to disguise accents that were less than genteel and he imagined they, particularly, would be delighted with living conditions in which their every need was provided for by an over-abundance of servants. Even those women who could not have been considered much above working class at home in England or America were ladies of leisure here. They rarely lifted a finger in the home and spent their days socialising, or playing croquet and bridge. It was a life far above their true stations and that applied equally to their husbands.

When Edward finally took his leave, it was well after midnight and he wandered down to the small pier, where several other guests were waiting for boats.

"Would you like to come with us?" Captain Bush called. "You're staying at Falcks's, aren't you? It's only a little farther up than us. My boatman won't mind." He indicated a handsome longboat with a Siamese oarsman that had drawn up beside the landing.

"Thank you, Captain Bush, much obliged."

As he spoke, the slight, shadowy figure of a Siamese woman glided silently past him toward the pier. When she neared the steps, she looked back and he recognised her immediately, even in the low lantern light. It was the serving girl who had caught his eye all evening. She was wearing the same panung, only now she had taken off the European blouse and replaced it with a brightly coloured sash that was loosely draped across her shoulders. He saw her breasts silhouetted against the light reflected in the water. An instant later, she turned and ran down the steps to her own tiny sampan, which was moored under the landing. She slipped into the little boat, paddled away and disappeared into the night.

∞∞∞

It was pitch black when he let himself into his room and he stumbled about—drunk on the alcohol and drowsy in the heat—until he found the desk on which stood a small kerosene lamp. He took off the glass cover, fumbled to light a match, then found the wick, which quickly caught the flame. As he was replacing the glass and adjusting the dial, he became aware that he wasn't alone. Slowly, he turned to face the intruder—and was brought fully to his senses when he saw who it was.

She sat on the floor with her eyes cast down and her hands held together in a prayer-like position in front of her chest.

"*Sawatdee ka,*" she greeted him, slowly raising her eyes to meet his.

Chapter 4

February 28th, 1868

Dear Charlotte,

      I hope this letter finds yourself and Elizabeth in good health. It will be winter by the time you receive it and I know how much you feel the cold. At least it does not snow in Melbourne, as it does in London.

      As you will realise, I am still in Siam, and I must tell you that I have found it to be the most remarkable place. My work is progressing well and I have, in fact, set up a small studio here in the house I have rented thanks to the good offices of the British Consul, Mr Knox.

      It is likely that I will be permitted to photograph the King himself, but I must await a royal summons, of course. Mr Knox believes there may be an opportunity in August. His Majesty is a keen astronomer and has apparently calculated the exact time and position of a solar eclipse which will take place during that month. A magnificent celebration of the occasion has been arranged on the coast in the southern part of the kingdom where the eclipse will take place and many of the foreign residents here, including myself as an official photographer, have been invited to join the expedition. Apparently, it is 140 miles from Bangkok and the journey will take several days by sea.

      My dear, this is a wonderful and exotic land, and to be perfectly candid, I believe I should like to stay for some time. I quite realise that my change of plans will greatly disturb you, but let me reassure you that I have the welfare of yourself and Elizabeth in *mind, and I urge you to consider what I have to propose next.*

Charlotte, we have not been without our difficulties throughout our marriage and I fully understand your position. That is why I am suggesting that you perhaps would rather not join me in Siam. The climate and conditions are not well suited to English ladies and many of those who bravely come here find it a trial. After a short time, they return home, frail and exhausted. If, however, you are set on joining me, I shall do my utmost to make your life here comfortable. You should have as many servants as you desired, and Elizabeth would be well cared for.

If you decide to come, please close up the house in Melbourne and terminate our lease. You may also arrange for our furniture and effects to be shipped here as well. Should you decide not to come, perhaps you would prefer still to leave Melbourne and return with Elizabeth to your parents in Yorkshire. You know well they would welcome the two of you and that you would want for nothing there. In many ways, it would be the more suitable of the choices.

Let me know your decision, Charlotte, by the next ship. Please give Elizabeth a hug and kiss from me.

Edward

Elizabeth, who had become sombre lately, wondering why her father didn't return, was almost too afraid to ask her mother what he said in the letter. She recognised the expression on Charlotte's face. "He's not coming, is he, Mummy?"

"No, precious," Charlotte replied, as cheerfully as she could. "He has a lot of work to do, and he's going to photograph the King of Siam. What do you think of that?"

"I think the King wouldn't miss a photograph as much as I miss Father. Doesn't he love me any more?"

She was an odd mix, Charlotte thought, of thinking beyond her age, then mixing it with childish petulance. "Of course he does, poppet. He loves you very much and tells me to give you a hug and kiss from him."

She stroked Elizabeth's soft cheek, then made her decision. "In fact, he has asked us to go to Siam to live with him."

Elizabeth's eyes brightened and she jumped off the chesterfield. "Oh, Mummy, that means we'll all be together. And we'll never have to be apart from Father again, will we?"

"No dear, never again," Charlotte murmured weakly.

Elizabeth skipped off to play with her dolls' house, leaving Charlotte alone with her thoughts. She read the letter once more, this time to ensure that she had read correctly. She could suppose only that he was doing the gentlemanly thing: providing her with an escape from the marriage if she so desired it. Divorce was out of the question, of course, but if she wanted to live apart from him permanently—and he from her —he seemed to be suggesting that this would be a way to accommodate that without bringing shame on their families.

Despite their problems though, she did not want to part from him permanently. She still loved him and she believed Elizabeth should be brought up with two parents.

What was he thinking? She was doubtful, but knew only one thing for sure. If she wanted her marriage to survive, she must go to Siam, even though he had given her almost no information about the country in his letter and no encouragement. Had he been so convinced she would not want to come?

This time, she was determined things between them would be better. She would have to make an appointment to see Dr Vickers.

∞∞∞

Kesri hadn't worked in more than a month and as she lay beside him with the morning light filtering through the bedroom shutters, she felt certain her life was changing for the better. But still she thought bitterly of the circumstances that had brought her there; of her father, swindled of what little money he had, compelled to sell himself and her mother into slavery to repay their debts.

Somtop had been a kindly tradesman who made spirit houses, the little wooden dwellings that every Siamese had outside their house in order to keep the spirits happy and dissuade them from moving into the main house. Than an unscrupulous merchant had tricked Somtop into forming a partnership, only to abscond with the deposits from a year's worth of orders before the materials had even been paid for. In order to make good the loss, to do the honourable thing and pay back the customers—and to avoid a long jail sentence —Somtop sold himself and his wife, Ning, into slavery. Kesri, born into perpetual servitude, was their only surviving child, her three brothers all having died of cholera.

Her parents eventually died without having regained their liberty, but Kesri had always been determined to secure hers by whatever means necessary.

And she had done so.

Not surprisingly, she dreamed of wealth, of marrying, and of being attended to by her own servants. But without family, and because of her past, she had little hope of becoming any Siamese man's first wife, never mind the first wife of a man of wealth and status. She knew also that to become a concubine or minor wife would be little improvement on the life she knew already as a servant.

Kesri was possessed of a determined spirit and she saw a way to fulfil her dreams by ensuring that one of these farang men fell in love with her. She knew that their strange religion permitted them only one wife and she knew they were attracted to Siamese women. Many, of course, had mistresses, but that was of little consequence to her. The number of minor wives or consorts her husband kept meant nothing; it was important only that she be the favourite at the very least —and preferably, the Number One wife.

Initially, she had found the foreigners extremely unattractive, repulsive even. The way they smelt was often enough to leave her nauseated. The Siamese bathed several times a day, but these farang sometimes refused to wash for days on end, despite the fact that they suffered dreadfully in the heat. However, as she served at more consular parties, she began to see that not all the farang were ugly. She was even able to tell them apart now, whereas at first, she considered them to be all alike. And even their smell was something she thought she could learn to tolerate in a husband, at least if she could make him wash every day.

For a long time, however, she had not been able to attract any of them, despite her best efforts. None had given her a second glance. She was merely a servant, an invisible utility.

But that was until the night of the consul's party, when this new farang—this green-eyed, fair-haired man she had never seen before—had seemingly become entranced by her. Those green eyes, so bizarre to her still, had pursued her all evening, sneaking glances as she passed near his group, watching her, she knew, from a distance, and gazing at her shoulders and hair as she served with her back to him. She dared not return his looks, but she felt them upon her at every turn. It was an opportunity that might not repeat itself and she would not let it slip by.

She had been with him more than a month now, and he had still said nothing about their future together. But she could wait.

∞∞∞

"We haven't seen you for quite some time, Mrs Fairburn," Dr Vickers said brightly when she was shown into his Collins Street rooms a few days after she received Edward's letter.

"No, Doctor, I'm pleased to say."

"How have you been?"

"Well, Edward has been away all this time, since just after I saw you last. So, naturally, there's been no trouble with the old problem."

"And now?"

"Well, he wants me to join him in the Far East, of all places. I've come to ask you what sort of medical supplies I should take with me."

She spoke without excitement, as if she were resigned to carrying out a recurring chore.

"The Far East, you say. Singapore?"

"No, Doctor. Siam."

His eyes widened. "Well, Mrs Fairburn, you understand there are many health risks in such a place. I really would *not* recommend ..."

"No, Doctor, I don't know anything about the health risks," she interrupted him, rather rudely, she realised—but she could not stop herself. "And no matter what, I have to go." She felt close to tears.

He spoke kindly. "My dear, I understand you have no choice—and you won't be the first European woman to find herself in such a place. But I must stress, once more, the advice I gave you after last time. You simply must not become pregnant again. It is dangerous enough for you to do so here, where medical practices are advanced, and where we have modern equipment. But to do so there ... well, I cannot answer for your safety. Not only the baby's life, but your own life would be in terrible danger in the likely event that things went wrong again."

"I understand, Doctor, but it's ... it's difficult."

The foreboding she felt on the last occasion he warned her not to become pregnant again, returned now. There was much more she wanted to discuss with him, but she could not permit herself to talk of such private matters, even to her own doctor. She wished one of those American lady doctors would come to Melbourne.

"Have you discussed this problem with your husband?" he asked.

"Of course. He says he understands. But it has ..."

She wanted to say that it had destroyed their marriage, that the fact that she could not sleep with her own husband without always the fear of becoming pregnant again had ruined their relationship. Instead, she said only, "It has created some tension."

He didn't push her to say more. "Well, as to Siam itself, all I can recommend is that you take quinine regularly—it seems to protect the body from *malaria*—jungle fever, you know. But keep away from swamps and stagnant water, just to be sure. Oh, and use nets around your bed to prevent mosquito bites. They're much more than an irritation—they can so quickly turn septic in such a climate and even poison the entire body. And I'd advise a tot of whisky each day to ward off the cholera. It's much more prevalent there, of course, than in London—and London's bad enough, heaven knows. There is, of course, a vaccine for smallpox, which … yes, you and Elizabeth have already received, I see from your records."

He went on to explain other diseases they might be exposed to, including leprosy, dysentery, and consumption. Bubonic plague was rife in Singapore and it was thus only a matter of time before it reached Siam, if it hadn't already. The list was frightening and he could do little more than explain the horrible symptoms of each. "I'm sorry to be so explicit but … are you still intent on going, Mrs Fairburn?"

"Doctor, I have no choice."

But she did. Had he not said that she could return home to England if she so desired?

Home. Or Edward. Her thoughts wandered.

It seemed so long ago that she had fallen in love, married when she was seventeen, and set out with him for what she believed would be continual adventure and everlasting happiness. She had been too young and naïve; too much in love to imagine that anything could go wrong for them. And she had thought nothing of the difficulties and discomfort of travel.

For a man, it was adventure, and she thought it would be so for her, too. But for a young bride accompanying her husband overseas, it was something quite different. Most were pregnant within a few months of marriage and then the weeks of morning sickness were spent rolling around in a cramped, airless cabin aboard a ship. A miscarriage at sea was far worse, and some women bled to death or died of hideous infections without adequate medical attention. But it was a risk she had taken often when she was newly married, to her peril. She was older now, and was prepared—determined, even—not to go through it again. She had Elizabeth to think of, her precious only child.

Dr Vickers urged her to make their stay in Siam as short as possible. He made out a prescription, which would be ready within the week, of quinine and other medical supplies to last six months. She thanked him and left the surgery feeling worse than she had since receiving Edward's last letter.

A week later, she terminated the lease on their house with some regret. They had lived in the two-storey double-fronted residence throughout their time in Melbourne, and Elizabeth had been born there. She had come to think of it as her own home, forgetting that it was rented. She realised now that they had never owned their own property because Edward could never settle, was always lured away by the prospect of one more adventure.

Elizabeth, too, seemed to have inherited her father's wanderlust. She had never lived anywhere else, but she didn't seem in the least upset to leave the house, even on the day they departed. And her eager, enthusiastic questions only served to further darken her mother's mood.

"What sort of house will we have in Siam? Will it be bigger than this one? Will Father be there to meet us?"

Charlotte prayed he would be, but she couldn't be certain. She wasn't even convinced they would be welcome.

"I sent a letter as soon as I knew what ship we'd be on," she told her. "We have to go to Singapore first, you remember. He won't know exactly what day we'll arrive, but I expect he'll ask someone to let him know as soon as the ship gets into Bangkok."

She walked round the empty house for the last time. Their furniture had been removed, the rugs had been rolled up, and bare floorboards were all that remained. The living room-cum-parlour looked cold and austere now, the kitchen had lost its welcoming air and the dining room bore little resemblance to the inviting place where she and Edward had once held elegant dinner parties for eight.

She could not bring herself to go back up the stairs to the bedrooms: her own, which she had shared with him and in which the joy of Elizabeth's birth had eased the sorrow of so many previous disappointments; and Elizabeth's, where her daughter had grown into an inquisitive and delightful seven-year-old.

When she had lingered long enough, she briskly took Elizabeth by the hand and said, "Come, it's time to go."

April 21st, 1868

Dear Mother,

You must have been wondering what had become of us, it is so long since I have written to you. I am afraid the truth is that I really have had so little news to tell you until now.

Elizabeth continues to grow and is quite a young lady these days. However, you have probably seen a photograph if Edward visited you, as I asked him to do. He didn't mention it in his last letter, but then he did not mention very much at all. That is, except for one rather unnerving prospect, which has caused me great dis-

tress and brought upheaval to our lives once more.

He has gone to the Far East, Mother, and writes to us from Bangkok, Siam, that he intends to settle there indefinitely. There is nothing for us to do but follow him, as always. I must admit to you that I go with much trepidation.

We know little of the country, but I am sure that medical and other facilities leave much to be desired, so I shall have to pray there is no recurrence of my old trouble. I must also divulge to you, Mother, that Edward did give me a choice. In fact, he almost insisted in his letter that we return to his family in England. I am most reluctant to do that, naturally, but how I yearn for the rolling green hills, the heath of Yorkshire, and the shops of London. And your own dear company, of course. I wonder what advice Father would offer if he were alive. He was always the epitome of good sense, was he not, Mother? I do so miss him still, as you must.

I am enclosing the rather incomplete address Edward has given me for Bangkok. There is no house number, but the residence is on a thoroughfare called New Road. It sounds very ordinary, but I am sure it is not.

I shall not burden you any longer with our fears and instead shall speak of lighter matters. I have heard that Mr Singer's American sewing machine is all the rage in the tailoring world. Nevertheless, I think nothing could replace your Mrs Elder's tiny, perfect stitches. In any case, Mrs Elder herself once told me that the sewing machine was a French invention and so not to be trusted. I was also alarmed to see drawings on the ladies' page recently of the new fashion discarding the crinoline—with skirts trailing in the dust. It appears most unattractive. Has it truly caught on, Mother, or is it only a few unconventional types? Do write back and let me know all the news, including that of the Queen and her family. Does Her Majesty still lead a life of seclusion? Such a tragedy for her to have lost her dear husband in such circumstances. Such a shame though, too, for her to remove herself from public duty.

Siam, too, is a kingdom, and since Edward's letter, I have read a newspaper article about the Paris Exhibition, which highlighted the Siamese section and the magnificence of its display. It is what drew Edward to the country in the first place. The Siamese King is, apparently, in favour of modernising the country, understands English, employed an English tutor for his children and even corresponds with Queen Victoria.

Perhaps Siam will be more civilised than I imagine, although it is said also that he has scores of wives in a huge harem, and goodness knows how many children.

I shall close now, Mother. The next letter you receive from me will be from Siam.

Your loving daughter,

Charlotte

Chapter 5

Kesri had been with him for more than four months now, but if she thought about it, she was little more than a servant to him still. She did his housework, cooked his meals, laundered his clothes—and shared his bed. What would become of her? What would become of her unborn child? When he knew the truth, would he cast them out? The only thing she could do was to be exactly what he wanted, and to wait and hope he could not do without her.

Charlotte, too, had little reason to think well of Edward that day. It had been a long voyage, and as they had approached the tropics, she had begun to suffer even more in the heat and humidity. That morning, as the *Chao Phya* steamed along its namesake river toward Bangkok, she had felt as if she were on another planet.

At mid-morning, they stopped at the village of Paknam, where vessels entering Siam had to gain customs clearance and surrender any guns on board. From there, it was a three-hour cruise along the river to the city. A little farther upriver from Paknam, they passed some thirty decrepit gunboats, each one flying the striking scarlet flag of Siam, emblazoned with its white elephant.

"Sad business, those gunboats," a British man, who had

lived in Siam for five years, told them. "They belonged to the second king, Pin Klao, who ran the navy. When he died the year before last, they were left to go to ruin."

She gazed at the banks of the wide river and was enchanted by the tropical foliage. The five other British passengers marvelled, too, at the scene unfolding before them, the discomfort of the journey quite forgotten in their wonder at seeing their destination for the first time.

"Look, Mamma, there are monkeys in the trees," Elizabeth remarked.

Charlotte looked up and, sure enough, Elizabeth was right. Chattering monkeys clambered and swung through the branches of the banana, coconut and mango trees that clustered along the banks.

The wooden houses on stilts, open to the river, scrambled with the dense vegetation for available space. Children jumped naked from verandahs and rickety wooden piers into the murky water, their skins glistening; women bathed serenely in sarongs or squatted as they washed clothes in the river; youngsters sat on the wooden jetties, smoking, giggling and teasing the skinny dogs that lay all around.

Boats of every description—small flat sampans, huge bulbous rice barges, dilapidated ferries, luxurious yachts, and modern cruisers—jammed the river, making the *Chao Phya*'s progress slow, but allowing them time to take in the extraordinary vista. It was the "River of Kings", life-blood of the entire kingdom. Brilliantly coloured birds darted across the bow and the people on the riverside waved to the strangers as they passed. The foreigners returned the greetings tentatively.

The steamer rounded a bend in the river and Charlotte caught her breath as the city of Bangkok came into view, a city that was as far removed and as exotically different as it was possible to be from London, California, Melbourne, or even other Oriental cities, such as Singapore.

Even as they sailed upriver, she had hoped that the jungle might give way to something familiar, but there was little to comfort her. She realised with a jolt that she was very much out of her depth, and then wondered how long she would be forced to stay. Her gaze was drawn upward from the riverbanks to the elegant roofs and golden chedi of what seemed to be a city of temples.

The sky was a dull, pale grey. It was the monsoon season and, although the rains would be heaviest in September and October, she could see already where the river had broken its bank in places and sandbags were piled up here and there. Canals, called klong, led off the river and as the steamer chugged slowly past, she caught glimpses of ordinary life among the thousands of floating houses. In these tributaries, the activity was even more chaotic than on the river itself. People were everywhere—fishing, swimming, bathing, or washing clothes.

On the verandah of each house stood a huge decorated jar—sometimes two or three—used for collecting and storing rainwater. She would learn later that these were called klong jars. For at least seven months of the year—from October to April or even longer—there was scant rainfall and the populace had to rely on what they had collected in the klong jars during the monsoon season. By the time the hot season was at its peak in April, the water in the jars was slimy and foul-smelling. But at least it was cleaner than the river water, which by then was brackish and a major contributing cause of cholera outbreaks. The very poor, however, were usually forced to drink straight from the river itself. That year, 1868, had been devastating, and thousands of bodies had piled up at Wat Saket, the temple where the dead were either cremated or left out for vultures and dogs to scavenge.

Charlotte knew none of this as they steamed along that early August day. She knew only that the sights that met her, although daunting, were fascinating. She saw Siamese women wearing what Captain Orton called panung. Many of the women were naked above the waist, although some draped a wide sash around their shoulders and torso that still allowed their breasts to hang free. She was taken aback at first and wanted to avert her eyes and to tell Elizabeth to look away. But then she sighed with something approaching envy as she realised how much cooler they must be in the climate than she ever would be. She hadn't even been bold enough to follow English fashion and discard her crinoline, but she had noticed one of the ladies on the steamer—who had just come from England—was without the contraption. What relief it would bring to allow her skirts to trail along, to be free of the steel cage that held out her dress, to be able to seat herself in any chair.

A crowd had gathered at the riverside, and the *Chao Phya* weighed anchor midstream as the passengers prepared to disembark. Charlotte scanned the dock, searching for the face she had not seen in more than a year.

"Father will be there, won't he?" Elizabeth asked excitedly.

Charlotte continued to focus on the people by the quay and the riverside, but they were too distant to identify clearly.

"He should be," she answered uncertainly. "But we can't be sure he received my letter in time. It could have been held up in Singapore. It could even be aboard this ship, I suppose."

Rowboats transported them from the steamer to the wooden quay and Captain Orton himself escorted Charlotte and Elizabeth. But Charlotte's confidence diminished even further as she surveyed the scene more closely. There were hundreds of Siamese milling around and only a handful of Europeans—there to meet the other foreign passengers, no doubt. Edward was not among them.

"Your husband doesn't appear to be here, Ma'am," Captain Orton said sympathetically.

"I'm afraid he can't have received my letter. I don't even have his exact address. It's somewhere on a street called New Road. He didn't have a house number. The letter was sent through the British Consulate."

"Don't worry, Mrs Fairburn. I've been to your husband's house a number of times. He's already well known for his lawn parties. I know exactly where it is. And New Road is the only real street in Bangkok. The rest of the place is built along the canals. I'll send someone immediately to let him know you're here."

"Thank you, Captain Orton. But really, it's not necessary to send a messenger. If you could just arrange some transport for us and give the driver directions, we're quite happy to go there ourselves directly."

"Very well, then. If you're quite sure. My victoria's already waiting." He indicated a small two-seater pony-drawn carriage with a driver perched up front. It waited some way off, where a narrow lane went up the road.

"I'll tell the driver where you want to go and he can return for me later."

"Thank you, Captain, that's so kind of you. And could you possibly arrange for our baggage to be sent on?"

"Of course."

He walked with them to the carriage, gave instructions in fluent Siamese, and assisted them up to the seats. He watched them go, thinking how mistaken he had been about her husband. Fairburn had soon cast off his British inhibitions —if not his woollen clothing—and had adjusted very well to life in Siam. Some might say too well. The captain wondered how Mrs Fairburn would react when she discovered he had taken a Siamese mistress. For she would find out, there was nothing surer. Everyone knew.

Elizabeth and Charlotte gazed out with apprehension as they rode through the narrow, muddy tracks. It was an unstable and uncomfortable ride, even when they came to what was, apparently, the main road, which was riddled with puddles and pot-holes.

Charoen Krung, also known as New Road, had been constructed only a few years previously, in 1861, when the city's small European population had petitioned King Mongkut to have a road constructed so they could go about in their carriages. Until then, there had been no roads at all in Bangkok. Because the city was situated on a delta and, as a result, flooded tiresomely for months during the monsoon, the risk of cholera was lessened if one lived on the river.

The Siamese didn't seem to mind the water at all and were happy to simply wade through the floods whenever necessary. Charlotte had experienced terrible roads in California and parts of Australia that turned to ankle-deep mud when it rained, so it didn't concern her unduly. But she certainly wasn't looking forward to several more months of rain.

She had never before seen such an array of refuse on city streets. When she peered down the tracks that ran off New Road, she saw all manner of rubbish strewn amid the tangled, overgrown bamboo and broad-leafed plants, a stench emanating from the mounds of rotting vegetable matter.

She noticed there were no proper bridges anywhere to be seen, but there were plenty of simple, rickety-looking planks for pedestrians to cross the numerous canals. Best, she determined at once, to go everywhere one could by boat.

There were few shops as she knew them, but then again, she couldn't really discern what many of the ramshackle, dusty buildings were at all. Surely they weren't dwellings? As they progressed slowly, she was horrified to see a gang of forlorn-looking prisoners, all chained together with heavy iron manacles and shackles on their necks, hands and ankles. Elizabeth had fallen silent and could only stare, open-mouthed, at the strange scenes before them. It was a strange mix: every so often, a mansion would appear behind a high fence, some even appearing to be in European-style architecture.

There were groups of Siamese here and there, squatting on the ground and either smoking or playing games to loud squeals of *"Euee!"* In unison, they stopped whatever they were doing and stared in utter astonishment at the European woman and her daughter. She felt hundreds of eyes follow the carriage. When they passed close to an elephant at the side of the road, she breathed in sharply, found Elizabeth's hand and held it tightly. A giggling group of children fed bananas to the huge animal, while the mahout perched, grinning, on top of the beast's neck.

But she had little more time to ponder the sights, for they soon drew up outside a two-storey house with a large expanse of lawn all round. The driver pointed to the house and nodded, and almost before Charlotte and Elizabeth could remove themselves from the seat—no easy task unaided for a lady wearing a crinoline—he was off again. They were on their own.

It was a rather plain, unremarkable house of dusky yellow stucco, of a modest size, with its pale green-grey window shutters all wide open, presumably to allow as much ventilation as possible. There appeared to be no glass panes in the windows at all, and as she looked up, Charlotte saw a small bird fly out of one of the windows on the second floor. It appeared well kept enough, however, although the vegetation from an empty property next door was encroaching on one side. It was really rather better than she had expected. She would plant some flowers to make it more like home. She loved roses, but supposed they wouldn't grow well in the tropics. However, she had seen some beautiful flowers —orchids of every hue apparently growing wild—among the trees on the riverbanks and in the small tracks off New Road. She remembered seeing the same blooms—orange, purple and pink—hanging from hooks on the houseboats and stilt-houses they had passed earlier. She wondered if there were many snakes, and then shuddered at the thought. She didn't mind insects or spiders so much, being well used to the enormous huntsman spiders in Melbourne—but snakes, she could not abide. Australia had some very dangerous varieties, but they were not much seen in the city. It was best not to think of them.

"Is this our house?" Elizabeth asked.

"I hope so, darling." She took hold of Elizabeth's hand

firmly and walked with her up the front path. She was uneasy. A feeling of anxiety tingled in her stomach, and she wondered how she could possibly be nervous about meeting the man she had been married to for twenty years. It was some time since they had seen each other, it was true, and she wasn't sure how he would feel about seeing her here, but it was ridiculous to feel nervous, nonetheless. She took a deep breath and knocked bravely, arranging her face into a smile of greeting.

A few moments later, the door swung open and her smile faded as she spoke falteringly. "I'm sorry. I must have the wrong house. I was looking for Mr Edward Fairburn."

The Siamese girl who had opened the door smiled to conceal her own shock. So, Mem Charlotte had come after all. It was what she had dreaded, but had quietly accepted as an eventuality. She answered as calmly as she could. "Yes, this is the house of Mr Edward. Come in, please. Mr Edward is home soon."

Kesri showed them into the front room. Charlotte took off her bonnet and gloves and handed them to the girl, whom she assumed to be a servant. "We would like some tea, please. And something light to eat."

"Yes, Madame." The girl pronounced the title in the French way, smiling widely to reveal her shiny black teeth, then took the bonnet and gloves and silently left the room. When she got to the kitchen, she threw them on the floor. She had prayed they would not come, and now they had, and she had immediately been treated like a slave. Edward would have to put this woman in her place. She considered herself his wife, now. Had their union not been blessed by a monk? She didn't object to him having more than one wife—it was only right and proper that a man of consequence should have a number of wives—but to be relegated to the role of servant was simply a step back to her past. With Charlotte around, there was little hope Kesri would fulfil her ambitions.

She went back with a pot of tea and a plate with the last of Edward's expensive imported English fruit cake—horrible stuff, in her opinion—and knelt beside Elizabeth, lowering her head as a sign of respect. She set out the refreshments on a low, Siamese-style table with short, curled wooden legs, next to the sofa. "You tired, Madame? You want to sleep?" she enquired politely.

"No, thank you," Charlotte replied coldly, thinking the girl was rather forward for a servant. "I shall wait for Mr Fairburn."

She had hardly said this when footsteps were heard and all eyes flew to the window. He was walking up the path, his velvet jacket unbuttoned, whistling merrily. But from the outside, he couldn't see anyone in the dim interior.

Kesri left the room, respectfully walking a few steps backwards from Charlotte before turning, and almost ran to meet him at the door.

"Kesri!" He kissed her lightly on the cheek. "You look very fetching today."

Charlotte, who could not see the entrance hall from the front room, thought this a strange way to greet a servant. But perhaps it was the custom here.

Kesri didn't allow him to embrace her as he normally might have done, but spoke formally and clearly, willing him to realise quickly. "Mr Edward, Madame is here."

He was puzzled at her tone and the way she had addressed him. "Madame? Madame who?"

"Madame Edward. Your Madame. And your … girl."

His jaw dropped in astonishment. He had heard nothing from her since he had written of his intention to stay and he had assumed she was on her way to England. He rushed to the front room and stood almost paralysed in the doorway, gaping at his own wife and child as if they were a mirage. As he moved into the room, Kesri closed the door but remained outside, listening to what was said.

Elizabeth ran to him and wrapped her arms round his legs. "Father, I've missed you so much. Promise you won't go away again."

Quickly attempting to come to his senses, he lifted her up and hugged her to him. "Dear little Elizabeth, of course I won't." He kissed her, then set her down in front of him. "Well, you're not so little after all. You've grown so much while I've been gone!"

"I can read the newspaper now, Father. Well, some of it, anyway."

He looked again at Charlotte while inwardly he reeled from the shock, his thoughts in disarray. He didn't know whether to be pleased or sorry she had come. But she had and she was his wife. "Hello, Charlotte," he said gently.

"The letter must have gone missing," she replied nervously. He made a movement toward her then and in a second, she was in his arms, feeling again the embrace she never realised she had missed so much.

"I didn't think you'd come."

"I didn't know whether you wanted me to."

"Darling, of course I did. You're my wife. And I could hardly bear to be away another day from my dear Elizabeth."

The family sat on the sofa together, Elizabeth snuggled against her father's shoulder, as they talked of the time that had passed—more than 18 months—since they had seen each other last. He told them about Siam and what they could expect of the climate and living conditions. "I'll make your lives here as easy as possible," he assured them. "You will find it difficult to adjust at first, but there's no need to worry unduly. Things will work themselves out."

"Who is the serving girl?" Charlotte interrupted lightly, almost as an inconsequence. Kesri's slim hips, dark eyes and flawless complexion had not escaped her notice.

Infuriatingly, he felt himself blush as he detected her suspicion. "That's Kesri, my maid. She's wonderful in the house and she'll be a great help to you, my dear. And whenever you want to go out, she can look after Elizabeth."

"Really?" Charlotte said dismissively. "Is she trustworthy?"

"Absolutely, though I wouldn't leave jewellery lying round. You know what a temptation it could be for a girl such as her."

"Yes. She does look awfully young, Edward."

"Well, ahem, yes, but she's very diligent, as you'll see."

∞∞∞∞

Kesri stood in the hallway, listening to their conversation, which she could understand a good deal of. She did not know what "diligent" meant, but she was certain it wasn't what she wanted to hear him describe her as. She had been right; he had referred to her as his maid. Furthermore, she was sure he had said that, given the opportunity, she might steal Charlotte's jewellery. Her face burned and she felt tears brim in her eyes, which she blinked back immediately. She hurried down the hallway and back into the kitchen, for instinct told her that she should remain as inconspicuous as possible. She knew he would not want his farang wife to know about her. Western women had peculiar attitudes about such things, and although Kesri had spent many months with the Protestant missionaries after she had gained her freedom, none of their ideas or beliefs had made any impression on her.

But at least she had learnt English from them and it had helped her find work. It had helped her find Edward. But for how much longer would she have him? Or, was the real question, how much longer would he want her? Was she again just a slave and a plaything who conveniently filled the place of both servant and wife? Perhaps she had been fooling herself all along. With her dream seemingly shattered, she could think only of the fate of her child. His child. The child he knew nothing of yet. Tears welled in her eyes.

∞∞∞

Charlotte stood and almost stumbled—she was still regaining her land legs. "Well, I think I shall go to our room and freshen up before I see the rest of the house. Can you have the girl bring me a basin of water?"

Edward also stood, suddenly panicking. Had Kesri left any of her clothes in his room? "Oh ... yes of course, dear. But ... I shall just ask her to make sure our room is ready for you ..."

"What do you mean, Edward?"

He had to think quickly. "Well ... I've been living as a bachelor for so long it seems, I'm afraid it's rather a mess. I often do my administrative work up there, so I'm sure there are papers and receipts and goodness knows what scattered everywhere."

"I see." She immediately sat down again, unconvinced, but unwilling to disobey him. "Then I shall wait here until it's ready."

"Thank you, my dear. I shan't be a moment."

He rushed out to the kitchen, where he found Kesri sitting at the table.

"Kesri, my sweet, it's very important that Madame not know about you and me yet," he whispered to her, leaning close. "Please, move everything of yours out of my bedroom immediately and into that back room." He indicated the servants' quarters. "It's only for a short time, until I tell her. Then you shall have a room of your own in the main house." He could tell she wasn't happy.

She looked at him balefully—and knew he was lying. This straight-laced farang woman, who must be 40 years old and looked it, would never accept her husband's concubine, let alone allow her to live in the same house. Edward would have to set up Kesri in her own house, she thought. She said nothing, however.

His next request was even more hurtful. "Kesri, could you clean the room, quickly? And Madame would like some water for washing, when you've finished tidying. And remember, please take everything of yours out to the back."

She simply made a gesture of acquiescence, stood and left. When the time came, she would see to it that he gave her a house of her own. It would suit her better, anyway. Then, slowly, she would entice him to spend more and more time with her, until he did not want to return home to his old wife at all.

She did as he asked. Her few nice possessions were gifts from him, more than she had owned in her life, but still a meagre lot. She bundled them up in a sheet, then hurried down the stairs and out the back of the house to the best of the maids' quarters. The tiny, dingy room had no windows or lamp and contained only a worn, dirty bid-roll, a scratched old side-table with a few ill-fitting drawers that no longer closed properly, and an empty candle-holder. Next door was a trough for washing and a lavatory set into the floor with a bowl of water and a scoop beside it. She did not mind this sort of toilet—in fact, it was actually more hygienic than that odd western seated arrangement—but she knew that in the eyes of those above her, she had been put in her place, a place she had believed she had escaped.

When she had arranged the room and her possessions as best she could, she delivered the basin of water to Charlotte, who had taken Elizabeth upstairs with her to sleep off the discomfort of the steamer. Kesri then went back to the front room, where she found Edward sitting alone in an armchair. Without a word, she closed the shutters and the room immediately became warmer as the breeze died away. Edward, deep in thought, did not realise what she was doing until she stood in front of him.

Without warning, she unbuttoned her blouse—which he insisted she wear in the house during daytime in case they had visitors—and let it slip from her shoulders, revealing her firm round breasts and her small brown nipples. Before he could protest, she had unwound her panung and it, too, slipped silently to the floor.

She stood before him, naked, her small yet curvaceous frame highlighted in the shafts of light that filtered through the closed shutters. Her hands moved slowly through her soft black hair, down her stomach, and between her taut thighs.

He felt a surge of desire but was well aware of the danger. "Kesri, for God's sake. We can't do this here. Not now."

She simply smiled and moved slowly toward him, deliberately letting her breasts brush against his face before she bent over to kiss his forehead with feathery lips. She then kissed him the Siamese way, delicately and briefly inhaling the scent of his cheek with her nose as her lips gently brushed against him. It was sensuous and he was weak with lust and fear. He was powerless to stop her, or himself, even though Charlotte—or worse, Elizabeth—could have walked in at any moment.

She straddled him, then quickly and deftly loosened the buttons of his trousers and slipped her hand inside.

"Kesri, not here," he whispered weakly in her ear. "Let's go to your room. No one will find us there. We can lock..."

But he couldn't finish the sentence. She had already manoeuvred herself so that he slipped inside her, and she began to move on him slowly and rhythmically. She raised her legs and linked them behind him, drawing him even deeper.

When it was over, she immediately stood up and he watched her put on her panung and blouse. She left the room as silently as she had entered and he knew he could never give her up. She was the only truly erotic woman he had ever known across several continents. She took him far beyond his wildest imaginings. Her gift was one that Charlotte would never possess: the ability to give herself totally to sensuality.

He didn't blame Charlotte for that, of course. It had never been her fault. But since he had come to know Kesri, he had realised how much he had missed during his marriage to Charlotte. And yet, dear Charlotte was the mother of his child and he could never turn her out.

Somehow, he would have to make it work so that he could keep both of them.

Chapter 6

Mr Knox had returned to England on home leave, but the acting consul, Mr Alabaster, had secured an invitation for Edward as the British Consulate's official photographic representative, with the promise of an added photographic session with the King himself. Edward's family was also invited and everyone had risen before dawn to prepare for the long journey south to view the eclipse.

Edward had finally managed to hire an assistant, a boy named Narong, who spoke a few words of English and who had once worked for a farang missionary family in his Northern home town of Chiengmai.

"Father, where are we going?" Elizabeth asked over breakfast of porridge and tea, prepared by their maid, Kesri, who Elizabeth thought was very pretty.

"A place called Hua Wan, near the seaside. Mr Alabaster says King Mongkut has ordered part of the jungle be cleared to put up a temporary town and palace. We'll have our own house on stilts while we're there. How does that sound?"

"Will there be any other children there?"

"Yes, I think so. Some of the King's sons and daughters are going. You might even meet Prince Chulalongkorn."

"Who's he?"

"He's the King's eldest living son and they say he'll be the next king. He's fifteen, but some of his younger brothers and sisters will be there, too."

"But I won't be able to talk to them. I can't speak Siamese yet."

"Don't worry, my dear. I've heard that the King's children all speak English. They had an English teacher for five years until last year. A Mrs Anna Leonowens, I believe."

"Eat up now, Elizabeth. We don't want to miss the boat," Charlotte said.

When they reached the dock, a large group of foreigners was preparing to board the Siamese gunboat, the *Impregnable*. Among those assembled were Mr and Mrs Alabaster and the other British Consulate staff, the American missionary Dr Bradley, and the American acting consul, Mr N. A. McDonald.

Edward and Narong unloaded the considerable amount of photographic equipment from the carriage. The inventory included the portable dark-tent, which fitted neatly into a wooden suitcase and in which the sensitising and processing chemicals were carried; a plate-box with two dozen plates; a case containing extra chemical supplies; two large tin cans to hold water used in coating the plates; a basket containing miscellaneous items such as towels, a glass funnel, filtering paper, a dusting brush, and a chamois leather cloth; and a case containing the camera lenses, the camera stand, and the camera itself.

As he and Narong struggled with their loads, he wished there were a new technique whereby the developing process did not have to be done on location. If it could be done at the studio, he would hardly even need an assistant. What freedom to be able to travel with only camera and plates.

The voyage to Hua Wan was uneventful and after only two days, the *Impregnable* reached its destination. As they were brought ashore to Sam Rot Yoi beach, Edward, Charlotte and Elizabeth, with the other Europeans, gazed in stunned amazement at the scene before them. For it was not the wild jungle they had imagined. Thousands of labourers, with the help of fifty elephants, had erected a town and palace extending along the beach-front for several miles. There were whispers among the crowd of foreigners gathered on the beach that the King had allocated a budget of tens of thousands of pounds for the expedition.

As they looked to the right, the magnificent royal pavilion stood surrounded by a fifteen-foot-high stockade draped in scarlet cloth. Some of the other buildings were pointed out by a Siamese courtier dressed in a shimmering red silk panung and a white muslin jacket—the jacket being a relatively new standard required by King Mongkut in one of his famous edicts, which were issued "by royal command, reverberating like the roar of a lion".

Adjacent to the royal palace stood the houses of government ministers, then those of the royal children, the consular officials and the other foreigners. To the extreme left, as they looked, were the accommodations of the French scientists, complete with a temporary observatory and removable roof for their telescopes. Ten accomplished astronomers had journeyed the 10,000 miles from France to view the eclipse from its best vantage point—this isolated beach in Siam. The French had arrived three weeks previously and—despite every convenience and comfort being provided—were already complaining of a lack of cooperation. The Siamese, they claimed, had dispatched spies to ensure that astronomy, and not some plot to annex Siam in the name of France, was their object here.

King Mongkut, a keen and accomplished astronomer himself, had predicted to the second when the full eclipse would take place, his calculations differing from those of the French scientists by two seconds. Meanwhile, the traditional Siamese astronomers refused to believe there would be an eclipse at all. The event was due to take place on the morning of August 18th and there were four days to wait, with all eager to see who would prove to be correct and more than a few betting on the outcome.

The Kalahome sent word to the master of the *Impregnable*, Captain Walrond, that Mr Alabaster was to remain on the ship until the other visitors had disembarked, because His Majesty wished to welcome him with an official reception. It was a great honour.

The crowd watched in awe as—with much pomp and ceremony—the second foreign minister and other important members of the court greeted Mr and Mrs Alabaster at the pier. Then they proceeded to the temporary palace, where King Maha Mongkut—known to the Siamese as King Chulachomklao—received them.

From his vantage point on the beach, Edward could see the King clearly. He was a slim, elderly man, taller than most of the other Siamese, although his height was hard to judge with certainty since his subjects prostrated themselves on the ground in his presence. He was, in fact, probably the first king of Siam whose subjects had actually seen him. Before his reign, it was illegal for members of the public to even look at the monarch. But Mongkut had been a monk for twenty-seven years before his coronation and—as he said himself—he knew many people from that time. He wanted his subjects to line the streets and he wanted to be able to speak directly to them if he so desired. They still, however, had to ensure that their heads were lower than his at all times.

His Majesty was dressed fabulously in a richly embroidered scarlet silk taffeta *panung* and a dark blue jacket with gold braid at the cuffs, lapels and Chinese-style collar. He wore a matching gold-braided hat and gold slippers. His wide smile revealed his new set of dentures, made for him by a Western dentist—a Mr V. D. Collins—who had travelled from China via Singapore when he'd heard, the year before, that the King would pay a thousand American dollars for a perfectly-fitting new set of teeth to replace his old ones made of red sappanwood.

Edward had heard the story from other expatriates of how Mr Collins had had terrible difficulties with the fit because the King refused to allow him to touch, or even to look at, his mouth, let alone to take a wax impression. His Majesty insisted on doing the job himself, the head being sacred to the Siamese, and that of the Lord of Life especially so. Several sets of teeth were made, but the fit on each one was so bad that he could not wear them. The King eventually allowed the dentist to take an impression of his mouth, with excellent results, and paid him 560 dollars, which Mr Collins accepted graciously, though it was not the 1000 dollars he had hoped for.

Mr Shaw had said that Collins had then become quite the adventurer, making a 43-day journey with his wife to Moulmein by elephant and boat. Mr Shaw and the other missionaries had been particularly concerned, because the Collinses spoke no Siamese or Burmese and the route they were to travel was virtually unknown to westerners. Indeed, Mrs Collins was the first European woman the villagers along the way had ever seen.

Edward noticed that one side of the King's mouth seemed to droop a little, as if he had suffered some malady, but that nevertheless, he had a warm, intelligent expression. He was old—in his sixties, but looking a decade older—and Edward felt he would make a most intriguing photographic subject. He was the first Siamese monarch to allow his image to be captured by the new medium of photography.

His Majesty fired the seven-gun salute to Mr Alabaster with his own hand—a rare honour indeed—and the members of the consular party then disappeared into the palace proper, where they were served refreshments in the vast audience hall.

The Fairburns were shown to their own house, a small but solid wooden structure that was more than adequate for their needs. A table was set in European style and several servants were in attendance. There were more surprises to come. They learnt that the finest European wines and champagnes were theirs for the asking: that a French chef was overseeing preparation of the food by forty Chinese and European assistants, and that an Italian maitre d'hotel would see to their every need. They were even more astonished at the extent of the King's hospitality when Edward ordered a bottle of champagne.

"Never mind that it won't be chilled, my dear," he said to Charlotte. "I feel like celebrating."

The champagne arrived in a bucket of ice.

"It's unbelievable," Charlotte said, gasping. "How on earth did they ..."

Edward laughed. He had known all along. "Shipped here from Singapore. Apparently, the only thing in short supply here is drinkable water. But then again, who wants water when one has champagne on ice, eh?"

He smiled at his wife once more and she thought that perhaps this excursion would help improve things between them. Meanwhile, Elizabeth watched them, delighted. She hadn't seen either of them looking so happy for a long time.

The next day was a French celebration—Emperor Napoleon III's Fête Day—and everyone entered into the spirit of the festivities. The ships in the harbour were bedecked with colourful ribbons, and salutes were fired throughout the day, officiated by the French expedition leader, Monsieur Stephan.

Charlotte and Edward stood on the beach and watched the sun set, as one of the two bands brought in to celebrate the occasion played a popular romantic waltz. She hadn't felt so close to him since Elizabeth had been born. It had been less than two weeks since her arrival in Siam and already she felt more content than she had dreamed possible.

The following day, a far more distinguished guest than Mr Alabaster arrived at Hua Wan: the Governor of Singapore, Colonel Sir Harry Ord, accompanied by Lady Ord and a large group of the Governor's officers and their wives. As their steamer, *Peiho*, appeared offshore, the King arranged to receive the Governor immediately. He was disappointed, however, when Sir Harry asked to postpone the reception until the next day, because they had arrived on a Sunday and he was a devout Christian.

Nevertheless, the King granted the Governor's request and the following day, Sir Harry was duly received with a seventeen-gun salute and a royal audience, at which His Majesty was seated on a throne surrounded by two hundred kneeling princes and officers attired in gold silk jackets.

Edward was disappointed not to be granted permission to photograph the meeting, but the governor later allowed him to take a picture of Lady Ord and himself by the palace entrance.

Edward also learned later that the King would agree to appear in a group photograph surrounded by his foreign guests. Edward would have preferred to photograph the King without the Europeans—alone or with the several wives who had accompanied him—but he felt reluctant to ask another favour. Now that the King knew who he was, however, he might allow Edward to photograph him alone at some future date. There was plenty of time, he reflected, now that he would not be leaving Siam in the foreseeable future. There was also the chance that he might even be given royal photographic commissions.

Edward spent the rest of the day setting up his equipment, assisted by Narong. Not the least important task was calculating the exposure time necessary in the overcast conditions typical of the monsoon season. Fortunately, his tintmeter, with the cumbersome name of Bing's Universal Self-Registering Actinometer, was the most accurate device available for measuring exposure times.

Although he had warned the subjects to remain very still during the process, the first plate was ruined when the King made a comment—out of Edward's earshot—that caused laughter throughout the group. It was unthinkable that one of His Majesty's quips would pass unnoticed, of course, and it was necessary to laugh heartily. There was nothing for it but to discard the plate and start again. Edward took six photographs, after which everyone was relieved to be able to move their limbs freely again.

The developing process revealed four of the plates to be worthwhile likenesses and he decided to make prints for the King and for each of the other subjects. He had waited so long, it seemed, to achieve his goal of photographing the monarch, that the actual realisation was something of a disappointment. The photographs were not particularly interesting artistically, but their central subject meant they were historically important. He took other photographs, of the French scientists (who were all complaining that there was no cheese available) as well as portraits of some of the important European guests.

The one concern of all present throughout the preparations was the weather. It was, after all, the monsoon season and menacing thunderheads had gathered above. They seemed to grow steadily blacker after the arrival of Sir Harry's party and loomed still, as the morning of the eclipse, August 18, dawned.

The King and the Kalahome were said to be almost frantic with worry that the spectacle would not be visible. Nevertheless, people busied themselves setting up telescopes in front of the dwellings.

Dr Bradley stopped to talk with Edward during the morning. "I believe your photographs were quite a success, Mr Fairburn."

"That's very kind of you to say so, Dr Bradley. I only hope the eclipse, too, may be successfully viewed. The King has set his heart on seeing it, I believe."

"With the Lord's help." Dr Bradley commented as he glanced up at the sky, where the cloud cover was thickening and a drizzle was beginning to fall.

Dr Bradley walked on, leaving Edward smiling politely and thinking how ironic it was that an American missionary should be asking God to grant a Buddhist potentate's wish.

Initially, when the King fired a cannon to signal the start of the eclipse at precisely 10.22am, nothing could be seen through the clouds. Moans of frustration and cries of "*Mon dieu! Mon dieu!*" were heard from the French section as the scientists began to fear they might have journeyed half-way round the world for nothing.

But suddenly, as if on cue, the clouds began to break up and the spectators on the beach were silent as the sky started to clear. Then, all at once, the eclipse was clearly visible in all its magnificence.

Dr Bradley and his party of missionaries cheered loudly, as did some of the Siamese at first. But then, in awe, they fell silent. Some of the Siamese ran into their houses as the Kalahome shouted, "Now will you believe what you have been told?" The King, beside himself with delight, almost danced for joy between his telescopes and fired the cannon once more to announce his victory. The cannon's boom was met by a blast of pipes and trumpets from his subjects.

The spectators, silent again as they gazed at the phenomenon, heard the distant sound of drums being beaten in the nearby village. The Siamese believed that an eclipse occurred when the evil back sky dragon, Rahu, attempted to devour the sun. In order to ward off Rahu, they beat gongs and drums, and crashed pots and pans together, lest the sun be consumed.

As the sun partially emerged, the French scientists quietly went about their calculations. They were relieved to have been able to witness the event, but were embarrassed that—for all their supposed superior scientific knowledge— the King of Siam had more accurately calculated the precise time of the total eclipse. Surely it was a fluke, each of them secretly concluded.

As the eclipse continued to cast an eerie light over its path, insects and other nocturnal creatures began to stir, deceived by the onset of the false dusk. Edward slapped yet another mosquito that had landed on his neck.

"Confounded creatures," he complained. "Don't suppose they do much harm, though. More of a nuisance than anything." Elizabeth's legs had been bitten and Charlotte, like the other ladies, had covered her feet with a large brown paper bag, drawn up round her wide skirt. Even the King hadn't been spared from the bites, and Edward had noticed him scratching at his arms.

They left in the *Impregnable* the next day with the other foreigners. Despite the heat and the mosquitoes, Charlotte was sorry to leave. It seemed at Hua Wan that she and Edward had begun to communicate again, to appreciate the qualities in one another that had brought them together in the first place.

"In spite of it all, we're still the same two people we were when we married," she had said to him the night before, as they lay side-by-side in bed. But then she turned and saw he was not listening. He had fallen asleep, still holding her hand. She smiled in contentment anyway, believing that she and her husband were perhaps falling in love all over again.

October 19ᵗʰ, 1868

Dear Mother,

All Siam is mourning the death of its esteemed ruler, or Lord of Life, as they refer to him, King Maha Mongkut. I do not know if you have read of this in the London newspapers, but it is such a tale of high drama that I shall describe it to you in detail. It is, in fact—as you shall see—fortunate that I myself am alive to tell it and it is also the reason I have not corresponded these last two months.

As you know from my previous letter, we were to travel to watch the eclipse at Hua Wan. I have included with this letter an article from the Bangkok Recorder *which describes the event much more eloquently than I could. The King certainly put those Frenchmen in their places when it was proved that his calculation of the eclipse was correct and theirs wrong. We were more than a little proud, and pleased to ally ourselves with the Siamese contingent, rather than with the French, who are bent on gaining far too much influence in this part of the world, anyway.*

We were amazed at the extent of civilisation in such an out-post and especially at His Majesty's hospitality. The entire expedition is said to have cost as much as £20,000—can you imagine! There was even ice for the champagne. Every important foreigner in Bangkok was invited and the King paid for the entire entourage, as well as for thousands of peasants to clear the area and construct houses for the thousand or so guests.

However, all the trappings of civilisation in the world could not protect the visitors from the diseases of such a place—none of which discriminate between servants, Europeans, or Siamese royalty. The King, Crown Prince Chulalongkorn (now the boy King), no fewer than eight of the ten French scientists, and I myself, among many others, came down with what is known as jungle fever (malaria, to be more precise in modern medical terms). Some became ill as early as the return voyage, while others are still succumbing only now. This is a terrible illness, Mother, and is quite often fatal. At least eight have died, as well as scores of labourers and servants. It is, as the name suggests, brought about by the bad airs of the jungle, I believe.

The King suffered his first fever on August 24th, the day of our return to Bangkok. Having developed the fever myself—albeit in a much milder form—shortly after we landed at the port, I can tell you it would be no way to pass into the Lord's hands. At first, one is burning hot, then icy cold, shaking from head to foot, yet still sweating in the extreme heat and humidity.

Dr Bradley administered quinine to me, which I took religiously, and I seem to have recovered well enough. Elizabeth and Edward are quite well. I think my daughter takes after her father and is of strong constitution, unlike myself. The poor King, being elderly I suppose, could not prevail, although Dr Bradley says that he lived weeks longer than he should have, by sheer determination.

Apparently, after first taking quinine and advice from his foreign doctors, and not making a quick enough recovery, he reverted to the traditional Siamese doctors, who are little more than witch doctors. Nothing more could be done because he refused to see either Dr Campbell or Dr Bradley for weeks.

When, finally, Dr Campbell was admitted, the King ignored his advice. The doctors believe that if His Majesty had taken quinine regularly from the first signs of the illness, he would most probably be alive today. Still others say he would not, for it is claimed he had made up his mind to die on his birthday, and did just that. Such a noble man he was, and we shall all miss him here, even though Edward and I did not know him personally. The Siamese burn their dead rather than burying them, but the King's body will not be burned for more than a year.

Shortly after he succumbed to the fever, his highest-ranking son, Chulalongkorn, was proclaimed King, the fifth in the current line, although because of his youth, being only fifteen, a regent has been appointed to rule until he reaches the age of twenty.

The young King is a handsome, intelligent boy who, they say, has already voiced strong opinions as to the modernisation of the country and the continuation of his father's good work in that respect.

Edward is sorely disappointed that he was unable to photograph the late King alone, but only with a group of other royals and dignitaries during the eclipse. He believed he had made progress in that direction and was even hopeful of gaining an audience. Now, as he says, he must start again with a new king, and not only that, but he must first gain an audience with the Regent, which is just as difficult, he supposes. Anyway, his photographic images taken during the expedition must be quite valuable, as they are among the last ever taken of the old King.

Other than that, Edward has started to do quite well in his business. He has even gained a reputation as the "ladies' photographer", managing always, as he does, to somehow photograph his subjects from their most fetching angle, masking their less admirable characteristics. There are several other foreign photographers in the city, so he by no means has a monopoly on commissions and must work hard for his clients within the limited expatriate community and within the top class of Siamese.

In addition, Mother, I do not think I am breaching any mari-

tal confidences if I tell you that we are renewed together. Edward must spend much time with his business, of course, and is often away from the house, sometimes overnight if he must be at a late appointment and stay at his host's house rather than risk the dark lanes home. However, I believe he is happy and content with us here and with our uneventful home life and our little lawn parties.

So, do not fret for me, Mother dear. I am, as you see, quite content at present. I look forward to your reply.

Your loving daughter,

Charlotte

∞∞∞

Charlotte thought it odd the way Kesri had just seemed to disappear. They returned from Hua Wan to find the house empty and the maid's room bare. Edward seemed distracted when she questioned him about it.

"Oh, didn't I tell you, dear? Kesri is no longer with us."

"Why? Where has she gone?"

"She ... she had to return home to her family. Her aunt is very ill."

"I thought she had no family, Edward."

"Er ... no close family," he answered quickly. "I believe the woman is really a distant older cousin she calls aunt."

"Well, I can't say I'm sorry she's gone. She was a good worker, but sometimes I thought she was ..."

"Hmmm?" Edward said vaguely, trying to sound as if he were not interested.

"Oh, I don't know, perhaps ... well, I sometimes had the feeling there was more behind her smile than we realised. I don't think she enjoyed being a servant. Edward, did you hear what I said?

"Hmmm? Sorry, Charlotte, what was that?"

"Never mind. I'll have to ask Mrs Alabaster if she knows

a girl who can replace her."

But Edward's thoughts were not on Kesri's replacement. He was still wondering how he had managed to retain a façade of normality throughout the entire trip to the south, especially after the news Kesri had given him only the day before they had left.

It had been her way of ensuring his return, of being certain he would still want her. But she had been very wrong, and now he reproached himself for what he had said and done that day in the studio when she had come to him with the news.

It had been only a week after Charlotte's arrival and he had thought, when Kesri let herself into the studio without knocking, that she was initiating one of their frequent, intimate interludes. Her revelation was a disaster.

"This cannot be true, Kesri. Tell me it's not," he uttered in shock.

"I tell you true," she insisted, her head bowed, understanding now that he was far from happy.

"Do you not realise that this is the worst thing that could happen to us at this time?"

She said nothing. She needed his support, and screaming and crying at him would not achieve that, she guessed.

"I thought you girls knew how to ..." he spluttered as she looked at him wide-eyed now. "Well, I thought ... I thought you knew how to stop these accidents occurring."

"In Siam, a man is not angry when his wife have baby. What you think would happen, anyway?"

"But Kesri, you are *not* my wife. Charlotte is my wife and it would bring shame to my family—cause a terrible problem —if everybody knew this child were mine. The child of our maid."

So, he had finally said it. She was not his wife. She was a servant.

She lowered her eyes again, maintaining her composure in the face of his frustration and anger. "But, Edward, everyone will know this baby not Siamese when he is born. Will be plain to see."

"Kesri, that's why you must leave this house. Nobody must know."

She turned her eyes pitifully up to his. If she did not proceed with the utmost of care, she would lose everything.

"Please, Edward, do not send me away," she whispered. "Do not. I do anything. Please, you think of our baby—maybe son for you."

But all he could foresee at that moment was the catastrophe of Charlotte discovering the truth and the public shame and humiliation if word were to spread, which it inevitably would.

Charlotte's suffering and devotion flashed before him and only deepened his confusion. She had offered herself to him again, although she knew it could endanger her life if she became pregnant. He had so far managed to rebuff her intimate advances, making the excuse that he was exhausted by the heat and that the developing chemicals he had to use in his work sometimes made him feel ill. But for how much longer could he deny her?

"I must send you away, Kesri," he continued. "I'm sorry, but there's nothing else to be done. You're a sensible girl—I'm sure you understand." He took her small hands in his. "Don't worry, I shall still see you and the baby. I will look after you and you'll have everything you need. But you must not tell anyone that I'm the father of your baby. You must go away someplace where nobody knows you."

Although there was still a possibility she would one day be with him, she was little comforted by his words. But, she thought, when he saw the baby, maybe he would change his mind. After all, Mr Knox had a Siamese wife who was Number

One.

"*Chai*, Edward, I do what you say. *Mai pen rai*."

It was her only choice. She had to remain calm and allow him time to reconsider. Her alternative was to make a public spectacle of the affair. But what purpose would that serve? He would deny responsibility, abandon her, and perhaps even take his family and leave Siam forever. At least this way, she and the child would be taken care of, even if it was not the outcome she'd hoped for.

"We're leaving tomorrow for Hua Wan to see the eclipse," he had told her, relieved that she was not going to make trouble. "When we get back, you must be gone. I'll see you have enough money to take care of yourself. You need not work. We'll return toward the end of the month and you may send a messenger here, to the studio, to let me know where you are. I'll visit you."

"You not divorce me?" she asked fearfully.

Edward sighed, realising that their paths would never converge. "No, Kesri. I don't believe in divorce. And anyway, I can't divorce you because we are not properly married. You're not my real wife. I've told you that quite plainly before."

Still she could not understand what he meant. If she lived with him and if their union had been blessed by the monks, as it had, of course she was his wife. And if he was willing to have her live with him before, despite his farang wife, he must not believe the missionaries who said that a man must have one wife only. Why would he not admit it?

She wondered if perhaps Charlotte had discovered their relationship and had insisted Kesri leave. But he had said it was because of the baby. A Siamese man would be proud in such a situation, because it proved his manhood. Why was Edward not pleased, particularly since he had only one other child and no son? But he said it was the worst thing that could happen to him. It was beyond her comprehension.

Chapter 7

Porntip waited until late the night of the garden party. The last guests had departed hours ago, and when she saw the upstairs lamps go out and she was sure everyone would be asleep, she slipped away down to the landing, her bare feet making no sound. She climbed into her sampan and stealthily rowed down the Chao Phya and then off to the Thonburi side of the river, into a narrow, anonymous klong.

A few minutes later, she moored her boat at another landing. Its stairway led to a floating wooden house, where a shadowy figure was waiting on the verandah.

"Come in quickly," Kesri whispered. "We have a lot to talk about."

Two months previously, in January, Kesri had given birth to her daughter after a straightforward four-hour labour. It was not her first child—a secret she had kept from Edward—so she had known what to do. She had immediately sent word to him via Porntip, who was her friend and also the Fairburns' new maid. He did not come for a week. After the midwife left, Kesri was alone with the baby and she felt deserted.

"His own daughter," she complained bitterly as Porntip sat down beside her on the rattan mat that covered the floor of the single room that was her home. It was, however, an improvement on the maid's room at the house. "And it's as if he doesn't want her."

Porntip tried to reassure her. "Of course he does, Kesri. But his wife barely lets him out of her sight."

"Then why doesn't he just tell her about me? Is he a man

or not? Is he not lord in his own house?"

"I don't know why he doesn't tell her. I can't imagine. But Kesri, they don't often share a bed, so passion can't be his reason for staying only with her."

"He doesn't need to lie with her, because he has me. I'm his secret wife. The wife no one must know about. For some reason, he's ashamed of me."

"What will you do, Kesri?"

"I don't know yet. But I will do something. I'll not be cast into the background, my child not acknowledged as his. Not for long. Will you help me, Porntip?"

"You know I will, sister," she replied, using the Siamese form of endearment between close friends.

"Good. We need to plan this carefully."

Once she had fully recovered from her bout of jungle fever, Charlotte found she had plenty of time on her hands. Because Edward worked such long hours, she needed something to occupy herself with. She had soon followed the other expatriate wives into charity work, which mostly involved visiting women and their children in poor areas, collecting clothing and other necessities for them and advising them on health care and whatever education could be provided for their children.

Most of all, she wished the women would end their custom of "staying with the fire", in which the mother of a newborn child would lie with a brazier of burning charcoal beside her stomach for several weeks. When the woman could bear the heat no longer, she turned so that her back could be roasted.

King Mongkut had abhorred the custom and it was said that his successor, Chulalongkorn, did, too. Consequently, "staying with the fire" was no longer popular at the palace, nor among the nobility. Nevertheless, the poorer people stuck to their tradition and still believed dreadful things would happen if they did not do it.

It was March and Charlotte was well established in her daily routine. In the mornings, before it became too hot, she would do whatever charity work she could manage, visiting mothers of sick children and going to schools and temples to distribute food and clothing. In the afternoons, she would visit friends to play cards, to take tea, and to catch up on all the news of the foreign community, then return home to meet Elizabeth after school and to rest before dinner. She went often to the residence of the consul, Mr Knox, who had returned from England, and his lady. Mrs Knox was a gracious, handsome Siamese woman of high birth, who spoke excellent English and loved to talk with Charlotte about her children. Her son, Tom, and elder daughter, Fanny, were at school in Europe, but the youngest child, Caroline, now eleven, preferred to stay in Bangkok with her parents.

Although Charlotte knew she would always feel like a foreigner in Siam, and she would never become accustomed to the year-round heat, she at least found the country and the people fascinating. She eventually discarded her crinoline, more out of expedience than to follow fashion, and she travelled through Bangkok mostly by water-taxi, the tiny paddle boats that bobbed, along with thousands of others, on the river and the klong network. She never tired of watching the people going about their daily activities. Nor, in turn, did the Siamese ever seem to tire of staring back at her, the children always smiling and waving. Sometimes, she wished she could jump into the water with them.

The Bangkokians were becoming more used to foreigners now. In the days when Ayuthia was the capital city, there had been a sizeable foreign population, but that was followed by a period of isolation from the late 18th century when Siam had been virtually closed to foreign trade. Since the 1830s, however, the foreigners had been coming once more to Siam —but the novelty of them certainly had not worn off for the locals. Charlotte, in her high-buttoned long dress, holding a matching parasol to shield her pale skin, was an incongruous sight among the throngs of Siamese, colourfully dressed in their comfortable panung, calling loudly to each other across the water and crowded into every space on every boat. A vessel barely more than three feet long might hold up to fifteen people. If it overturned, the passengers simply swam to the nearest landing, sat in the sun to dry themselves, and waited for another boat.

Charlotte did not like to bother Edward during the day, when he was working. Although his studio was on the property, in a room at the back of the house, he had his own entrance and Charlotte knew he preferred not to be disturbed while he worked. Many members of the European community brought their families to be photographed and as word of his talents spread, he even made customers of some of the Siamese.

It was only a few years previously that no Siamese would even have allowed their portrait to be painted, let alone permit themselves to be photographed. They believed that the reproduction of a person's likeness—whether on a coin, a drawing, a portrait, a sculpture or a photograph— would remove a part of their soul and thus shorten their life.

Photography was introduced to Siam even before King Mongkut's time, during the reign of his predecessor, Phra Nanklao, probably by the French missionary and adventurer, Père Larnaudie, who happened to build the first rice mill in Thailand. However, because of the common superstition, the presence of a camera could still immediately disperse a crowd, especially beyond Bangkok. Following King Mongkut's example, however, the wealthy and titled classes were now quite comfortable before the camera and it was soon considered essential to have one's portrait taken.

Most of the professional photographers in Bangkok

were Chinese, but there were a few Europeans. Westerners preferred to patronise one of their own, so Edward soon found he had more than enough business. In fact, he was often booked up for several weeks in advance. He was also hoping to lend his services to His Majesty and to the government, in order to officially document the rapid advancements taking place in Bangkok.

Establishing contacts was a drawn-out process, however, and to do so, one had to secure invitations to the right social events. That was why he encouraged Charlotte to work with the likes of Mrs Knox, rather than with the missionary wives who meant nothing to the Regent and were merely tolerated.

While the Regent, Somdech Chao Phya Sri Sriyawongse, did not favour foreigners, it was known that the young King was very enlightened and was already planning to use the foreigners to hasten the modernisations he wished to bring to Siam. However, because he would not gain his majority for some years, it was necessary for foreigners such as Edward to be patient, to wait, and in the meantime to secure what private work they could.

Edward told Charlotte he was still trying to gain an audience with the Regent, but it was not easy. Sri Sriyawongse had many more pressing matters to concern him than the granting of his time for one English photographer with no political connections. It was rumoured the French were preparing to colonise Siam, as they had Cambodia, and the hated French consul, Gabriel Aubaret, had been removed before King Mongkut's death.

But the French were still considered a threat—as, in fact, were the British, who now governed Burma—and Charlotte could not help but marvel at the ability of the Siamese to keep the great powers at bay. They possessed no navy to speak of and could not possibly have defended themselves in the event of an annexation. That left their diplomatic skills, which must be of the first order, she thought.

∞∞∞

The Fairburns' lawn party guests were a select few, invited for 3pm to play croquet, to try their hand at archery and to share an afternoon tea of tropical fruits, and drinks cooled by water kept in a trough in the shade. Among those invited were the Alabasters, the Bradleys, and Joseph Shaw, who taught at Elizabeth's school.

Charlotte had met Joseph only a few times, at school soirées, and although they did not know each other well and had never had the opportunity to talk at length, she immediately felt him to be a kindred spirit, someone to whom she could talk easily and in whom she sensed great empathy. She also detected, behind his kind expression and soft eyes, some sadness that seemed a permanent burden to him. They had not exchanged even the slightest of personal information before, but she found that the informal atmosphere of the party made her bold enough to enquire about him.

"I haven't met many of the English missionaries," she remarked as they stood in the shade of a large tree. "Most of the missionaries here seem to be American."

"Well, yes, the Americans do have a strong representation here," Joseph replied. "But, actually, I'm not exactly English. I'm from New Zealand. My parents are English originally, but I was born in Auckland."

Well, then you and I can feel homesick together for the Antipodes. We spent many years in Melbourne. Elizabeth was born there."

"Oh yes, I remember your husband saying you'd lived in the Australian colonies. How are you settling in here?"

"Much better than I expected, Mr Shaw. The heat is debilitating, of course, but with the shipments of food coming from England so frequently, we're really rather well looked after."

Indeed, life in Siam was much more agreeable than she had imagined it would be. Socially, it was as busy as Melbourne, and because of Edward's family background, they were accepted by the consular staff into their elite circle.

She had found, to her surprise, that class divisions among the foreigners in Siam were almost as obvious as in England. In Bangkok, the foreign community was split into four cliques, with the consular staff considering themselves superior to the merchants, the sea captains, and the missionaries. They were not strict divisions, however. An urbane or well-off sea captain might be invited to a consular party, if he were considered to be of sound breeding. And a consular officer might stoop to socialise with merchants and the like if he thought it could benefit him economically, or perhaps just for an amusing diversion.

Although it was far easier in Siam for certain people to fabricate backgrounds—and so, if they were guileful enough, to be admitted to cliques they would otherwise never have been—true impostors were nearly always discovered, or at least treated with suspicion. Charlotte heard of an English school teacher named Anna Leonowens, who had left the previous year after more than five years tutoring the royal children. Mrs Leonowens, accompanied by her young son, Louis, was a widow of a British officer, or so she said. Captain Tom Leonowens, she claimed, had died of sunstroke after a tiger hunt in Singapore. She claimed to be from an impoverished but genteel Welsh family. One young British attaché, who also came from Wales, was puzzled when she seemed to know so little of the country, or indeed of England, where she claimed to have gone to school and lived for a time after her marriage. "I think there is more—and less—to Mrs Leonowens than she has let on," he mumbled to a colleague, though no one said anything openly. Still, she was gone now and would be quickly forgotten.

Charlotte, of course, did not suffer Anna Leonowens's

problem. Having been born to a family of reasonable social standing, if reduced means, and having made what was considered a brilliant marriage, she was immediately recognised by the British as a lady, a member of that class of landed gentry whose younger sons so often made their lives abroad, as Edward had done.

Charlotte could call upon the advantage, also, of having travelled abroad a great deal. She was used to things not being as they were at home and was, in that respect, not as delicate as the Victorian ladies who arrived in the tropics straight from their English drawing rooms. She could hoist up her skirts and pick her way across a road ankle-deep in mud—as she had done in the goldfields on numerous occasions—without a second thought to propriety, all the while speaking the most beautiful Queen's English. In this way, she was admired by some of the foreign women in Bangkok, although a few thought her perhaps just a touch vulgar for it.

To add to her contentment, Edward seemed more satisfied than she had ever seen him. He made no demands of any sort on her, yet he remained mostly cheerful and considerate. In fact, feeling guilty, it was she who sometimes suggested they retire together to the bedroom, only to be assured by him that such a sacrifice on her part was unnecessary. Still, she did notice that he sometimes seemed distant and distracted. They had a new maid, who was friendlier and more obedient than Kesri, though Porntip barely spoke any English and was not nearly as efficient as her predecessor.

The climate was the thing Charlotte found hardest to tolerate. Though it was only early March and everyone was remarking how the cool season had lingered this year, for Charlotte the heat and the mosquitoes were almost unbearable. The loathsome creatures were everywhere, even finding their way through the nets covering her bed and biting her as she slept. Despite the temperatures being much more comfortable in the cool season in the early morning and at night, it still reached eighty or even ninety degrees in the afternoons.

And it was just such an afternoon as she stood on their lawn in conversation with Joseph Shaw.

"But tell me about yourself, Mr Shaw. How long have you been here?"

"Six years, Mrs Fairburn. Since 1862, in fact."

"Six years! Good gracious. Have you returned to New Zealand during that time? I presume your family is still there."

"Yes, they're still there. But no, I haven't been back." He paused, as if he were not sure what to say next.

Was she imagining it, or was there a wistful, melancholic look about him?

"You must have been young when you came here," she said to fill the silence.

"I was only twenty-one."

"It must have been difficult for you, alone in a strange land, no wife beside you."

Joseph smiled a little and briefly looked heavenward. "I had help, Mrs Fairburn."

"Of course. But what did your parents think of you running off to Siam to become a missionary?"

"Actually, it was my father's idea." A shadow seemed to cross his face for an instant, but then it was gone. "He's a minister, you see. He and my mother went out as missionaries to the Maori in the thirties."

"How fitting that you're carrying on the family calling then."

"I suppose you could say that, but I hadn't really thought of it that way before."

She thought this a strange comment, but it intrigued her and she persisted, nonetheless. "But why Siam? Why did your father not keep you with the family in New Zealand? I'm sure there's still work to be done there, is there not? Or perhaps somewhere else closer to home? You're such a long way from your people."

Joseph hesitated, then spoke as if picking his words carefully. "I suppose he wanted to teach me to have ... humility. You see, I don't believe we'll ever succeed to convert much of the populace here. Missionaries in the South Pacific have had such astounding success—entire populations have been converted. Not so here in Asia, I'm afraid. So here, we will, in a way, always be doomed to fail." He cleared his throat, embarrassed to have spoken so frankly to a woman he barely knew. However, he felt at ease with Charlotte, and he continued. "My father met some Presbyterian missionaries in America many years ago, when he and my mother visited California on their way to Hawaii. They were among the first to work in Hawaii, but then the need for missionaries to go farther afield seemed much stronger, and as New Zealand was part of the Empire, they decided it would be more patriotic to travel on. But they did keep in contact with their friends, who obtained a position for me. Sadly, both those good people died of cholera last year, within six days of each other. I was quite lost for a while without them."

"Yes, Mrs Bradley told me they've lost many of their recruits to illnesses since she arrived." She lowered her voice. "Do you know that her husband has been here since 1835? His first wife died of consumption in 1845, so he took his three children, went back to America and returned with a new bride in 1850. He introduced the first smallpox vaccines here and the first printing press. It's the stuff of novels, is it not?" She paused, looking slightly embarrassed. "I'm sorry, Mr Shaw. I'm forgetting myself. I'm sure you know all this already and I'm sure you have no time for such nonsense as novel-reading."

Before he could answer, Charlotte excused herself as another couple arrived at the party. She circulated among the guests, making sure everyone had a cool drink, but she couldn't help feeling curious about Joseph. She wondered why he hadn't married. He wasn't particularly handsome, but he was tall and straight-backed, with an intelligent face. He had only a small moustache and no side whiskers, and his fine brown hair wasn't very well cut. But this seemed only to add to his look of sincerity and goodness. She felt he was someone who could be trusted. He would have made a wonderful minister, she thought, wondering why he hadn't been ordained.

∞∞∞

Porntip came to Charlotte one day soon after the party and said in the newly acquired English she had learned since starting her job with the family: "Madame, my friend have baby. You come?"

The girl had never approached her so directly before and Charlotte was surprised. "What's the matter with her, Porntip?"

"She no happy, Madame. She no have husband. She ... I not know how say ... she ... *ther ngao maak*. Only her."

"Lonely? She's lonely?"

"*Ka*," she assented.

"But she has friends, hasn't she? Family?"

"No family. Porntip only friend."

"But why?"

"Baby farang—Angrit!"

"The poor girl." Now she began to understand. "And the English father. He's deserted her?

Porntip looked confused, and Charlotte tried again, more simply. "He's gone? Man gone?"

The maid nodded.

"Very well. I'll come immediately. If the baby has an English father, that makes it a British subject. He'll have to do the decent thing by her."

But she was speaking to herself. Porntip understood little of what Elizabeth said, except that she had gained Charlotte's attention, meaning her task was almost complete.

She took Charlotte downriver in her boat and they soon arrived at a floating house, which Charlotte noticed was well kept and clean. Through the open front, she could see a young woman with her back to the klong. The woman was holding a bundle in her arms and gently rocking it.

When Porntip and Charlotte climbed from the sampan to the house, the woman turned to greet them. Charlotte gasped when she saw it was Kesri.

"Hello, Madame," Kesri said, her eyes cast down as she continued to rock the little bundle in her arms.

"Kesri! I had no idea."

"No, Madame."

Charlotte knelt down beside the former maid. "Kesri, I'm here to help you. You need not feel ashamed."

"No, Madame."

"Please, let me see your baby." She was beginning to feel very afraid.

Kesri smoothed the wraps back from her daughter's face and Charlotte looked down at the little girl, who was peacefully sleeping. At first, she thought Porntip had made a mistake. It was a Siamese child, she was sure. True, the skin was quite pale, but she was still very young, and Kesri herself was not dark. The baby had Siamese features: the tiny snub nose, the black eyebrows and lashes and a fuzz of black hair on her head. Then, the baby stirred, yawned and opened her eyes and Charlotte was so startled she drew in her breath sharply. The child's eyes were the purest colour of green.

"She's a very beautiful baby," Charlotte managed to say as a feeling of panic and despair shot through her.

"Thank you, Madame. It is sad her father does not want her."

"Has the father seen her? Does he even know about her?"

"Yes, Madame, he knows. He sees. But he has problem."

Charlotte thought she knew what Kesri meant—and Kesri knew that Charlotte was beginning to fear the worst.

"Is he married already, Kesri?"

"*Ka.* And he say his wife not want second wife in house."

"If I'm to help you, Kesri, you must tell me his name." She was almost numb, stricken with fear at the prospect—the certainty—of Kesri confirming what she already knew must be true.

Kesri indicated a pile of triangular-shaped cushions and Charlotte sat against them awkwardly, unaccustomed as she was to sitting on the ground. Kesri sat beside her with the baby and Charlotte noticed her very European-looking silver locket.

"A gift from the baby's father?" she asked. But Kesri looked away and said nothing. Charlotte let it pass.

"Kesri, when was the baby born?"

"Two months ago, Madame."

She counted back the months, realising that Kesri must have been working at the house when she had conceived. There could be only one explanation. She was almost shaking now and her voice began to break.

"Was this ... was this man a friend of ours, perhaps, who took advantage ..." But she was clutching at an improbable hope and she trailed off as a wave of dread swept through her.

She remembered the way Edward had greeted Kesri that first day, and she remembered other things too: the looks between them and Kesri's resentment toward her.

When she spoke again, it was almost in a whisper. "Kesri, tell me his name, I beg you. Tell me his name!"

Kesri lifted her head and looked straight into Charlotte's eyes, her chin held high.

"His name, Edward Fairburn. His daughter here, Anchalee Kesri Fairburn. Elizabeth has sister now, *ka*."

Chapter 8

It began a few days after they set sail: the vomiting, the diarrhoea, the muscle cramps, the overwhelming weakness. She knew she had the dreaded cholera, and as the steamer lurched from wave to wave, her energy drained away. There was a British doctor on board, returning home to England after eight years in Siam, but he could do no more than sponge her with alcohol and administer a little opium to ease the pain.

"You must try to drink, Mrs Fairburn" he urged, holding some water to her lips. Whisky was the only alternative, but he had tried that already. He could do nothing for her. Not there, in the middle of the ocean and at that stage of the disease.

She took a sip, then immediately vomited again. Her tortured eyes opened for a moment, as the helpless doctor gently wiped her parched lips. "Where is she?" the poor woman whispered.

"Don't worry, she's in good hands," he improvised, knowing nothing of her situation. "But she needs you and you must try to get well for her sake."

It was futile to try to save her, but he wanted to show her some last kindness in her final hours.

She mustered all her strength to force out the faint words. "My daughter—I'll never see her again."

Then she drifted back to that day when she had lost everything and everyone she loved …

∞∞∞

Edward had known the game was up when Charlotte had stormed into the studio without knocking as she usually did. Intrusions irritated him, but he thought better of his reaction when he saw the anger and distress on her face. Jars of chemicals shook on the tables and shelves as the door slammed behind her.

Tears had begun to well in her eyes, but she managed to calm herself enough to speak. "How could you do this to me, Edward? I am mortified. How could you?"

"What's this? What's wrong, for heaven's sake?" But he knew what it must be.

She could only repeat herself, louder, shaking within, but staring at him intently.

"Sit down, Charlotte; you're hysterical."

"I am not hysterical," she said, gritting her teeth to regain her composure.

"Well at least tell me what's wrong." He was buying time. She knew his secret, obviously. Only, how could she have discovered it?

"I know, Edward. I've seen her."

"Seen who, dear?"

"Don't you dare call me that. It's obvious that I am not your *dear*, isn't it?"

"Well, whatever are you talking about?"

"You know, damn it." This time she shouted and it was the first time he had ever heard her curse. "I've seen Kesri. And the baby. Your baby."

He took a deep breath and sat down. "Is this what she told you? That the child is mine?"

"Yes. And I believe her. The baby has your eyes." She remained standing, her bonnet still on, having come directly from Kesri's houseboat.

"It could have been any foreigner. Green eyes aren't rare. These girls … you know how they lie."

"No, I do not. The only person who is lying is you, Edward. There is no doubt in my mind who the father of that poor child is."

He sighed. There was no point in denying it any longer. "I suppose you had to find out some time, Charlotte," he admitted.

"But why, Edward? Why? In all our years together, you have been a loyal husband." She looked straight at him. "Or so I thought. Maybe you have not. Maybe this sort of thing has been going on for years and I've been too blind to see the truth."

"Charlotte, I swear to you, this is the one and only time." But he could not look her in the eye.

"I don't know how I can believe that, Edward. But tell me one thing. Supposing what you say is true, then why now? Why with this … this young girl—our *employee*? Why?"

"Do you really need to ask?"

"What do you mean?"

"I'm a man, Charlotte, like any other. I'm not a priest. I can't be celibate. I need a woman."

"Edward, you have a wife," she uttered in a shocked whisper.

"A wife in name only," he replied. "A wife whom I cannot lie with, for fear of the consequences. Kesri gave herself willingly to me, with no guilt, no sense of sacrifice. She wanted me for myself. For her, it wasn't a duty."

Always, always the same thing. Their problems were ever the consequence of the one burden, this one disappointment, this one misfortune. Charlotte saw it as her great failure. His words cut so deeply, he might well have sliced her to pieces. There was only silence now, and he felt a familiar surge of guilt as she collapsed into an armchair, her head in her hands.

∞∞∞

At the beginning, newlyweds Edward and Charlotte Fairburn were brimming with excitement at what the future could hold. They had remained in England only two months after their marriage, before setting out for California and the gold rush. But Edward was no ordinary prospector. He could have stayed in the family business in England, making a comfortable living and never having to worry about money. But he could not bear the thought of joining his father's bank, as his brothers had done, and nor did he have any desire to become an officer in the army, which was what his father had suggested when his son told him he wanted to see the world. He decided he would make his own fortune—he and Charlotte together. At his father's insistence, he agreed to accept a private income, but only until he could manage on his own. What he really needed more than anything was adventure.

Charlotte was already pregnant when they boarded the steamer for California, but she hadn't told him before they left, not wanting him to feel obliged to postpone his plans. He was delighted when she did tell him, their first night at sea, and all went well until two days before their arrival at San Francisco.

In choppy seas, the deck was unstable, but that morning, Charlotte was suffering so badly from nausea that she had begged him to take her for a walk on deck. There was a sudden lurch and they were both thrown to the floor. She fell heavily on her stomach and retired straight to bed.

That afternoon, she awoke soaked in blood and suffering severe stomach cramps. The ship's doctor confirmed what she already knew; she had lost the child.

No sooner had she recovered in San Francisco than she found herself pregnant again—but she miscarried at four months, when Edward was away at the goldfields. She cried herself to sleep, alone in her misery.

Edward never did have much luck finding gold in California, and they were glad after all of the stipend from his father, ensuring they were never short of money or basic comforts. Then Edward discovered photography and, after his investment in a camera and other equipment, did well enough thanks to the steady stream of cashed-up prospectors who were eager to have their "pitchers took" on their claims and with their finds. He had, at last, discovered a natural talent and although he didn't really need to work, he was thrilled that his new venture provided him with both satisfaction and the opportunity to become financially independent of his family.

After her fourth miscarriage, Charlotte was advised not to become pregnant again. Nevertheless, she lost another child at sea in 1851 while they sailed to Australia to follow the gold trail. She carried the next baby—a girl—to full term, but she was stillborn. The marriage Charlotte had entered into with such joy, such passion, had become a bed of misery, although she still loved her husband deeply. She wanted so desperately to give him a child and she felt she had failed him, though he assured her she had not.

It was not until thirteen years after their wedding that she finally gave birth to Elizabeth, in Melbourne in 1861. As soon as she knew she was pregnant, she took to her bed, determined not to lose this child, though she knew it could happen anyway, no matter what she did. She stayed in bed for the full term, rising only for half an hour each day.

After Elizabeth was born, their marriage seemed renewed. Both felt the fulfilment they had so long been denied. But Charlotte knew she should never allow herself to become pregnant again. She was drained, physically and emotionally, and her face and body seemed a decade older than her thirty-one years.

He said he understood, and they agreed that his conjugal rights should be taken only once a month—and each month she prayed she would not conceive. Her prayers were not always answered. She became pregnant again in 1866, and as before, she took to her bed. She watched herself grow with both mounting excitement and fear as the months passed, and she saw Edward filled with anxiety each day when he asked how she was. At six months, she went into premature labour. The child—a son—was another stillbirth.

It was the end of their physical relationship. He could not bear to inflict any more pregnancies on her. Charlotte turned away from even his comfort-offering embraces, sorrowful and bitter at what she saw as her failure to be a proper wife.

He left for England shortly after and she felt it was mostly to escape her, and to run from the guilt he felt every time he looked at the lines of strain and disappointment on her face. But still, something made her want to try again, to save their marriage, and perhaps, to become closer again. She wanted his love and respect, not his guilt and pity. Her marriage vows meant everything to her and she was willing to risk her life for them.

∞∞∞

So many years later, in the deafening silence of the studio in Bangkok, everything they had built together was falling apart. Even so, she spoke quietly and reasonably, hoping for an explanation she could live with.

"Edward, I offered myself to you without restraint. I told you I was willing to take the risk. I wanted our marriage to work."

"But at what cost?" he challenged bitterly. "Do you think I could live with myself if you died in childbirth simply because I could not control my desires? It would make me little better than a murderer. Even if you were to have another miscarriage and live, I couldn't bear making you suffer so much again. And all those dead babies—our children ..."

Tears of grief and frustration coursed down her face and she could not speak.

He took his chance to try to explain. "Charlotte, darling, don't you see? This woman means nothing to me. I don't feel for her what I feel for you. I don't love her, but I have needs, and she's content with filling them."

"Don't speak to me that way of her—the mother of your child," she cried out, her anger and disillusionment deep and draining.

"Charlotte, this is the way things are done here."

"What are you saying?"

"You'd be surprised at how many European men have Siamese mistresses. More often than not, their wives know about it. They give them what's called a pink ticket ..."

She could not believe what he was saying. "But it's wrong, Edward. It's wrong. They don't do it because they want to. They do it because their husbands bully them into it. Simply because you are here, doesn't give you licence to behave in this way. And what about the child?"

"Charlotte, can't you see reason? Having Kesri here would make our lives together more peaceful, more satisfying. There'd never be any pressure on you. You'd have all the status that went with being my wife, and none of the demands of married life that bring you so much pain."

She stood in dismay, staring at him for several seconds before speaking again. "There is neither status nor honour in being the wife of a man who'd ask me to accept his mistress. I have loved you for so long, Edward, but suddenly, it's as if you are a stranger to me. It's as if that love were obliterated, had never been and will never be again."

"You're tired and overwrought, Charlotte. Why don't you go upstairs to rest and I'll have Porntip bring you up some tea?"

"I don't want tea!" she shouted. "And Porntip—will she too be joining your harem? Edward, do you not see? You cannot brush this aside. It is over."

"What do you mean?"

"I mean that I cannot and I will not accept this woman as your mistress. How could you even imagine that I would? You must provide for the child, I suppose. But you must agree never to see the mother again."

"No!" Now he was angry and he rose from his seat and stepped towards her. "You've no right to forbid me to do anything."

"I have a moral right to ask this of you. To *demand* this of you. I'm your wife before God."

"And, as such, you must obey me."

"So, you'll not give her up?"

"No."

"Then our marriage is finished, Edward. I'll return to England as soon as it can be arranged." She sounded braver than she was.

It took him by surprise. "Charlotte, don't be rash. Don't do anything you will regret. Take some time to think this out. Please, my dear …"

"I don't need more time," she cut him off abruptly. "This will not change. I simply cannot accept her, or any other woman. It's high time Elizabeth went home to school, anyway. She's running wild in bare feet, speaking Siamese half the time and climbing trees. She'll be much better off in England."

"You are not taking Elizabeth with you. If you go, you go alone." He was sure this would make her change her mind.

She had not expected his reaction and now it was she who was caught off guard.

"You cannot stop me, Edward."

"Yes, I can. And I will. You're a wife deserting her husband. No British court would award you custody of our daughter. Elizabeth stays here."

"And you're a man committing adultery," she responded. "What sort of life would she have here with a father devoid of moral principles?"

"Better than the life she'd have with a mother who deserted her husband. You realise society will shun you, don't you? I couldn't abide my daughter being subjected to that."

Now she began to panic. Fear engulfed her as she realised she would lose Elizabeth. "Please Edward," she begged, as tears spilled from her eyes, "I've done nothing wrong. Nothing. Why are you hurting me this way?"

He was trying desperately not to allow her to manipulate his guilt. "It's *you* who is hurting me, Charlotte. A wife's place is with her husband and he is the head of the family. Think what shame you'll bring on us by leaving this way."

"Shame? How can you speak of the shame I'd bring on *you*? You've brought shame enough on yourself to last a lifetime. You can explain my absence by saying I had to return to England for health reasons. In time, they'll find something else to talk about. Perhaps the former maid and her green-eyed baby."

"You're jealous, that's what it is. You're jealous of Kesri having a baby because you can't have another!" As soon as he had said it, he wished he had not.

"You are insane," she replied through her shock and her tears. "You don't even deserve the dignity of a reply." She walked out of the room and into the burning afternoon sunlight, leaving him alone in his studio.

He felt a terrible guilt, like a gnawing pain deep in his stomach. It had been this way all their married lives. Would it ever stop? Would he ever be free of the burden of her pain?

∞∞∞∞

It was Joseph Shaw's day off and he was relaxing in a hammock that his houseboy, Simon, had rigged up between two shady trees. He was taking to it more and more on his rare days off, despite the risk that a snake might one day drop on to him from the branches above. There were plenty of reptiles around, including cobras, and five-yard-long pythons that enjoyed feasting on new-born puppies, according to a neighbour.

Here in the garden, Joseph was indulging in a pastime he was a little ashamed of, a pastime he felt would not be quite approved of by the more pious members of his church: he was reading a novel. George Eliot's excellent volume, *Adam Bede*—the story of a simple girl led astray from the man who truly loves her by a man she can never hope to marry—was one he was particularly fond of. He had read the book before, but although it was now ten years old, it had not lost its attraction. His supply of new novels was exhausted and he was reading again the best of his old ones—which he kept discreetly out of view in a locked teak cabinet in his living room—while he awaited a shipment from England. He had a standing order to be sent the latest releases from London. He hoped his next parcel would include something new by Anthony Trollope. In books, he could forget the sadness and loneliness of the real world, and become lost in a dream world in which he himself had no part and in which he, therefore, could do no wrong.

He was engrossed in the book when Simon arrived beside him pointing to the house.

"Sir, Madame Fairburn here."

Joseph could speak Siamese well, but Simon wanted to improve his English, so they always conversed in that language, unless Joseph needed to explain something complicated.

He was surprised. "Mrs Fairburn is here, to see me?"

"*Khap*," Simon said, nodding. "She say she must speak with you."

"Of course. I'll come immediately. Please bring us some lemon squash, Simon."

As Simon returned to the house, Joseph put his book down carefully on the hammock, took his jacket—which was hanging on a nail on one of the trees—and hurriedly ran his fingers through his hair. He walked briskly up to the house and when he greeted Charlotte in the living room, immediately noticed how disturbed she appeared.

"Good afternoon, Mr Shaw, I ..." She was almost breathless. "I'm sorry, please forgive me for intruding."

He smiled warmly. "Not at all. You're most welcome any time. But you look a little flustered, Mrs Fairburn, if you don't mind me saying so. It's the heat, no doubt. Simon will bring us a cool drink."

"Yes, thank you, that's very kind. And you're quite right. I *am* flustered. In fact, more than flustered. But I'm afraid it's not the weather, Mr Shaw."

"How may I be of assistance, Mrs Fairburn?"

"To tell you the truth, Mr Shaw, I don't think anyone can do anything to help me. But I wanted to talk to someone. I feel I can trust you."

"Absolutely, you can. But please, take your time." He sat on a chair opposite her. "You look pale. It's not Elizabeth, is it?"

"No, no, it's not Elizabeth. Well, that is to say, it's not her directly. But it does concern her."

"Go on, Mrs Fairburn. Whatever's troubling you, I'm sure there's a solution."

"But that's just it, Mr Shaw. There is no solution."

Joseph became alarmed. "Whatever is it, Mrs Fairburn? Your health is all right, is it not? And Mr Fairburn? Is he in good health?"

"Oh, yes," she replied cynically. "*He's* in good health."

"Then ...?"

"I may as well come straight to the point, Mr Shaw." She hesitated only firefly. "My husband is having an affair with a Siamese girl."

Joseph wasn't completely surprised. It happened frequently and he knew some of the wives even tolerated it. Affairs were common in the West too, of course. But he was sorry for Mrs Fairburn, who seemed such a decent, honest woman. "Are you absolutely sure?" he asked, just to say something.

"Yes, he's admitted it. But the worst of it is, they have a child. Or rather, she has a baby that she says is my husband's. And he doesn't deny it. In fact, he … he …" She almost broke down and had to take a deep breath before she could go on, dabbing at her eyes with a handkerchief. "He refuses to put a stop to the affair. He actually believed I would consent to him continuing the relationship."

"That would be a most heinous way for you to exist," Joseph agreed, before pausing for thought. "You know, Mrs Fairburn, your husband isn't a member of this parish. He's never attended services, so I can do little to influence him, except to offer you my prayers."

"Mr Shaw, I didn't mean that I wanted you to do anything. His mind is made up and I doubt anyone can change it. He's not a religious man, unfortunately. I do not wish him any ill and I do not wish to cause him any hardship. He is still the father of my own daughter. But I cannot countenance this relationship. The only thing left for me to do is to leave for England immediately."

"Mrs Fairburn, I cannot officially condone your leaving your husband, you understand. But in private, may I say that I'm perfectly sympathetic to your decision. Is there anything I can do to help you?"

His kindness almost made her burst into tears once more, but she took a deep breath and nodded. "There is one thing, Mr Shaw, that's leaving a terrible ache in my heart, more so, in fact, than my husband's infidelity. He forbids me to take Elizabeth back to England with me. He says that as I am the one deserting him, the law will uphold his right to custody of our daughter."

"I'm afraid he's correct, Mrs Fairburn. Unfair as it may seem, unless you can prove his adulterous affair—which would involve a public court case, lawyers, witnesses and so forth—he's entitled to keep Elizabeth here with him. British subjects must abide by British law here, according to extraterritoriality arrangements. I'm so sorry."

"Oh, Mr Shaw, I can hardly think of how meaningless life will be without her. But still, I *cannot* stay. I will not. I don't want to stand by and watch my husband with his second family. Equally, I don't want my daughter brought up in such circumstances. But a public court case is out of the question. I will not give her up, though. I intend to speak with his brothers back home, and to see if they can influence him to change his mind."

"Quite so. Is there anything at all I can do?" he offered again.

"There is one thing, Mr Shaw. Elizabeth looks up to you. She thinks you're a wonderful teacher. Would you watch over her? Could you talk to her from time to time, to be a sort of godfather, I suppose? I'm very sorry to ask such a thing, but you're the only one here I can trust."

"I'd be more than happy to," Joseph agreed instantly. "And if she ever needs help for any reason, I shall give it her without question. You can be sure of that, Mrs Fairburn. I give you my word."

∞∞∞

She sat with Elizabeth in the bedroom she and Edward had shared only briefly. A large trunk was open on the bed. She knew that the next day would be the saddest of her life; her marriage was over and she was farewelling her only child for who knew how long.

"But Mummy, why must you go to England? I don't understand."

"Darling, I've told you. My health isn't good and I must return to a cooler climate. Siam is an uncomfortable place for me and I must get well again."

"Is it like when you told me you used to get sick before? And my brothers and sisters went to heaven?"

"Not quite like that, Elizabeth. Just that I am hurting so much inside."

"Will England make you feel better?"

"I hope so, sweetheart."

"Why can't I come?"

"Dearest, it's a very long journey. Besides, you have to go to school." For her daughter's sake, she fought back the tears.

"Does that mean you'll be away for a long time, like Father was?"

"Yes, Elizabeth. Perhaps longer."

Elizabeth began to sob. "Don't you want me any more, Mummy?"

The tears that had been threatening all day finally rolled down her face uncontrollably. She clasped Elizabeth to her. "Of course I do. I love you more than anyone in this world. When you're older, you'll understand more why I had to go."

The next day, Elizabeth stood on the pier with her father, silently waving farewell to her mother as Charlotte boarded the boat that would take her to the ship waiting across the bar. Edward didn't wave. Elizabeth hoped the vessel would somehow be forced to turn around. But it wasn't to be. Her mother was gone.

The captain had been through it before and he knew the routine well. It had become something of a standard procedure, but it was never easy. He picked up his steel-nibbed fountain pen and began: *It is with much sadness that I must inform you …*

Mrs Fairburn had been thirty-eight years old, and the

captain had heard she had had to leave her only child in Bang-kok as she set out alone for England.

Chapter 9

Each day, she waited for her mother to come home. Might she reach Singapore and decide not to continue to England after all? Her father was quiet these days and would hardly answer her when she asked such questions. When she *was* brave enough to ask about Mummy, his only reply was to tell her to stay quiet at the table, or to stop interrupting him.

Less than a week after Charlotte had left, Kesri returned to the house with the baby.

"This Anchalee. Your sister," she said as she handed the child to Elizabeth.

Elizabeth thought for a moment. "My sister?"

"*Chai*. Your sister. We come back now, live with you."

Elizabeth was suspicious. "But how can Anchalee be my sister? My mother didn't have another baby. And if she did, she wouldn't have just left it with you."

Kesri's expression darkened and she snatched Anchalee away. "I talk with your father." And as she angrily left the room, she said something under her breath that Elizabeth could not understand.

Elizabeth couldn't imagine what she had said to make Kesri react like that. But how could the baby be her sister? It didn't make sense. But she was sorry all the same and she went out into the kitchen to apologise. She found only the maid there.

"Porntip, where's Kesri?"

"She rest," Porntip answered.

Elizabeth started toward the back door, meaning to go

out to the maids' quarters, but Porntip shook her head and held her back. "*Mai chai, mai chai,*" She said, pointing to the ceiling.

Elizabeth was confused. "She won't be there if she's resting, Porntip. Only our rooms are up there."

Porntip looked at Elizabeth, almost with pity, and Elizabeth wondered if the maid had understood her.

Finally, Porntip just nodded her head. The girl would find out for herself soon enough, she thought, and it wasn't Porntip's duty to tell. She didn't know how to explain it in English, anyway.

In fact, Porntip had already noticed Kesri was treating her differently. No longer, it seemed, was she a trusted confidante, but more someone Kesri felt she could give orders to Porntip was beginning to regret her part in the scheme. Mem Charlotte had been kind and undemanding, and Porntip realised now that Kesri would not be so generous.

Elizabeth climbed the stairs two at a time, and when she looked round the doorway into her parents' bedroom, her mouth dropped open in astonishment. Kesri was lying on the bed, tickling Anchalee and giggling. She had pulled back the bedspread and was lying across the bed on Mummy's best white linen sheets.

Kesri looked up. "Yes, Elizabeth?" she said irritably.

Elizabeth was speechless. She didn't know what to make of the scene, only that it didn't seem right.

Kesri stood up, leaving Anchalee gurgling on the bed, and went over to the dressing table. "What you want, Elizabeth?" she asked again. "You want to say sorry? So say. Then go."

She picked up Charlotte's silver brush and began to groom her hair, all the while watching Elizabeth in the mirror. Elizabeth knew how much her mother had loved that brush. Her father had given it to Charlotte as part of a set when Elizabeth was born. The little girl wondered why her mother had left it behind if she loved it so much.

Very deliberately, Kesri then took the stopper out of one of the little coloured-glass perfume bottles and dabbed the scent behind her ears. Elizabeth felt sick and she hurried from the room, down the stairs and into the front garden, where she lay in the long grass beside the fence, sobbing and not caring what snakes might lurk there.

It was in this condition that Joseph Shaw found her. He knelt beside her so his head was level with hers and wiped her eyes with a big white handkerchief. "Hush, hush. What's the matter, Elizabeth?"

My mother ... has gone ... away," she spluttered, still shuddering from crying so hard.

"I know," he said, aching for her. "And you must be very brave. Just remember that she loves you and she will write to you soon."

"If ... she did ... she wouldn't ... have gone ... away." She was sobbing less, but still distraught.

"I know it's hard for you to understand, but you must believe she loves you and always will. And perhaps, when you're older, your father will let you go to England to visit her."

She found hope in his words. "Do you think so?"

"Why don't you ask him? Your father loves you very much, too, and I'm sure he wouldn't want to see you unhappy like this."

His words only brought on a fresh round of tears. "No, Mr Shaw, he doesn't care about me any more. Whenever I talk about Mummy, he tells me to be quiet. He doesn't want to talk about her at all. And then... and then ..." She looked up at him mournfully.

He set her down on the lawn and sat beside her. "What is it, child?"

"I saw Kesri in Mummy's room, lying on her bed and using her brush and her perfume." But before Joseph could think of a sympathetic reply, she told him even more disturbing news—to which he could not respond. "And, Mr Shaw, she told me that her baby is my sister. I don't understand. I don't know why she said that. She's telling fibs, isn't she?"

Joseph determined to speak with Edward as soon as possible. The child was so confused, she hardly knew where she was. He stood up and brushed grass from the legs of his trousers. "Well, Elizabeth, since I'm your visitor, do you think we should go inside and have some tea?"

"Are you my visitor? I thought you came to see Father."

"No, I came to see you."

She managed a weak smile. "I don't think I've had a visitor before." She slipped her hand in his as they walked into the house and she asked Porntip to bring them some tea. "I have a visitor," she said importantly.

They went into the front room and chatted about her school work and the subjects she enjoyed most. When Porntip brought in the tea, Elizabeth poured the cups herself and they continued talking. Usually, she would have liked milk or juice rather than tea, but she suddenly felt like a grown-up, with her own visitor. Joseph tried to ensure Charlotte was not mentioned.

The conversation ceased when Kesri entered the room with Anchalee. "*Sawatdee ka*, Mr Shaw," she said, surprised to find him here with Elizabeth.

"*Sawatdee khap*, Kesri. How are you?" He remembered her from the mission and from the party at the British Consulate.

"I'm fine, Mr Shaw. Meet Anchalee." She held out her baby for his inspection.

He had no choice but to take the child from her and was startled to see the baby's bright green eyes. It was Edward's child, there could be no mistaking it. "She's very beautiful, Kesri." He held the baby for a moment before handing her back. Elizabeth remained silent.

Kesri hugged Anchalee to her. "You come for Edward?"

"No, I'm here to see Elizabeth."

Kesri laughed to conceal her agitation. "Elizabeth? But

she is only a girl." There was something dubious about the situation and she didn't like it.

"Yes, but she's my pupil. And her mother asked me before she left to come to see if she was well from time to time."

Kesri gave him a funny look and spoke dismissively. "You can see—she is fine." Then she left the room without ceremony.

Elizabeth watched her go and then whispered, "I don't know why she's so angry with me. I don't think she likes me."

How could he explain the situation to an eight-year-old? The truth was, he could not—and besides, it wasn't his place to do so.

"Perhaps I will have a word with your father before I go, after all," he told her as he stood up. He sent her off to read one of her school books in the garden, hoping it would provide some distraction, at least for a short while, then went out to the studio, where he found Edward cleaning his equipment and preparing for a family portrait session later that day.

Edward greeted him jovially. "What can I do for you, Mr Shaw? You haven't come to have your portrait taken, have you?"

"No, thank you, Mr Fairburn. I was in the neighbourhood and thought I'd call by. Elizabeth treated me to a cup of tea."

"Did she really? She's becoming quite sophisticated in her old age, isn't she?"

"Indeed," Joseph laughed politely. "I also met Kesri. And the baby."

Edward abruptly became irritated. "Oh, yes. No doubt you've heard the rumours and were curious to see for yourself?"

"That's not why I came," Joseph replied quickly. "Actually, I hadn't expected Kesri here at all."

"I think of her as my wife, now," Edward commented almost casually as he went on with his preparations.

Joseph felt very uncomfortable. "Your … your wife? But

you already have a wife, Mr Fairburn."

"Not here, I don't, Mr Shaw. Charlotte made her decision. It was she who abandoned her family."

"You didn't give her much alternative though, did you?" Joseph was shocked at his own forthrightness.

"And what interest do you have in all this?" Edward shot back, now visibly angered.

"I didn't come to moralise, Mr Fairburn, if that's what you're thinking. But I *am* concerned about Elizabeth. She's very confused. Did you know Kesri told her that Anchalee was her sister?"

"No, I didn't." Edward was taken aback slightly and this comment curbed his anger. "She shouldn't have. Not yet. It is, however, the truth."

"Mr Fairburn, she'll hear the whole truth from someone, sooner or later. Or she'll put it together herself eventually," Joseph continued. "I realise it's none of my business, and I don't like to intrude, but she's also wondering what Kesri is doing in her mother's bedroom. Far be it for me to advise you on what you should tell your daughter, Mr Fairburn, but I think you'll have to talk to her soon."

Edward did resent the intrusion and—even more—the fact that it was the truth. But he was forced to relent.

"You're right, of course," he said, sighing and slumping on to the sofa. He gestured toward the armchair and Joseph sat opposite him.

"I didn't want Charlotte to leave, you know. But things hadn't been good between us since she ..."

At that moment, Elizabeth knocked briefly at the open door and entered the room.

"Elizabeth, I've told you not to disturb me while I'm working."

"Yes, Father, I'm sorry. But a messenger brought this letter. It says 'urgent'. I think it's from Captain Orton on the boat." She handed the envelope to her father.

"All right, my dear. Thank you. I wonder what Captain

Orton can have to say that can't wait until he returns."

"Maybe it's about Mummy?" Elizabeth asked hopefully. "Maybe she's coming back."

Edward did not reply, but was certain that would not be the reason for the letter. Missives of this kind usually meant bad news.

April 20th, 1869

Dear Mr Fairburn,

It is with much sadness that I must inform you of the death of your wife, Mrs Charlotte Fairburn, on board the Chao Phya at six o'clock on the morning of April 20th, 1869.

Shortly after we set off, Mrs Fairburn developed a fever and Dr Matthews on board diagnosed cholera. He worked to save her through the day and night, but to no avail.

Mrs Fairburn passed away quietly in her sleep and she was given a proper Christian funeral service by myself, followed by a burial at sea.

I enclose the death certificate, completed by Dr Matthews. I shall visit you on my return to Bangkok to answer any questions you might have.

May I express my condolences, Mr Fairburn, to yourself and to your daughter, Elizabeth, and may your dearly departed wife rest in peace.

Yours sincerely,

Captain Orton

Edward stared at the letter, dumbfounded, the truth not sinking in. Without a word, he handed the page to Joseph.

Elizabeth noticed his expression and was alarmed. "Father, what is it? What's wrong? Why do you look like that?"

A numbness came over him and a distant look entered his eyes. For a few moments, he could not seem to remember where he was. He saw a vision—like an old, faded photograph —of a young woman on her wedding day, laughing gaily as she looked into his eyes. She was full of joy and it was as if her life were just beginning. But then the edges of the picture turned brown and started to curl.

Elizabeth pulled at his sleeve. "Father, tell me what it says," she screamed, terribly frightened.

Joseph had also read the letter by now and he, too, was shocked, but he knew he would have to be strong for Elizabeth.

Edward spoke unsteadily and it was almost as if he really were somewhere else. "Will you tell her, Mr Shaw? I cannot." Then, slowly, like an old man, he walked from the studio back to the house.

"Mr Shaw, tell me, please," Elizabeth cried. "What's happened? Is it my mother? Is she ill?"

Joseph spoke listlessly. "Yes, my dear, it is your mother. Come, let us sit on the sofa together and I shall tell you as gently as I can."

She sat down and he turned to face her. Elizabeth's green eyes looked fearfully into his.

"Elizabeth, your mother is no longer with us," he began.

"Mr Shaw, I know that. She is going to England."

"No, Elizabeth, I'm afraid she's not. Your mother was very ill, but she's at peace now."

"Then she's coming back?"

"No."

"Then she's ... she's ..." Elizabeth could not bear to say it as she finally understood.

"I'm so sorry, Elizabeth. Your mother passed away on the ship, of a fever."

She didn't bother to wipe her tears away. "It's not true. I don't believe you. My mother's coming back. She's coming back."

"Oh, my dear, as terrible as it may seem, she has departed this life."

"No!" she cried, not wanting to believe, yet understanding deep down that it was true.

"I'm so sorry. We don't know much yet, but Captain

Orton says she was not in pain when she died."

He knew this to be untrue, that the captain had attempted to spare them her agony. He had seen people die of cholera, racked with pain and exhausted from dry-retching when there was no more fluid left in their bodies to expel.

Cholera claimed so many in the tropics: missionaries, royalty, the poor, adults, children, Europeans and Siamese alike. There had been an epidemic only the previous year in Bangkok, and this year, things were not much better, although people said 1849 had been worse. Elizabeth sat there still and silent, but the tears continued to stream down her face.

∞∞∞∞

Kesri was sitting in the nursery with Anchalee, rocking her to sleep, when Edward walked past in the hallway. Even in that brief moment, she saw that something more than usual was troubling him. When she was sure the child was well asleep, she followed him quietly into the bedroom, sneaking up as he lay face down on the bed. Softly, she began to massage his back in the way he always loved. But then suddenly, without warning, he reared up and pushed her roughly aside.

"Can you never leave me alone, woman?" he shouted angrily.

She was shocked and looked at him in confusion, taking a moment to recover.

"Should I go?"

"Go, stay, do as you please. Just don't bother me. Not today."

"Edward, what ...?"

He sat on the side of the bed now, his head in his hands. He looked up at her once more but did not need to say anything. His expression told her what to do and she left the room as silently as she had entered.

Back in the nursery, she lay next to Anchalee, alone and afraid. Was he tired of her already? What if he rejected her? Had he met someone else? What would become of her and Anchalee if he had? And how would he react to her latest news?

She had planned to tell him her special news today, but now she realised it would not be wise to do so. She could not risk her daughter's wellbeing for anything.

Chapter 10

She had already decided she should tell someone, a person who would believe her and who would help her. Father had become ill-tempered over the last few months, and she was wary of approaching him for fear of making him angry. It wouldn't have been difficult. In any case, he seemed to have so little time for her now. He was either out on his photographic business, or busy in his studio most of the time.

Only a few days after it had happened, her chance came when Mr Shaw arrived to visit her while Kesri was out. She told him what she had seen.

"Well, Elizabeth, that's certainly strange. And you were right not to keep it to yourself. I wouldn't like to guess the reason for it, but you have to be certain of these things before you make accusations. Do you understand what I'm saying? Are you sure that's exactly what you saw?" he asked her gently.

"Yes, Mr Shaw. Father always gives her money—whatever she needs."

"Then are you sure the money you saw her with wasn't given to her by him?"

She hadn't considered that. "No," she answered hesitantly.

She thought for a moment and then became more animated. "But she tried to hide it when she saw me. I don't think she'd do that if Father had given it to her. And I did see her take the silver things and come back without them."

"I do hope there's a logical explanation for this, Elizabeth. But I think what you must do is tell your father what you saw, just as you told me today. He should know about this."

She was silent for a moment, then looked up fearfully. "Are you afraid to tell him?"

She nodded. "He'll be angry with me. I know he will."

"Would you like me to come with you?"

She nodded again, but she was still uncertain whether or not she was doing the right thing. Together, they went over to Edward's studio.

She repeated exactly what she had told Joseph and her father's reaction was just as she had feared. He was already annoyed at yet another interference by Joseph.

"I don't believe it, Mr Shaw. The child's obviously making this up."

"Well, I don't think she is, Mr Fairburn," Joseph replied firmly. "Perhaps you should examine the silverware case yourself."

Edward hesitated because he had never taken much notice of what was in that case. There were so many small pieces that he'd be unable to tell if any were missing. It had always been Charlotte's collection.

"No, it's preposterous," he went on. "Why should Kesri need to steal and sell our silver? She can have whatever she wants. Shame on you, Elizabeth. You're either fabricating this deliberately, or you're beginning to believe your own vivid imagination."

She wished now that she hadn't said anything to anyone. "I'm only telling you what I saw," she pleaded miserably.

"I believe she's telling the truth," Joseph continued on her behalf. "Elizabeth isn't the type of girl to lie about something like this."

"Thank you, Mr Shaw," Edward responded brusquely. "But I think I can deal with this matter myself, now."

"Of course," Joseph said lightly. He turned to Elizabeth. "You've nothing to worry about as long as you tell the truth."

"Yes, Mr Shaw. Thank you for helping me."

"I'll see myself out." Joseph nodded at Edward and was

gone.

Edward turned his full attention on his daughter. "You've some explaining to do, young lady. Just what possessed you to start spying like that?"

"But I wasn't spying, Father, I wasn't. When I saw Kesri take the silver the first time, it was by accident. She didn't know I was there when she came in. I wasn't hiding, I was there all the time, reading. I was scared she'd shout at me if she knew I was there, so I kept quiet."

"Well, spying on someone and then telling tales to other people is not acceptable behaviour."

"I'm sorry, Father. I didn't know what else to do."

"What you should have been doing is paying less attention to your imagination and more to your reading and your needlework."

"I'm sorry," she whispered.

"Off you go then. And there'll be no more talk of stealing and secrets. Is that understood? You need to show some respect to your stepmother."

"Yes, Father."

She went to her room and lay on her bed, confused and upset. She *had* told the truth, and he hadn't believed her. She remembered vividly what she had seen that afternoon, from her vantage-point sitting in the window seat in the front room, hidden behind the curtains. It was two months after they had received the tragic news about Charlotte, and she had accepted the fact that her mother would not be returning. She had felt very alone.

Her father had immersed himself in his work and hardly spoke to her. He seemed to have time only for Anchalee—five-and-a-half months old and a beautiful baby with dark, slightly wavy hair, skin that was perfectly balanced between the complexions of her parents, and startlingly green eyes.

Elizabeth was thinking again of the day, less than a week after the dreadful letter arrived with news of Charlotte's passing, when her father had explained that Kesri was no longer their maid.

"What is she then, Father?" she had asked.

She'd realised things were different since Kesri had returned with Anchalee, but she hadn't been able to work out exactly how.

"She's my wife, Elizabeth."

"But Father, she can't be your wife. Mother is your wife."

For some reason, she no longer referred to her as "Mummy" since she had died. Not to her father, anyway.

"Elizabeth, dear, your mother is gone, which makes me a widower. Do you know what that means?"

"No, Father."

"It means I no longer have a wife. I'm lonely without a wife, and Kesri and Anchalee need us. Don't you think it would be nice if they stayed?"

"Is that why Kesri was in your bedroom, using Mother's things? Because she wanted to be your new wife?"

"Yes, that's right. And I hope you'll treat Anchalee as your sister from now on."

Elizabeth found she actually liked having a sister and it was true that Kesri had been friendlier to her lately. She seemed to trust Elizabeth more and allowed her to look after Anchalee for hours some days.

Carefully, Elizabeth reconstructed to herself all she remembered of the day she saw what Kesri did. She recalled that as she sat behind the curtains, she had heard a noise in the room beyond. Someone had come in, and Elizabeth peeked through a tiny gap. She saw Kesri. Elizabeth was about to say hello, to surprise her, when the words stuck in her throat.

Kesri went quietly to the whatnot—the rosewood cabinet Elizabeth's parents had filled with souvenirs and treasures from their travels—and removed several silver pieces. She put them in a small sack she carried, glanced at the door, then selected a silver candlestick from the crowded sideboard. She put it, too, in the sack, then crept quietly from the room.

Elizabeth couldn't believe her eyes. She then heard the front door close and, from her window seat, saw Kesri go down the path, holding the sack. Elizabeth sank in the seat, hoping Kesri would not turn and see her. But Kesri didn't look back as she hurried toward the boat landing.

Elizabeth jumped up and flung open the curtains, looking incomprehensibly at the spaces where the silver pieces had been. Kesri hadn't taken much, and Elizabeth was sure no one would even notice the difference. But why? The pieces were not dirty. Porntip could have cleaned them, anyway. They were not in need of repair. Perhaps her father already knew about it. Perhaps he had told Kesri to take them somewhere. She decided not to tell him just yet.

Perhaps because she was on holiday from school at the time—a result of the cholera epidemic—she allowed it to slip from her mind. Nothing happened for two more days. Kesri played with Anchalee, preened herself in front of the dressing-table mirror and dressed up in the clothes Charlotte had left behind. The dresses were far too big for Kesri, who wore them without petticoats, or even any underwear, and she was so slim, she had no need of a corset.

"You like my dress?" Kesri asked one day as Elizabeth watched her from the bedroom door. Kesri swirled the skirts round her.

"Isn't it too big for you?" Elizabeth answered honestly.

As usual, her every comment sent Kesri into a black mood. "Go to the kitchen, look after Anchalee from Porntip. I am going out."

Elizabeth did as Kesri asked, again feeling intimidated. But she was always content to look after Anchalee, anyway. She sat in the front room, bouncing the baby on her lap, giggling, and as she did so, it suddenly occurred to her. As she looked into the baby's eyes and saw again how green they were, she realised she knew only two other people with eyes exactly that colour—her father and herself.

She stopped playing for a moment as she pondered the

anomaly, and Anchalee became agitated. "Oh, I'm sorry, baby," Elizabeth crooned, holding her closer. "Hush, hush, don't cry. You really are my sister, aren't you?"

But then she thought about it more. Anchalee had been born before Elizabeth's mother had died, before she had even left for England. That meant ... not the same mother? But it was all too much for an eight-year-old's mind to grasp.

She heard the front door close softly, and when she looked out the window, she saw Kesri, now dressed in her usual panung, hurrying down the path with the small sack in hand. It jolted her memory, and she became suspicious again. She put Anchalee on the floor while she went to the sideboard and searched it. Everything appeared to be in place. Then she went through to the dining room and looked in the cupboard. There was a dust-rimmed space where a silver platter had been. She thought she remembered it from Melbourne. They didn't use it often, only if they entertained a large number of guests for dinner, and it would not be missed immediately, or maybe not at all. She believed her father wouldn't even know what silver they had, because he had never been much interested in domestic concerns.

She played with Anchalee until the baby fell asleep, and after an hour or so, she heard the front door open again and Kesri's footsteps on the stairs. She decided to ask her about the silver platter.

She gently laid Anchalee in the little wooden cradle that had once been her own, then climbed the stairs to her mother's room—as she still thought of it, despite Kesri having made it her own.

Elizabeth had taken to going barefoot in the house, like the Siamese, so Kesri didn't hear her coming up. When she put her head round the open door, she saw Kesri reclining on the bed, counting coins from a small pouch.

Kesri looked up, not pleased to see her. "What do you want, Elizabeth? I am busy." She hastily scooped the coins together and returned them to the pouch. "Why do you look that way, Elizabeth?"

"Nothing, Kesri. I'm sorry," was all she could say. Sorry my father doesn't know you're a thief, she thought.

"You go play with Anchalee," Kesri snapped.

"She's asleep."

Kesri paused momentarily. "So, go tell Porntip to make *khao pat moo* for me."

"Yes, Kesri." But she could not seem to move. Her legs were rooted to the spot and she was staring at the little money pouch.

"*Pai, pai!*" Kesri gestured impatiently for her to leave, and Elizabeth finally came to her senses and did so.

She brooded all afternoon, thinking of reasons why Kesri had stolen the silver and why she might need money Elizabeth's father didn't know about. What secret was she hiding? Elizabeth didn't like what she had seen and she was convinced it was not right.

∞∞∞

And so, too, was Edward, after Elizabeth's revelations. He hoped the matter could be left to rest, but the problem was —although he was reluctant to admit it—that Kesri's behaviour troubled him greatly. He realised he did not fully trust Kesri.

After all, how much did he really know about her, except that she had been taken in by missionaries for a short time after her parents died? She had never volunteered any more information and he had never asked for any. In fact, they seldom talked seriously together at all. Their relationship was based on sensual pleasures and little more. On the rare occasions he would initiate a sensitive conversation, particularly with any regard to herself, her family or her past, she would smile beguilingly, slip off her panung, and that would be the end of it.

He reflected carefully and was forced to admit to himself that something was amiss. She had been moody and preoccupied lately, and she was eating more and gaining weight. There was one obvious reason, but when he asked her if she was expecting again, she had denied it and had changed the subject.

Perhaps she had a lover, he thought, suddenly feeling panicky. He knew the Siamese women did not find the farang men handsome, but he had thought she might be an exception. Perhaps she was not, after all. Perhaps she meant only to extract enough money from him so she could disappear with a young Siamese lover. He knew that some of the Siamese mistresses of expatriates even had husbands and families elsewhere and that they regarded the foreigners as nothing more than a source of income. Some self-righteous expatriates—most of them missionaries or scorned wives—claimed this as just retribution for the foreign males who, they said, used the Siamese women purely to satisfy their selfish and sinful lust. Edward knew this was true in many cases, too, but he did not include himself in that category.

There was only one course of action left open to Edward.

Chapter 11

Narong followed at a safe distance, ducking into doorways or behind vendors' carts whenever it appeared the woman might look round. All he had to do was follow, keep out of sight, and report back where she had gone and who she had seen. He was not, under any circumstances, to reveal himself. And he would not, with the promise of an extra month's pay if he completed the task satisfactorily.

He followed her deep into Chinatown—a place she would not normally have reason to go—down the narrow, crowded lanes, past the tiny shops selling medicines, Chinese silk, all manner of bric-a-brac and religious icons. They passed goldsmiths, where highly skilled tradesmen beat gold sheets into paper-thin squares and sold them to worshippers who used them to make merit at the Buddhist temples. They passed gambling and opium dens, many with the doors almost closed on their dim, smoky interiors, guarded by grim-faced men.

When she reached her destination, she looked from side to side then cautiously knocked at the door to a dirty, tumble-down wooden building. The door was answered by a European or possibly American foreigner, which was something of a surprise to Narong, who now loitered at a nearby noodle soup stall. The foreigner, too, looked warily up and down the street before ushering her in and closing the door quickly behind them.

Narong now knew she was in trouble. He could not guess for certain what kind of trouble, but there were, however, only a few possibilities. She already had a farang man, so did not need another, unless she had lost a lot of money gambling and had been reduced to selling herself to repay her debts. But that seemed unlikely. Siamese men were prolific gamblers, but the women rarely indulged and she, especially, did not seem the type. Too smart, certainly.

Narong ordered a bowl of soup with plenty of fish sauce and chilli, and sat on a small wooden stool next to the cart. His father was Chinese and Narong spoke the language well.

"Who's that foreigner?" he asked the stall-holder in Cantonese, indicating the grubby building.

"Who wants to know?" The old woman eyed him suspiciously as she prepared his soup.

Narong grinned and said nothing more until he had finished eating, all the while keeping a careful eye on the doorway in case she should make a hasty exit.

When he went to pay the woman, he asked again about the foreigner. He held out his hand and she stared greedily at the white porcelain hexagons and discs embellished with blue Chinese characters. They were *pee*—originally produced as gambling tokens but also used widely as currency throughout Bangkok—and to her, they represented at least three days' clear profit.

"I might tell you," she hedged, as if not interested in the derisory sum on offer.

Narong dug deeper into his pocket and extracted another *pee*—another day's profit in his upturned palm.

"He's a doctor," she said, reaching out to grab the *pee* from his hand.

But Narong was too fast for her and closed his fist, trapping the coins. "What sort of doctor?"

Now she was agitated and wary. "Who wants to know?" she said again.

"Just me. I may have a client for him."

"He's very expensive."

"Why? What does he do? Is he some sort of magic doctor? Does he deal with the spirit world?"

"No, but he does deal with the future."

"What do you mean? What sort of doctor is he?"

"Let's just say he takes care of unwanted consequences of romantic liaisons."

Narong understood. But why would Kesri have need of such a doctor? Unless, he thought, she had a Siamese lover to whom she had fallen pregnant and—because she would not have been able to pass off the baby as Edward's—had to seek an abortion.

Still, he did not really care about such things and did not think much more of it. His task complete, he loosened his grasp and poured the tokens into the old woman's impatient hands. He hurried directly back to the house, eagerly anticipating his own easily-earned reward.

∞∞∞

When she arrived back home from Chinatown that afternoon, she found Edward in the front room, alone, waiting for her. He looked furious and she prepared for the worst.

"Where have you been?" he demanded without any greeting.

She felt weak and disorientated and she knew the ball of rags between her legs would be soaked with blood by now.

"To the market. Now I am sick, *mai sabai*. I will go to bed." As she spoke, she averted her eyes from his so he wouldn't see the horror in them.

"First, tell me where you've been. Tell me the truth, Kesri." His voice was cold yet subdued.

She had never seen him like this before, and as she looked into his eyes, she understood that he already knew. There was a rushing noise in her ears—like the crash of waves on a beach—and a whispering in her head that she could not escape: *jai barb poo-ying, jai barb poo-ying. Evil woman*, it said.

"Tell me!" he shouted suddenly.

She couldn't answer. Then, as if from a great distance, she felt his arms grip her shoulders and shake her violated body. All the blood and guilt inside her seemed to rise up to drown her, and she slumped from his grasp to the ground.

∞∞∞

Later, he sat by her bedside in a torment of rage, frustration and confusion.

She was pale and weak, but pronounced by Dr Bradley to be as well as could be expected after such a procedure.

Edward felt cheated. "Why, Kesri? Tell me why you did it. Why did you do this to our baby?" There was a pause. "Or was it not mine?"

She looked up at him, tears swimming in her dark eyes. "*Chai* ... yes, yes ... your baby, Edward," she answered, almost in a whisper.

"Then why in God's name would you do this? An abortion in some filthy, back-street kitchen? It's lucky you're still alive, lucky that money-grabbing quack didn't manage to kill you in the process."

"I do not think you can understand why." She tried to sit up, but fell back against the pillows, exhausted. She closed her eyes for a moment and took a deep breath.

"Before, I have nothing. Then I have Anchalee ... and you. You have two daughters, but all men want son. If I have boy, I think you love him more than Anchalee. Maybe you give your son everything and Anchalee nothing. Then Anchalee suffer, like me."

"But Kesri, what you're saying doesn't make any sense." There was no sympathy in his voice. "I'd love all my children equally. You must know that. There must be some other reason, something I can believe. What is it?"

She sighed. She would have to tell him the whole truth. "If I have another baby, and another, and another, and so on, I will no longer be beautiful for you. Waist grows thicker, woman grows older. Maybe you will be tired of me, maybe you get another wife. Then you have more children with other wife and mine get nothing, because she will be younger and favourite."

For an instant, Edward could see her side, and he knew there was truth in what she said. But he could not accept what she had done. A woman belonged to her husband and should not be permitted to destroy his child.

"Kesri, you lied, you stole from my house and used the money to murder our child. I cannot ever forgive you."

"Please, Edward, I will do anything. We can have another baby if you want."

"No, Kesri, there can be no more children. Dr Bradley says you've been too badly damaged." He looked dejected and weary now, then stood as he said his next words slowly and quietly, as if to confirm to himself that it was the only course open. "There'll be no more of anything for you and me," he said. "We're finished, Kesri. Finished. I cannot love you any more. You've killed my child. Do you know how desperately some women wish to have children and lose their unborn babies again and again and again? You insult every one of them. I cannot even look at you."

Tears slid across her cheeks and on to the white linen pillowcase. "Please, Edward. I am so sorry. But we have a good life together, with daughters. Please ..."

"No, Kesri." He gestured for her to stop talking, not allowing himself to feel guilty for treating her this way. "I don't want anything more from you. I'm sorry." The apology was out of his mouth before he thought about it, and she seized upon it.

"Edward," she cried, desperately clutching him with a weak hand. "Anchalee. How can I take care of Anchalee?"

He stared at her and wondered if he had ever really loved her. It had been nothing more than a shallow relationship, he realised now. But she was right: there was an innocent child, already born, to think of.

"Of course she must be cared for," he said at last. "None of this is Anchalee's fault. She is my daughter, and I love her. Nothing can change that. And she's a British citizen, of course. I cannot allow her to go with you. You'll leave her with me, and she'll have everything I can give her. Everything, that is, on the condition that you leave and do not return. You'll have an allowance to live on—I'll not see you starve or go back to service—but you'll not see Anchalee or me again. That is my final and only offer."

His words crushed her, and she could only moan in pain and despair as the tears seeped from her eyes, shut tight in anguish.

He did not relent. "As soon as Dr Bradley says you are well enough, you must take your things and leave. I rue the day I ever forsook my dear Charlotte for you," he added, as much to himself as to her. Then he left the room.

Her fight was gone. Drained, irreparably damaged, and with no one to turn to, she realised that this one mistake had cost her everything she had dreamed of—and, for a time, believed she had attained. It was a terrible error of judgement. The dream was over.

In the following days as she lay there alone, recovering from the abortion, she contemplated her future. She wanted her daughter to have the life she herself had never had, but she was consumed with thoughts of vengeance. She knew it was Elizabeth who had engineered her demise, the evil little sneak. Eventually, she vowed, her daughter would know the truth of what Elizabeth had done, of how Elizabeth's betrayal had left Anchalee motherless, too. She would somehow ensure that, one day, Anchalee despised Elizabeth enough to want to ruin her.

∞∞∞

Two weeks after Kesri left the house, Edward decided it was time for Elizabeth to return to England. She complained bitterly when he told her.

"No, Father, please don't send me away. Please."

"Elizabeth, your mother was right. Siam is no place for you. I believe you must return to England to school."

"But I love it here. I don't want to go to England. I've never been to England. At least let me go to school in Australia if you must send me anywhere."

"Elizabeth, we don't have any relatives there to take care of you, and you can't go alone. In England, you can live with your grandparents, at least during the holidays. You'll go to the best boarding school we can provide, and you'll be taught how to be a lady. It's high time you stopped running round like a little savage."

She was shocked at his words. He sounded just like all those other men at church. "Won't I ever see you again?" she asked fearfully, thinking of her mother. She had begun to think people did not return from long journeys abroad. Or if they did, everything was different.

Of course, my dear. I shall doubtless make a trip home one day. And when you've completed your education, you may return here, if you like. Although by then, I'm hoping that perhaps Grandmother will have found you a suitable young man to marry."

This was even more upsetting news for Elizabeth and seemed like proof he wanted rid of her. Since Kesri had left, he hardly spoke to anyone. It seemed to Elizabeth that he was blaming her in some way, and although she was not really sure what had happened, she was aware it was something terrible. She began to think that she should have kept it to herself when she saw Kesri taking the silver.

Suddenly, she brightened. "Will you send Anchalee away one day, too? Can she come to boarding school?"

"Well, if she wants to go to school in England, she can, I suppose. But you'll be almost finished school by the time she begins and soon to marry and have a family of your own, no doubt. And remember, she is half Siamese. She might not want to go."

"Just as I don't want to go. Oh please, Father, I'll be good, I promise. I won't make a sound. I'll work hard at school, I'll stay in my room, I'll look after Anchalee. I won't ever bother you. I'm sorry, so sorry about the silver, about Kesri, I never should have ..."

"That's enough, Elizabeth. It's final. You're going and that's that. No more arguments."

And she did go, only one month later. Edward engaged a Miss Smith—a teacher returning to England—to escort her.

As Elizabeth waved goodbye to her father and to Siam from the deck of the *Chao Phya*, she tried not to think about the fact that it could be years before she saw him again. She tried not to see the tall coconut palms gently swaying in the tropical breeze, the vendors in their little boats plying their wares up and down the river, or the naked children diving and swimming in the murky water. She was leaving Bangkok as a child, and she knew that when she returned, she would be an adult.

Part 2

April 1882-November 1886

Chapter 12

Sam balanced *Far East Adventures* on one hand, feeling its weight, then opened it again at the foreword. He wondered what his father would have thought. He could imagine him saying, "Well son, now you're done with travelling, it's time to make some girl an honest woman. Come home and settle down. I've a nice little business here. You could do worse."

His father had never known about the book. In fact, he had heard little from his son over the last ten years. Sam had left home as a teenager, and he regretted losing contact with his father. And now, it was too late.

Sam read the cover and the book's opening again.

Far East Adventures
By Samuel Taylor II

Foreword

Even as a boy, I knew that an ordinary life was not for me. I would lie on my narrow bed in the living quarters above my father's saloon, dreaming of adventures in distant lands and of life on the high seas. I believe I must have inherited this adventurous spirit from my father, although most people remember him as a steady, honest working man rather than as an adventurer.

Samuel Taylor I left England for California in 1848 in search of gold. He did not discover the riches he sought, but he did marry a beautiful Mexican señorita, my mother. I was only two years old when she died of scarlet fever in 1852. My father's wan-

derlust seemed to die with her, and he decided it was his duty to provide a steady home for his son. He bought a saloon in the then sleepy pueblo of Los Angeles, and there he stayed.

I studied hard and learned how to stand up for myself when I was called a "dirty Mexican half-caste". I was kept away from the drinking customers, but sometimes I would sneak down the stairs at night and sit outside the back door of the bar, listening to the tall tales the men told. My yearning for adventure grew.

In 1865, during the Civil War, I finally persuaded the Union Army to let me join up. I lied that I was eighteen and was ready to fight. Unfortunately for me, Lee surrendered to Grant on April 9th of that year, and I never reached the front. I returned home, worked hard, saved my money, and read every travel and adventure book I could lay my hands on. When I did reach eighteen, I said goodbye to California, and I have been travelling ever since.

This book is the result of the past seven years I have spent journeying in Southeast Asia, the Far East. During that time, I have mostly earned my living through journalism for publications in London and Europe, as well as the United States. But there was much more I wanted to tell about my experiences abroad, and this volume, I hope, will bring my readers a little closer to the world I have come to love. I will start with the city to which I have returned again and again, perhaps the most Oriental of all cities: Bangkok, Venice of the East, the City of Angels.

Samuel Taylor II
Bangkok, 1881

After his father died, there was nothing left for him in California, so he had arranged for the saloon to be sold. He would never have gone back to it. Siam was where his heart was now.

He leaned back in his chair and sighed with satisfaction. His book was finally published and he was pleased that his author's copies had arrived this week, when Bangkok was celebrating its centennial. His publisher said in the covering letter that he expected significant sales in New York and San Francisco, and—later in the year—in Great Britain too. Furthermore, he wanted to know how long it would take Sam to produce a second volume of travel tales.

There was an additional, more personal note to Sam from his editor, Jonathan Taite, with whom he had established quite a rapport, despite the fact that the two had never met:

... If you have not done so already, you must read Mr Butler's new travel book, The Alps and Sanctuaries of Piedmont. I have enclosed a copy, understanding the difficulty of acquiring new English volumes in your part of the world. You must be due for furlough soon, and I would enjoy meeting you in person ...

Sam tapped out a quick reply to the publisher on his typewriter. He was fond of the machine, although he had initially cursed the thing many times as another heavy item of baggage he had to contend with on his travels. He had taught himself to use the Remington and Sons machine, eventually mastering the odd QWERTY-style arrangement, composed that way from 1873 in order to separate letters that often occurred together and so prevent keys from jamming as they struck the roller.

He sealed the letter in an envelope and addressed it in large, clearly-legible print. The mail service was not particularly reliable. First, the letter would have to be taken to the American Consulate, where it would be hand franked. From there, it would travel to Singapore, then take a circuitous route to New York. There were rumours that the service would improve soon, with special stamps coming from Singapore, and more mail ships to and from Europe and North America. But for the moment, it was a matter of hoping for the best, and being patient.

Sam put on his sports coat, left his room at the Oriental Hotel and went down to the landing nearby to hire a boat to the consulate. It was only a short distance upriver, and he asked the boatman to wait to take him back.

Like most foreigners, he found the riverside activity fascinating, and when he returned to the Oriental after handing over his letter, he lit a cheroot and leaned against the wooden railing. He looked up at the plain two-storey teak building with its verandahs and tiled roof—wondering if he could not perhaps secure more comfortable lodgings—then turned and gazed down into the brown water below, marvelling that in all the filth, fish not only survived, but seemed to thrive.

A short distance out from the bank, the carcass of a dog floated by, half submerged. Not far away, children dived into the water, laughing and shouting, and a woman squatted on the steps of her floating house, using the river as the family laundry basin. On the landing itself, men sat together in groups, smoking and talking, and mangy dogs skulked around, looking for scraps.

Furlough, his editor had suggested. Yet, Sam could not even imagine what he would do on vacation in California. Likely go insane, or become a raving drunk like most of the other failed adventurers who found their way there. No, he did not need to return home. What he needed, he decided, was some excitement.

The steamer was due in from Singapore today, and most of its European passengers would disembark at the landing. They generally preferred to stay at the Oriental because of its proximity to the British Consulate and its location next to the river, with its cooling breezes. In addition, many of the long-term foreign residents lived in the area and so would alight there with their trunks and wooden cases.

Soon, however, he was so engrossed in watching a beautiful Siamese woman bathing nearby—wrapped from neck to ankles in a sarong designed for the purpose—that he did not see the first lot of Europeans from the steamer until the boat was almost level with the landing. He recognised two of the people on board as Edward Fairburn, one of Bangkok's most prosperous photographers, and his daughter by a Siamese woman.

What was the child's name? She must be twelve or thirteen, he thought, and she would certainly break some hearts one day with her perfect golden complexion and startling green eyes.

He had never before seen the other young woman. She sat between Fairburn and his daughter, tranquil and composed, yet looking this way and that, as if rediscovering a scene she was familiar with but had not seen for a long time. As the boat pulled closer to the pier, she made some comment to Edward. Then he realised, she must be the other daughter, the one by his English wife who had died. He couldn't recall the elder daughter's name either, but he looked at her with more than a passing interest. She would be in her early twenties, and he knew from local expatriate gossip that she had been sent away to school in England when she was quite young. The result of bad behaviour, perhaps? Looking at her now, he could scarcely believe the elder Miss Fairburn capable of any sort of misbehaviour.

She was pristine in her high-necked white dress, which was old-fashioned in comparison with that of the other young English women, who now wore brighter colours. She held a white and pink-trimmed parasol above her head, and she wore a small hat fastened beneath the chin with pink and white ribbons.

He wondered how she had managed to keep her dress so white during the long journey from Singapore. She must have kept it in a separate case, specifically for her arrival. She hadn't seen her father for many years, he guessed, so it was no wonder she wanted to impress him. Still, she appeared as if she had been dressed by her grandmother—straight-laced, with no sophistication or artistry about her costume. It was the outfit of a virginal young woman, he thought—which was almost certainly what she was. The English guarded their daughters as if they were the crown jewels.

As the boat drew up alongside the pier, the younger girl jumped out on to the landing with ease. Edward helped his elder daughter from the boat, and she made a careful exit on his arm.

"There are so many new buildings. I can hardly recognise Bangkok," Sam heard her exclaim.

"It's true," Edward agreed. "But you'll soon get your bearings again. Really, not much has changed."

"Well, at least the Oriental Hotel is still here. That's one landmark I do remember."

"Yes, it's still here." He looked up at the decaying building. "Although perhaps due for some renovations."

The trunks were off-loaded, and as the three walked toward him, Sam noticed she was quite tall. She certainly towered over the Siamese women, most of whom were little over five feet tall. He nodded a greeting to Edward and tipped his hat to the girls as they approached.

"Afternoon, Mr Fairburn," he drawled. "And ladies."

"Mr Taylor," Edward replied, shaking Sam's extended hand briefly. There was a pause and Edward realised the man was waiting to be introduced. "Ahem. You've met Anchalee before, and may I introduce my elder daughter, Miss Elizabeth Fairburn."

She looked at him, then quickly away again, and he smiled to himself at her flushed cheeks. Was it merely the heat, the result of the exhausting journey—or was it a blush?

When she looked at him again through long lashes, he was struck by the same green eyes as Anchalee had. Not as dazzling on her pale face as they were on her younger sister's, but engaging, nonetheless.

"Charmed, Miss Fairburn. I hear you've been away for some time."

"Yes, Mr Taylor. More than thirteen years, actually," she said, her English accent very proper indeed.

"Well, I trust you'll be attending some of the centennial celebrations?"

"I ... I'm not really sure." She looked enquiringly at her father, before adding, "I expect so."

There was a moment of silence before Edward ushered them on. "Come, Elizabeth, Anchalee. Excuse us, Mr Taylor."

"Of course, Mr Fairburn. We'll meet again soon then," he called to her as she turned away, her cheeks scarlet again. He watched her all the way as Edward escorted them to their waiting carriage.

The rickshaw drivers, who were stationed at the landing, laughed good-naturedly as they attempted to lure the foreigners into their vehicles for a reasonable fare to their destination. Edward waved off their advances without humour, and Elizabeth could sense that he had been irked by Mr Taylor's presence. She wondered why.

Rickshaws had been introduced to the city in 1871, and enterprising Chinese operators continued to import them from other Asian countries, including Singapore and Hong Kong, usually after they had been rejected as too dilapidated for service in those places. There was a plethora of them available along New Road and its side lanes, and the Siamese had readily taken to riding in them for convenience, even for very short distances. They were used for every purpose, including transporting household goods from one road to another and for carrying pigs and poultry to market.

Foreigners, however, generally eschewed the rickshaws, most preferring to run their own carriages. It was an expensive investment, but labour was exceedingly cheap, so after the initial outlay for horses and carriage, it wasn't difficult to maintain a stable with several employees.

Edward had two carriages: the larger one they were now getting into, which could comfortably seat four and had room for luggage, and a smaller victoria he had owned for years, with room to accommodate only two, plus the driver.

Sam, however, wasn't concerned with carriages or rickshaws as he watched them leave. He was far more interested in one of the occupants of the departing vehicle. She had intrigued him. One word from a man and she was rendered almost speechless. He saw in her a challenge he couldn't resist.

But there was the problem of her father. Fairburn would never permit his daughter to become acquainted with a journeyman writer who had been brought up in a saloon, was of no fixed abode, who lived in hotels, and who had a reputation for enjoying life in whichever way he desired at the time. Sam had known many women, but had been serious about none of them. None had managed to command his attention for much longer than it took to lead her to his bed. And that usually wasn't long. But this Englishman's daughter might require a little more attention and effort, not to mention ingenuity to get her alone.

It was strange about her father, he thought. If the rumours he had heard were true, when Fairburn came to the city in the 1860s, he had been no saint. By the time his wife and Elizabeth had arrived, he had already taken a young Siamese mistress. The wife discovered they had a baby, refused to share her husband, and left him—only to perish on the voyage back to England. Or so the story went.

Fairburn and his Siamese mistress had then apparently had a terrible argument, resulting in him banishing her, but retaining custody of their daughter, Anchalee. Almost immediately, he had sent his elder daughter back to England.

No one seemed to know exactly what had become of the Siamese mistress, although rumour also had it that she had died a year or so later of a broken heart.

After that, Sam thought, Fairburn must have been overwhelmed with guilt. Perhaps he believed he was responsible for the deaths of both women—which, indirectly, he was, it seemed. Whatever the truth, he had turned to the Church and had become increasingly involved in parish activities at the little riverside chapel run by the American Protestant missionaries. He had returned to England only once during that time, leaving Anchalee with a missionary family until he returned.

Sam wandered back up to his room, where he sat at his desk and contemplated the first chapter of his new book. He planned now to write exclusively of Siam, and intended to make the perilous journey north to Chiengmai, along crocodile-infested waters on overloaded boats and on elephant-back through dense forest where the risks of tiger attacks, jungle fever, and venomous snake bites were great. It was a journey totalling 500 miles, which could take many weeks, even several months, to complete.

Few foreigners went to Chiengmai, and he was convinced it would make for a first-rate adventure story. There were, however, a number of brave missionaries there, and Sam's friend, Louis Leonowens, also wanted to make the trip.

Louis had lived in Bangkok as a boy, when his mother, Anna, taught English at the Grand Palace. He had left with his mother in 1868, but as a young adult he'd made his way to Australia, where he'd spent time on the goldfields. In 1886, when he was 25, he returned to Siam to become a captain in the army of his boyhood friend, now King Chulalongkorn. At present, he was in Australia again to purchase horses from New South Wales to ship back for Chulalongkorn's cavalry.

Sam and Louis had been friends since their first meeting and Louis had even offered his friend a commission in the army. Sam had admitted to himself that the generous annual salary was tempting.

"But Louis, I'm afraid I'll have to turn you down," he'd said to his friend. "All that discipline, all that attention to detail, putting on a uniform every day, and all those men relying on me. It's not for me. Now, if you go to battle and need a correspondent to travel with you, I'd be the first to volunteer."

Sam placed a sheet in the typewriter and began ...

Chapter One: Bangkok
So much of Asia has been tempered, dare I say spoiled, with

things Western, that the true adventurer is often disappointed when he arrives at some Oriental outpost only to find there many of the comforts of home. However, there remains at least one Asian port that has not suffered the effects of a colonial invasion, one that remains wholly Asian, wholly itself: it is Bangkok, the capital city of Siam. Here, the visiting Occidental has never felt so foreign, so alien or so overwhelmed by the Far East in all its tropical, spicy splendor. Here, the adventurer can ...

Can what? He got up from the desk and stepped over to the window. The publishers were keen to have another book right away. He had enough notes at least for the first chapter on Bangkok and for several on Siamese life and customs. He had been to some of the country's most beautiful southern coastal areas in the seven years since he had first come to Siam, but the bulk of the book would remain unwritten until he travelled farther into the hinterland.

As he looked out his window at the bustling scene below, the image of her face came to him again: her fine fair hair, her green eyes, the white dress and the white-gloved hands holding the matching parasol, and the unblemished skin that seemed almost as white as the dress until she blushed at his first glance. She seemed the antithesis of her equally beautiful younger sister. And he knew he must have her. Once the innocence had left her face, she would no longer distract him, he was sure, and he'd be able to get on with his work.

"Damn," he swore under his breath. Unlike many other authors, he prided himself on being able to work when required, not having to search too hard for inspiration nor wait for some mythical muse. There were few—only very few— distractions that could bring his work to a halt, and it now seemed that she was one of them.

The room was stifling, even with the window open, and he could feel the onset of a thumping, heat-induced headache. To prevent it taking hold, he needed some fresh air, a drink, and a diversion. He picked up his jacket from the back of the chair and slung it over his shoulder.

If he were lucky, perhaps he could still secure an invitation to the centennial ball at the British Consulate.

Chapter 13

Who was that man, Father?" she asked casually as the carriage trundled roughly along New Road to the house.

"I introduced you. Samuel Taylor." His response was terse.

It was clear to her that he didn't like the man and she wanted to know the reason. "Yes, but who is he? Or perhaps I should say, *what* is he?"

"A journalist, I believe, and"—he spoke as if this were distasteful—"quite well known in his field. Why do you want to know?"

"Oh, no reason, Father. I was just curious about him."

"Well, don't be. The man has a reputation for thoroughly enjoying the company of Bangkok's young ladies—Siamese and European—and you'll stay away from him. He's a philanderer and he's trouble."

She hardly heard her father's reply. In her mind's eye, she saw again the tall, broad-shouldered and olive-skinned man with eyes that were almost jet black and wavy black hair rather longer than was fashionable. He was a world apart from the insipid aristocrats she knew in England. She was intrigued to uncover more about him, and to meet him again.

"And how is James?" her father said, quickly changing the subject of the conversation. She did not answer and he nudged her gently to rouse her from her reverie. "Elizabeth?"

"I'm sorry, Father, I was miles away. What did you say?"

"James."

"James?"

"Yes, James. Your fiancé."

"Oh, of course. James. Sorry, I'm not myself. It must be the heat and the long journey. James is quite well, thank you."

"Have you set a wedding date yet?"

But before she could answer, the carriage had drawn up at Edward's imposing, two-storey colonial mansion, and her attention was immediately drawn to it.

"This is wonderful, Father. Your description didn't do it justice, I must say."

The European-style house, built in 1880, was constructed of teak, with a white granite stairway leading up to the front door, and green painted shutters on each window. It was solid and comfortable, with five bedrooms and two modern American-style bathrooms upstairs, and a parlour, sitting room, billiard room, and dining room downstairs. In Siamese style, the kitchen was detached from the house, at the back with the staff quarters.

Compared to the way most of the population lived, it might well have been a palace. Elizabeth had noticed, as she had journeyed along the river, that the houseboats and rickety stilt dwellings along the banks had hardly changed in the years she had been away, only there were more of them.

She had noticed, also, several scorched areas where many houses had been burnt to the ground. Fires were frequent and there was no dedicated fire brigade. Soldiers would be called to any major conflagration, but it was generally too late to prevent widespread damage. Flames quickly leapt from house to house via the palm-leaf-thatched roofs, and hundreds of people could lose their homes and possessions within minutes.

Anchalee, who had hardly said a word during the carriage ride, jumped out ahead of her sister and led her quickly up the path, eager to show her round the house. Edward went out to the kitchen to ask the maid to prepare tea. The rooms were full of furniture that Edward had imported from Europe at great expense. There were seven different types of wallpaper from England, a marble-topped tea table with curled, dark wood legs, a baby-grand piano, Italian gilt mirrors, and even a billiard table.

Elizabeth was delighted to find, in the parlour, the old rosewood whatnot her mother had loved all those years ago, with the same pieces still displayed inside, as if it had not been opened all these years. "I didn't know this would still be here," she said. "How lovely." She ran her fingers along the wood of the cabinet lovingly.

Anchalee wasn't looking. "We have lots of new imported furniture. Father's regularly summoned by the King to take photographs of the royal family, so he's become very successful."

"I suppose His Majesty is quite grown up. When I left, he wasn't much older than you are now."

"Yes, and he has many children of his own. And many, many wives."

"Oh, really," Elizabeth mumbled in surprise. She had almost forgotten that aspect of the culture and wondered how the Siamese women tolerated it.

Anchalee knew intuitively what Elizabeth was thinking. "Don't you like that idea?"

"What idea?"

Well, in Siam it's prestigious for a man to have many wives."

"How can you say that as if it's acceptable? I'm sure the wives themselves don't like it."

"Oh, but they do. If your husband has other wives, you don't have so much work to do yourself."

Elizabeth laughed involuntarily, amused at Anchalee's precocity. "You didn't learn that at the missionary school. I forget sometimes that you're only half English." She gasped as she realised how insensitive that sounded, and apologised. "Oh, I'm sorry. I didn't mean—" she began.

But Anchalee seemed unconcerned, immediately taking Elizabeth's hand and leading her out of the parlour. "Come upstairs and I'll show you your room. It's the best one and we've been saving it for you all this time. It's got a lovely view of the river."

Elizabeth smiled, her remark forgotten. She hadn't seen Anchalee since she was a baby, except in photographs sent by Father, and it was still hard for her to believe that this almost-grown-up thirteen-year-old was really her half-sister. At twenty-one, Elizabeth felt more like an aunt or an older cousin. The only similarity between the two was their green eyes, though Elizabeth thought her own looked nothing out of the ordinary, whereas Anchalee's were thrillingly exotic.

The room was as lovely as Anchalee had said, with a white lace bedspread and masses of draped mosquito netting round the bed. There was a window nook with a seat that looked out over the water, and the dark teak floor was so highly polished she could see herself reflected in it. There was a large oval mirror over a dressing table, on which sat a fine china basin and jug for washing.

Elizabeth was delighted. "It's perfect, Anchalee. Did you arrange all these lovely white orchids in here?"

"Yes. They're growing in our garden."

Elizabeth sat on the edge of the bed and patted the space beside her. "Come and sit next to me." She took Anchalee's small hands in hers. "It's been a long time since I've seen you, Anchalee. You wouldn't remember, but we played together when you were a baby. You were so beautiful and I loved you from the start. And now you're almost a young woman. We'll have to watch out when the boys come calling for you!"

"Elizabeth, you're so prim and proper." Anchalee jumped off the bed, giggling. "Is that what they taught you at finishing school? I've already got a boyfriend. But don't tell anyone. He's Siamese, and Father wouldn't like that."

"Wouldn't he?"

"No. He says I have to marry a farang." She wrinkled her nose at the thought. "He forgets who I am, sometimes."

"I think he's probably just concerned for your well-being, Anchalee. Anyway, you're much too young to be talking about such serious things."

"Lots of Siamese girls get married at fifteen—or younger."

"But you're not Siamese, Anchalee."

"Aren't I?"

"No, because your father is English and that means you are too."

"Hmmm," she replied lightly and smiled, her small, even teeth gleaming white.

"And I'm glad to see you haven't started that awful pastime of chewing betel nut," Elizabeth said in mock seriousness.

"I probably would, if it weren't for Father. But he'd die if I did. Anyway, the King doesn't like it and most of the younger people have given it up. White teeth are actually becoming quite fashionable. Well, you must be tired. I'll let you rest. See you at dinner."

With that, she skipped out like a child, leaving the door open behind her.

Elizabeth sat by the window, reflecting on the contradictions she saw in her younger sister. On the one hand, she could be sweet and immature. Yet on the other, she seemed earnest and precociously knowledgeable. She was sure Anchalee had only been joking about having a boyfriend. She was much too young, surely.

But how could she advise Anchalee when she, herself, had had so little contact with men, having been taught privately at her grandmother's house by a middle-aged spinster, then at an exclusive girls' boarding school, and lastly, finishing school in Switzerland?

Her grandmother had held an elaborate coming-out ball for her when she was eighteen, and she had attended a fair number of functions since then. But she was always chaperoned, always under her grandmother's eye, and the young men she met were frightfully formal. It was at one such ball that she had met Viscount James Claridge.

James, who was heir to his father's earldom and a fortune, had fallen instantly in love with her and had begged her to marry him only a few months later, at another ball where they had managed to steal a few moments alone together in the garden. She accepted immediately. After all, hadn't everyone told her what a marvellous catch he was? And indeed, James seemed everything a woman could want. He was tall, handsome, wealthy, and titled. He was charming, witty, and he adored her. Her grandparents thoroughly approved of him, of course. Even so, for some reason she had held off setting a wedding date, even though they had been unofficially engaged already for six months.

"It's hard to explain to you, James," she had told him then. "I do want to marry you, but there's something I must do first. I must return to Siam."

"I see, my dear. But why don't we get married and go there during our honeymoon?"

What he had said made sense, as always, but still she felt that she should wait.

"Don't ask me why, James, because I don't know myself. But I feel I must go back alone. I feel as if I've left something unfinished there. I'll not be a whole person and I'll not be ready to marry you until after I've been back. Can you understand that?"

"Not really, but if that's what you want, then so be it. We'll be married as soon as possible after your return. It's just, well, I was rather hoping Her Majesty might attend our wedding, and we'd need to give the palace some notice."

She kissed him gratefully on the cheek. "Thank you,

James. You've been wonderful. I'm sorry to be so infuriating."

"But remember," he added, a hint of warning in his voice, "don't stay away too long. I'm thirty and it's time I married. My father's getting old and he wants to see his grandchildren before he dies."

She realised he wasn't joking and the smile left her face. Still, she would not be deterred. "James, I don't want to hold you to anything," she had said then. "We haven't made a public announcement about our engagement yet—only our families know. If you find someone else ..."

And she had gone, promising to write as soon as she arrived in Siam.

At first, she had thought it might be a mistake and that she would regret leaving. She was filled with a sense of relief when she felt no pangs of homesickness—or of missing him. The feeling of freedom she had experienced as soon as the ship set sail remained with her. She began to feel, to her own surprise, that she had not been in love with him at all. And now that she was back in Bangkok, she truly felt as if she had come home. Already, she knew she didn't want to leave.

Even though she had spent only a short time in Siam as a child, she had never forgotten the warm breezes, the palm trees, the gentle people, the colour and the contrasts. She had always felt like a stranger in England, a guest in her grandparents' huge, sprawling mansion, in which half the rooms were closed off, their furniture draped in dust-laden white sheets.

∞∞∞

Now, as she sat in this new bedroom, reminiscing, she felt herself blushing at the memory of another man, the one they'd met as she arrived. His dark good looks and his confident, casual air were etched in her mind. She tried to busy herself opening drawers and closets, ready for her unpacking, which she preferred to do herself. But the vivid memory of the man remained. She smiled to herself and leaned back on the soft bed. She was home.

As soon as her trunks arrived, she found her new pink silk skirt and blouse, and asked the maid to iron them before she washed and changed for dinner. She and Father had much to talk about. She had not seen him since he'd visited England five years before.

∞∞∞

"You seem to be very involved with the Church these days," she said to Edward at the table later, while their maid, Noi, served the first course of spicy seafood soup.

"I am, indeed. Does that surprise you?"

"Well, to be frank, Father, yes it does. You always called them 'interfering busy-bodies' in the old days, as I recall."

He looked a little uncomfortable. "I found the Church late in life, it's true, and not before I'd made some regrettable mistakes. But I believe I'm at last on the true path."

Elizabeth coughed suddenly and breathed in sharply at the now unfamiliar taste of chilli.

Anchalee could barely suppress a burst of laughter at the combination of her father's comment and her sister's reaction to the spices.

"You sound like you're giving a sermon right here in the dining room, Father."

"Don't be impertinent, young lady," he admonished Anchalee. His words were harsh but his tone was not. Elizabeth could see he adored her half-sister.

The naughty girl laughed again, but nevertheless had to admit to herself that her father was a happier man these days. For a long time, she had not heard him call out in his sleep as he used to when she was younger.

And what of Joseph Shaw, Father? Remember, he was my school teacher. Is he still here, or has he retired back to New Zealand?"

"Retired? Good heavens, no, Elizabeth. He's younger than I am. He'd be only forty now. Retire? Whatever gave you such an odd notion?"

Elizabeth smiled at her mistake. "Isn't it funny? When I was a child, Mr Shaw seemed so old to me. But he must have been only in his late twenties then. I always imagined he was about fifty when I was seven or eight. He must be married with a family now, is he?"

"No, he's never married. But he's doing very well in his work. He's even brought a few converts into the fold."

"Is he a minister now?"

"No, he never seemed to want to pursue ordination, for some reason. He's one of the Church's most valuable missionaries and a wonderful teacher. The local people love him, even if they don't want to convert to our religion."

"They don't want to become Christians because they're already Buddhists," Anchalee pointed out matter-of-factly. "Buddhism is a much older religion than Christianity."

"Anchalee, simply because Buddhism is older doesn't mean it's better—or the more correct path to the truth." He swiped at a mosquito that hovered directly in front of his face.

"But Father, you're always saying that with age comes wisdom," she responded quickly.

He couldn't muster an adequate reply and instead resorted to his usual chiding. "Young ladies, Anchalee, should make polite conversation—especially at the table—and not try to outdo their elders and betters."

Anchalee, well-practised in the art of goading her father —or anyone else, for that matter—simply smiled as the maids began clearing the table ready for the main course, a roast of beef complete with Yorkshire pudding and peas.

Edward wiped the sweat from his brow and swatted another mosquito on his hand. "Confounded things," he grumbled. "I hear one of the American families actually as a mosquito-proof dining room. They have special nets on all the doors and windows that allow in the air, but not the mosquitoes. Now they dine in perfect peace."

"No, they don't," Anchalee remarked. "Their cook is truly dreadful. She's always burning the meat and undercooking the vegetables, or making mush of the whole lot."

"Anchalee, how do you know these things?" he asked in exasperation.

"I have big ears," she replied. "And you forget that I speak Siamese. I hear the gossip from the maids."

"Well, you know far too much, if you ask me. And you shouldn't be listening to servants' gossip. Perhaps Elizabeth can teach you to be more ladylike. I've given up."

But he wasn't angry, not really, and Elizabeth noticed Anchalee smiling to herself for the remainder of the dinner.

"Anyway, my dear," Edward addressed Elizabeth again. "How long do you intend staying with us?"

"I'm not sure, father. I didn't have a set time in mind."

"But what of James? Is he in agreement?"

"Father, James is not my husband yet. He has no say in the matter."

"But he's your fiancé. Surely..."

"Not officially, Father. You know that. We decided to wait until my return."

"Why don't you write to him and ask him to come to Siam? You could even be married here. It would be quite fitting for you to wed from your father's home. We have a lovely church beside the river, not far from here."

She thought of James and his grandiose plans to have Queen Victoria attend their wedding, and knew that Bangkok would not do. "No, Father. I'd rather wait. To tell you the truth, I'm not sure if I'm ready to marry James immediately."

"*What*? You're twenty-one, girl. You should have been married a year or two ago and have given me a grandson by now. I can't understand why you've waited." He shook his head wearily.

"I can't explain it myself, Father. I can say only that the time wasn't right."

"Well, young Claridge is a patient man. There'd be many a woman—younger than you, I might add—who'd be only too ready to marry the Earl's heir. You'd be making a grave error to let him slip through your fingers."

Elizabeth made no reply, but steered the conversation toward less personal topics. "Anchalee tells me King Chula-longkorn is well established in his own right now."

Edward could see that the subject of her marriage was no longer open for discussion, and he reluctantly followed the new conversation thread. "Yes, he's doing wonderful things for the country. He's outlawed slavery and decreed against people prostrating themselves before their superiors, including himself. Unfortunately, that custom is so ingrained, they can't help themselves and most still do it. But at least no one dares at official ceremonies in his presence.

"It's said, also, that he plans to travel to Europe. He's already been to Batavia, Singapore, India, and Burma. I think he's the most widely travelled Siamese monarch ever. He was to have gone to America and Europe about two years ago, in fact, but the trip was cancelled at the last minute. Still, he'll go eventually, I'm sure. In some ways, he's very enlightened."

Anchalee looked at her father sharply. "Only in some ways, Father?"

"Unfortunately, yes. We had hoped he would take a stand against polygamy. But I'm afraid he's as polygamous as his father before him—more so, in fact. He has at least thirty wives, I believe—some say as many as ninety, others two hundred—and all manner of children, as you can imagine. And some of his wives are his half-sisters."

"Father, they'd be old maids if they didn't marry him. You know that Siamese princesses cannot marry below their rank. Besides, they are not brought up together once they grow beyond earliest childhood. And people who say he has two hundred wives are liars—or perhaps just stupid."

"Anchalee, how many times must I tell you to hold your tongue? Especially at the table. Anyway, it's an abominable custom," he continued.

"I wish you wouldn't talk like that, Father. At least we Siamese are honest about such things. How many men in England are hypocrites who have one lawful wife and who also keep a mistress—or two—hidden away? I believe the custom is especially rife among the upper classes."

"You, young lady, would do well to remember you are British. You are also much too impertinent for your age." He sighed, feeling the conversation turning too close to home for his own comfort. "You'll not speak of such matters."

But she didn't relent, knowing precisely just how far she could bait him without making him genuinely angry. "It's only the truth. And I know some members of the Church who keep Thai mistresses their wives don't know about."

Edward turned red. "Now that really is enough from you, Anchalee. You're simply showing off now that your sister is here."

But, he wondered, did she know the truth about her own mother? Or was this conversation just coincidence?"

Sensing her father's discomfort, Elizabeth quickly changed the subject again. "And what of the former Regent?" she asked. "I can't recall his name."

Edward was relieved to move on. "Yes, Chao Phya Sri Sriyawongse. Well, as you know, he relinquished the regency when the King turned twenty-one—in 1873, as I remember. But he's still chief minister, and although he's very old now and not in good health, he's still a powerful man."

"And didn't something awful happen to one of the queens recently?" Elizabeth asked as she helped herself to some fresh fruit—pineapples, pawpaw, and rose-apples—that Noi had set out. She loved catching up on all the news of Siam.

"That," Edward said, getting up from his chair, "is a tragic story I shall tell you over coffee."

When all three were settled in the comfortable, over-stuffed chairs in the sitting room, Edward sipped his black coffee thoughtfully, then began the story.

"Queen Sunanda was the King's favourite wife—and his half-sister, I might add. She was only nineteen, already had one daughter, and was expecting her second child last year. Anyway, she was on her way with her court to the summer palace at Bang Pa-In. She and her daughter, just a toddler not even two, were travelling along the river in a small royal boat being towed by a larger one when, without warning, their boat capsized. The queen and the child were drowned."

"But how?" Elizabeth asked. "The royal family never travels anywhere alone. There must have been many people there at the time."

"There were indeed," Edward confirmed. "Their attendants stood and watched as they died. They believed they could do nothing to help the queen or the princess."

"I don't understand, Father. Why not?"

"No one helped her because of an old law that says commoners are not permitted to touch members of the royal family. The punishment is death."

"But surely, in those circumstances, an exception could have been made," Elizabeth said, incredulous. "Or someone could have thrown her something so she could have saved herself."

"That too is against the law. The boatman must swim away. And if someone throws a lifebelt, he and all his family must be executed—or so the antiquated law has it."

Elizabeth was even more shocked. "I can't believe it—it's preposterous. I'm sure the King wouldn't condone such a law."

"I'm sure also," Edward agreed. "The King even imprisoned the chief attendant. But the law is the law to the common people and they dare not risk going against what they've been brought up to believe is correct, even in these modern times."

Anchalee had been sitting quietly, but now she spoke. "Father, all these laws have a reason for existing, as English laws do. I'm sure there are ridiculous old laws in England, too, that don't seem very sensible today. It was very sad that the queen was allowed to die and I'm sure the King would have granted a royal pardon had someone saved her. But you must remember, our history is long and the people learn respect from a very young age. You can't expect them to change so quickly. They believed they had no option."

"Anchalee, you shouldn't take everything as a personal insult. And must I keep reminding you that you are as much English as you are Siamese? More so English, in my opinion."

"Which allows me to see both sides," she answered stubbornly.

They fell silent for a few minutes as they sipped their coffee, which was served from the same elegant pot Elizabeth remembered from her childhood. When she was finished, Elizabeth set down her cup and stood up, smiling at her father and sister.

"All this travelling has caught up with me. I think I'll retire for the evening, if you don't mind."

"Of course not, dear. You must be looking your best for the ball tomorrow. The cream of Bangkok society will be there," he said haughtily.

"It's wonderful to be back," Elizabeth said, thrilled at the idea of attending the ball.

"Goodnight, then, my dear. And don't rush to get up in the morning. Noi will bring you breakfast on a tray."

Chapter 14

Elizabeth felt the other guests' gaze upon her as she entered the ballroom on her father's arm. She was in her element at a social function such as this, and although naturally shy, she had been trained to make an eye-catching entrance and to conduct herself with aplomb at any ball.

Tonight, she knew she looked her best. She wore an exquisite gown of pale blue-grey satin ruched over a fashionably high bustle at the back and falling to form a short train. The skirt had a mass of tiny rows of pleating in front. The neckline —her first décolletage, wide and low—was a special departure for her, and she loved the way it revealed her pale neck, extending to where her bust began to swell. She had carried it with her from England, but hadn't dared to wear it on board. It was the first dress she had bought without her grandmother's approval, and she felt daring and sophisticated, even though many women in the room had opted for lower necklines than her own, some leaving little to the imagination. The long sleeves of Elizabeth's dress were edged with rows of lace, and she wore a double strand of pearls with an amethyst clasp at her throat. Her grandmother had presented the piece to her for her twenty-first birthday. Her fine, light brown hair was piled on top of her head and threaded with grey satin ribbons.

"Mr Edward Fairburn and Miss Elizabeth Fairburn," announced a page dressed in purple silk panung and white jacket with gleaming gold buttons.

A young, recently-arrived single woman was always a source of interest in expatriate society, particularly, of course, to those young men who were not yet married—but also to the women, who were keen to glimpse the latest fashions from Britain and the United States. Elizabeth was revelling in the atmosphere, but suddenly felt the attention drawn away from her. A stillness engulfed the room as if all in attendance were holding their collective breath as the announcer presented, "Miss Anchalee Fairburn".

In the glory of her own entrance, Elizabeth had almost forgotten that her sister was right behind them. Anchalee had insisted on entering the room alone, and Elizabeth could only marvel at her attention-seeking tactic. She had chosen a simple emerald-green taffeta dress with a fitted bodice and ground-length, draped skirt. Her figure was developing and her newly acquired bust was accentuated by her nipped-in waist.

But it was her face that gained her the most attention. In contrast to every other woman there, she had left her hair undone, and it fell straight, dark, and luxuriant past her shoulders to halfway down her back. Her perfect complexion needed no rouge or powder, and her full lips were a natural, subtle shade of burnished rose. Even in the low gas light, her green eyes sparkled. She smiled at the guests, revealing her perfectly white, even teeth. Whispers of appreciation seemed to ripple through the room, and she graciously curtsied to her audience and joined her father and sister.

Edward had initially been reluctant to allow her to attend the ball, but she had pleaded and cajoled until he'd finally relented. Now he wondered to himself if it had been a good idea. He realised she had matured lately, but he had no idea that in her grown-up gown, with the low lighting, she would look every bit the woman she was not. Still, at least if she were here with him, he could keep a watchful eye on her. The maid, Noi, had let slip that Anchalee sometimes went out for hours at a time while he was away, and he was concerned about where she was going and what company she was keeping. Hopefully, Elizabeth would be a steadying influence on his younger daughter.

The orchestra began to play the opening waltz, and Elizabeth danced with her father while Anchalee watched from the side. Within minutes, a young British officer had asked Anchalee to partner him, and Elizabeth was surprised to see how elegantly and confidently her sister danced.

"Where did she learn to waltz like that?" Elizabeth asked her father.

"An English woman runs a dance school in Bangkok for girls. I thought it would be good for your sister to go and meet some other young women. She spends far too much time with servants and anyone else who'll speak with her in Siamese."

"You'd never guess she's only thirteen," Elizabeth whispered.

"No, and that's what concerns me. In some ways, it might be best if she is married young. Then I wouldn't have to worry about her so much."

"Married!" Elizabeth exclaimed. "But she's only a child, Father."

"I know," he said, sighing. "But some Siamese girls are still married very young. It wouldn't be thought of as immoral if she were to marry at, say, fifteen."

"I suppose you're right. Even in England, it's not that rare for girls to be married so young. But why anyone would want to surrender their freedom at such an age of wonderful youth is beyond me."

The waltz finished, and Elizabeth and Edward left the dance floor for drinks. They saw that Anchalee's partner had been replaced by another equally dashing young man, and Elizabeth wondered what either would say if they knew how young she was.

Elizabeth herself then accepted an invitation from the officer who had just surrendered her half-sister to his colleague, but some way into the dance they were interrupted when a man tapped her partner on the shoulder and cut in. Elizabeth felt weak and her breath caught in her throat as she recognised him.

"I knew we'd meet again," he said in a low voice as he held her closely—rather too closely for her comfort. His hand seemed to burn through the flimsy fabric along her back, and she felt as if the room were resounding with her heartbeat.

"You are looking especially beautiful tonight, Elizabeth," he said.

His words took her by surprise. She usually found the way Americans used first names so soon after introductions quite ill-mannered and distasteful. But from him, it somehow seemed appropriate. In any case, she was unable to object because she seemed to have lost her powers of speech. She could only look up into his dark eyes as he towered over her.

As they danced, the room seemed to spin, and all that mattered in the world was him. The music faded into the background until she was in a distant place, whirling with him in a misty paradise.

He smiled at her then, and she noticed the creases at the sides of his eyes, fine white lines in his deeply-tanned face. Unlike all the other men in the room he was clean-shaven, without moustache or side-whiskers, which was considered terribly unfashionable. But to her, it looked wonderful. The black shadows on his upper lip and around his chin seemed strangely distinctive, and she imagined how rough his skin would feel on hers.

The music stopped, and she was brought back suddenly to reality.

"Thanks for the dance. See you later," he said casually as he escorted her from the dance floor. And he was gone, just like that.

She could only stand motionless at the edge of the dance floor, not knowing what to think or why he had left her so quickly. She wasn't upset so much as bemused. Had she been so intoxicated by the combination of the tropical night air and a single glass of champagne that she had lost her wits?

"Elizabeth, there you are," her father said as he arrived

beside her. "Would you like another glass of champagne?"

She felt flushed, as if she had been caught unawares in the midst of some guilty pleasure—which, in a sense, she had. She nodded, and he handed her a crystal coupe. He rarely drank himself these days, preferring instead the tropical fruit punches, though he didn't begrudge other adults the pleasure.

"Having a good time, dear?"

She nodded again. "Why yes, of course, Father."

"Have you met anyone interesting?"

"Yes ... yes, so many interesting people to meet. But I think Anchalee is meeting more people than I am."

Anchalee was across the other side of the ballroom, sipping champagne and surrounded by a group of handsome young men.

"The little devil. I told her she wasn't to have any champagne. She's much too young."

"Anchalee doesn't seem to think she's too young for anything," Elizabeth remarked, and Edward looked at her quizzically.

"Well, she's not like the other girls her age, is she?" Elizabeth added.

"No, unfortunately," he was reluctantly forced to agree. "But although she purports to be so sophisticated, I'm certain she's actually very naïve. That's what concerns me, Elizabeth. She could be vulnerable to the first young man who comes along. A handsome face, a few whispered compliments, and Anchalee could well allow herself to be ... well, to be ruined, so to speak."

Elizabeth blushed again. Her father could have been talking about her. She would have to come to her senses over this American, for she realised the magnetism he held for her. If a single dance with him could render her breathless ...

"Elizabeth, what do you think?"

But she was too distracted to reply. Edward sighed in exasperation. "Elizabeth! Why don't you join your sister over there? And do try to prevent her acquiring another glass of champagne."

As she made her way round the room, she found herself scanning the dance floor, searching for him. She saw him dancing with a beautiful blonde woman, the young wife of a British consular official. He held the woman as closely as he had held Elizabeth, and he wore that same charming smile. He was probably telling her how beautiful she looked tonight. She could only wonder at what the woman's husband thought of the spectacle. Mr Taylor leaned closer to whisper something in the woman's ear which made her blush and giggle. Elizabeth felt a stab of jealousy and quickly turned away toward her sister, thinking that if he danced with every attractive woman in that fashion, then she could mean little to him. He had simply moved on to the next young woman.

"Elizabeth," Anchalee called. "Come and meet my new friends."

She joined the group, successfully taking Anchalee's champagne coupe and handing it to a passing waiter. One of the young men asked Elizabeth to dance and they took to the floor. But both the music and the man before her became distant distractions as she moved mechanically, her feet automatically picking out the right steps. She couldn't help looking past her partner, trying to catch a glimpse of *him*. Her eyes located him with yet another dance partner, the daughter of a Portuguese merchant. Her own partner smiled politely when the music ended, but did not ask her for another dance. She was suddenly aware she had ignored him, and was sorry she had seemed rude. Too late though, the young man had already moved on.

Mr Taylor alone commanded her attention that night, and yet it was ludicrous; he hardly seemed to acknowledge her presence. After only one dance with him, one breathtaking dance, the spell had been broken. Yet she was sure there had been an attraction between them. Had he already forgotten her?

She fretted that for the remainder of the evening she

would merely have to watch from the side as he partnered every other young, and even not-so-young, woman present.

"Elizabeth, are you feeling all right?" Anchalee asked. "You look pale."

"Yes, I'm fine, thank you. But I think I need some fresh air. I'll walk outside to the terrace for a while."

"Would you like me to come with you?"

"No, no thank you. I'm quite fine, really. You stay here and enjoy yourself. And Father says no more champagne."

Anchalee looked guilty. "Oh, he noticed, did he?"

"Yes, so you'd better be on your best behaviour from now on, or there'll be trouble."

"I can deal with Father," she stated confidently.

"I'm sure you can." Elizabeth raised her eyebrows knowingly as she walked toward the french doors that led to the wide terrace.

Outside, flickering lamps burned, and several couples stood closely together in private conversation. She looked out to the lush gardens that were landscaped with both native and non-native trees, bushes, and flowers. But she hardly saw them. What she saw instead was his face—and in her imagination, she traced the contours of his wide brow, high cheekbones and sensuous lips.

She had been standing on the terrace for only a few minutes when she was startled by a deep voice very close behind her.

"What, tired of the party already?"

She gasped, turned quickly and found herself looking into the dark eyes she had just been dreaming of. She went pale, then her face flushed with embarrassment at her thoughts of only moments before. "I ... no, Mr Taylor," she stammered. "I mean, I just came out here for a little air." She tried to smile and was sure he could sense the hammering of her heart and the quickening pulse at her neck. As he grinned, she felt that he was reading every thought that raced through her mind.

"The name's Sam. Mr Taylor was my father."

"Was?"

He leaned on the railing beside her. "He died last year in California."

"Oh, I'm sorry." She paused. "And your mother?"

"She died when I was two. So, I'm an orphan, you see."

"That must have been difficult for you, losing your mother so young."

"Not really. I don't remember her at all. Besides, I was always the independent type."

She wanted to tell him about her own mother; about how much she had missed her when she died. But she was afraid he wouldn't be interested. There was another awkward pause and she could still feel her heart beating as if it were trying to burst from her chest. "So, your family is from California, then?" she finally managed to ask.

"That's right. I'm a born-and-bred Los Angeleno. My father went to California to find gold."

"Oh, how extraordinary," she said, delighted to discover they had something in common. "So did mine."

"Did he find any?"

"No, but he became a photographer in California, on the goldfields. And now … well, of course, you know my father already. I was forgetting. And your father—did he find gold?"

"Nope. But he did find my mother, who he always said was better than gold. He never did get over losing her."

She felt a little more confident, now they had something to talk about. "It's odd. You—um, you don't look American."

"You mean, I don't look like a *white* American."

"No, oh no … I'm sorry. That's not what I meant." She hesitated, embarrassed. "It's just that I—well, I imagine your father was Italian … or Spanish, perhaps?"

"No, he was English."

"Please forgive me for prying. You must think me very impertinent."

"Not at all. And if you're referring to my complexion," he said with amusement, "I inherited that from my mother. She was Mexican."

"Oh, I see." And although she hadn't intended it to be, she was immediately sure that her reply had sounded disdaining to him. Ashamed, she could not look him in the eye.

"Does it matter to you?"

"In what way should it?" she asked, attempting to sound as if it were a trivial matter.

"I don't know. Some people don't like half-breeds." As he spoke the derogatory word, his voice had a sarcastic edge to it, and it seemed as if he were testing her in some way.

She became flustered momentarily, then realised the perfect response was at her disposal.

"My sister is a … a half-breed, as you put it. I prefer not to use that word, though."

"Oh yes, Anchalee; I'd forgotten that." He smiled. "Anyhow, enough about me. Tell me about you."

She was relieved to have salvaged some dignity from the encounter. But was he really interested, she wondered, or was he just toying with her?

"There's not much to tell, really. I was born in Australia and came here with my mother to join my father when I was still a child. My mother was travelling back to England for— a sojourn, when she became ill and died on board the ship. So, my father sent me back to England to school. When I wasn't at school, I lived with my grandparents. And now, here I am, back in Siam. It's so good to be home."

"That explains it," he said, grinning.

"Explains what, Mr Taylor?"

"Yesterday, when I saw you at the pier. The way you were dressed."

She considered his tone rather too familiar. "What can you mean?" she asked coolly.

"Oh, don't take it the wrong way, honey. You looked enchanting, but…"

"Yes, Mr Taylor?" she prompted as calmly as she could, shocked at his indecent familiarity.

"Well, you looked like you'd been dressed by your grandmother."

She turned away in embarrassment yet again and looked out over the gardens.

"You're right," she admitted quietly after a moment of silence. "My grandmother always chose my clothes."

"But not tonight."

"I beg your pardon?"

She almost jumped out of her skin as he ran a warm fingertip along her neckline, along the top of her exposed décolletage. But she didn't push him away.

"I mean this," he said.

She could only stare at him with wild, wide eyes, and she felt a cold sweat envelop her.

He withdrew his hand. "I'd like to see you again, Elizabeth."

She felt sick, and the heat now seemed to rise up to choke her. She took a deep breath. "I don't think that can be possible, Mr Taylor."

"Don't you want to see me again?"

"It's not that, Mr Taylor. It's just that ... well, there's someone in England. I'm ..."

"I don't see a wedding band."

"No, I'm not married. But ..."

"But what?"

"My father wouldn't approve."

"Don't tell him. You're old enough to make your own decisions."

She was speechless.

"So, you'll meet me?"

She needed only a second's thought. "Very well," she replied impulsively.

"You can come to my hotel."

She was shocked. "Mr Taylor, that is an outrageous proposal. You know well that I cannot possibly be seen … Really! I've a good mind to inform my father of your … your …" She trailed off as he seemed to look right into her soul, his dark eyes not leaving hers.

There was a hint of a smile at the corners of his mouth. "Of course. I'm sorry. I have a friend with a house. We can meet there. Say, Tuesday at one o'clock?"

She couldn't believe what she was hearing but still found herself nodding in agreement, as if in a trace. She knew it was dangerous, yet she was unable to refuse.

"I'll write down the address and give it to you before the end of the evening."

"But my father—."

"I'll be discreet," he assured her. "Trust me." Then, with a brilliant smile, he left her, sauntering back inside, no doubt to request the company of another beautiful woman on the dance floor.

His parting words were an enigma. Could she trust him in any way? Her common sense said no, but her burning skin told her that she wanted—needed—to see him again.

"Where on earth have you been?" Edward asked when she arrived back inside.

"Oh … just out on the terrace, Father. I needed some air."

"Well, I think we'll be leaving shortly. Anchalee shouldn't be out too late."

She began to panic. It was still early, and she didn't have the address yet. "Oh, Father. Couldn't we stay just a little longer?" she pleaded. "It's my first night out, after all."

He smiled, realising how much he had missed her all these years. "Very well, then. But only a little longer."

She excused herself to use the powder room, and on the way back, in the long hallway leading to the ballroom, she saw him sitting in the shadows on one of the decorative teak chairs.

As she walked in his direction, he stood up and nodded to her. "Miss Fairburn," he said formally, for the benefit of several other people nearby.

"Mr Taylor," she replied, and as he brushed past her, she felt a small piece of paper being pressed into her hand.

She had no time to examine it then but simply tucked it into her sleeve to read later.

Chapter 15

Joseph greeted her at the door of his two-storey home—the same house he had lived in all his years in Bangkok. He was surprised at how she had changed. "Elizabeth, you've grown so." He smiled and offered his hand.

"Mr Shaw. It seems so long since I saw you last." She took his hand warmly in hers.

"Not at all," he said as he ushered her into the hallway. "It seems like only yesterday you were a little girl lying on the grass with a broken heart."

"You still remember that?"

"Of course. How could I forget? It was a difficult time for you."

"Thank you for the letters you wrote when I first went away. They helped a lot when I felt homesick and missed my father."

"Were you miserable?" he asked as they went into the sitting room.

"Not so much after the first year. I got used to it. Everyone was very kind to me in England. But it wasn't the same as being here."

"And now that you're back?"

"Well, I feel as if I've come home."

"Please, do sit down."

Joseph's houseboy, Simon, brought in a pot of tea on a tray and set it on the table. There was sugar in the milk jug, and milk from Joseph's own cow in the sugar bowl.

"Simon tries so hard," Joseph said. "I haven't the heart to

tell him."

Elizabeth smiled at him. He was still the kind, generous person she remembered.

"How did he acquire an English name?"

"Well, the truth is that I had to buy Simon. He was a slave, you see," Joseph answered with distaste. "Of course, I freed him immediately and offered him a paid job, which he accepted. He wanted a Christian name when he was baptised."

"He's a convert, then?" Elizabeth asked, surprised. The missionaries still had so little success in Siam.

"Yes," Joseph replied proudly. "He was my first. Others have come and gone in the years since then. Many are Christians for a short while, then revert to Buddhism. But Simon has remained."

"Your work is still difficult, then?"

"As difficult as always, I'm afraid. I'm beginning to wonder if Christianity will ever take root in this country. The missionaries in New Zealand and Hawaii have had almost complete success. Here, we can't claim even a handful." He shrugged. "Still, this is my home now and has been for a long time. And I won't give up the Lord's work."

"Are you ever lonely?" she asked as Joseph poured the tea. "I mean here, by yourself?"

"You mean without a wife?" he said, smiling again.

"Well, yes, I suppose that is what I mean."

"I've never found the right woman, Elizabeth. One cannot simply decide to marry, can one?"

"No, I suppose not. But perhaps you will find that right person. There's time enough still."

"I have my work. That keeps me occupied."

"Of course."

"And what of you? I hear you have found a most suitable young man to marry."

James. She did not know what to think or to say about him any longer. How could she contemplate marriage to one man, when she was so attracted to another?

"Well, we haven't made an announcement yet, Mr Shaw."

"Oh, I understood from your father that you were to set a wedding date on your return to England. Your father is delighted that there will be a title with the marriage."

"I know—he's anxious for me to make the engagement official."

"And you?"

"Well, in truth, I still haven't committed myself wholly."

Mr Shaw always seemed to have a way of eliciting the truth, just like in the old days, but until she had uttered the words, she had not fully realised that was what she thought. But it was true, and she knew it as soon as she had spoken. She had not committed herself to James, and she was no longer sure she wanted to.

"Well then, I expect you must consider carefully. And you've come far enough away if you were seeking some time to think alone," he added.

She smiled politely. Joseph could not realise how far from the truth he was; for Bangkok was where temptation was at its peak. She had already decided she would not meet Sam the next day as she had promised. She could not trust herself with him, nor could she trust him with her; that was only too evident in the way he looked at her—or, rather, in the way he looked at every woman, she reminded herself. Her father had been right when he warned her against him.

"Elizabeth, are you all right?" Joseph asked when she fell silent. "You seem a little preoccupied. I'm sorry, perhaps I shouldn't have pried."

"Oh no, it's fine, really," she answered quickly. "I'm sorry. I suppose I'm still tired from the journey. And still getting used to the climate again."

"Of course. The heat is one thing we can always rely on in Siam."

"But Bangkok has changed so much since I was last here.

It's amazing that Siam has retained its independence."

"Yes, indeed. And I believe it will remain so, if the British and the French can be kept at bay."

"Do you really believe it's best for Siam to remain independent?" she asked, surprised. Her education in England had taught her that colonialism and empire-building were to be celebrated as the most glorious achievements of the nineteenth century.

"I do," Joseph stated firmly. "Although mine isn't a popular view among the expatriates. Of course, I'd like to see a conversion to the Church, but the people are very resistant to change. It will take time and perhaps we will never achieve very much."

They talked further, and he told her of comings and goings over the years that her father had not known of. When they had finished their tea and exhausted polite conversation, Elizabeth stood to go.

"Well, thank you very much for the refreshments, Mr Shaw. It's been a most pleasant afternoon."

He escorted her to the waiting carriage. "I'll see you at church on Sunday, no doubt."

"Until Sunday," she replied, smiling as he helped her in.

He watched the carriage until it was out of sight, thinking to himself that she had become an extraordinarily refined young woman, and that she would make some young man a most suitable wife. In fact, he thought, as he walked up the steps of his front verandah, she was exactly the sort of woman he should have married fifteen years ago, if only there had been such a lady then. He had no doubt that a wife would have helped him immensely in his work. And yes, he secretly admitted to himself in answer to Elizabeth's question, he had been very lonely. However, a helpmeet in life was not to be his, it seemed. It was his cross to bear, his punishment for that lamented indiscretion so many years ago.

∞∞∞

Edward was far from pleased at what he had heard from Elizabeth. To have a daughter married into a family with a hereditary title, which her husband would inherit, would have suited Edward very nicely, and it would have provided opportunity for him even in distant Siam.

He thought of well-repeated stories about Mr Knox having secured his promotions because he was related to Lord John Beresford and Lord Ranfurly in England. Knox had originally been a soldier with no diplomatic training, yet had risen to become British Consul-General in Siam, and had been knighted for his services.

Edward's father, too, had been knighted by Queen Victoria, and although in his younger days, Edward had dismissed the title as inconsequential, he would now have liked one for himself—or at least the trappings and connections which accompanied the honour. If Elizabeth were to marry James, who knew what doors it could open? And she was his only hope. Anchalee was the beauty of the family, that was certain, but a girl whose mother was of the serving class was of no consequence at all in hierarchical Siamese society, nor would she ever marry into the British aristocracy. Anyway, he was sure Anchalee would never consider such a prospect, even if it were offered. His hopes lay with Elizabeth marrying James, and he was sure that His Royal Highness the King of Siam would accord him more time and credibility if she did.

While Edward had photographed the King several times with various wives and children and was often called to duty at official receptions, he was still regarded as little more than a casual employee. But he wanted admittance to the inner circle, perhaps to be appointed a special advisor in some capacity, or as the official royal photographer. In any case, and in the meantime, he would let certain people know just whom his daughter was to marry. It was sure to be influential, assuming Elizabeth saw sense.

∞∞∞∞

Anchalee heard her sister in the hallway and stopped her as she began to run up the stairs. "How was your outing?"

"It was fine, thank you, Anchalee. But I feel quite tired. I think I shall go upstairs and rest." She gave Anchalee a weak smile and turned to continue up the stairs.

"Elizabeth? Is anything wrong? You look different."

She stopped and turned back. "No, nothing's wrong."

But Anchalee noticed the thin voice and the tight, awkward smile which was not reflected in her eyes. Her expression appeared almost as if it had been painted on, and her eyes were unusually bright, as if she were about to cry.

"I'm just weary. I think it must be the heat. I'll see you at dinner." And she continued up the stairs. Anchalee had an uncanny knack for seeing through people, and she knew that Elizabeth had not told the truth. She went up the stairs after her, but found her bedroom door closed. Crouching, she put her ear to the keyhole and could hear muffled sobbing.

Inside, Elizabeth lay on her bed with her face pressed into the pillow. She was deeply upset, and no matter how hard she tried to put the events of the day out of her mind, she simply could not.

∞∞∞∞

It had been a mistake, from the moment she had accepted the note at the ball to the moment she had sat down at breakfast that morning and asked if she could use the carriage that afternoon. Edward hadn't looked up from his newspaper —it was months old but was British, a rare luxury. He replied distractedly, "Of course. More old friends to see?"

"No, I just thought I'd like to go for a drive," she had said. And at that point, she had actually been telling the truth. Or at least she thought she had been.

She still believed she had no intention of keeping the appointment, but she did want to get out of the house and see some more of the city, a diversion she had thought would take her mind off Samuel Taylor, at least for a while.

She was beginning to resent the power and attraction he held over her. She wanted to forget him and to think instead of James. Yet, when she tried to picture her would-be fiancé's face, the image was vague. She couldn't even remember the colour of his eyes.

After lunch, she had gone up to her room to change. She asked Noi to prepare her blue and white striped cotton visiting costume. It was light and cooler than many of her other outfits, with close-fitting long sleeves, a draped skirt, a fitted bodice, a bow at the high neck, a row of buttons down the front that would take the maid ten minutes to fix, even with the special button fastener Elizabeth had brought from England, and a matching dolman jacket which fell to just below her hips.

Noi helped her arrange her hair in a neat coil close to her head, and when she was dressed, she surveyed her reflection in the full-length mirror. Elegant, yes, but still so dull. Why had she allowed her grandmother to buy her clothes for so long? She would love to wear the new brighter colours that were the rage in London now, but instead, almost all her clothes were in old-fashioned pastel colours—lilac, pink, or blue—or just plain white. How could she expect to hold his attention with such dowdy dresses? "Curse the man," she said aloud. What did it matter what he, or any man for that matter, thought of her? Everyone believed she should marry James and be done with it.

She picked up her white parasol, tucked a white lace-edged handkerchief into her sleeve and was on her way. She carried a small silk purse containing a few coins as well as the paper he had written the address on: not that she would need it, since she was not going there.

"Just go slowly up New Road, please," she ordered the driver, in Siamese. She was quickly reacquainting herself with the language, a case of necessity when few servants spoke English.

As they drove along in the victoria at a leisurely pace, she found it impossible not to think of the note. It was inevitable that her hands, as if of their own mind, eventually opened the little drawstring purse and extracted the simple slip of white onionskin paper on which the address had been written hastily, by the look of the ink blots on it. Idly, she wondered if it was one of those newfangled pens with its own ink vial that could so easily leak.

But back to the present. The place, just off New Road, was quite close to where they were. She worried that he would think her rude for not keeping the appointment—which was, after all, a lady's prerogative—then she began to fret over what he really thought of her. He would simply move on to the next young woman if she showed no interest. Perhaps he would even forget they had arranged to meet, anyway. It was entirely illogical that it pained her to think of him with another woman, but she had been given her opportunity and had declined to take it.

"Driver, turn around, please!" she called spontaneously. "Go back the other way." She pointed the way they had come, hardly knowing what she was doing. "I have an appointment to keep," she said to herself in English, as her heart began to beat alarmingly fast. The beads of perspiration that had already formed on her forehead ran down the sides of her face, and she dabbed at them with her handkerchief.

"*Leoh saai*—turn left," she called when they reached the side road she thought was the correct address. She would just go to the door and tell him she would not be keeping the appointment. She would apologise politely but not go in, and she would at least see him one more time.

"Wait for me here, please," she told the driver when they arrived at what she hoped was the house. It was similar in style to her father's but about three times the size. The garden was sumptuous, but becoming unruly. She noticed that the windows on the second storey had been thrown open. Perhaps his friends had not lived there long. She rang the doorbell, expecting a maid to answer, but when the door swung open and it was Sam himself who stood there, she took a step back in surprise. In his arms, he held a white thread of a kitten that stared at her without blinking. She was startled to note that the kitten had two different-coloured eyes: one orange, one blue. She recognised immediately that it was the famed *khao manee*—diamond-eyed—breed that His Majesty King Chulalongkorn favoured. But she'd heard the cats were reserved for royalty ...

He smiled widely, as if there were nothing incongruous about him opening the front door while holding a kitten. Gently, he set the cat down, and it skittered away a few feet down the long hallway, then stopped, turned, and resumed its stare, eyes glinting in the half-light.

She looked back at Sam. His dark eyes, too, were penetrating as he appraised her. "I wondered if you'd changed your mind." He opened the door wider and she noticed he wore Siamese-style silk slippers. He motioned for her to come inside, but she remained where she was, looking at him, again lost for words. "Well? Please do come in."

"I ... I can't. I'm sorry, but I ..."

He smiled again. "Do I scare you?"

"Of course not," she answered swiftly, irritated by his arrogant tone.

"Well then, at least come in for a cup of tea. We won't be disturbed. The servants are taking a siesta, I believe—or whatever they call the Siamese equivalent."

She looked puzzled and a little concerned. "I thought you said your friend lived here."

"He does, but he's away in Singapore for a number of months on His Majesty's business, no less. He asked me to look in on the house from time to time, and that's what I'm doing today. The gardeners are supposed to be keeping up the grounds. I'll have to have a word to them."

She found herself removing her shoes and placing them in the shoe-rack just inside the door. He held out a hand, which she took without thinking, and she was in the hallway. The big house smelled slightly musty.

"It needs airing, as you can tell. The servants have their own quarters in an adjoining building. I'm afraid all the furniture's under dust covers, except for a small sitting room next to the kitchen. We'll have to sit in there."

She realised he still had hold of her hand, and she snatched it away. It was all too odd. "Really, Mr Taylor, I don't intend to stay. My driver's outside."

"Well, he can wait then, can't he? He won't mind a nap, I'm sure. And I've told you before, Elizabeth, my name's Sam. Or Samuel, if you want to be really formal."

She followed him along the dark hallway, into a comfortably furnished room—not large, but not as small as he had intimated—that contained a sofa and two armchairs, a sideboard, and a low, finely-carved teak table in the Siamese style. She saw no evidence of tea.

He noticed her expression as she surveyed the room. "You're right, of course. I lied about the tea, I'm afraid. Would a glass of sweet sherry do instead?"

"Thank you, that will be fine."

He poured the drink from a crystal decanter, then a whisky for himself from another, and offered her a plate of miniature cakes. She took one, though she had no appetite, but she was reluctant to drink the sherry. She wanted all her wits about her.

"You look uncomfortable, Elizabeth," he said in a mocking tone.

"That's because I am," she answered directly, setting down the sherry, but still holding the cake, not knowing what else to do with it. He had neglected to provide plates.

"Well, don't be. My intentions are strictly platonic on this occasion." He sat next to her on the sofa, and she found the very proximity of him almost overpowering. It was all she could do to stop herself from jumping up and running out to the carriage. Yet she remained riveted to her seat, unable to look away.

She felt a pressing need to somehow take control of the situation, to establish some authority. As fate would have it, at that very moment, the kitten padded in, perched at the base of Sam's feet, tail wagging, concentrating on its bid for world dominance, then took an almighty leap. Unfortunately, it did not make it to Sam's lap, but landed like a gecko about three-quarters of the way up his leg, clinging to his trousers with its sharp little claws. Chuckling, he hauled it up to his lap, where it immediately curled into a ball and feigned sleep, though one eye remained open in case there should be enemies.

Despite her unease, Elizabeth was fascinated. "The kitten likes you."

"At least someone does—or something, I should say."

She ignored his attempt at humour. "The eyes—isn't it a *khao manee*? Reserved for royalty, I thought."

"Hmmm," he answered. "Let's just say my friend has friends in high places. He's a diplomat and this kitten's mother was a gift from His Majesty, who is also my friend's distant relation. Turned out she was pregnant, though my friend had to leave almost immediately. She had two kittens, both with the lucky jewel eyes."

"Oh! How lovely." Elizabeth looked around for the mother.

"There's a sad story. She gave birth to two kittens, but the other died shortly after, unfortunately. We don't know why. Then, five weeks later, we found mamma cat lying outside in the garden, close to death—we think bitten by a cobra. There are a few around here."

Elizabeth shivered, despite the heat of the day.

"We did what we could, but it was hopeless. At the time, this little one was asleep in its box in the kitchen. That was a few weeks ago. Now she thinks I am mamma."

He picked up the small warm bundle and held it out to Elizabeth. She took it and put it in her own lap. The kitten did not purr, but instead looked up at her, as if to say, "And *who* are you?" Then it decided it had important business to attend to, suddenly jumping off, sliding down the couch and skittering out the door.

She smiled then. He was surprising—she had not imagined this soft side to him. Then he had to go and ruin everything.

"So why did you come here today?" he said. "What were you expecting?"

"I—nothing. I was expecting nothing at all," she stammered, disarmed again. "I don't know what you mean. In fact, I wasn't even sure myself that I would come. Now that I'm here though, I find this meeting, shall we call it, rather an unusual way to court."

"Be careful, Elizabeth. I can hear grandma's warnings. The old lady still has quite a hold on you, hasn't she?"

She sat up even more stiffly. "I'll thank you not to speak of my grandmother that way. You don't even know her."

He laughed. "You're right, honey, I don't. But looking at you, I can guess."

"You're very insulting, Mr Taylor."

"I'm sorry, I don't mean to be. I guess I've had to stick up for myself most of my life and it's given me too sharp a tongue. What do you think?" But before she had a chance to answer, he continued. "And anyway, what makes you believe I'm courting, as you put it?"

"I'm sorry, Mr Taylor, if I've misunderstood. But when a gentleman asks to meet a lady, it's my understanding that he's

—well, he's—." She blushed scarlet, unable to say what she was thinking.

"Looking on her as a possible wife?" he finished for her. "Don't get me wrong: you're a very attractive young woman. But I don't court anyone. I'll be straight with you. I'm not looking to get married. Those aren't my intentions toward you and are unlikely to be so in the near future. I'm sorry to have to spell it out that way, but I don't want you getting any false hopes. Then again, I guess some woman, someday, will persuade me that it's not such a bad idea."

With a jolt, she realised what she was doing—dallying with a man her father disliked, alone, at a strange residence. And he had openly admitted that he did not have decent intentions toward her. Not to mention the fact that she was already promised to another. He must think her a fool.

She stood abruptly and began to put on her hat and gloves, trying desperately to retain at least some of her dignity.

"Well, in that case, Mr Taylor, I think it's time for me to leave," she stated primly.

"I hope I haven't offended you," he said, still slouched on the sofa.

"Not at all. I'm only glad we understand each other."

"Meaning?"

"Well, as I told you last time we met, I'm engaged to be married. So, you see, I'm not looking to be courted, either."

"You could have fooled me," he said infuriatingly. She knew she should leave immediately, but somehow, she couldn't.

"If you find me amusing, Mr Taylor, I can assure you the feeling is *not* mutual."

He only laughed again. "No, it's not exactly amusing that I find you. Just so *verah propah*," he added in a mock upper-class British accent. Before she could retort, he jumped up and stood very close to her. "I'll walk you to the door," he said abruptly, as he stood up.

She looked away. "Thank you, but I can see myself out."

"I'm sure you can."

He remained where he was, not moving an inch, and she was at a loss over what to do or to say to him next. Then, slowly, his head moved toward hers, his arms closed around her, and before she realised what was happening, his lips were on hers. He wasn't holding her forcibly at all, but still she could not seem to tear herself away. She felt his tongue prising her lips apart and she felt her own arms reach up and clasp him around his neck, while her mouth opened to his. She closed her eyes, and, just as that night she had danced with him, a sense of unreality swept over her. But when he pulled his lips from hers and pressed her tightly to him, her head resting against his chest, she soon came to her senses. What was she thinking of, letting this virtual stranger take such intimate liberties?

"Let me go," she demanded, almost in a whisper. "You must let me go now."

He released her immediately, and she stood beside him, not daring to look into his eyes again. For if she did, she was afraid she would not be able to leave. "I must go," she said, hastily rearranging her crushed skirt and tucking up strands of hair that had fallen during the encounter. Silently, he stood aside for her, and still without looking at him, she said, "I cannot see you again. Not like this. Not ever."

She turned and hurried from the room, down the hallway and out to the waiting carriage. Sam sat down again thoughtfully and poured himself a second drink. *She'll be mine before another month has passed,* he thought to himself, *but only if she wants to be—and I think she does.*

Outside the bedroom door, Anchalee was more than

curious to discover if her sister would confide in her. She stood up, smoothed her skirts, then knocked lightly. The sobs stopped and there was a long silence. Anchalee knocked again.

"Who is it?"

"It's only me. Can I come in?"

"Just a moment." There was another interval before Elizabeth called out that she was ready.

Anchalee opened the door to find her sister seated at her dressing table, brushing her hair. But she noted that the covers of the bed were rumpled on one side and that Elizabeth's eyes were red and puffy.

"Elizabeth, have you been crying?"

"No, of course not." She spoke to Anchalee's reflection in the mirror. "It's just the air outside irritating my nose. Such a nuisance."

"But you're inside now."

"What?"

"I know you've been crying. I heard you through the door."

"Oh, so you've taken to spying on me now?"

"No. I was just worried. What's the matter?"

"I told you, nothing. I'm just homesick. For England. For James."

"I don't believe you."

"Anchalee, please."

"It's a man, isn't it? Are you in love?"

"What do you mean? That's nonsense. In love with whom?"

"Your answer should have been 'James'. But I can tell by the look in your eyes. It's that other one, isn't it? Sam Taylor. You've been to visit him today."

For an instant, Elizabeth's hairbrush paused in mid-air, but only for an instant. She continued brushing her hair, and her strokes were faster and harder than they had been a few seconds earlier.

"I don't know what you're talking about, Anchalee."

"Yes, you do. I saw the way you looked at each other at the ball. And I saw you on the terrace with him. And then you met him in one of the hallways."

"How do you know all this? You *have* been spying on me, haven't you? You little minx."

"Of course not. I told you, I saw you in the hallway. You didn't see me, because you had your back to me. You've been with him this afternoon, haven't you?"

Elizabeth put down the brush. "All right, I had afternoon tea with him. There, I've told you."

She turned from the reflection to face her sister. "And you must never, never breathe a word of this to Father, nor to anyone, do you hear me? If you do, I'll deny everything, and you and I will no longer be friends. Do you understand?"

Anchalee was stunned at her sister's gravity and was silent for a moment. "Of course I won't tell." Then she smiled as she asked, "So, what happened? It was more than tea, wasn't it?"

"Anchalee, that's quite enough. I don't appreciate your insinuations."

"I'm sorry. But I can always tell."

"Well then, you'd know there is nothing *to* tell. And in any case, I'll not be seeing Mr Taylor again."

"Was that what he said?"

"No, I did. He's entirely unsuitable."

"I don't think that would bother him."

"Now what do you mean?"

"I've heard about Sam Taylor."

"Well, I'm not concerned with anything you've heard about him, actually, because I haven't the slightest interest in him. And that's the end of the matter."

"Half the women in town are in love with him. The other half have probably already been discarded by him."

"Anchalee, that is not a fitting way for a young lady to talk."

"I'm not a young lady, I'm a child, as everyone keeps reminding me. Anyway, what I said about him is the truth. You should be careful with him. I don't want you to be hurt."

Elizabeth suddenly smiled, despite the situation. Anchalee really was a most engaging girl, and she had a good heart. "Now I'm receiving advice about men from a thirteen-year-old, am I? Anchalee, I am eight years older than you, and I know very well how to conduct myself with men. As I said before, the matter is over. But thank you for your concern. I'm sure you mean well."

"That's all right," Anchalee said, jumping out of her chair with childlike vigour. "See you at dinner."

Anchalee went to her own room and thought some more about Elizabeth and Sam. She could guess what he had done to upset her so much, but was certain Elizabeth would not surrender easily to a man. She was convinced that if Elizabeth had allowed him so much as a kiss, she would be very distressed. Even at her young age, Anchalee sensed the hypocrisy of a society that permitted men to act as they pleased, but which condemned women as immoral if they behaved in a similar fashion. There was something unjust in it, she knew, and, as usual, she wished her own mother were there to explain things to her.

She knew little about her mother, only that her name was Kesri and that she had died years ago, not long after she had married Father. No one would speak of her or tell her why she had died so young. She reached under her mattress and took out an old, cracked photograph of a beautiful Siamese woman with her hair done the old-fashioned way in a top-knot.

∞∞∞

Edward had insisted he had no photographs of Kesri, but Anchalee knew it was not possible that a photographer could have no pictures of his own wife. Anchalee had asked him some time previously if she might look through the boxes of pictures of her as a child, hoping there would be at least one of her mother—or, better, of the two of them together. But she had discovered nothing. So, she had waited until one day when she knew he would not return until late in the evening, or perhaps even the next day. She had sneaked into his bedroom, found the studio key in a drawer in his dresser and let herself in.

It had taken hours of searching through the boxes of dusty old prints and photographic plates. There were several pictures of young Thai women, but none had any identification on the back. Then, just as she was about to give up, she found it. The picture was in two halves, torn across the centre, as if someone—he, she assumed—had meant to discard it. On the reverse of one of the halves was the inscription *Kesri, 1868* in her father's handwriting. She carefully pasted the picture back together and looked at her mother's face for the first time in her memory.

Kesri was very young—she looked as if she were still a teenager—and she was beautiful, too, with a sensuous mouth and smooth, perfect skin. And yet, she did not have youthful eyes. Anchalee saw sadness in them, as if her mother had suffered much during her short life. A man, she thought, would see only her beauty, not her sorrow.

She replaced all the boxes carefully in their original positions and returned the key to Edward's room. She was always mindful to keep the picture hidden in her room, as she was convinced her father would be angry if he knew she had it. It seemed to her that he wanted no reminder of Kesri—he certainly never spoke of her—and he was intent on raising Anchalee as an English girl, barely acknowledging the fact that she was half-Siamese.

But despite his efforts to the contrary, she had picked up the Siamese language easily, and she spoke and read it as fluently as she did English. She was determined that she would eventually discover exactly what had happened to her mother.

As she lay on her bed, pondering these things, it occurred to her that the one person who might help her was her sister. Elizabeth had been only eight when she had left Siam —but that was old enough, surely, to remember people and events. She was there when Kesri was alive and was bound to know something. But Anchalee knew she would have to tread carefully. Because of the way others had reacted to her questions about her mother, she was wary of asking anything important until she had gained Elizabeth's trust. Perhaps this trouble her sister was having with Sam Taylor could be turned to her own advantage, she thought.

$$\infty\infty\infty$$

At dinner that night, Elizabeth was pale and withdrawn, and she only picked at her food.

"Elizabeth, is something wrong?" Edward asked. "You're not eating."

"No, Father, I'm fine," she answered quietly, her eyes cast down.

"Are you sure you're not ill?"

She looked at him blankly. She didn't want to lie, but she couldn't possibly tell him the truth. "No, its …"

"She's been suffering from some sort of irritation," Anchalee interrupted. "From the air since she was out this afternoon."

"Oh, is that all? Well, I should prescribe an early night, young lady."

He went back to his meal, and Anchalee looked across at Elizabeth, who smiled slightly in appreciation.

∞∞∞

April 18ᵗʰ, 1882

Dear Marjorie,

How long it seems since I saw you last, waving goodbye to me at the Liverpool docks. I have been in Bangkok for only two weeks now, yet so much has happened, I wish I could have you here to talk to, my dear confidante.

The city has, of course, changed markedly, with innumerable modernisations, thanks to His Majesty the King, who has many innovative ideas for the development of his country. It is a particularly exciting time here at the moment, because it is the Bangkok centenary, and there are many social functions to mark the event. We attended a ball, just the day after I arrived, and only yesterday we visited the Siamese National Exhibition. Well, such a magnificent display even Europe has hardly seen the likes of, every foreigner here is saying. His Majesty has been to view it, and pronounced it quite extraordinary.

But now, dearest Marjorie, I am simply bursting to speak to you of another matter which, no doubt, in the months it takes this letter to reach you, will have been resolved one way or another. I have met a man, Marjorie, and not just any man. I can see your knowing smile now, but I believe this man has completely overrun my emotions so that I can think of none other. Without divulging too much at this time, I can tell you he is an American—yes—and a writer, and is also the most arrogant, insulting, yet intoxicating man I have ever met. To complicate matters, I do not believe he has any honourable intentions toward me, at least not yet. Isn't it exciting?

The problem, of course, is James. Father regards him as such a good catch that I shall be fortunate indeed to be able to extricate myself from our engagement. I rather believe that Father is quite taken with the idea of his daughter married into the aristocracy *and the advantages that might bring him. What to do, Marjorie? What to do? Nothing like this has ever happened to me before. James was always so proper and Samuel—that is his name, so romantic—is not.*

You will think me awfully liberal to speak of such matters, so I shall turn now to my family instead, almost like a new family to me, it is so long since...

She went on to describe Anchalee to her old school friend, as well as their house and the multi-hued tropical flowers in their garden.

She had, it seemed, made a surprisingly rapid recovery from the emotional distress she had been suffering only hours earlier.

Chapter 16

On a muggy Saturday afternoon a few weeks later, Elizabeth and Anchalee decided to visit the King's Garden, near the Grand Palace, which was open to the public one day each week. The King's band played as usual, and a large proportion of Bangkok's foreign community could be seen wandering among the spacious, well-kept grounds, which were luxuriantly planted with various tropical species, some of which were quite rare.

It was a weekly social event that both communities looked forward to. The foreigners met to trade news and gossip, or to play tennis and croquet on the lawn with Siamese noblemen, and the Siamese public were provided the opportunity to gaze at the peculiar-looking foreigners with their eccentric fashions and habits.

"Shall we walk through the bamboo garden?" Anchalee suggested.

"Very well," Elizabeth agreed. She loved the long aisle of lofty bamboo trees, many of which were more than thirty feet tall. There weren't as many people at the gardens as usual that day, perhaps because the rains had arrived without delay that year, and the ladies were afraid of ruining their gowns in a deluge.

Elizabeth and Anchalee were delighted to have the entire 300-foot length of the aisle to themselves. They linked arms and walked around companionably.

"It feels like we're a long way from the city, doesn't it?" Anchalee remarked excitedly. "As if we were in the jungle somewhere, having to keep a look-out for tigers and mad elephants and ..."

But as she was talking, she felt her sister stop suddenly beside her. Along the path in front, Anchalee saw why. Elizabeth tugged at her sister's arm. "Let's turn around and go back," she whispered.

"Don't be silly—he'll see us," Anchalee said, resisting Elizabeth's efforts.

"I don't care, I don't care," Elizabeth insisted urgently. "Please, Anchalee. I can't face him now."

"But Elizabeth, if we turn back, he'll be walking in the same direction, and he'll surely catch up and want to walk with us. What will you say to him then? If we keep walking this way, we can merely nod and keep going."

"You're right, of course," she conceded, and Anchalee saw her sister's face had become ashen. "I can't avoid speaking to him, can I?"

"No, you can't. Not unless you want to look foolish. And I don't suppose you want to appear that way to him, do you?"

"Absolutely not." She took a deep breath, as if preparing to dive into an icy river.

"Aha, the Misses Fairburn," Sam said amiably, tipping his cap as he approached. "I wondered if I'd come across you two here today."

"Did you?" Anchalee responded casually, seeming neither intimidated nor embarrassed.

Sam smiled at her in an open and friendly way that seemed quite unthreatening to Anchalee. Elizabeth hadn't said a word, and Anchalee nudged her almost imperceptibly.

"I trust you're well, Mr Taylor?" Elizabeth asked, as coldly and imperiously as she could.

"Just dandy, Miss Fairburn," he replied in that infuriatingly mocking tone.

Elizabeth brought the encounter to a hasty conclusion. "Well, we must be going. If you'll excuse us, Mr Taylor."

"Of course," he answered nonchalantly, without even

attempting to linger. And he strode off in the other direction.

"You see, it wasn't so bad, was it?"

"It was most awkward."

"Don't worry, you'll see him again," Anchalee added playfully. Her sister was so obviously in love with this man that the younger girl couldn't resist the temptation to tease just a little.

"But that's just it, Anchalee. I don't want to see him again. Ever."

"Oh, and why not?"

Elizabeth still hadn't realised her sister was mocking her. "You are only thirteen, Anchalee. I shouldn't expect you to understand. But he's just too ... too dangerous."

"Dangerous?"

"Yes. He's entirely unsuitable for me and would not do at all as a husband."

"You don't have to marry him. Just because you're in love with him doesn't mean there has to be a wedding."

"I am not in love with him, Anchalee. I detest him. He's everything I despise in a man and more."

Anchalee smiled to herself, trying desperately not to break into laughter, delighted that she had managed to fluster Elizabeth. She was thoroughly enjoying the over-reaction, which simply confirmed everything Elizabeth had been denying.

"He has no breeding at all. The son of a saloonkeeper—or some such thing—and a *Mexican* woman. No, he wouldn't do at all. It's quite out of the question," Elizabeth continued vehemently.

Anchalee made no reply, and Elizabeth quickly realised how clumsy her comment had been. "Oh, I am sorry, Anchalee. I didn't mean he was unworthy because his mother wasn't English. I ..."

"Don't worry," Anchalee stopped her, smiling. "I know you didn't."

Anchalee wanted to talk about her own mother. It was

on the tip of her tongue to ask how much Elizabeth remembered, to ask what Kesri had been like. But she felt it was too
soon. There was also the danger that Elizabeth would say she
had been too young to recall Kesri. Then the subject would be
closed, and Anchalee would be no nearer the truth.

They walked on in uneasy silence, and when they
reached the end of the aisle and were out in the open again,
they saw that the clouds had gathered overhead, low and dark.
In a couple of minutes, there would be a downpour.

"Perhaps we should walk to the orchid house and shelter in there," Anchalee suggested.

Elizabeth agreed, still feeling guilty over her tactless
remark, and they walked briskly to the long, two-storey
greenhouse that contained thousands of lovely orchids on the
ground floor and many more varieties of tropical plants on the
roofless upper floor.

As they hurried towards the building, the sky flashed
with forked lightning, and rumbled ominously with thunder,
a cannon-roll never equalled in volume outside the tropics. A
moment later, the first drops fell—each one heavy as it burst
on the skin—but their timing was perfect, and they managed
to leap inside just before the rain descended in sheets like a
waterfall.

The orchid house was hot and humid, but there were
only a few leaks from the roof, and it proved sound enough
shelter. Several other people had also taken refuge inside, although they were widely spaced apart in the 200-foot-long
building. It was packed with orchids of every colour and size.
Some were in hanging pots with long tangled roots and stems
of flowers that escaped the confines of their vessels to block
the view along the pathway. They didn't grow in soil, but apparently took sustenance from the humidity alone. Anchalee
silently wandered off, and Elizabeth—preoccupied with the
beauty of the flowers and plants—didn't notice. She was also
unaware of quiet footfalls behind her.

As she walked on in the sultry atmosphere admiring the

displays, she felt trickles of sweat running down her back. She came across one area that was even more overgrown than the rest, where a large painted porcelain pot had been knocked over, its foliage obstructing the path further. She lifted her skirts above her ankles to climb over it, but as she did so, her foot caught the edge of a pot, and she began to fall.

She would have landed on her face, had not a pair of strong arms suddenly reached out from behind and caught her around her waist. Immediately, she knew it wasn't Anchalee, and when she looked down, she saw tanned, masculine hands holding her. Above them were the arms of a dark velvet jacket.

She was not released when she'd regained her balance, and, as she turned slowly, her mouth became dry as she saw that it was he who held her. She cleared her throat but her voice was still shaky. "Mr Taylor. Thank you for your assistance. Now please remove your arms from my waist. Where is my sister?"

"She saw a friend and had to hurry off down there." He pointed back along the path, but still did not release her. "She'll be back soon enough."

"Well then, I must go after her. Father does not allow her to be out alone." There was a pause. "Please unhand me, sir."

"If that's what you want," he said, and did so.

She was shocked and confused at the same time. "Someone will see us and think we ..."

But she had become trapped in the intensity of his stare, and felt herself being drawn into his embrace again. Before she could think straight, she had brazenly joined her lips to his. Her knees felt as if they might buckle and finally, she sank into his arms and allowed him to gently tease her lips apart as she shivered with pleasure.

"I must see you alone, in private," he whispered.

"Yes," she agreed, after not even a moment's thought, her concern at them being seen momentarily forgotten.

"I'll send a message to you."

"But how are we to meet? You know my father wouldn't

permit it."

"Shhh," he stopped her. "Is Anchalee to be trusted?"

"Yes, I think so."

"Good. Then she may be able to help us. Your father won't mind if you go out with her. Then you can meet me once you're away from the house. I'll take care of the place."

The sound of footsteps and women's voices in conversation came from behind them, very close. Regaining her senses, she sprang away from him and stepped aside guiltily as two elderly European ladies walked past in single file. She trembled as she realised how she could have been discovered in a most compromising position. The women both looked back at her sharply, as if to say, "Where is your chaperone, young woman?" before they disappeared along the overgrown path.

"I'll see you soon," he said as he touched her cheek briefly, sending tingles up and down her spine. He turned and was gone, leaving her alone and still trembling.

A few minutes later, from the opposite direction, Anchalee returned.

"Sorry, Elizabeth, I saw a friend from school. I had to run down and see her, or I would have missed her. I hope you weren't lonely."

Elizabeth wondered if Anchalee knew Sam had been there; she wondered if, in fact, her sister had engineered the meeting somehow.

"No, not at all," she replied. "Actually, I've been thinking about Mr Taylor. There's something I'd like to discuss with you."

∞∞∞

Edward hadn't felt well for weeks now, but still he tried to ignore the symptoms. In fact, if he were honest with himself, he had not been in good health for months. He had given up his nightly pipe, at first trying—and failing—to convince himself that the breathlessness and the nagging cough were only a consequence of his tobacco habit. He concentrated all his energy on his work, as he planned to mount an exhibition of photographs taken in Bangkok. A photographic exhibition was a rare event in Siam, and he had been promised royal patronage by the King's agents. But in order to warrant the show, he needed to produce a variety of new images, from which they would then select the most remarkable and suitable for public display.

Despite the greater ambitions of his younger years, Edward had managed only one exhibition in his career. It had been a modest but critically successful show, of pictures taken on the goldfields in California and Victoria, as well as some of Siam, staged in Yorkshire when he had returned to England to visit Elizabeth. Perhaps because of it, he had briefly entertained the notion of returning to England permanently and establishing a studio in London.

But he had soon realised the foolishness of the idea. His brothers still considered him a hopeless failure—rather an embarrassment to them, actually—and his parents, elderly now but still involved in their social circles, made it clear they were not impressed by his liaison in Siam, which had produced the "other daughter".

Very soon, he reached the conclusion that he would be almost completely isolated if he went back to England, and he certainly did not wish to reach old age alone there, sadly reminiscing about his years in the tropics.

So, he had returned to Siam and had laboured hard to finance the large house they now lived in, without having to make recourse to his inheritance in England.

In moments of waking torment, when the rest of the household was asleep, the certainty of his coming death would haunt him, and he would remember the events of his past that would have been best forgotten, but which seemed to rear up to taunt him more and more lately. He tried without success to deny them—he was desperate to finish his work for the exhibition while he was still able. But he knew the end was nigh.

Chapter 17

The message arrived in an envelope addressed to Anchalee. Inside was a smaller envelope with Elizabeth's name on it, and when Anchalee brought it to her sister, Elizabeth tore it open at once.

Be with Anchalee tomorrow, midday, at the Oriental dock. A boatman will take you to our meeting point, the typed message read. There was no signature, but she hardly needed to be told who the author was. Neither was there any endearment or romantic connotation. It was safer that way, of course.

When Elizabeth had enlisted her help, Anchalee had seemed delighted. But now it was the younger sister's turn to be hesitant about the arrangements. "Are you sure you want to do this?" Anchalee asked.

"Of course I'm sure," Elizabeth replied more confidently than she felt. "It's the only way. Perhaps he'll even ask me to marry him."

Anchalee recoiled with an expression of amazement. "I don't think that's quite what he has in mind."

"What do you mean?" Elizabeth felt a tingle of unease, which she tried to dismiss, but which lingered nevertheless.

"Just that you ought to be careful."

"You'll be with me. What could possibly happen?"

"Of course," Anchalee said, smiling. "You're right. We'll go. And Father won't think it strange if we go out together."

And he did not. Anchalee explained to Edward at the dinner table that night how she would show her sister the river and some of Bangkok's more famous temples the next day.

"That's a fine idea," Edward agreed. "But, young lady, you'll have to go back to school soon. This is your last week off with Elizabeth."

Elizabeth didn't enjoy having to deceive her father and was glad to be able to change the subject with his sudden concern over Anchalee's education.

Anchalee was far from impressed with her father's dictum. "I was hoping you'd have forgotten about that silly old school, Father. I really don't need to go any more," she complained.

"Nonsense, girl, you're only half educated. I don't hold with that old-fashioned idea that women shouldn't be schooled. Gives them something to occupy their minds with, instead of constant silliness. No, certainly not. You're far too young to leave."

"Too young, too young. That's all I ever hear," Anchalee moaned, pouting.

"Count yourself lucky, then. For one day you'll hear the words 'too old'," Edward said wryly. He could never seem to reprimand her seriously, no matter how impertinent she was, and Elizabeth was beginning to enjoy their continual verbal sparring.

Elizabeth dressed carefully next morning, telling Noi she would manage herself, after the maid had helped her with the tight corset. She found that she was actually savouring the experience of preparing herself for him. She wished she had had time to visit Anchalee's seamstress, Mrs Smythe, at her shop, but she would have to make do with what she had.

She selected a dusky-pink shot-silk gown, draped over the bustle and falling in soft folds to the ground. It featured one of the new higher bustles, which Elizabeth thought was particularly flattering. The bodice had a double row of buttons, with a high stand-up collar and long sleeves with turned-back cuffs. She wore white silk stockings and pink silk shoes with a Louis heel, and carried a matching pink parasol. Her corset—the one with the white French lace—was the tightest she owned, and it ensured her waist measured no more than nineteen inches. The outfit was completed with a tiny straw hat trimmed with pink satin rosebuds.

There was a tap at her door as noon approached, and Anchalee entered, dressed in a simple white gown that would have made her look her age, if not for a rather low, square neckline. She looked Elizabeth over. "You look beautiful. What a fancy dress."

"Is it all right, do you think? Not too much?" Beside Anchalee, she now felt overdressed.

"It's perfect, of course. You always seem to know just what to wear."

Elizabeth felt suddenly giddy, and she had to reach out to grip the side of her dressing table for support. "I can't believe I'm doing this. A secret rendezvous. Who would have believed it possible?"

"You're not having second thoughts, are you?"

"If I thought about it at all, Anchalee, I wouldn't dare do this. It's totally out of character for me and it goes against all my principles. It's just that … I can't not do it."

"You can make exceptions to rules if it's for passion. People do that all the time," Anchalee stated precociously, and it sounded as if she'd read it in a novel. This time, however, Elizabeth did not protest her sister's choice of words. The boatman was waiting for them as the note said he would be. He was sleeping, and once they had roused him, they set off in the brightly painted craft.

They went upriver in the direction of the old capital city, Ayuthia, but long before they left the environs of Bangkok, the boatman turned off into a narrow series of klong. It was a long time since Elizabeth had made a trip on the waterways like this, and when she had, as a girl, it had always enchanted her.

The activity here was merely on a lesser scale to that of the River of Kings, and as their boat progressed on the swathe of brown water, passing clusters of bamboo and thatch huts amid the dense vegetation and the coconut groves, they were always alongside the wooden floating houses, each with its own spirit house in front. Colourful panung and sarongs hung on lines strung across almost every home.

Many of the waterside inhabitants were taking their midday meal—bowls of white rice with chicken curry or simply fish sauce and chilli—while some went about a variety of daily chores, and still others dozed in the noon heat. Impish children were everywhere in the water, and monkeys still frolicked riotously in the trees, although Elizabeth thought there might be rather fewer than she remembered as a child.

The sun beat directly down on them, and they were glad of the boat's striped canopy. It offered little protection from the heat, but with a breeze in their faces from the movement of the boat, the discomfort was not too great.

As they entered a quieter stretch of a narrow klong, the boatman suddenly stopped the vessel and manoeuvred it alongside a handsome, polished-teak houseboat. A maid appeared and helped them climb out, and the boatman then went on his way again. Elizabeth and Anchalee stood on the wooden verandah, and the world seemed to stand still, with only the immediate sounds of water lapping the sides of the boat, and tropical birds chattering high in the coconut palms.

The woman went to the opposite side of the houseboat, closest to the bank, and Elizabeth wondered if Sam were there, or even if he had decided to keep the liaison at all. The silence was disconcerting, and she began to panic at the thought of what they would do if he did not come. But then the door to the living quarters opened and he was there, dressed Siamese-style in dark panung and a white cotton shirt that was open at the neck.

"I hoped you'd come."

"I told you I would," she answered nervously. His appearance had shocked her initially, but now she found herself unable to look away from him.

The woman appeared again and spoke in a low voice to Anchalee in Siamese. Elizabeth, who had forgotten most of her childhood Siamese, couldn't catch what the woman was saying. Then Anchalee disappeared round the side with her, leaving Elizabeth alone with him. He walked toward her slowly, and she could not break his stare. He held out a hand to her, and she took it, allowing herself to be led toward the open door and into the dark interior. He shut the door and locked it behind them.

Edward turned over the likeness again and looked at the face of the woman he had once adored but had then cast out so heartlessly. When he had discovered it in Anchalee's room, he had been angry with her for taking something that was not hers. But then he realised how selfish he had been. For Kesri *was* Anchalee's, more than she had been his, and he regretted that he had denied his daughter her right to a mother. It was only by chance that he had discovered she was in possession of the picture.

When she had asked to borrow the photographs of herself as a baby and a child, he agreed with the provision that she return them tidily. She had not, of course, and he knew what condition they would fall into—dog-eared, lying round her room, pushed into the edge of her mirror, or used as bookmarks—if he did not reclaim them. He made a note to let her keep her favourites but to return the remainder.

One day in his studio, his eye had caught the row of boxes of old prints he had discarded but could not quite bring himself to throw away. He hadn't touched any of them for years, yet one was slightly askew. The maid rarely cleaned in that area, and when he examined the boxes more closely, he could see marks in the dust on the lids. Someone had opened them recently, and it was obviously Anchalee.

She had asked for the pictures of herself only after he had told her that no pictures of Kesri existed and—he surmised—she must have been hoping he had overlooked one or two in the old boxes. When she hadn't found what she wanted, she had taken the key to the studio without his permission—everyone in the house knew where he kept it—and looked for herself.

Could she have found what she had been seeking, he wondered? It was so long since he had seen a picture of Kesri, he couldn't remember whether he had kept any. He recalled, on the day she had left, smashing a number of photographic plates in anger, tearing up prints and tossing them into a fire, but keeping back the last one—although it, too, had been torn in two in his frustration and fury. What had he done with the pieces? Had he put them into one of the boxes, and had Anchalee found them? Did it matter? Somehow, it did, and he had to know. He was possessed of a sudden urge, too, to see Kesri's face once again.

He locked the studio and went into the house and up to Anchalee's room. Where would be start? He was reluctant to rifle though her cupboards and dressing table, but guessed that perhaps the image was in one of her books. What was that anthology of poetry she was always dipping into? That ridiculous, romantic verse that filled her head with notions far too sophisticated for a girl and highly unsuitable?

Ah yes, there it was. He pulled out the volume from the shelf and shook it gently. He had been right. The photograph, its pieces glued back together, fluttered out and landed on the wooden floor. The face he had not laid eyes upon in thirteen years looked back up at him. He, in turn, gazed at her image for a few moments, then turned the print over. On the back was written, in his own hand, simply, *Kesri, 1868*.

It was this discovery, as well as Anchalee's brooding, her regular questions, and her occasional, contrived remarks, that had brought him to his decision. Of course, when she was younger—and with her mind so preoccupied with the carefree pleasures of childhood—there had been no effort on her part to discover the truth about her mother. But now she was maturing quickly, and so was her inquisitiveness.

He had hoped that the photographs of her as a child would have been enough to satisfy her curiosity, at least for a while longer or at least until she was older and, perhaps, better able to cope with the truth. But they proved only to spur her on. The situation was reaching the point where he could deter her no longer. With this growing realisation, a shadow seemed to be cast over him as his guilt returned to haunt him at every turn.

Kesri had been so beautiful and had seemed willing to cater to his every whim. But then he would recall how she had spat on his trust in her. God had punished them both. She had been banished and barred from ever seeing her child, and he had been compelled to live with the guilt, all these years, that his actions had deprived both his daughters of their mothers.

Joseph Shaw had told him, less than two years later, that Kesri had died of consumption. At the time, Edward had believed it was her due for murdering their unborn child. But now he pondered the wisdom of that view. At least Anchalee would have known her mother's undoubted love, had he not banished her.

Now, also, he saw that it had been wrong of him to separate Anchalee from all knowledge of her mother. In his heart, when he looked back on his life now, he saw much wrong—and he feared that he would not be worthy of God's mercy. He hoped his daily prayers would save him from eternal damnation.

He stopped to cough into a handkerchief—he kept several in his pocket these days and washed them himself—then returned the tatty photograph to the book and replaced it on the shelf. He could no longer deny Anchalee her right to know.

Equally, he knew he could not be the one to speak of her mother. The past was still too painful. There was someone else, he decided, who would be able to perform the task much better than he could.

That afternoon, he called on Joseph. It still surprised him that the man he had once thought of as an adversary—who had disapproved of his lifestyle—had now become something of a trusted confidant.

"She asks so many questions," he told his friend as they sat in the garden, sipping lime squash. "I cannot discourage her much longer."

"Why not simply answer her questions?" Joseph suggested. "With discretion, of course. She needn't know every detail."

"She's so desperate to know about her mother," he said, sighing. "She's had a happy life so far, and she's wanted for nothing. But she feels a certain emptiness, I know." He paused to take a sip of his drink. "She has an old photograph of Kesri. I thought I'd destroyed them all, but this one has been pieced together from torn remains. I don't know why I saved the pieces, but I must have put them in one of the old boxes, and she found them."

"Every child needs a mother figure, Edward. And although she may seem mature for her age, she is still a child."

"It's easy to forget sometimes. I put it down to those novels and that poetry she's always reading. That romantic nonsense seems to give her all kinds of ideas. She's far too impressionable. Highly unsuitable reading material—for anyone, if you ask me."

The missionary blushed slightly and looked away for a moment, his own passion for reading romantic novels and poetry like a guilty secret.

Edward seemed not to notice as he continued. "But I don't want her to grow up feeling I've denied her the knowledge she has a right to. It's true, I've told her very little about her mother, but I thought she'd eventually give up trying to find out."

"So, what do you plan to do?"

"Well, I must confess that's where I hope you can help me. I find that I'm still unable to think of Anchalee's mother without—emotion—let alone to speak of her. To my shame, I *cannot* forgive Kesri for what she did. But nor can I forgive myself for what I did to her. She was so young at the time, and sometimes now I think she shouldn't be blamed for what happened. And yet, I *cannot* accept her actions. I cannot forgive, Joseph, and that is a terrible sin."

"Many of us, in youth, do things we regret forever," Joseph said quietly.

"That's why I must ask a favour of you."

"By all means, if I can be of any help."

"Would you talk to her? Tell her how lovely her mother was and how much she loved her daughter. Please don't tell her what happened—the unfortunate incident that led to her dismissal, I mean. Simply say that she and I were unable to get along agreeably, and that we decided, for Anchalee's sake, that it was better to part. Will you do this for me, Joseph?"

Joseph contemplated Edward's request for a moment, then nodded his agreement. "Very well, Edward. Ask her to come to see me tomorrow."

Edward thanked him and they talked for some time until he had to leave for a portrait session at his studio.

Joseph continued sitting at the table in his garden after Edward had departed, and he finally decided it was time to give Anchalee her mother's bequest. Although it was still six months until her fourteenth birthday, Kesri had instructed him to hand over the letter to her daughter before then if he thought it necessary or appropriate.

He went upstairs to his study and opened the safe where he kept his few valuables and private papers. There were— among other things—his birth certificate, his letter of appointment to Siam, and a picture of a young woman that was faded and yellowed now after twenty years. The early photographic processes provided poor quality images, he reflected, in comparison to those of the present day. Even so, it was a fine likeness. She still looked beautiful and regal to him, with her long, thick, wavy hair, and her moko—the facial marking that Maori wore that determined whakapapa, or family line. For a moment, he thought about what could have been, what should have been, but what was denied both of them.

He put aside the picture and its painful memories, and picked up the large envelope he had come for. It was also yellowing at the edges, but the address—in the careful handwriting of someone unaccustomed to English script—was still clear.

He recalled the day, more than twelve years before, when Kesri had come to him with this letter, and he had written on another piece of paper, the script for her to copy on the front: To Miss Anchalee Kesri Fairburn. *Private and confidential. If the addressee be deceased, this envelope and its contents are to be destroyed, unopened.* He had promised her he would never open it or read it, nor allow anyone but Anchalee to do so. And he had kept his word. It was time to carry out Kesri's last wish.

Chapter 18

She was almost too astonished to respond when he handed it to her. "A letter from my mother? Then she's ..."

"No, Anchalee, I'm sorry," he interrupted her quickly. "She died a long time ago. You've always been told the truth about that."

She turned the envelope over and over in her hands, then stared at the handwriting, touching it and tracing her name. She could hardly comprehend that it had been written by her own mother.

She had been a little put out that morning when her father had insisted she go to Mr Shaw's house for some sort of talk. She had assumed he had persuaded Mr Shaw to berate her about something she was doing that Edward deemed "Ill befitting of a young Christian lady", and she prepared herself for a tedious lecture. But now she was wide-eyed with curiosity.

"Before you open it," he added, "I must tell you what happened to lead to this. Yesterday, your father came to me, concerned that you were so inquisitive about your mother. I don't know why it suddenly upset him so much after all this time, but that's beside the point. Anyway, he asked me to tell you something of your mother. He considers you have a right to know, now that you're older."

"Why doesn't he tell me himself, Mr Shaw?"

"Well, Anchalee, it's still very painful for him when he remembers your mother. And, indeed, he still grieves for Elizabeth's mother, too. He was quite upset when we spoke yesterday, and he prefers that I talk to you."

"Does he know about this letter?"

"No, he doesn't. He and I have become friends over the years, it's true, but this was a matter of honour. I promised your mother I would speak of it to no one but you when the time came. Nobody has laid eyes on its contents but her. After you've read it, you may tell your father about it or not, as you see fit."

Anchalee, seated in his front room on the well-worn brown leather chesterfield, was mesmerised by what he was saying.

He cleared his throat to continue. "Well, I don't quite know where to begin. Kesri—your mother—was very young when she met your father. No one knew very much about her before then, except that she'd spent about eighteen months with the American Protestant missionaries after somehow buying her freedom from slavery when she was sixteen. They taught her to speak English, and she was an extremely bright and willing pupil, although she was never interested in the religious tuition.

"Because she was literate in her own language and could speak English, she was employed as a servant by some of the foreign families. In fact, she worked on a kind of freelance basis, showing a lot of ingenuity for one so young. Anyway, during a party at the British Consulate, at which she was serving, she met your father."

"What happened?"

"Well, she became his ..." He hesitated, slightly embarrassed. "Well, I'm afraid that at that time, your father was still married to Elizabeth's mother, although she hadn't yet arrived from Australia. However, when Charlotte—Elizabeth's mother—left for England later, she died tragically at sea. Your mother and father were then married, although they had a Buddhist ceremony and the union was never blessed by the Church."

"And then I was born?"

"Yes, you were born. And both your parents loved you

very much."

"Then why did she leave me?"

"She didn't want to. But it was the best thing at the time."

"How could it have been?"

"Well, your parents found they were ... how shall I say it? Incompatible. They couldn't get along, and they agreed it was better they parted permanently. You must remember, Anchalee, that they were from very different cultures, and sometimes it wasn't easy for them to understand one another. Not only in conversation, of course, but in the very way they thought about things."

"But what happened to her? Why did she never come to visit me?"

"She became ill with consumption about six months after she left, and that's when she brought me this letter. She knew she was very sick, and sadly, she did die a year later. I was told she passed away peacefully in her sleep."

"You were told? By whom?"

"By Porntip, the maid who used to work for your family."

"I remember Porntip. Why did she never tell me anything? Why did she keep it a secret from me that she knew my mother? Did my mother do something awful? Was she a ... a criminal? Or a madwoman?"

"No, no, nothing like that. I suppose, my dear, that they decided it was best not to tell you anything."

"You mean, Father decided it was best," she said sullenly.

"Yes, well, perhaps the letter will explain things in more detail."

"But Mr Shaw, you still haven't told me what she was like." She again turned the letter over and over in her hands, desperate to open it, yet at the same time, stalling, for fear of what she might read within.

"Oh. Well, she had black hair, of course, done in a top

knot, as was the style of the day—."

"No, no, Mr Shaw," she interrupted. "Not what she looked like. I have a photograph of her. But what was she *like*? As a person, I mean?"

"Well, I'm afraid I didn't know her at all well personally, Anchalee. So, I cannot really tell you. But I imagine she was very determined and resourceful. I hardly remember her from her time at the mission, and she was rarely seen in public with your father."

"Was he ashamed of her?"

Joseph was feeling very uncomfortable. "No, it wasn't that. Only ... well, why don't you wait and see if she explains that in her letter, too?"

Anchalee nodded. She suspected there was much more to the story than Joseph was telling her. "And Elizabeth? Did she like my mother? Her own mother died, so it must have been nice for her to have a new mother."

"Elizabeth was very sad, naturally, when her own mother died, and I don't think she had time to get used to having a new mother. But she loved you, from the moment she first saw you. She used to carry you round with her all day."

"But she left me, too."

"She didn't want to go. Your father understandably decided she should be educated at home in England."

"I see. Did you know Elizabeth's mother?"

"Yes, quite well."

"What was she like?"

Joseph vividly remembered poor Charlotte and her plea for him to look after her daughter. "Mrs Fairburn was a gracious, noble lady, and it was a tragedy that she passed away so long before her time."

"You said she died at sea?"

"Yes, she was on her way back to England."

"Why? Was she going away for long?"

"Well, it was said she was in need of a cooler climate."

"Oh, I see." Anchalee paused before asking quietly,

"Shall I read the letter now?"

"Yes, I think that's a good idea," Joseph agreed, getting up from his seat. "But first, I have something else to give you. He reached into his pocket and withdrew a small package wrapped in paper, which he held out to her.

Wordlessly, she took it, and quickly unwrapped it. It was a silver locket, old and tarnished, but beautiful to her because she knew at once that it had belonged to Kesri. She opened the clasp, and inside were two tiny pictures: her mother on one side, and herself as a baby on the other. In the corner of Kesri's picture was a tiny lock of black hair. Tears filled her eyes as she slipped the silver chain over her head and tucked the locket inside her dress.

"I'll leave you here alone, now," Joseph said as he left the room. "Call me when you're ready. Take as long as you like."

Anchalee turned the envelope over and over in her hands. It was a letter from the grave, a legacy. It was what she had been waiting for all these years without knowing it.

Carefully, she slit the top of the envelope with Joseph's silver letter opener, and took out a thick sheaf of pages written in the familiar Siamese script. The top sheet was dated *January 10th, Buddhist Era 2412—1870 on the Christian calendar—at Krung Thep (Bangkok).* She unfolded the pages and spread them on the desk before her. She was so glad her mother had written in Siamese and not had the letter translated into English. For in her heart, Anchalee felt Siamese, not English, and she wanted to communicate with her mother in what she had always thought of as her native tongue.

She began to read, imagining as she did so, her mother in this very room, so many years ago, sealing the letter. She felt Kesri's presence strongly for the first time. It was almost as if her mother had somehow materialised before her and was speaking the words of the letter to her in person.

It took her a long time to read the letter, pausing often to wipe the tears from her eyes and cheeks. When she had finished, she looked up from the pages, too stunned to cry any longer. She sat for a long time, staring at the pages, their words still searing through her. Then she clutched the letter to her chest, her knuckles white. "All this time, I thought you were my friend, Elizabeth," she cried out loud.

At first, Joseph, beyond the closed door but not far away, thought Anchalee was calling to him, but he quickly realised that she was not.

∞∞∞

Edward could wait no longer. In early October, he put his plan into action, having received assurances from his daughter—albeit rather weak ones—that she was still planning to marry James Claridge. Edward's intention was to hold the exhibition early in the new year, and he hoped that his letter to the King would be fruitful.

Chapter 19

The sickness in the mornings, the slight thickening of her waist, the tenderness and swelling of her breasts, and the absence of her monthly bleeding—all told of the consequence of her actions. She had suspected for some time, and—bizarrely—had even welcomed the idea on occasion, with the hope that it would force his hand, that it would elicit from him the commitment she so desperately wanted. Surely, it would.

It had been September when she had first given herself to him, although they had been close many times before then, in his borrowed houseboat on the klong. Since then, she had been stealing away—always with Anchalee as chaperone—whenever she could, at least two or three times a week. The irony of the affair was that when they met at social events, she would have to affect that she knew him only slightly, as Mr Taylor, the American writer.

But now, she felt the first stirrings of fear as she faced the reality of her situation, rather than her romantic ideal of it. It was love, she was sure, on his part as much as hers—or she at least tried to convince herself it was so. At the height of their passion, he told her how much he wanted to be with her, how he yearned for her when she was gone. There had been no mention of marriage, but she felt sure it must be only a matter of time.

He was busy writing another book about Siam, he had told her, and he had strict deadlines to meet. She had been sure that if she waited until he'd posted his manuscript, he would propose to her—and she would accept, no matter what her father thought or how strongly he objected. She would agree, in fact, even if Edward forbade it. The fact that she was carrying Sam's child would mean only that they must marry earlier, before he had completed the book. But she would promise to give him all the time he needed to write once they were wed. She had longed for the newly fashionable post-wedding trip everyone these days was calling a "honeymoon", but she was prepared even to forego that for him. She was capable of amusing herself during the days, and she would eventually be too busy caring for their child to worry about how many hours he spent at his typewriter.

James would be heartbroken, she supposed, and she resolved to write to him soon to cancel their arrangement. She would probably be married before he even received the letter. Her father, she knew, would be furious. He continued to pester her to set a date for the wedding to James, and she continued to stall him, bewildered at her own inability to tell him the truth: that she had no intention of marrying James, or of returning to England at all.

She planned to tell Sam of her condition the next time she met him, and she prayed he would not be angry. She had dared not tell Anchalee the secret, nor had she written to Marjorie, believing it best that she carried the burden herself. Besides, Anchalee wasn't aware of what happened during her trysts with Sam—she couldn't be, she was only a child. Elizabeth had told her younger sister only that they talked and took tea. Anchalee had never said anything to indicate she did not believe Elizabeth.

She felt nauseated again and rushed to the basin that stood on the washstand. She vomited violently, just as there came a light tapping on the door. Without waiting for an answer, Anchalee opened it and stepped into the room.

"It must have been something I ate," Elizabeth claimed, wiping her mouth with a towel. She was pale and shaky.

Anchalee stared at her.

"I'll call the maid," she said calmly.

∞∞∞

Joseph was surprised when he answered a knock on the door that afternoon, and Anchalee stood alone at the step.

"Nice to see you again, Anchalee. Please, come in. what can I do for you? Is it something about school? Or the letter, perhaps?"

She looked round suspiciously, as if she expected there to be spies, then said in a low voice, "No, Mr Shaw. Elizabeth asked me to come to see you on her behalf. She says it's a matter of some delicacy."

"In that case, you'd better come into my study." He was perplexed by her request, but didn't forget his manners. "Would you like some tea?"

"No thank you, Mr Shaw. I should be going home as soon as possible."

"Certainly." He showed her into his book-lined study, which she would have expected to be full of heavy religious tomes. There were some, but she was surprised to see there was also a selection of the latest novels by Henry James, Thomas Hardy, and George Meredith, among many others. His collection had grown over the years and he no longer felt the need to conceal his books when members of the parish visited him at home. Indeed, there were now so many that it would have been impossible to do so.

When they were both seated—he at his desk, and Anchalee in the leather chair facing it—she removed an envelope from a pocket concealed in her dolman jacket and handed it to him.

"This is the letter from Elizabeth. She said it was self-explanatory, but if you have any questions, I'm to answer them."

"But why hasn't she come herself?" he asked, even more

puzzled.

"Well, she was very embarrassed. And ... well, it's all in the letter, Mr Shaw."

Joseph put on his reading glasses and opened the white envelope.

November 15th, 1882

Dear Mr Shaw,

We have known each other for many years, and you have always been a good friend to me, and to my mother before me. Because of this, I should like to ask for your help with the most painful matter, which I have chosen to write about in this letter, rather than to discuss in person, because of its sensitive nature. It concerns myself and a gentleman of my acquaintance, Mr Samuel Taylor. I believe you know him slightly.

For some time now, Mr Taylor and I have been meeting secretly, chaperoned by my sister, Anchalee. Though nothing improper has occurred, I know my dear father would not approve of these meetings and would, in fact, expect me to marry Mr Taylor immediately for what he would consider my indiscretions.

I am ashamed to admit the truth, Mr Shaw, but you see, I find that after several of these meetings, my initial feelings for Mr Taylor have cooled considerably, and I no longer believe him to be a suitable candidate for marriage. However, I do not wish to hurt his feelings, as I am positive he feels deep affection for me and plans very soon to ask for my hand. I should like to save him from the mortification of rejection.

If you could see your way to helping me extricate myself from this unfortunate arrangement, without his knowledge, I would be eternally grateful to you. What I ask, Mr Shaw, is that you might somehow persuade Mr Taylor to leave Bangkok for a time.

I understand that you are seeking someone to accompany supplies to the mission in Chiengmai in the north. I know also that Mr Taylor himself is keen to make a journey north in order to obtain more information for his book about Siam. I am sure he could be persuaded to join this expedition, which I understand is ready to depart soon. Because we cannot meet openly, he would then have only to write me a note to advise me he was to be away for so many months.

I believe that if such a distance of time and place were put between us, I could reject any advances he might make on his return, without embarrassment to either party.

My dear Mr Shaw, I am deeply sorry to burden you with this inconvenience, but I can think of no one else I could trust so well. You may speak freely of this matter to my sister, as she is aware of everything that has occurred and of my intention to end this inappropriate liaison.

Obviously, I would ask that you make absolutely no mention of this letter to Mr Taylor. Because I feel so embarrassed and ashamed over this whole matter, Mr Shaw, I would also greatly appreciate it if you and I never mentioned it, or indeed this letter, either to each other or to any other party, at any occasion in future. I thank you profusely for your help.

Your sincere and affectionate friend,

Elizabeth Fairburn

He read the letter twice before finally removing his reading glasses and putting them back in their case. "Well, poor Elizabeth has got herself into an unfortunate situation, hasn't she? I do hope he's not made any … unseemly advances, so to speak."

"Not to my knowledge," Anchalee lied. She had never, for one moment, believed Elizabeth's stories that nothing happened between her and Sam at their secret rendezvous.

"In that case, I shall do my best to do as she asks. I agree it's best to keep Mr Taylor away from her. Although why she agreed to meet him in the first place is beyond me. He is, as she says, most unsuitable."

"So you *will* help her, Mr Shaw?"

"Of course. As I say, I shall do my best. But how shall I get word to her if I've been successful?"

"There won't be any need," Anchalee said. "The expedition leaves very soon, does it not?"

"Well, your request is most timely. It could be ready the day after tomorrow, and certainly within three days."

"Then if she receives a letter from him within three days to inform her he's departing, she'll know you've succeeded. If she doesn't, she'll know he's still here in Bangkok. Even if he didn't send word, expeditions are always a matter of some interest in the expatriate community—I'm sure she will hear about this one and who is on it. As you can imagine, she's most anxious to dispense with the matter as quickly as possible. And she wishes never to speak of it again."

"I understand. She has my word that I'll mention it to no one, and that I'll never refer to it in conversation with her."

"Thank you, Mr Shaw. She'll appreciate that very much."

∞∞∞

A letter arrived for Elizabeth that day from England, and it was one she hardly dared open. It was from James, and she was convinced he would be urging her to return so they could set a wedding date.

In all that had happened to her during the last few months, she had hardly thought of him, let alone written. She would have to reply to him straight away, informing him, as gently as possible, that she no longer wished to marry him. Finally, she slit open the envelope and found only one sheet inside. It had taken more than four months to reach Siam.

July 7th, 1882

My dear Elizabeth,
You have been away a relatively short time, yet it seems like a lifetime. Much has happened since you left, and it

is my unpleasant duty to inform you on one of those events.

There is no easy way to write what I have to tell you, Elizabeth, so I shall say it directly. I have fallen in love with Lady Cynthia Asquith-Brown, and we are to be married early next year. We are a most suitable match.

Elizabeth, you know that I shall always have only the fondest memories of you, and I never meant to hurt you in any way. But for some reason, I am thinking that perhaps this news will come as something of a relief for you, rather than anything else. The truth is, I feel it is time I married, and I do not want to delay any longer. I simply cannot wait for you. My father, as you know, is in failing health, and his only wish is to see me married and settled with a family of my own before he passes on.

I sincerely hope that this news does not come as too much of a shock to you. With deep affection,

I remain your loyal friend,

James T. Claridge

Slowly, she put down the letter on her dresser, and as his words sank in, she began to smile for the first time in several days. Now, all that remained was to send a brief letter of congratulations to the bride and groom, and the matter would be concluded. She sighed with relief. Perhaps this predicament was not so dreadful after all. Perhaps she and Sam could marry quickly, and—in time—people would cease counting the months between their wedding and the birth of their child. Her father would be livid, but he would have no choice but to accept the situation since it was James, and not she, who had called off the engagement.

Sam paced his room and fretted over how Elizabeth would react when she received his letter. She would be distressed at his leaving, but it was simply too good an opportunity to miss. As Joseph Shaw had explained, Sam's only responsibility would be to ensure the supplies reached the missionary families in Chiengmai, and he would otherwise be free to write through the entire journey. It would provide ideal material for his book.

She loved him, he was certain of that. She was not the kind of woman who entered lightly into an intimate relationship with a man, and this had been her first. And he was forced to admit to himself that he cared for her more than he had for any woman before. Since the day he had first met her, on the jetty by the Oriental Hotel, he had known there was something special about her, even though he could not define what it was. She was not the most beautiful woman he had known. Nor was she the wittiest, nor the best lover. In fact, she had been completely inexperienced in that way, which was not generally what he liked in a woman. And yet, he wanted her and somehow found himself longing for her company when they were apart.

He had never felt this way before, and it troubled him greatly. He wondered if he were actually falling in love with her. If he asked her to marry him, he knew she would accept immediately, with or without her father's approval, and he knew she would be a devoted and faithful wife. But he needed this time away to be absolutely sure, to test himself. It was strange for him to even contemplate a permanent relationship and he needed to get used to the idea.

∞∞∞

How could this be happening to her? The words in his brief message echoed in her head, as if he were speaking them over and over. *I will be gone for up to six months ... gone for up to six months.*

"Oh, God help me!" she said aloud, throwing herself on

her bed and burying her head in the pillows. It was unthinkable that anyone know of her condition, even though it would soon be impossible to conceal. She was ruined, and she broke down in a fresh series of choking sobs.

She was aware of abortion, of course, and suspected it was available in Bangkok in some disgraceful back alley, just as it was in England. But she had heard so many whispered horror stories—of contaminated instruments, of damage so severe that women bled to death, and of women who underwent the procedure left almost certain never to bear children again—that she was afraid even to consider it.

The likely scenarios spun through her mind. Her father would eventually have to be told, and the only possible course of action was that she be sent away and the baby adopted out to a good family—perhaps missionaries. She would return, explaining that the extended absence was for reasons of health. No one would give the story any credence, and she would probably never marry. She would stay home and care for her father, and then, the best she could hope for was to become a nanny to another family's children, until she was too old to work any longer and was sent away to sit in a rocking chair alone until she faded away to obscurity.

She could not even envisage her father's reaction. He would never trust her again and would never look at her with the same fondness. He was already disappointed at her failure to marry James when she had the opportunity, and he had not spoken to her in the few days since she had told him. Now he was to discover she was carrying the illegitimate child of a man he despised. A bastard child. The word rang in her ears, for that was what her child would be, no matter how much she wanted it to be otherwise.

She spent the next week in misery, despairing over what would become of her. When she was no nearer a solution after seven days than she was at the beginning, there was only one thing left to do.

∞∞∞

It was in church that Joseph found her. She wore a dark dress and was huddled in one of the pews, her hands clasping her Bible, her eyes closed. He didn't disturb her at first, as he went quietly about his duties setting up for the minister's evening service. Eventually, she opened her eyes and wiped the corners quickly with a sodden handkerchief. Her face was pallid, and there were dark shadows under her eyes.

He moved toward her in concern. "Elizabeth, what on earth is wrong?"

She avoided looking him in the eye and was about to say, "Nothing at all, thank you, Mr Shaw. Everything is quite in order."

But she could not. Instead, she collapsed back on to the wooden pew, her tears falling uncontrollably.

Joseph rushed to sit beside her and took her hands in his.

"Elizabeth, what is it? Something dreadful has happened. Please, you must tell me what it is." He was also confused. Sam had gone, so should she not be happy?

She continued to sob. "I … simply cannot. I cannot, Mr Shaw. I cannot tell you."

"Come now. It can't be that bad. You've shared your problems with me before. This one, too, can be fixed, I'm sure."

She wondered fleetingly what he meant, but supposed he was referring to her childhood problem with Kesri, so long ago. Anyhow, her sobs subsided as a result of his gentle sensibility. "Mr Shaw, I cannot tell you. I … I cannot even imagine what you would think of me."

"My dear, I could never think badly of you. And no matter what it is, I'm sure I can help. Why don't you come along to my house? A cup of tea will make you feel much better. Or perhaps you're in need of a sherry? You know I'm not a drinking man, but in some cases, for medicinal purposes ..." He stood up. "You were right to come here for guidance. But right now, I think you may be in need of some mortal help."

She nodded, dabbed at her eyes once more, and agreed to his suggestion. He was quite possibly the only person who could help her. She had no one else to turn to.

When they arrived at his house, he poured the sherry in his study, and she drank it down at once. It did seem to calm her, and although pale, she was now composed and prepared to accept whatever advice he gave her. But first, she had to confide in him.

"I'm afraid, Mr Shaw, that I've become rather a different person of late than the girl you once knew," she began. She spoke slowly and deliberately, and he could tell it was painful for her to say the words. "I've disgraced myself in the most terrible way."

"Does this have something to do with—."

"Yes," she cut in before he could say the name. "The cause of my trouble is a man. Or, rather, the cause is my own stupidity brought about by my ... my emotional attachment to this man."

"Has he harmed you, Elizabeth?"

"Not exactly. The truth is, I am—." She broke down again, unable to say the words.

It dawned on him then, and in a flash, he knew she had lied in the letter about the nature of the relationship. He didn't wish to reproach her or become righteous—he, of all people, he thought wryly. He wanted only to help, and his heart went out to her.

"Elizabeth, I understand how difficult it is for you to speak of this. But you must answer my question. Are you with child?" He asked the question gently and his concern was evident in his eyes.

She looked up at him, her tears flowing again uncontrollably, and he wanted to reach out to her, to comfort her, to rescue her. She nodded, then buried her head in her hands, rocking back and forth like a frightened child herself.

Not knowing what else to do, he simply sat beside her on the chesterfield and put his arms around her. She wept on his shoulder until she had no more tears to cry. He felt guilty, as if he had added to her grief. After all, it was he who had sent Mr Taylor upcountry, although it had been at her bidding. But even so—and against the Church's teachings—he still believed that marriage to Sam Taylor would not have been the best solution for her, even though she was carrying his child. The man was a rogue who would only hurt her and eventually desert her, he suspected.

When her sobbing eased and her tears ceased at last, he drew back and patted her hand gently.

"That's better. You mustn't cry any more. I will do all I can to help you, Elizabeth," he promised with rather more confidence than he felt. "But what I don't understand is the reason for the letter."

She thought he somehow knew about the letter she had received from Sam about going away.

"He didn't know of my condition then, or I'm sure he would never have agreed to go. I am sure he would have married me, Mr Shaw. But now he'll not return for six months or so, and it's … it's unthinkable that I could wait here for him in my condition. I don't know what to do."

"I'm afraid I must accept some of the blame for this," he said, sighing.

"How do you mean?"

"Well, as you know, it was I who suggested to Mr Taylor that he join this expedition. If only I'd known of your condition sooner, I could have prevented him leaving."

She wondered why he thought she would know. Sam had not mentioned that in his letter. But she was too upset to dwell on the details.

"Please, don't rebuke yourself, Mr Shaw. This is entirely my own doing. I have no one to blame but myself."

They were silent for a while and then Joseph spoke again. "I think you should say nothing of this for now, Elizabeth. Your father will have to be told eventually, of course. But if you allow me perhaps a short time to consider your situation, there may be something that can be done to make things easier."

She was sceptical that anything at all could save her. She was resigned to her fate, but thanked him just the same for his compassion.

When she was gone, Joseph could concentrate on nothing else. There *was* a solution, but it was such a frightening idea to put to her, that he began to worry if he could even utter such a thing.

It was a most brilliant idea, and Edward wished he'd thought of it himself. He did not, however, intend to let authenticity of authorship stand in his way. The German, Helmut Klein, had enjoyed his share of preferential treatment from high-society patrons, had staged several talked-about exhibitions, and was still ten years younger than Edward. Klein still had time enough to make a name for himself, whereas Edward did not. He had thought his hopes dashed when Elizabeth had announced she would not be marrying James. But now this golden opportunity had arisen, and he planned to take advantage of it before Klein could.

Chapter 20

One shot and it was over. The great beast lay shuddering at Sam's feet, then was still. It had taken him by surprise, by the side of a river, just a half-day's trek out of Chiengmai, and it had left him shaken, realising this could have been his end.

They had left the boat to make camp where the bamboo jungle almost met the water, and he had walked into the forest along a rough path, noticing the axe marks in the dense undergrowth where other travellers had fought their way in, perhaps to pitch tents for the night or to forage for wild fruit.

Fortunately, it was the cool season, and their small party—himself, two English adventurers, and twenty Siamese soldiers-cum-porters—had been spared fevers of the monsoonal wet season and the withering temperatures of the hot season. It was still too hot for the comfort of most foreigners, although it was cooler up in the hills, especially at night.

Snakes and marauding elephants were a constant menace, but the greatest fear was the silent and deadly tiger. An unwary traveller could be mauled or carried off before even having the chance to draw his gun. Sam had seen it happen on several occasions during his travels, and had heard a story of a tiger dragging off two Siamese at the same time—a tall tale, probably, but still.

He had thought he was too canny for it to happen to him, and he was only fortunate that a frightened monkey, believing itself the tiger's prey, had screeched and scurried up a tree. By the time Sam had swivelled, rifle aimed, the cat had begun its quick padding toward him. It was only twenty yards away, only a moment until it would spring, jaws open—and he would surely have known no more.

His first shot, between the eyes, took the beast down. He fired off a second, which glanced off its head—but the cat had already fallen dead in its tracks. He was glad he had kept his marksmanship skills up to scratch, and glad too of the heavy gun he always carried on expeditions such as this. The 1876 Winchester lever-action .45/70 was the most modern weapon available for American big-game hunters, and weighed more than nine pounds. It had a range of up to 600 yards, and could bring down a charging buffalo. It had saved his life more than once.

"Good shot, man! A prize for the home hearth, eh?" Hearing the shots, one of his companions, Terence McConnell, had come running from the camp. He was followed by another man, Sir Horatio Noone, a gentleman adventurer who was rather put out that the tiger wasn't his own kill. Both carried the Englishman's hunting gun of choice, the double-barrel .50 calibre elephant rifle, favoured because it had two barrels. Cartridges often misfired, and if this happened, the second barrel was bound to fire.

Although he carried a sportsman's rifle, Sam wasn't a recreational hunter—far from it. Target practice, self-defence, and food when necessary were reasons enough for him to carry such a weapon. He found shooting animals for fun to be a detestable hobby. And he really didn't like these two pompous Englishmen.

"A prize?" he said. "I don't think so. I wouldn't want anyone to think I'd killed it for pleasure. Have it if you want."

"I say, that's jolly decent of you, old chap," Noone edged up to the animal, poking it with his foot. "Not a hunter, then, eh?"

"As I said, not for pleasure."

Noone decided the American was not only mysterious, but downright odd. It was quite unusual for a man to own up to being squeamish about hunting. Not that he thought Sam was any sort of coward. The American had already proven otherwise.

When they had set up camp and got a good fire going, Sam filled a pot with water from the river and set it over the flames. When it boiled, he poured it down the barrel of the Winchester. The new shotgun cartridges were a great advance but upon firing, a large volume of smoke was released, filling the barrel with soot. The fulminate of mercury primer in the back of the cartridge was corrosive, and it was necessary to flush the barrel with a stream of hot water at regular intervals. Sam then took a collapsible rod with a looped end for an oil-soaked cleaning rag, and ran it up and down inside the barrel. There was something soothing about this process, and he preferred this ritual to having to fire the gun itself. He also ran a rag over his revolver—an 1878 double-action Colt army model—which, at .45 calibre and weighing only two pounds and ten ounces, was better suited to dispatching humans than big game. The most often-used item in his personal arsenal, however, was his bowie knife—adapted from the Scottish dirk —with its ten-inch blade and double-edged point. It was the quickest, most effective way to deal with a serpent that ventured too close, or an intruder set on ambush. Sam ran a finger along the edge of the razor-sharp blade. He would keep it beside him at night, within easy grasp of his right hand.

Later, when the others were already snoring in their bed-rolls and the Siamese watchmen were crouched in small groups, smoking, at the edges of the camp, Sam sat with his leather-bound writing pad in the light of the dwindling fire, deep in thought and writing from time to time. There could be no more hesitation. The letter had to be written, otherwise she might not wait for him. He would have to risk the unreliable mail service and pay a villager to take the letter to Chiengmai, in the hope it would then proceed to Bangkok.

20th November, 1882

Dear Elizabeth,

Forgive me for leaving you so suddenly without giving you any indication of my intentions toward you. The truth, though, is that I have come to know my own mind on this matter only since setting out on this journey.

Elizabeth, allow me to be quite frank with you, if I may. I guess I didn't realize, until I departed, how much I had come to enjoy and depend upon your company, for I am afraid now that I might lose you. I don't know if that is just the loneliness of a jungle at night getting to me, or if it is something to do with the fact that this day, I came very close to death. If not for a stroke of luck, I would have been carried off by a tiger and consumed for sure. Fortunately, I managed to shoot the beast before it could lay its paws on me, and I suppose this event reminded me of my own mortality, and the fact that I am no longer a young man. I am beyond thirty years of age, Elizabeth, and find that I now have a sudden yearning to be settled, to have a "home hearth", if you like, to quote another man's very words to me today. I want you to be part of my dream.

What I mean, Elizabeth, if you will excuse my boldness (for which you have so often chastised me), is that on my return to Bangkok, I will seek your permission to ask your father for your hand in marriage. Until then, my darling, look after yourself and think only of my return.

Your admirer,

Samuel Taylor II

She took the carriage and went as quickly as she could when Joseph's message summoned her ten days later. They had been the longest ten days of her life. So many times, she had been tempted simply to go to his house, to beg him to do something, anything. She had certainly prayed that she would miscarry the baby, though she knew that was a sin worse than the one she had already committed.

Joseph was bright-eyed, but nervous. He had thought long and hard about what he would do next and had prayed for guidance. He was still doubtful about whether it was the most sensible approach—or the most ridiculous notion he had ever entertained. He bade her sit beside him on the chesterfield, and she did so, staring at him beseechingly.

"Mr Shaw, I cannot contain myself any more. I've been hoping for a miracle—I'd even dreamed that perhaps Mr Taylor would find reason to cut short his expedition."

Joseph shook his head. "No, I'm afraid that's not going to happen, Elizabeth. And I must stress the fact that you'll have to forget about Samuel Taylor. He's somewhere in the jungle and won't be in communication for months. Your solution cannot lie in him."

He spoke confidently—like the school teacher he was— yet he could feel the slight tremor in his hands, and he knew that he was delaying what he really wanted to say.

She was so downcast, he did not want to prolong her torment any longer. He decided to ask the question he meant to, even if she thought it ludicrous.

"There is one solution," he offered, choosing his words carefully. "One that would save your reputation and your dignity, and would ensure that your child was born legitimate."

"I very much doubt that anything can save me now, but I will consider whatever you suggest, Mr Shaw."

"Please, Elizabeth, call me Joseph. We've known each other a long time."

"Yes, we have … Joseph. And I'm most grateful to you for everything. What is it you suggest?"

He felt his mouth go dry and his heart beat faster. More than anything, he hoped she would not be shocked or offended. He hadn't even seriously considered the possibility of her agreement. He decided it best to be direct and end the matter there and then.

"Elizabeth, would you … could you, consider marriage to me?"

Stunned and speechless, she could only stare at him, open mouthed with surprise.

Already, he felt it had been a terrible mistake, daring to hope she could be his wife. But an explanation was necessary, and he was compelled to continue. "I realise I'm much older than you, Elizabeth. I'm now forty and you're …?"

"Twenty-one." She was too astonished to say any more.

"Quite. But, my dear, although I'm not young, or adventurous, or handsome, I believe I'd make a good husband to you. The child we could bring up together, and I swear to you I'd never treat it as any less than if it were my own flesh and blood. If we were married quickly, there'd still be time to say the birth was simply premature. People would suspect, of course, but let them, I say. They'd eventually forget."

"But Joseph, a marriage cannot be purely for convenience. There must be deep affection, surely, some considerable feeling…"

"Elizabeth, I do have a deep affection for you. And, lately, I've found myself thinking of you more and more often as a dear friend. I admit, the idea of our marrying had never occurred to me before, simply because I didn't think you would even consider someone such as myself."

He stopped, believing he was only making the situation worse. "Perhaps I shouldn't have asked you. I've spoken out of turn. Please forgive me; this has been a dreadful error."

"Joseph, I too have a deep affection for you, although the idea of marriage to you had never remotely occurred to me, either."

"Of course not," he said, quietly.

She drew away and could not look at him. Tears began to sting her eyes. "I feel so ashamed. I'm a fallen woman. I've been with another man, and I wouldn't be fit to be your wife. Any man's wife."

"I know this has come as a shock to you, Elizabeth, and I sense that you will decline my offer, but …"

She tried to interject, to say something sympathetic,

but he raised a hand to quiet her. "Please allow me to say that I, too, have something to confess. You see, you could say equally that I am a fallen man. In fact, I'm not at all who you think I am."

She looked at him with new surprise, not sure of his meaning.

"There is something about myself that I must tell you, Elizabeth, before ... before you finally reject my proposal."

He paused, then resumed his confession.

"I've not spoken of this matter for twenty years, although I have thought of it every day. But if you were to be my wife, as I very much hope, then you should know everything about me. There should be no secrets between us."

"I'm listening," she said, intrigued now.

"As you know, I grew up in New Zealand. My parents went there as missionaries and I was born there. I never felt called to serve the Church myself, but I was a firm believer, and always attended services. I wanted to be a writer, in fact, and I planned to go to England to study at university. But that wasn't to be. Anyway, I befriended a young Maori girl— a chief's daughter—whose family had converted, and whom I saw regularly at church."

"Joseph, if you'd rather not tell me this, please don't feel obliged to."

"No, my dear. Painful as it is, I want to tell you. I've spoken of it to no one else, and it's time I did. Her name was Aroha—it means 'love' in the Maori language—and I fell in love with her, although I knew that neither my father nor hers would approve a marriage between us. But I didn't care, and my love made me reckless. Well, in due course our affair was discovered—by my extremely pious father, in the worst imaginable circumstances—and to this day, he has never forgiven me. I receive a small income from him twice a year, but there is never any letter. My mother sends an annual Christmas note, but she's always formal in her correspondence, as if she's merely performing a duty and I am a distant relative."

"And what happened to Aroha?" she asked, touched by his story.

"Aroha was expecting our child. Even then, my father wouldn't hear of us marrying, and I didn't have the courage to elope with her as I should have. Instead, they sponsored me to become a missionary and to come to Siam, where they said they hoped I'd spend a long time repenting my sins.

"I wrote to Aroha every week for months, but never received a reply. Eventually, I received a brief letter from her sister, who'd been educated at a mission school, informing me that Aroha had died in childbirth, and that the baby—a girl—had been stillborn. She told me never to contact the family again; that they'd refuted the Church, and had withdrawn to their tribal *marae*."

Elizabeth saw his eyes glisten with tears as he finished the story. "I'm very sorry for you, Joseph," she whispered. "You've suffered terribly!"

"But not as she did. And I will feel forever that I was responsible for her death and for that of the child. That is why I've never been ordained. I've never felt worthy."

There was a pause while both gathered their thoughts. "And you never wanted to be a missionary before ... the events?" Elizabeth asked.

"Well, no, at the time I didn't. I was certain I'd hate the life. But as I accepted the fact that Aroha and I would never be together, I grew to love my work here. I found it occupied all my time and came to offer great fulfillment. It's become much more than a penance, and for that much, I'm grateful."

He was waiting now for her answer. She took a deep breath and walked to the window, looking out at the garden. It was true he was much older, but many women married men twenty years their senior. She knew Joseph to be a good, gentle person who would keep his word and treat her child as his own. And what was her alternative? To bear a bastard child and have it adopted out, never thereafter having the opportunity to marry decently. Despite what she had said to Joseph, in her heart she was doubtful that Sam would ever commit himself to her. Otherwise, he would never have left so readily. But despite this, she still wasn't certain that marriage to Joseph was the solution to her predicament.

He began to apologise again for even contemplating the idea of proposing to her, but this time it was she who silenced him.

"Joseph, I'm grateful—more than I can tell you—for your offer and it's far more than I deserve. But I must say that it has taken me by surprise, and I feel I need some time to think it over. I'll go now, and I promise to let you have an answer very soon, either way."

For a moment, he sat without reply. He had dared to hope—but no, she was letting him down kindly, he could tell.

"Of course, I understand. Please take as long as you need, and I'll accept your answer graciously—whatever you decide. I only hope I've not caused you any offence."

He fell silent again as she thanked him awkwardly and left the room, still dabbing at her eyes with her handkerchief.

∞∞∞

Far away, out in the jungle, Sam gave the sealed letter to one of the Siamese porters, who came from a nearby village and had always shown himself—as far as Sam could tell—to be reliable and trustworthy. He watched as the man disappeared into the jungle, on his way, Sam supposed, to hire a raft downriver.

The messenger ran down the track, and when he was out of view, tossed the letter away into the jungle undergrowth, pocketed the coins that Khun Gun—as the men had nicknamed Sam on account of his excellent marksmanship—had given him, and made haste back to his moobahn, his home village, well pleased with himself. He was an important man in his own village, being the son of a revered elder. He hadn't seen his wives for two years, and he was tired of the nomadic life, working for these white men for next to nothing. Nevertheless, the money Sam had given him would buy them some stock and perhaps even allow him to go into business as a trader. He wouldn't waste it on hiring a raft. It was only a letter, after all; the man could write another.

Edward knew his plan could have been a disaster, with embarrassing repercussions. Instead, it had turned out rather well. He had taken a great liberty, and it was only after he had sent the letter that he fully realised what he had done. He hoped Helmut Klein had been too drunk to remember the night they had talked at the bar of the United Club—and had unwittingly divulged his idea. Klein had already been well on the way to oblivion that evening, and Edward had bought him several generous shots of schnapps to help him along. Klein talked on and on about how it would be possible to gain entrée to the inner circle of the court, and how much His Majesty would enjoy the companionship of a fellow photographer.

Now, it seemed, the King's imagination had been inspired by Edward's offer of photography lessons and had invited him to the new royal residence at the Grand Palace —the Chakri Maha Prasad—to begin the tuition. The palace had been completed only that year, to coincide with Bangkok's centenary, and Edward had not yet been admitted to the King's private chambers, although he had photographed members of the royal family at various functions during the year and had attended several parties in the vast reception rooms.

It was a hugely imposing building, and—because of King Chulalongkorn's admiration of European culture—had been built mostly in Italian Renaissance style, although it was designed by a British architect. The roof, however—unlike any building to be seen in Europe—was traditional Siamese, with orange, green and yellow-tiled tiers that supported three golden spires.

The most splendid room was the central throne hall, featuring magnificent crystal chandeliers, marble and gold fittings, and a nine-tiered white-and-gold pagoda-like canopy above the throne.

Edward, however, now found the pomp and ceremony of receptions held for foreign envoys and the expatriate community rather tedious. What he wanted was to see how the King really lived and to become known as His Majesty's personal photographer. It was to this end that he had written with the offer of the lessons.

He had originally planned to use the fact that his daughter was engaged to Viscount James Claridge as a lever to attract His Majesty's attention—perhaps in the hope that he would be the guest of honour at a reception to celebrate the upcoming nuptials. After all, Claridge was related distantly to Queen Victoria and his father had been a frequent guest in royal circles.

It had been a shock when Elizabeth had told him of James's letter. But at least it had not been she who had broken off the engagement, as he had feared. Edward supposed he could not blame James: a man in his position needed a wife, and Elizabeth was half a world away.

∞∞∞

Days later came a shock that had nothing to do with the Palace. Edward was still reeling from the impact of the words.

"Are you serious, Joseph? Does Elizabeth know?"

"Yes, of course. She's happy to accept my proposal, providing you give your permission."

Edward was astonished. "But when did all this happen? I wasn't aware of any … romantic feelings, let alone courtship between you two."

It was an awkward moment for Joseph. "Well, I think Elizabeth and I have always felt quite close, even when we didn't see each other for years. And when she returned, we realized—quite suddenly, in fact, yes—what our true feelings for each other were. Yesterday, I asked her to marry me, and today she has agreed. Which is why I have come to see you now. I am sorry, Edward, I should have come to you before proposing, but I wasn't at all sure she would accept, you see …"

"Good Lord!" Edward exclaimed, perplexed by the strangeness of it all. "I apologise, Joseph, I don't mean to appear rude. It's just that this is something of a shock. How extraordinary. Well, though, I have no objections, I suppose, if that's what she wants. I mean, if that's what you both want."

Elizabeth, who had been listening at the parlour door, now entered the room. "It is, Father. We want to be married just as soon as possible, don't we, Joseph?"

"Yes, indeed; we're both agreed on a small service and reception, so, yes, as soon as possible."

Edward, who by now sat dumbfounded in an armchair, could hardly respond.

Finally, he did. "In that case, as the two of you seem intent, I think I must give you my blessing." Then, almost absent-mindedly, he suggested that the new year might be a good time for the wedding.

Elizabeth glanced quickly in alarm at Joseph.

"Well, we were hoping rather sooner than that," he said. "In fact, as soon as the banns can be read."

"Neither of us wants a big wedding," Elizabeth added. "Just a small reception here at home."

Edward was now almost completely detached from reality. "Of course, dear. I'm not a believer in long engagements myself. The banns shall be read on three successive Sundays, as usual, and you can be married the next week."

"Thank you, Father," Elizabeth said warmly, kissing him on the cheek.

At last Edward managed to collect his thoughts. "My dear, will you excuse us?" he asked Elizabeth. "There are some matters I must speak to Joseph about."

She smiled with relief. "Of course. I shall see you this evening, Joseph."

When she had left, Edward asked Joseph to sit down.

"I'm sorry, Joseph, but I must ask you this. Is Elizabeth..."

"I give you my word," Joseph assured him, "that nothing improper has occurred between myself and Elizabeth."

Edward leaned back in the chair, relieved. "Of course not. I don't know how I could even think that of you. Please forget I asked."

∞∞∞

From their first session, King Chulalongkorn was entranced with the gentle art of photography, and his intelligence and creative spirit had seen him master the basics much sooner, Edward had to admit, than he himself had done. After only a few weeks, the King was already making his own prints in a darkroom he had set up in the new palace.

During the course of the lessons, he allowed Edward to photograph him in his private rooms—alone and with family members—eating dinner, entertaining his children, and smoking a cigar. Edward was ecstatic. It was the highlight of his career, and he was hoping the King would give him permission to use the photographs in a special exhibition he was planning. More than anything though, Edward hoped he would still be well enough to complete a suitable body of work and organise the event.

Chapter 21

It was true, there was no passion—she never felt her pulse quicken when she saw him—but she liked and admired him enormously, and she was sure she could be happy with him. Besides, there had been no other way.

She could hardly believe they were married. It had all happened so quickly; the nuptials that morning and the luncheon reception afterwards in the garden of her father's house. By mid-afternoon, they had arrived at Joseph's own home—their home together, now, as a married couple. He did not intrude as she excused herself to change from the ungainly crinoline into a more comfortable day dress. They passed a pleasant afternoon in the garden, talking and sharing their views as they always had on everything from food to Mr. Darwin's book, *On the Origin of Species by Natural Selection*, which had created a crisis of faith since its publication in 1859, with many people questioning the importance—nay, the very existence—of God.

Later, Joseph appeared to doze in the shade, but she wondered if he was really asleep, or if he, too, was bemused by the whole event and needed time to reflect upon it.

As she reviewed the formalities of the day, it seemed so strange to her, as if it had happened to someone else. Anchalee's words echoed through her mind. "Congratulations, Mrs Shaw," she had said—and for a moment, Elizabeth had not realized her sister was speaking to her. She imagined her surreal wedding day as if she were reading a newspaper item about some other woman's marriage:

The wedding of Elizabeth Ann Fairburn, daughter of Mr Edward Fairburn, professional photographer, of New Road, Bangkok, and Mr Joseph Peter Shaw, missionary teacher, was celebrated this day at the Protestant Chapel, Yannawa, followed by a reception for forty friends and family at the father-of-the-bride's residence. The maid-of-honour was the bride's half-sister, Miss Anchalee Fairburn; and the best man, the groom's friend, Mr John A. Eakin, a teacher at King's College.

The bride wore a white satin gown, ruched to show a pleated satin underskirt, held out prettily by a crinoline, giving the ensemble a traditional look. She wore a long veil and orchids in her hair, but no jewellery, except for the plain gold band given her by her husband during the ceremony. The maid of honour wore a green satin frock in similar style to the bride's, but without the crinoline. The gowns were made by the Bangkok seamstress Mrs G. E. Smythe, in what was said to be a supreme effort in the short lead-up to the wedding.

Official photographs after the 10.30 a.m. ceremony were taken by the bride's father, Mr Fairburn, at his home studio, after which an elegant luncheon was served under a marquee in the garden. The reception was blessed with what was, for Bangkok, an exceptionally mild day, even for the cool season, the temperature climbing no higher than 78 degrees. Soon after the bride and groom cut the three-tiered wedding cake at 2.30 p.m., they departed by carriage for the groom's home.

Elizabeth was startled from her reverie by the arrival of Simon, who announced that a light supper was served in the dining room. The newlyweds went inside and sat opposite each other, making polite conversation. But neither was concentrating on the chatter, nor on the lightly grilled fillets of fish with steamed rice and lime wedges.

When the plates were removed, only half cleared, Elizabeth said she would retire for the evening, and she hoped he could not see her blush. Unfortunately, as she left the table, the chair caught the hem of her dress, and there was an awkward moment as she tugged to free it. She glanced at her husband, and, suddenly, he was grinning with mirth, taking years off his countenance. She smiled back: perhaps it would all be all right after all.

Upstairs in the bedroom—their bedroom, she reminded herself, knowing his arrival must be imminent—she hastily changed into a long white cotton nightdress with a full, gathered and tucked skirt that concealed her now slightly protruding stomach. Her pregnancy was the reason, also, that she had chosen the old-fashioned crinoline style for her wedding dress. Sitting before the mirror of her intricately carved teak dressing table—a wedding gift from her father—she brushed out her hair and noticed how long it had grown in the eight months since she had arrived in Bangkok. That arrival seemed like a lifetime ago. And now, here she was, expecting a baby and married to a man who wasn't the father of her child, a man who, otherwise, she would never have thought of—even remotely—as the one she would be tied to forever.

She knew she shouldn't, but she thought of Sam now. When he returned to Bangkok, he would no doubt hear the news. What would be make of the marriage and the baby? She prayed for the child's sake, as well as for her own and Joseph's, that it would have her fair colouring, so no questions could possibly be asked. She wondered how she would cope with the memories if the face of the child she would look at every day was the image of that other face.

Would Sam have married her if he had known? She wanted to believe he would have, but reason told her that he would not really want to be saddled with a wife and child. He didn't seem the type, and had told her as much. Why had she been so gullible? Why had she not resisted more? Because she had been in love with him. Blindly in love. From the novels she read, she knew this was the sort of passion that came only once in a lifetime. But unlike in novels, real-life romance had real-life consequences. A man could do what he liked and waltz off on his next adventure; a woman, on the other hand, could make one error of judgement and, forever after, she would never be able to escape it. She knew this marriage would not fix everything forever. As a woman, she knew that some time, somewhere, somehow in the future, her past would catch up with her.

There was a light tap at the bedroom door, and her husband entered. Sitting at the dressing table, she continued to brush her hair, hoping the long, rhythmic strokes would calm her nerves.

"My dear," he began awkwardly. "I understand that in your condition, you might not want ... well, that you might prefer to sleep alone. If you wish, I'm happy to sleep in the guest room until after the baby is born."

His frankness startled her, but when she saw his earnest face, her heart went out to him. "No, Joseph," she said resolutely. "You are my husband: of course I want you here with me. You've saved my life, my reputation. I am so grateful."

He sat on the edge of the bed. "I hope our marriage can be based on much more than gratitude. You owe me nothing, Elizabeth. I cannot erase from my mind the fact that it was my actions that made this step necessary for you. Even though it was at your request, if I'd known of your condition when I received your letter, I should never have sent *him* away."

She frowned, confused, and set down her brush, turning to face him. "My letter? I don't understand ..."

"I know you asked me never to mention it again, and I know how painful it must be to you. But we are man and wife now, and we must always speak with perfect candour."

"But what letter, Joseph?"

"The letter Anchalee brought from you, explaining how you wanted to extricate yourself from his influence."

His words confounded her. What could he be referring to? She knew of no such letter delivered by Anchalee or anyone else.

She tried to keep her expression neutral, but inside, her stomach was in knots. "Do you still have it?" she asked lightly.

"Why yes, it's locked in my desk."

"Joseph, could I see it—again?" she said, remembering to add the final word. Noting his concern, she elaborated. "I was so confused at the time, you understand. I can hardly remember what it was I wrote."

"Of course," he said, bemused. "One moment."

He returned quickly, and handed her a white envelope.

She opened the pages and lay them on the dressing table before her, seeing immediately that the handwriting was not her own, though it was a good attempt at a copy. She turned away from her husband as she read the lines, trying to conceal the increasing horror she felt.

In her name, it was written that she no longer believed Sam to be *a suitable candidate for marriage*, that she wanted Joseph to help her *extricate* herself *from this unfortunate arrangement*. Then the most telling words of all: *You may speak freely of this matter to my sister, as she is aware of everything that has occurred and my intention to end this inappropriate liaison.*

She saw now what had really happened. Her own sister, Anchalee, had sought to ruin her, to send away the father of her unborn child. Anchalee must have guessed when she witnessed Elizabeth's morning sickness. But why? If it had been a malicious act, what had Elizabeth done to make her sister hate her so? Or could it possibly be that Anchalee had in fact not realised Elizabeth was pregnant and merely acted on what she imagined, misguidedly, were her sister's best interests? The latter seemed unlikely.

The existence of this letter changed everything. For, as Elizabeth now realised, Sam had not meant to leave her—and if he had not, she would have told him of the pregnancy, and he would now in all likelihood be her husband, even if he had not wanted to be.

But right now, her actual husband's hand was on her shoulder, concern in his eyes. "Is everything in order, my dear?"

How could she tell him? How could she reveal that this

had all been a terrible mistake; that she had wanted to marry Sam with all her heart, before and after she fell pregnant? That she still did? But it was all too late. She could not allow Joseph to discover the truth after he had been so honourable. It would be too cruel. It was done, and could not be reversed. She resolved that he must never know the letter was a forgery: she must take care to dispose of it at some stage, so he could never notice her handwriting was slightly different to the hand of the one who had so carefully and deceitfully written the letter. The other problem, of discovering why her sister had done this, could wait—but she vowed to find out the truth one day.

She tried to smile to mask her shock and torment as she turned to look up at her husband. "I'm sorry, Joseph. You must think me so strange. I expect it's my condition—it does tend to bring on such vagueness of thought, sometimes, that I hardly know where I am." She knew this was untrue, but it was all she could think of.

"Yes, of course. But you must now forget the misery of the past, Elizabeth. Put it far away from you. We are one now, and I shall always stand by you. That is my vow today. I hope you know that."

Neither said another word as she stood slowly to meet him, determined to do her duty. He kissed her tenderly and wrapped his arms around her. She buried her head in his neck, feeling as she always did with him: warm and safe.

He led her to the four-poster bed with its draped mosquito nets and down-filled patchwork quilt, and they set beside each other. He turned to face her, and she smiled to reassure him. Then he pulled back the quilt and extinguished the lamp next to the bed, before taking her in his arms.

Chapter 22

King Chulalongkorn enjoyed the new art of photography so much that his family and subjects were becoming accustomed to being summoned for a photo session, sometimes taken by one of several foreign professional photographers who had made their abode in Bangkok, and sometimes by the King himself, who engaged them to tutor not only himself, but any members of the court who wanted to learn, including his ladies. He had willing subjects in his many children, who had been known to hide and then cheekily leap out from behind silk curtains as the scene was being set for a portrait, demanding to be photographed themselves.

Though His Majesty indulged the foreign photographers for the most part, Edward Fairburn worried him. Mr Fairburn was a patient and courteous tutor, but that meant nothing in itself, because everyone was patient and courteous in the King's presence. King Chulalongkorn, known for his astuteness, simply did not trust the man. There was something about the Englishman that led him to think that beneath his gentlemanly exterior lay a scoundrel. Discreet enquiries were made, and His Majesty paid particular attention to a story that was reported back to him regarding a certain well-known competitor of Mr Fairburn named Helmut Klein.

The sounds of her agony filled the house, at times high-pitched and piercing, at others descending to a low moan. The doctor could be heard from behind the closed door, urging her on. Joseph paced the hallway outside, unable to tear himself away from the evidence of her pain, thinking the torture would never end.

It was three in the morning and she had been in labour since eleven o'clock the previous morning. The doctor had emerged at one point, about five hours earlier, to tell him that it would be a long night, and that perhaps it would be best if he went out for a walk, or even away to stay with friends. But Joseph could not leave her. He had had no idea that giving birth was like this, and as the hours dragged on, he thought of another woman, long ago, bleeding to death without him and because of him. It seemed to him so unjust that woman should have to bear the seed of man in this way.

Suddenly, the screams ceased, and the silence was somehow more frightening than the noise. He grew cold, thinking the worst. She had filled his life so completely in the six months since they had married, that he could not imagine life without her. The silence was finally broken by the child's cry, and then the bedroom door swung open.

Dr Newhaven stood before him, smiling, holding a bundle wrapped in a blanket. "Your son, Mr Shaw."

Gingerly, Joseph took the baby from the doctor and looked down at the tiny red face, the eyes shut tight, the tuft of black hair on the crown of his head. He felt an instant love and a complete bond with this child, this son who was not his own. Then he looked back at the doctor, suddenly concerned again. "My wife ...?"

Dr Newhaven immediately reassured him. "She'll be fine, Mr Shaw. She's weak, and she's lost some blood, but all she needs is rest and nourishment. She's still awake. Why don't you take the baby to her while I go and wash up? This is a special and private family moment for the three of you."

On entering the room with his tiny—now squirming—bundle, Joseph was alarmed to see her looking so deathly pale, so exhausted. But she smiled when he entered the darkened room as he sat beside her on the bed, taking her hand in his. She soon became drowsy, but before she fell asleep, she managed to whisper, "He's your son, Joseph."

"I shall never think of him as anything else. I love him already."

She smiled for joy. "And his name will be Joseph," she added. "Joseph Edward Shaw."

It was over. So much work had come to nothing. The King refused to grant him permission to use any of the photographs he had taken in the private quarters of the Palace. And yet, others had been allowed to do so.

Although the arrangement had seemed to Edward to be working rather well, His Majesty through an envoy suddenly cancelled their lessons after three months, with no stated reason. Edward presumed that more important matters of state were demanding the King's attention, and that they would resume when His Majesty was able to spend more time on his hobby.

Strangely, no more royal summonses were forthcoming in the next three months, and when Edward sent a polite letter to His Majesty, via his assistant, enquiring after his family and suggesting they meet once more to share photographic knowledge, he received no reply. For some reason—he could not fathom what—he had been excluded.

When an official note did arrive one day, carried by a court underling, it informed him that His Majesty wished it known that any photographs he had taken in the private quarters of the palace were to remain unpublished, and that permission to exhibit them had been rescinded. When he asked the assistant why, the man said, rather vaguely, that it was for reasons of security.

Shortly after, he heard that Mr Klein had been appointed the official royal photographer and had taken over the King's informal photographic lessons. Edward burned with shame that his deceit had been discovered.

∞∞∞

There was a rap on the front door, and Anchalee ran to answer it before the maid could get there. She was bored, and a visitor—any visitor—would be a relief, even if it were Elizabeth and her pampered son. According to her sister, the three-month-old was so intelligent he was already saying "mamma", but Anchalee could decipher only ordinary baby babble.

When she opened the door, she took a step back in astonishment. Then she couldn't help but be pleasantly surprised at the caller: the day might not be such a tedious one after all. "Well, hello, Mr Taylor," she said as nonchalantly as she could muster. "We thought we had lost you forever to the jungle."

Sam wasted no time on pleasantries. "Is your father home, Anchalee?"

"No, he's not, I'm sorry."

"Good. Then tell Elizabeth I want to see her immediately, will you?"

"You'd better come in."

She smiled sweetly, opening the door wide and stepping aside to allow him into the hallway. This would be even more fun than she had imagined.

He removed his cap and strode into the parlour in front of her, as if it were his own home.

"You look as if you've just got off the boat," she said.

"You're not far wrong," he replied, turning back to her. "Got back this morning. How is your sister, by the way?"

"She's wonderful. In fact, she says she's never been happier."

There was an unmistakeable tone of mischief in her voice as she showed him into the front room.

"Oh, does she now," he said, following her joking tone. "Well, I'll have to be the judge of that. Call her down, won't you —or should I go upstairs to get her myself?"

"I don't think that would be of much use. She isn't here."

"Damn, I was hoping to see her right away. What time is she due home?"

"Oh, I should think she's home right now." She was thoroughly enjoying this game. It was the moment she had been waiting for.

"But you said she was out."

"No, I said she wasn't here."

He was now becoming less amused by her antics. "If you're trying to entertain me, Anchalee, it's not working. This is the Fairburn residence and I should like to see Elizabeth Fairburn."

"There is no such person—well, not any longer." He paled, and she took pity on him. "Oh, nothing untoward has happened, don't be concerned. It's just that Elizabeth is no longer a Fairburn, and she now lives elsewhere."

"What do you mean?" he snapped, frustrated by her immature frivolity.

"I *mean* that she didn't see any reason to wait for you." Anchalee whirled around and plonked down girlishly on the sofa. "She married Joseph Shaw shortly after you left."

Her statement had the desired effect. It was the first time she had ever see Sam caught completely off guard.

"She married Joseph Shaw? The missionary? The teacher—*her* former teacher, in fact?"

"The very same. Odd, isn't it? Anyway, they have a baby now. A little boy." She paused for a few seconds. "Born quite prematurely, apparently."

He sat down in an armchair and wondered if she were joking at his expense. It wouldn't have surprised him.

"This is unbelievable. Are you having me on?"

"Ask anyone, if you don't believe me. We could hardly believe it ourselves when she told us the news of their engagement. But they consider themselves very fortunate. The baby was born so early, but thankfully, he didn't seem at all below weight."

He looked at her suspiciously. "All right, young missy, you've had your game. Now tell me where she really is."

She went to the sideboard and picked up two framed photographs, then handed the first to him. "See for yourself. Here's their wedding photograph."

He looked at it briefly, but his attention was immediately drawn to the second image she handed him—of Elizabeth with the baby in his christening gown.

"Is that ... their son?"

"Yes, that's Joe."

"When was he born?"

"Three months ago, on the 30th of June. Everyone believes it's a miracle he didn't die, being so early."

She revelled in Sam's torment, not hesitating to deliver the final blow. "It's very strange though. Elizabeth has green eyes and Joseph has light blue eyes—but Joe has dark brown eyes."

"And what do *you* think?"

"About what?"

"Do you believe the baby was premature?"

"Of course. Why wouldn't I?"

Same shrugged. "Well, that's that then."

"What's what?"

"Anchalee, are you always so trying on a man's patience?"

"Ah, you've finally noticed something about me. And yes, I usually am."

He picked up his cap. "Give my regards to Mrs Shaw when you next see her."

"Oh, I shall. You can be sure of that."

"I'll see myself out."

She smiled to herself after he had departed, thinking that he really was a most attractive man.

∞∞∞

He returned the next day, before she had even had the opportunity to pass on his regards to Elizabeth. It was another duty she was looking forward to. They went into the front room again and she poured him a whisky from her father's cabinet. She suspected he had been watching the house, because as soon as Edward left for a photographic assignment that morning, he arrived at the door.

"I want you to do me a favour, Anchalee."

She handed him the glass and took a seat on the sofa opposite him. "A favour, Mr Taylor?"

"Sam to my friends, Anchalee."

"Am I a friend … Sam?"

"Of course. And you might be an even more valuable one if you can help me out." He took a sip of the whisky and leaned back in the armchair, eyeing her closely.

"I assume this has something to do with Elizabeth," she said, sounding bored.

"Yes, it does. I want you to arrange for us to meet."

He was sure he detected the trace of a smirk on her face.

"My sister is a married woman now, so I'm sure she won't agree to meet her old … what exactly would you call yourself? Paramour? Suitor doesn't seem quite right, somehow." Anchalee had already begun to think how she could engineer such a meeting.

"I know she's married," he replied. "But I still need to see her. I feel I owe her an explanation as to why I was away so long. Will you do it?"

She affected a show of dwelling upon his request—as if it were a terrible dilemma—and after a few moments' consideration of nothing whatsoever, she agreed. "Very well."

"Good. Now, where can this meeting occur?"

"Well, why not here? Then it could look accidental, and she wouldn't be suspicious. She comes to see me every Friday for the entire afternoon."

"And is your father at home during these visits?"

"Not until at least three o'clock. He has lunch with his cronies on Fridays."

"Perfect. I can arrive looking for your father on the pretence of a photographic job for my book. And be sure to ask her to bring the baby with her."

"She always brings him anyway. She imagines I would want to see him. But why should you be interested?"

"Anchalee, you ask far too many questions for a child."

"I'm no child," she protested. "I'll be fifteen in just over three months."

He laughed at her petulance. "Well, young lady, I'm thirty-three this month, and from where I stand, nearly fifteen is merely a child."

She pouted, annoyed that he had managed to unsettle her. He would know otherwise in due course, she thought—and she was prepared to wait for however long she had to.

∞∞∞

Elizabeth's quiet investigations had revealed nothing. For all these many months, since she had discovered the existence of the forged letter, she had tried to work out why Anchalee had been so devious. She could not, of course, say anything that would let her sister discover that she knew, but her guarded questions were met only with vague answers.

Once, when she had asked Anchalee what she knew about their respective mothers, her sister had looked at her sharply, but only for a moment. Then she'd smiled, shrugged, and said she thought the past should remain exactly where it was.

On the surface, Elizabeth appeared to be the perfect wife and mother. She and Joseph had a loving relationship, and she made sure the household was efficiently run. She refused to have a nanny for the baby, preferring to spend all her time with him. Often, she was unable to prevent herself gazing at his face—she was aware that every time she did so, she saw his real father's reflection, just as she'd feared.

Joseph was as good a husband as any man could be, and —thankfully—was not overly demanding. Night after night, while he slept soundly, she lay beside him awake, enmeshed by mounting fury and disbelief at what had befallen her. Meanwhile, she dutifully visited her sister once a week, and continued her secret quest to find the truth.

On Friday, Elizabeth arrived as usual with Joe, and he smiled and gurgled as soon as he saw his aunt. He seemed to have a special liking for Anchalee, who couldn't understand why—she never gave him any encouragement.

Elizabeth pushed the beautiful imported English perambulator into the front room and adjusted Joe's white broderie anglaise quilt that had once belonged to her mother, and which had, in fact, covered herself when she was a baby.

"We just missed the rain, by the look of the sky," Elizabeth said. It was the monsoon again, and it rained heavily almost every day.

She managed to rock Joe to sleep, and they sat in the

front room for a chat, Anchalee cheekily helping herself to a pre-lunch sherry, which Elizabeth declined. There was a knock at the front door.

"Are you expecting another guest for lunch?"

"No. But Father did say someone might call about a time for a photographic session." Anchalee went into the hallway at once to open the door herself, and Elizabeth heard her talking familiarly in the hallway.

"Oh, it's you! What a nice surprise. Do come in. Elizabeth will want to say hello."

Elizabeth stood, smoothed her skirt and turned to greet the visitor. She nearly collapsed back into her chair when she saw him. She felt as if her legs would buckle under her.

He stood in the doorway for an instant, then walked toward her. "Hello, Elizabeth. It's been a while."

"Sam ... Mr Taylor. I didn't expect to see you ..."

"No doubt," he cut her off curtly. "I've only just returned from Chiengmai."

Anchalee quickly made her retreat, her job done. "I'll go and see how lunch is progressing," she said breezily on her way out.

Elizabeth sat down again and reminded herself she needn't feel ashamed or nervous before him. After all, he was the one who had seduced then abandoned her. There was silence for only a moment before she spoke coolly. "You left without warning."

He sat, and she could see her frank words had disarmed him, though there was little hint of contrition in his voice when he spoke.

"I sent you a letter."

"A letter!" She sank back into the sofa. "It was less than I expected of you."

"At the time, I had no choice," he argued. "You know it was impossible to visit you here."

"If it's possible now, why was it impossible then?" she retorted.

"That's unfair," he protested. "Besides, nothing was re-solved and I said I'd see you when I returned. And I told you in the next letter exactly what my intentions were. You didn't think me worth waiting for?"

"What do you mean, your next letter?"

"The one I sent during the expedition—it should have come here via Chiengmai. You did receive it?"

She shook her head, puzzled. "I don't know what letter you're referring to. All I know is that you left, informing me with a rather vague note and leaving me to ... Well, anyway, it doesn't matter now."

He was distracted and barely seemed to be listening to her. "Damn the man!" he almost shouted, seemingly to him-self. "Damn him to hell. Jesus, can't anyone be trusted? I should've known better."

He then realised where he was, and seeing her alarmed expression, moved to the sofa and sat beside her. For a fleeting moment, she thought he was going to take her hands in his, but he did not.

'I'm sorry, Elizabeth. Please excuse my outburst."

For a few seconds, he simply looked at her, and she felt the magnetism once more. She was desperate to tell him the truth, that they had been tricked into a life apart. Yet she knew she could not. From now on, their relationship would, of necessity, be one of formality and distant acquaintance-ship, a veneer to disguise their real feelings and the tragedy of being forced to live their lives without each other.

He had spoken of his "intentions". She had no doubt now that if he had known she was pregnant, he would have married her. But if she had known he meant to marry her on his return, would she—could she—have waited for him, despite the baby and what people would say? Could she have thumbed her nose at conservative society, borne a bastard child, and suffered being called a harlot, if it meant ultimately being with him forever?

But no. She realised only too well that she would never

have been able to do that. She lacked courage, always had—and she was ashamed to admit to herself that social appearances had taken precedence over her love for him.

She knew she must be rid of him. "Please, Sam, I think it's best that you leave. I made a terrible mistake, but I have a new life now. I'm happy with Joseph—no doubt you already know of our marriage."

"Yes. But why, Elizabeth?"

She faltered. "Because … because I love him."

"I don't believe you."

"Well, it's the truth. And it's really of no interest to me whether you believe it or you don't."

He suddenly noticed the pram at the corner of the room when the baby whimpered slightly, and she could only watch as he stood and approached it.

"He's asleep. Please don't disturb him."

He looked down at the sleeping baby, at soft black hair and olive skin. "Very dark-haired, isn't he?"

She sensed bitterness in his voice, and was certain he would see the truth. She could feel her hands shaking. She held them together tightly in her lap.

"It's only baby hair," she said nervously. "It will lighten in a few months when his real hair grows in."

"Really?" He walked toward the sofa and stood before her. "Can you swear to me, without any doubt, that this is Joseph's son?"

She looked up at him and hesitated for only a moment before replying confidently, "Yes, Sam. He is Joseph's son."

He stared intently into her eyes, and she looked back unflinchingly, holding her breath—so afraid he would see through her. He must not know the truth, or she was sure he would make trouble and ruin them all.

At last he spoke. "Then we have nothing left to discuss, do we?"

She shook her head slowly, still looking into the deep brown eyes she had once fallen in love with. She knew she was still in love with him, that a part of her would always love him. Now, though, it was hopeless to do so, and she prayed that she could take this secret with her to the grave.

Without another word, he turned and walked away, and she heard the front door open and close, then his steps down the path becoming fainter. She sat transfixed, as if she had been turned to stone, until Anchalee appeared again.

"Has Sam gone already?" her sister asked in a clear expression of disappointment.

"Did you know he was coming?" There was irritation and suspicion in Elizabeth's counter-enquiry.

"Of course not." Anchalee paused to affect a sudden realisation. "I'm sorry. I shouldn't have asked him in. I thought you wouldn't mind, now that you're married."

"Of course I don't mind. It doesn't matter at all." Elizabeth looked away, as if to dismiss it as a triviality. She hoped she had given no indication of the depth of her discomfort.

Elizabeth was quiet during dinner at home with Joseph that night. She looked pale as she pushed the food round her plate.

"Not hungry?" Joseph asked.

"Just tired, that's all." She put down her knife and fork. "Joseph, truthfully, are you happy with me?"

His eyes widened. "Elizabeth, what an extraordinary question. I am, most definitely. You must know that. I couldn't be happier."

She seemed to relax a little, then took a deep breath.

"Joseph, I think there's something that might make you even happier than you are now."

He looked slightly perplexed.

"A child Joseph, of our own. Yours and mine."

"We already have Joe. I've told you, I consider him my own."

"Joseph, I'm going to have a baby."

"You mean…"

She was smiling now and crying at the same time. "Yes, I'm expecting. Isn't it wonderful?"

∞∞∞

It wasn't the only time she saw Sam that week. A few days later, he was at her own house, and she was alarmed when Simon ushered him in. She didn't need to utter the question, as her feelings were obvious to Sam by the expression on her face.

"Don't panic," he said immediately in the lazy, almost insolent manner she knew so well. "I'm here to see *your husband*. About the mission to Chiengmai. I have my report to give him."

"Oh, of course." She had almost forgotten that his part in the expedition had been at Joseph's instigation. She was also sure Joseph would not have asked Sam to come to their home. "I'll call him down."

"There's no need," he said, raising a hand. "Simon has gone to get him."

"Well then, please sit down."

"Where's the baby?"

"Joe," she answered with emphasis, "is asleep in the nursery."

At that moment, Joseph entered the room. He and Sam exchanged an uneasy greeting which was little more than a mere acknowledgement of each other's presence, and Elizabeth could feel the underlying tension. She excused herself hurriedly and wondered how her husband felt having to deal with Sam.

Joseph led Sam to his study and sat behind his desk, putting distance between them. Sam sat in the leather chair opposite as Joseph eyed him closely and wondered what he had been saying to Elizabeth. He was also piqued that Sam had arrived at the house unannounced.

"I gather the mission was a success, Mr Taylor."

Sam wondered how much Joseph knew of his affair with Elizabeth. Had Joseph purposely sent him upcountry in order to leave the way open for him to marry her himself?

"A success, Mr Shaw. Your people up there are well settled now."

"I'm most grateful. The entire mission is grateful. Your fee will be forwarded to you in due course. Did any other matters arise from your journey?"

"The mission families gave me a bag of mail to send on for them. I've already taken it to the consulate." From an inside pocket, he extracted an envelope addressed to Joseph, and passed it to him. "The rest you'll find in my report."

"Thank you. A written report will be most helpful."

Sam stood to go, and said curtly, "I most offer you my congratulations on your marriage. And on the birth of your son."

"Oh, well, thank you again. Both events have been a great joy to me indeed." Joseph then changed the subject. "Would you be available for further excursions to the north?"

"Only if you don't want me back in Bangkok in a hurry."

"Oh?"

"I'm returning to the north very soon—for some time, I expect. Joining up with a government expedition to charter the Siamese boundaries. Might even look into the teak trade while I'm up there and join the Borneo Company."

It was a trade he in fact had no intention of pursuing, but he said it to gauge Joseph's reaction. The man's obvious relief at the prospect of being rid of him told Sam all he needed to know.

"I see." Joseph smiled slightly for the first time since

Sam had arrived. "Well, in that case, I wish you *bon voyage*, Mr Taylor."

Sam nodded, saying he would see himself out—leaving Joseph hoping that this new expedition would, indeed be lengthy, if not permanent.

∞∞∞

She felt unusually tired as she sat resting in the window seat in the front room, and he asked if she would like him to stay with her. But she told him no; that he should go on to his mission meeting. She was also suffering from cramping pains in her back. She had been lucky not to have any morning sickness with this pregnancy, so could not understand why she felt to awful now. She was past the first three months and should be feeling fine.

Nevertheless, her cheerful air reassured him, and he kissed her goodbye, promising to be home in time for an early dinner. She sat for a while before slowly going upstairs, as the gripping pains in her stomach intensified.

When Joseph did arrive home at four o'clock, the house seemed unnaturally quiet. Then he remembered that Simon had the afternoon off, and the only other servant—the cook-cum-housekeeper—would be at the back working in the outdoor kitchen.

Elizabeth was not to be found in the front room, and he thought she must have decided to take a nap before dinner. He was right. When he climbed the stairs and entered their bedroom, he saw her lying on the bed, seemingly asleep. He was surprised to see she had been so tired she had not changed out of her day clothes. He sat beside her and pushed back the strands of hair that had fallen across her face, noticing that her forehead was damp and there was a sheen of moisture on her skin. Her breathing was shallow and fast, and she was perfectly still.

"Elizabeth?" he whispered, prickles of alarm spreading through his body. "Elizabeth, wake up—what's wrong, my dear?"

Thinking that perhaps it was simply his imagination—that she was perspiring only because of the heat of the afternoon—he decided to loosen her skirt and blouse. He turned her gently on to her side to undo them. As he did, he gasped in horror and sprang back from the bed. The back of her dress and the quilt were saturated with blood. She was unconscious, not asleep, and he knew in an instant the child was lost. But more terrifying than that, even, was the prospect that she herself was in grave danger.

Chapter 23

Chiengmai is the principal city of Upper Siam—or Lanna, as the old kingdom was known—and is enclosed by ancient battlements dating from the thirteenth century. The town itself has broad streets, hundreds of glittering temples, and a population of around five thousand. The people from this part of Siam consider themselves Lao.

The city is set beside the Mae Ping River, on fertile land framed by mountains and forests. It has been isolated from Bangkok for so long that the people of Chiengmai hardly know the country's capital exists—and indeed, they have had their own rulers and have considered themselves a separate entity through much of history. Bangkok certainly plays no part in their daily lives, being more than four hundred miles distant, through some of the most difficult terrain I have ever encountered.

A telegraph line between Bangkok and Saigon in Cochin-China opened, after much pressure from the French government, on July 16th, 1883. However, there are, as yet, no railways, no telegraph, and no reliable postal services between Chiengmai and Bangkok.

With modernizations being uppermost in King Chulalongkorn's mind, changes will come quickly. With them, the country will gain much, of course, but something of its unique character, born of complete parochialism, particularly in Chiengmai, must surely be lost in the process. It is this uniqueness, this stunning character that I have found in my travels, that I would like to help preserve in some small way by telling my readers how it is in 1884, and how it shall never be again.

Sam wished he were still up north, but he had been away for nine months—as long as he'd dared, because his editor in New York would be screaming for his next chapter by now. He had returned to Bangkok to find several letters, months old, from his publisher. Each one noted fine sales for his last book and entreated him to be quick about providing new material while his name remained in his readers' minds.

It would take him some time to write enough for a new book, but in the meantime, his publisher would take each new chapter and sell syndication rights to newspapers and periodicals in America and England, thereby ensuring a steady income for them both. Eventually, the work would be republished in handsome, leather-bound book form.

He had made good progress in the two weeks since his return. There was much he could not write, of course, lest it offend good Christian sensibilities. He was well aware that most of his readers would—at least outwardly—thoroughly disapprove of some of his activities, and because he was a popular author whose work was often serialised in family magazines, he had to consider the readership if he wished to continue to receive the substantial quarterly royalty payments.

He put aside the pages and leaned back in his chair, the leather creaking. It was early evening at the run-down Oriental Hotel, and he could already hear the Scottish merchant seaman in the next room singing to himself, the bottle clinking as he poured himself another whisky.

The Oriental was managed by a former mariner, so attracted sailors who had heard of it from other seamen, as far away as the Caribbean. It had a chequered history, and by the condition of it these days, Sam didn't think it could remain in business much longer. The original hotel had burnt down in 1865, and the current building was a utilitarian, two-storey wooden rectangular design with verandahs on each level and an exterior staircase.

Sam had ceased renting houseboats or houses in his vain attempts at domesticity. He had lost his sudden desire to settle almost as soon as he had acquired it. Perhaps it had been only a whimsical notion borne of his desire for one woman, now unattainable. He wanted to be ready at a moment's notice for a new adventure, for if he remained in one place for too long—especially here—he was sure he would be consumed with thoughts of her and of his stupidity in losing her.

Not that the memory of her had prevented him from seeking subsequent conquests. There had been many, and he had taken physical pleasure in women wherever it was to be found and whenever he felt the inclination and could find a willing partner. There were plenty of jaded expatriate wives seeking excitement in their otherwise tedious lives, not to mention the missionaries' daughters—or the missionaries' wives, for that matter—and the exquisitely delicate Siamese women. Throughout the country he had been offered daughters for the night or forever, as he saw fit. He did not object to a temporary arrangement, unless the woman herself refused him, but a night or a week almost always sufficed before he tired of them and moved on. On one occasion, he had even won a girl in a gambling game at the home of the chief of Chiengmai, Chao Luang Intanon. He spent the night with her, so as not to offend his host, but he could see she was reluctant, so they ended up just talking and sleeping.

He picked up the pages of the manuscript once more and read on, taking up his gold-nibbed fountain pen to make corrections.

The expedition was launched on January 16th, 1884, an auspicious date according to King Chulalongkorn's astrologers. Among the party were Mr Louis Leonowens, British head of the King's cavalry; Mr James McCarthy, an English surveyor on loan from the Indian government who had returned from three years' work in the Siamese jungles only in November past; and myself, a Mexican-American of no particular talent, save that, perhaps, of being able to record the journey for posterity.

During the dangerous north-eastern expedition, McCarthy —with a staff of seven young Siamese surveyors and the Bangkok harbourmaster's twenty-one-year-old son, George Bush—was to map the boundaries of the Siamese and French holdings. It was an important task to the Siamese in terms of national security and diplomacy, and quite a measure of the respect given McCarthy and Leonowens in a country that has been notorious for its distrust of foreigners.

Our route was made perilous indeed by tribes of Haw invaders from Yunnan in China, and Leonowens's orders were to protect the surveyors by driving out or—if necessary—eliminating the Haws. To enable Leonowens to accomplish this, he had been provided with two hundred infantrymen. Unfortunately, from the outset it was obvious—even to a person such as myself, untrained in military disciplines—that most of these men would be of no use in the event of a battle. Leonowens was not at all sure what particular training they had undergone, but it certainly did not appear to be in the art of warfare. The arts of sleeping, eating, and gambling, however, they appeared to be well acquainted with. Trained Siamese soldiers had a reputation as fearsome warriors, and most of this group were nothing like trained Siamese soldiers, that was for sure.

Sam smiled as he remembered the expression on Captain Leonowens's face when he decided to encourage the troops by organising target practice. They had passed through some Mao hilltribe villages beyond Nong Khai and were heading toward Chiang Khan in their pursuit of the Haws, who were said to be only a day or two's march ahead ...

However, the sight of the sacked temples and burned houses, and stories of the villagers—men, women and children—who had been slaughtered without mercy, had unnerved the men so much that they would run off into the forest, forgetting their guns, at the slightest unexplained noise. They did not consider this uncourageous, just common sense. Most had wives and children at home.

Siamese families are very close and even the men are as devoted to babies and children as the women—and they had no intention of being killed in the line of duty. For this, I certainly did not blame them. Self-preservation is, after all, my own philosophy, also. [Sam hastily wrote a note to himself here: "Perhaps not good to admit this lack of heroic quality in self? American and British readers will be disillusioned"].

So, target practice was arranged, and it was a disaster. Leonowens was at first livid, then shocked almost to disbelief, as he discovered the sad fact that most of his men had never fired a rifle. When he demonstrated for them, expertly hitting his target with the first shot, most of them fell to the ground, terrified of the explosion. He retired to his tent in disgust.

Later, he picked out the best of them—about thirty who had at least fired a gun before—and sent packing the remaining 170 to travel on and set up camp in the Lao province of Luang Prabang.

Sam had been reluctant to involve himself in much of the fighting. He would rather have observed from a hillside above and written his impressions for dramatic passages in his book. However, his passive approach was not always possible, for it was evident that Leonowens needed all the assistance he could muster.

We were sure—Leonowens, myself, and the tight band of thirty men who had become his devoted followers—that we would soon be embroiled in battle. The Haws were less than two hours ahead, and we were gaining rapidly. McCarthy, by the way, calmly continued his own surveying duties, using our camp as a base but often disappearing with his small team for days on end, and upon his return—somehow catching up with us if we had moved on— rarely commenting on anything more than the weather, or what birds or other animals he had seen along the way. Never have I met a man so suited to the task in hand, so dedicated and unfazed by the myriad physical discomforts of the tropical jungle. I could tolerate these for months at a time, but McCarthy could endure up to three years at a stretch without, apparently, feeling the need for contact with civilisation.

We had, so far, managed to avoid much hand-to-hand fighting, because with our limited resources, Leonowens had decided it was best to rely on scare tactics and to chase the marauders over the borders whenever possible. Predictably, though, they were becoming suspicious of our actual numbers, we could tell, and one night, a small band of them doubled back from their camp, several hours to the north of us, and infiltrated our own jungle bivouac. Three of them crept in past the watchmen and would almost certainly have murdered us in our beds.

Leonowens, sleeping in a bed roll two feet from myself, has, however, a sixth sense regarding such things, and just as two advanced—one to strangle him, the other to smother me—he leapt up, his pistol at the ready, and fired a shot, mortally wounding one man before the other could turn and run. At the same time, my grip instantly tightened on my knife and I sank the bowie deep into the man's chest. His eyes widened in the shock of one who realizes he is about to die. He fell to his knees and then, sickeningly, on to his chest, from where the knife had protruded. He was dead within seconds. The third, on hearing the shot and the groan of the man I had stabbed, managed to flee, and disappeared into the jungle. His escape was unfortunate for us because he would report back that we were, indeed, a small camp, and not the army they suspected us to be.

It was decided, after that encounter, to pursue them and engage in full battle as a surprise tactic. We pushed on with our elephants for the next two days through the jungle, which the Haws had laid with sharpened bamboo snares. These inflicted serious wounds in some of the soldiers' feet, which slowed us considerably.

Our elephants were overloaded and exhausted, and the crossing of rice paddies became laborious. The men had to make a sort of woven bamboo mat for the elephants in order to allow them passage across the paddies. It looked hopeless at first to myself and Leon-owens, but this ingenious invention actually worked quite well.

We negotiated a heavily-jungled mountain range, and when we reached the town of Muang Ngan, we found it nearly deserted except for one small boy, shivering in terror, who attempted to hide under some pig carcasses. We managed to reassure him that we were his King's men and would not harm him, and he told us that most of the villagers had fled in terror when the Haws arrived, but that many had been killed, including his parents, whose poor bodies lay side by side outside their shack.

The boy had tried to run away, but twisted an ankle, and had hidden in a large half-full water jar until the invaders had passed on. Surprisingly, he spoke to us in French, telling us that two foreigners in the town—French missionaries—had escaped. The boy looked morbid when we made to leave, and he begged to be taken along with us. Leonowens agreed, adopting him as a kind of mascot for the force.

The expected battle did not eventuate that time. The Haws apparently decided a confrontation was best avoided, and had, infuriatingly, broken up into small groups, retreating on their fast ponies back over the borders. Meanwhile, once we reached Ta Tom, we sent the elephants and mahoots back to Nwang Kai without us. The animals had completed their task and were now more of a liability than anything else. Since we had consumed most of the heavy goods we initially carried with us—canned condensed milk, coffee, hard biscuits and salted meats—we were now travelling comparatively lightly, so had less need of the elephants.

Apart from our weapons, which were the heaviest items, each man carried in a canvas bag his bed-roll, pillow, and mosquito net, plus a blanket for the cool Northern nights. Each man had also the following: a small tent, although we used them only if it was raining; a lamp with a supply of oil, as well as candles; a medical kit *with bandages, quinine and fruit salt for stomach disorders; and a set of clothing fit to be worn in a town amongst mixed company. Porters carried two small boats. Leonowens and I carried water filters and used them religiously, although the Siamese seemed perfectly fine drinking directly from the rivers.*

It was becoming well known in Bangkok that Leonowens was something of a hero, after effectively chasing the Haws from Siam, as the story went. After his success, he returned directly to Bangkok to marry Caroline Knox, daughter of the British Consul, Thomas Knox. The wedding took place on August 29th, 1884. Sam was happy for Leonowens, and for a short while fancied the same stability for himself.

To those in the city, the expedition—in its retelling—had become a glorious adventure, which perhaps it was. But Sam knew just how perilous it had been, and he had feared for his own life several times—if not at the hands of Haws, then from disease or misadventure.

The swirling waters of the Mekong had resulted in Leonowens's and McCarthy's boats colliding one night. They had moored them and decided to sleep on them, for some reason. Luckily, McCarthy awoke to a slight noise, discovering that the stern of Leonowens's vessel had turned and connected with his own, and that both had broken their moorings and travelled some way from the camp. They had great trouble in separating the two while avoiding being swamped and drowned.

In addition, when Leonowens's group had re-joined the other men at Luang Prabang, it was to find most of them laid low with jungle fever, contracted most likely from the swamp adjacent to their camp, they supposed. McCarthy and most of his party were also stricken, despite Leonowens immediately moving them to higher ground, and young George Bush was a sad fatality. The dour McCarthy took all these events in his stride, commenting little and always keen to proceed with the job at hand.

As Leonowens headed back to Bangkok and the hardy

McCarthy planned to continue his surveying in the district, despite the onset of the rainy season, Sam decided to re-acquaint himself with Chiengmai. Without the company of others or the thrill of military operations, he had found the arduous daily climbs entailed in cartography to be rather monotonous. He needed a bath, a strong drink, and some engaging company.

A British Vice-Consulate was established in Chiengmai with the signing of a new treaty in 1883, and Mr Edward Gould, a veteran of 11 years' service in Bangkok, was appointed to the position, arriving in the northern outpost in May, 1884. I knew Gould slightly, so decided to visit him and see how he was coping.

Sam had never liked or admired Gould in any way—and the feeling was mutual, he was sure. Sam found the tall, thin British parson's son to be supercilious, uncompromising, and obsessed with his own importance. And he imagined Gould found him, in turn, to be lascivious, undisciplined, and far too swarthy for his liking. Gould was a fool and a bore. What Sam wanted, however, after the rigours of months in the jungle, was some social sport, and he thought Gould's floundering might amuse him.

But first, I decided to call on the chief, the Prince of Chiengmai, to pay my respects. I had met Chao Luang Intanon when I was last in the city, and we had got along exceedingly well. He is a complex character, but a most wonderful host, and I enjoyed several evenings at his home. He served sumptuous feasts, and his guests were entertained with performances of classical Siamese dancing by dancers whose graceful beauty is unequaled in the Orient. There were also exhibitions of Siamese-style boxing, in which the pugilists are permitted to use fists, legs, feet and elbows to overcome an opponent.

The Prince resides, with his household, in a palace magnificently decorated with great chandeliers, gilded screens, and silk-

draped chairs (although the Siamese themselves rarely sit in Western-style chairs, preferring to crouch or kneel on the floor. This is, no doubt, partly because inferiors are required to keep their heads below those of their elders and superiors at all times). Siamese houses of the wealthy often have front rooms decorated in European style, in which they receive visiting Occidentals. However, these rooms are a façade, and beyond them, where the Siamese live, one finds a more traditional scene.

Sam, in fact, felt the chief was rather a kindred spirit. His vaguely-described "household" was, actually, a harem of beautiful wives and concubines, headed by the principal wife, Caho Radchabut, whom the other women appeared to be very much afraid of. There were also many other women in the harem in various capacities as attendants, companions, servants and ladies-in-waiting.

The evening's entertainment began with Siamese-style boxing bouts, the outcomes of which the assembled guests gambled on furiously. Sam enjoyed the classical dancing, more for the sight of the supple, beautiful women—some of whom came from nearby Burma and Laos—than for the art itself.

The prince made it clear that Sam could have his choice of the unmarried women, or several at once if he so desired, and he had accepted the offer, enjoying the company of 17-year-old Burmese twins for several pleasurable early-morning hours.

However, the real business of the evenings began after the dancing and boxing, when dice games were played by the Siamese noblemen and wealthy visitors. The games continued until daybreak, with seemingly endless supplies of money, replenished frequently from each nobleman's heavily guarded stashes of silver and gold coins, and brought by servants who attended, throughout the night, to the gamblers' every need.

The Siamese are not, as a rule, great consumers of alcohol, although they do distill a potent rice liquor called samshu that can have a debilitating effect on the unacquainted. I had always assumed that the people of the region would consume great quantities of tea, having seen many areas of land in the surrounding mountains covered in the crop. McCarthy, however, informed me that the tea grown here—some wild, some cultivated—is not drunk, but rather chewed, much like tobacco in the United States, or betel nut in other parts of Siam. The tea leaves are harvested, steamed, rolled, and then buried with salt in the ground. A wad can be sucked all day, and is, apparently, an excellent stimulant.

It had been a magnificent adventure—superior to anything he had read in a novel—and there was still much to write. But he felt there was something missing in his life. He needed to discover again the true *soul* of an adventurer. To do that, he knew he must do something about his decline: he must see Elizabeth, and the child he was convinced was his son.

Chapter 24

Incredibly, she was maturing into a voluptuous young woman, and he could barely keep his gaze from her, even though at the same time he lambasted himself for being so weak.

"You look five years older than the last time I saw you," he said futilely.

"No, just a year. I'll be sixteen in a few months."

She went over to her father's drinks cabinet. "May I pour you a drink, Mr Taylor? Scotch?"

"Yes, you may. And you know it's not Mr Taylor. Sam will do just fine. We Americans don't stand on ceremony."

She poured him a generous measure of whisky, and a sherry for herself, knowing his eyes were upon her.

"So, what have you been up to while I've been away, Anchalee? Or must I call you Miss Fairburn now that you're so grown up and that there is no longer an elder Miss Fairburn?"

"Anchalee will do just fine," she said, cheekily imitating him. She handed him his glass. "We Siamese don't care much for surnames, you know. Too recent an addition to our identities."

He laughed out loud. "I'd love to be here for your father to hear you say that. So, you consider yourself Siamese, rather than British?"

She scowled, and answered him thoughtfully. "I was born here, and I have as much Siamese blood as British. Actually, let's call it by its proper name—Thai blood. I have never been to England, nor am I likely to."

Despite her seriousness, her low-cut, green silk dress revealed a deepening cleavage, and she felt his glances sweeping over her body, even though he tried to hide his interest. Though she had no practical experience, she was instinctively aware of how much power she could have over him. She planned to use it.

He leaned back and rested one arm along the back of the sofa. Despite her confident maturity, which was as transparent as his crystal glass, he harboured a suspicion that there might be more to her than met the eye. For a start, she had deliberately set out to unnerve him.

"Rather a daring neckline for one so young, isn't it?" he said.

"Do you think so? This was made for Elizabeth, but she thought it inappropriate in her condition, so she gave it to me. Father said I was not to wear it for a year, but … well, here we are."

She swept a delicate finger slowly along the neckline, which served only to emphasise the swell above her bodice—and he knew she was teasing him with her feigned innocence.

She looked at him then back down at that bodice, and his eyes followed hers as she surveyed the pleasing aspect. "I had to have the bodice let out and the waist taken in, but otherwise it was just right."

But the dress itself was of no interest to him whatsoever. His eyes still lingered over her form, and he imagined her without the frock at all.

When she looked directly at him, he caught himself.

"Ah … Elizabeth. Is she expecting again?"

"Yes. Due in May, she thinks. She's so brave to try again."

"What?"

"She lost the last baby. It was just after you left again. She and Joseph were distraught. She's desperate for them to have a large family, which she tells me shouldn't be that difficult, if you know what I mean."

"Well. You must pass on my condolences. For the lost

baby, I mean. So, they're happy together?"

"Very much, she says."

"And the child—the boy?"

"Young Joe's fine. He's walking now, of course. And he's the image of his father." She looked away in mock distraction.

Sam said nothing for a moment and shifted on the sofa to a safer position away from Anchalee.

"Speaking of fathers, where's yours?" he asked.

"Oh, he'll be down soon. The maid went to tell him you were here. I think he'll be most interested to hear more about your travels, although I'm sure he won't be told the whole story, will he?"

"And what would you know about whole stories, young lady?"

"Oh, you know, all the details considered unsuitable for polite conversation in social settings. Especially those concerning the fairer sex." She raised her eyebrows in a knowing expression and emphasised the last word ever so slightly.

He laughed out loud again. "I'm not fooled by you—really, I think you have no idea what you're talking about. But someone needs to teach you to hold your tongue."

"I've tried," Edward called out jovially as he strode into the room. "But I haven't been very effective."

Sam stood and they shook hands. Anchalee had quickly reverted to the girlish bearing she adopted whenever her father was around.

"Anchalee, why didn't you tell me Mr Taylor had arrived?"

She looked slyly at Sam out of the corner of her eye. "I told the maid to tell you. She must have been waylaid."

Edward noticed the glass of sherry on the table beside her. "And I've told you about helping yourself to the liquor. You may pour a drink for a guest, but you may *not* pour one for yourself, until you are twenty-one or married (if your husband agrees), whichever comes first."

"Father, I wasn't drinking it. I poured it only for appearances, to look sociable."

"Yes, but it's still unseemly for such a young girl to have a glass of sherry beside her, whether or not she drinks it."

"I'm not a child any more. I'm old enough to be married, technically and legally," she pouted. "Why, Mrs Jones was only fifteen when she married that old man of twenty-eight last year."

Yes, yes, I'm only too well aware of that."

Sam smiled to himself during the encounter, but quickly straightened his expression as Edward turned back to him to apologise for his daughter's cheekiness. As they went through to the dining room, he glanced at her and shook his finger in playful disapproval—and was startled when she, like a child half her age, poked out her tongue at him.

During dinner, the two men talked of the North and of their respective adventures in various parts of the world. Anchalee was bored with their masculine one-upmanship and stifled a yawn on more than one occasion. She was barely able to get a word in through dinner. Only when the meal was over did Edward address her directly, and then it was to say that he and Sam would retreat to his study for cognac and cigars. His cough had seemed to improve lately, and he had taken to the occasional after-dinner smoke once more. He suggested she might like to sit with her needlework in the front room. "Or, perhaps you should like to retire early," he suggested. Imagine if she'd replied, *No, I'd like to smoke a cigar in the study with you and Mr Taylor, especially Mr Taylor.*

"I'll be in the front room, Father, amusing myself."

Half an hour later, she still sat curled up in the window seat of the front room, immersed in a novel she had borrowed from Elizabeth. Edward maintained that novels were

not suitable reading material for girls—only further encouraging their silly notions of romance and excitement—but she
ignored him, as usual, and read them anyway. Joseph had a
wonderful collection, and Elizabeth said she could help herself to whatever took her fancy. This particular novel, a new
one about pirates and adventure on the high seas, was called
Treasure Island, and her father would have deemed it particularly improper.

"I thought adventure stories bored you." Sam's voice beside her made her jump.

"And I thought you were smoking cigars or something
with Father."

"I told him I needed the water closet."

"Well, this isn't it, is it?"

"Never mind that. I wanted to ask you something."

Her plan seemed to be working. "Yes, what is it?"

"It's about Elizabeth."

"Oh, her," she said, deflated. Her plan *wasn't* working.

"Yes. Do you think you could possibly arrange for me to
see her one more time? There's something I need to ask her."

"I could, but it wouldn't do any good, you know. I'm
sure she'd refuse to see you."

"How do you know?"

"I've already asked her. I mentioned that you'd returned
from Chiengmai again and asked her if she'd like me to arrange a meeting between you. She said no, most definitely not.
In fact, she said she never wanted to set eyes on you again if
she could avoid it." She looked him straight in the eye to dis-
pel any doubt in his mind—of which she could see there was
plenty.

He sighed. "Well, I suppose it's for the best."

"She really is very happily married, even if it did seem
like an odd and hurried match at the time. I'd advise you to
forget the past—forget her. After all, you don't want to cause
any *trouble,* do you?"

He had to stifle his laugh in case Edward heard him from

the study. "And what would you know about such matters?"

"More than you might imagine." She looked down at her book again, as if to dismiss him.

His eyes ran over her once more, and he sat on the sofa and loosened his collar. "How old are you again?"

She did not look back at him. "I told you, fifteen. I'll be sixteen in a few months. Many girls my age are already married."

"Fifteen going on twenty-five," he said wryly. It was becoming increasingly difficult to deny to himself that she intrigued him.

"Won't my father be wondering where you are?" she said dismissively.

"What do you think he'd say if he knew I was in here with you?"

She sat beside him, so closely she could feel his warmth. "He'd probably scold me for leading you astray."

For one fleeting moment, his hand touched hers. He stood abruptly then, remembering he must return to the study. "Perhaps I'll see you at the King's Garden on Saturday afternoon?" he added.

"Perhaps, but don't count on it."

"Who's counting on it?" he added with a grin as he left the room.

She smiled to herself. This was proving easier than she had anticipated, after all.

Physically, he seemed to have rallied. The grating cough and the weak spells became fewer, and he attributed them to some other illness. Perhaps they had been due to the worry that accompanied the high ambitions he had held for his photographic work, and the distress at eventually being discovered. He accepted that his photographic aspirations would never be realised, and he wanted now only to enjoy time with his family. With Elizabeth happily married and Anchalee his constant and witty adversary, he wanted for little, after all.

Business had not been so good lately, and he began to notice some members of the expatriate community—always those he suspected of never having liked him anyway—looking at him with disdain, or simply ignoring him. He knew he had done wrong, but still he could not bring himself to go to Klein to apologise. Instead, he carefully put into storage the wonderful photographs of King Chulalongkorn, knowing that they would never be seen publicly in his own lifetime, but that perhaps one of his descendants would be able to make use of them.

Sam was strolling toward the orchid house, and she saw him before he saw her. It was a perfect opportunity. She turned to her father, who was chatting with an acquaintance, an English businessman who supplied him with photographic equipment.

"Father, I'd like to visit the orchid house."

"Of course, my dear. I won't be a moment."

"Oh, I'm quite able to go by myself. Why don't you stay here and enjoy your conversation with Mr Brightman? I shan't be long."

He nodded his approval, tuned back to his friend, and she sauntered off in the direction of the enclosure.

The air was heavy inside and she wished she could take off her shoes and stockings and walk barefoot. It was so much of an inconvenience to have to wear these ludicrous English fashions. They were so uncomfortable, so obviously unsuitable for Siam. When she was married, she thought to herself, she would dress as she pleased—definitely not "like a young lady", as her father continued to insist upon. Or perhaps she would go about the house naked, even. She was sure her husband would not mind.

She wondered which floor Sam was on. Likely the upper terrace, as it was open to the air, and cooler. She was right. He was sitting on a cast-iron two-seater, and he raised his bowler hat to her as she stepped toward him.

"Fancy meeting you here." He smiled knowingly.

Her plain, deep blue dress of shot silk was now clinging to her in the humid heat, accentuating every curve.

"Why don't you sit down and cool off?"

She did so, sitting just a little closer than what would be considered a respectable distance, and he caught the aroma of rose water and something sweeter on her moist skin.

"I didn't come here because *you'd* be here," she told him. "Father decided we should have a day out."

"Did you follow me in here then?" he asked, amused.

"Of course not. Why should I want to follow *you* anywhere?"

He simply smiled and gazed directly into her startling green eyes.

"How on earth did you emerge into the world with eyes like that?"

She held his gaze without blushing or looking away. "Courtesy of my father. Or hadn't you noticed?"

"I can't say the colour of Edward's eyes has ever intrigued me."

He then lowered his voice and leaned toward her. "If we weren't in such a public place, I believe I'd be compelled to kiss you."

She looked away, as if entirely disinterested. "Well, I don't see anyone here."

"Are you daring me?" He looked around, and then back at her, grinning.

"Not at all," she replied. "I've no desire to be kissed *in that way* by such an old man."

"Old! You watch your tongue, young lady, or I might have to teach you a lesson or two." Suddenly, he grabbed both her wrists and pulled her into his arms, kissing her thoroughly on the mouth, and noticing she did not resist in the slightest.

However, she yielded for only a few seconds, then abruptly wrenched free of his grasp and stood up.

"Excuse me," she said brusquely, "I've already learnt *that* lesson. But I'm not a girl to be toyed with in the garden shed. You'll have to speak to my father if you wish to see me again. Goodbye." With a toss of her head, she walked away, leaving him amused and pondering the fact that she had become an object of such fascination to him.

He had never thought of her as a prospective conquest until very recently. She had always been the little sister, engaging and undeniably destined to be a beauty, but far too young to consider romantic involvement with. But now—as was only too evident—she seemed to be a woman in almost every sense.

Elizabeth was lost to him now, and he was certain of how seriously she would take her marriage vows. She would never leave Joseph. Yet, she was still the woman he dreamed of. While he had been away that past year, he had thought seriously of no other but her, and he had hoped that somehow, when he returned, he would discover her free again. But it was not to be.

His thoughts wandered back to Anchalee. She was young and wild, but he had dealt with perilous situations before—and only recently, at that. His thirst for adventure had not been slaked and the prospect of a dangerous liaison with Anchalee filled him with excitement. It was a challenge he could not resist. She had dared him—and he was certainly a gambling man.

Chapter 25

Elizabeth felt a rushing in her ears as her legs buckled under her and everything went dark. The next thing she recalled was waking up on the sofa with Joseph fanning her face and reviving her with smelling salts.

"Elizabeth, what has happened? Shall I call for the doctor?" he said fearfully.

"No, no, I'm quite well, really. It's just my condition. It sometimes unbalances me for no reason I can determine." Her pregnancy was showing now, at five months, although her generously-gathered skirt did much to conceal it.

"I think you should rest for an hour or so before we go home," Joseph suggested.

She still felt disorientated, and she struggled to remember what had happened before she had fainted. It was Anchalee's sixteenth birthday—January 10th, 1885. There had been a meal, a cake, candles, then... Then it all came back, like a horror story, and she realised she would have to feign her congratulations for the sake of appearances.

She wanted to cry out what she knew to be the truth —that her sister had precociously plotted to tear Sam away from her. But she knew she could not reveal anything without hurting too many others.

Her father knew nothing of her relationship with Sam, but how much pain would this bring Joseph, having him so close? She wanted now only to go home, but she had to be careful not to arouse suspicions. What could she possibly say to the bride-to-be?

Anchalee ushered the men from the room. "Go to your billiards game, and let poor Elizabeth have some peace and quiet."

When they had gone, it was Anchalee who spoke first, sitting beside her and wiping her sister's brow with a damp cloth. "I do hope it wasn't the announcement of my engagement that upset you."

Elizabeth attempted a smile. "No, of course not. Why should it have been? Our ... friendship ... was long ago. And anyway, it was brief, of little consequence."

"Well it has worried me that perhaps you still ..."

"That was more than two years ago, Anchalee. I am a wife and mother now, and I love my husband. I have no feelings toward Sam, one way or the other."

"Then you don't mind?"

"Of course not." She managed to smile, but the expression masked a storm of emotions—shock, disbelief, anger, and a sense of further betrayal—that swirled within her. But she would never give Anchalee the satisfaction of knowing she had caused uch pain. She wondered why she had not seen the reason for her sister's deception before. Half-sister, she reminded herself. "When is the wedding to be?"

"As soon as possible. February 20th. And since you've been so gracious, and so kind in your well wishes, would you be my matron-of-honour?"

It was impossible. She could not bear that responsibility, and she had to make an excuse quickly. "I'd love to, naturally. But in my condition, I couldn't guarantee my health, and I wouldn't want anything to spoil your day. Perhaps you could choose someone else."

Anchalee sighed, suddenly the petulant child again. "But there's no one else I'd rather have. You're my best friend as well as my sister. And here's a secret: despite my skiting, I really don't know anything about ... you know, married life. Sam has been a perfect gentleman, so far. Please help me understand what will happen on our wedding day! I really do need you by my side, dear Elizabeth."

∞∞∞

In the snug billiards room, Joseph and Edward discussed the same subject: the upcoming wedding.

"Are you sure he's a suitable choice for Anchalee?" Joseph lined up his cue and sank another ivory ball.

"No, to tell you the truth, I'm not absolutely sure. But you know how headstrong Anchalee is when she wants something. She's almost impossible to discipline—a trait she inherited from her mother, I'm certain of that. Do you know, Joseph, she had the audacity to tell me that if I didn't agree to the marriage when Sam came to ask for her hand, she'd elope with him, or—worse still—she'd simply live with him without benefit of clergy." Edward cleared his throat then, remembering his own past. "Well, what I mean is, that for a woman in English expatriate society, what the right-thinking members of that society think of her is important. She could be ruined and never marry. There was nothing I could do but give my consent."

Joseph took another shot. Missed. "I must agree that she's certainly wilful—and probably a little reckless, too. However, she does look happy. Then again, the emotions of the young can be fickle."

"Indeed," Edward agreed, sipping his port. "But at least if she is married, I will no longer have to worry about her. And even though I don't entirely approve of Sam, he *is* eighteen years her senior. She needs an older husband. I fear that a younger man simply couldn't control her."

"He doesn't strike me as the responsible type. Where is he tonight, anyway? One would have thought a newly engaged man would be present at his fiancée's birthday dinner." Joseph regretted the biting words as soon as he had uttered them.

"Well, that's true enough," Edward answered. "But Anchalee says she told him he needn't come, apparently. I don't think family dinners are his particular interest. And she said he had to work on his latest manuscript. I think she has romantic ideas about writers."

Joseph tried to keep a neutral expression, wishing he could change the subject, as Edward continued.

"I admit, I once thought him a scoundrel. But I've come to know him better lately. He is a talented writer, we know that. And at his age, of course he has a past—some would perhaps call him rakish. I prefer to think of it as the result of an adventurous spirit." He was now almost chuckling. "In fact, dare I say it, I almost see something of my younger self in him. On the matter of Anchalee though, I always thought it would be a rare man who would catch her attention for long, but I think they are of similar character. And I'm certain he has enough substance to hold her."

"Perhaps it's for the best, then," Joseph concluded as he prepared the table for the next frame. Edward mistook his strained look as merely concentration on the game, and the effects of the port. Joseph rarely drank alcohol, but had consumed four glasses already.

The old Scottish sailor from the next room wasn't such a bad sort after all, Sam thought hazily. The two were propped up on stools at the United Club bar, and—after their eighth whisky—Sam had told him groggily that he should be at his engagement announcement at his fiancée's birthday dinner.

"Hah! Then we have tae hae one mair wee dram, laddie," the old salt drawled, ordering "two large doubles!"

"An nain ay yer waterin' doon tricks wi' 'em," he slurred to the bartender, before looking back at Sam with as intense a gaze as he could muster. "Marriage! A fine institution."

Sam nodded heartily. "Are you married, Jock?"

"Hah! Ye wouldnae catch me faillin' intae that trap." He leaned close to Sam and looked at him with squinted eyes. "Dae ye love her, man?"

"No, I love another."

"Hah! Then that's all reet, laddie." Jock bellowed. "She willnae be able tae get the best ay ye. This calls fae one mair drink!"

Two hours later, things were even less lucid to Sam. He excused himself, leaving Jock—who actually seemed to have sobered up—to entertain another drinker they had met at the bar. Sam lurched into a rickshaw waiting outside, and soon found himself stumbling up the stairs toward his dim room at the Oriental. The next morning, he would not remember how he got home.

At the time, however, all he could think of was *her*. As he drunkenly tried to visualise her face, he realised that he had failed her and would likely never have her again. He fumbled to insert the key in the lock, then suddenly lurched back to the stairs and vomited over the railing.

February 20ᵗʰ, 1885

Dear Marjorie,

It is my sister Anchalee's wedding day, and I have been compelled to tell them, falsely, that I cannot attend the ceremony owing to my present condition. I write this letter to you from my father's house at the very moment the nuptials take place. Anchalee was disappointed, of course, when I made my excuses, but although I am actually quite well physically, I feel that I simply could not go through with it, and I do not wish to spoil everyone's day. I will explain all this, dear Marjorie, but you will first want to know what she wore—and having said goodbye to her just before she set out, I must admit that a more stunning bride was never seen. The dress was of ecru silk with a straight skirt and a fitted bodice—rather low cut but with a soft tulle overlay for modesty, and three-quarter sleeves. She wore a white tulle veil without any other decoration on her head. Rather plain, in fact—dare I say, unfashionable, even—but Anchalee's beauty needs no adornment. She carried a bouquet of tiny jewel-like orchids in gold, mauve and white.

And now my explanation, Marjorie. I must tell you, dear friend, that the man she has married, Samuel Taylor, is the very same I wrote you of some time ago with respect to myself. I must tell you also that when Anchalee made her announcement, I was filled with grief and heartache; my despair has hardly diminished since then.

As you know, Marjorie, he had departed on that long expedition to the north of Siam, and believing myself abandoned, I married Joseph. I can hardly believe, upon his return, he chose my own half-sister, of all people, to be his wife.

Everyone says they make a delightful couple, and I can hardly make comment about the difference in age between them, my own husband being so much older than myself.

Joseph and I continue to pray for a happy event around April.

She put down her pen, wishing she could write the truth to Marjorie. She had told her friend that although she had married in the despondency of her abandonment, she loved Joseph deeply nevertheless, and let her think that their baby, Joe, was the natural issue of their marriage. Marjorie herself was married now, and quite possibly pregnant too. Her letters had become few and far between in the exigencies of distance between them.

Elizabeth folded the pages and put them into her writing compendium. She would have to finish the letter another day, for the wedding party and forty guests would be back to the house soon, and she would have to go downstairs, at least for the cutting of the cake.

Her pregnancy had also furnished her with an easy way to excuse herself from becoming overly involved in wedding preparations, and she was glad she had managed to avoid Sam during the weeks leading up to the event. She no longer even knew what she felt for him. She had written the truth to Marjorie about her feelings for Joseph: she had grown to love him dearly, for his kindness, his gentle ways, and his acceptance of her child as his own. Who would have thought, also, that he would be such an accomplished and considerate lover? It was a shame she could feel no physical passion for him, though she certainly considered she did her duty as his wife. She accepted her situation as the price she had to pay for her sin. She wondered time and time again what Sam would have done had he known of her condition before he had left for Chiengmai.

Physically, Elizabeth felt well. This pregnancy had been much easier than the last from the start. She felt confident now, at six months, that she would not miscarry. She prayed that she had not inherited her mother's weakness after all. But she lay listlessly on the bed in what was now the guest room at her father's house, the very room that had once been her own before her marriage. The blinds were drawn, and as the clock in the hallway chimed the hour, she knew that the man she loved and her sister were now man and wife.

When she heard the party's arrival downstairs, she waited, breathless. Perhaps they were not married after all; perhaps someone would rush into the room, crying out that there had been such a commotion at the church, that Sam had not arrived; or, that he had arrived, but had left before the vows!

But no such messenger came. There was no avoiding it any longer. She would have to put on her new turquoise silk dress and offer her felicitations to the happy couple. From now on, whenever she needed to see her father, there would be the chance that she would see Sam, for he and Anchalee were to live there until they bought and fitted out a suitable house of their own.

Somehow, she managed to tolerate the company and hold her emotions in check, and it was a great relief to her to be able to keep up appearances. She found, however, that she could not face Sam. She had nothing to say to him, but she would have to offer her congratulations if they came face to face. Instead, she managed to avoid him. She glanced at him on only a few occasions during the course of the afternoon—a dark figure in his black morning coat and grey striped trousers —and each time she did, just as she felt he was about to catch her eye, she turned away quickly to engage someone in conversation, or to see that their drinks were refreshed.

At one point, when it seemed as if he would come over to speak to her, she felt a prickling panic. But she was saved when his best man, Mr Louis Leonowens—newly married himself, and full of good cheer—chose that moment to slap his friend heartily on the back, put yet another glass of champagne in his hand, and propose a toast to the beautiful young bride and her gallant groom. There followed short speeches from Edward and then the groom himself.

With all attention on the happy couple, Elizabeth found she was able to drift away and climb the stairs once more to seek sanctuary in her former bedroom and wait for Joseph to take her home.

She never did finish the letter to Marjorie. The next day, she tore it up, knowing she would not write again soon, if ever. She felt as if she were deceiving her old friend, thus it was better to maintain silence.

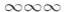

It was a stifling hot April night, and she awoke soaked in sweat. As she had done the previous night, and the night before that, she prayed that her unborn child was safe. For the past week, she had felt no movements within her. But the baby was due any day, and it had been such an uneventful pregnancy, she had not wanted to alarm Joseph by telling him her suspicions. She prayed she was wrong. Neither had she told Anchalee, now newly pregnant herself, news that had devastated Elizabeth anew.

Her back ached and she could not even lie down comfortably. The hot season had sapped her energy, and there had been no respite from the unbearable temperatures. Even at night, it rarely fell much below eighty degrees.

She had begun to wish she could go back to England. For despite her initial joy at returning to Siam, she realised bitterly that the last three years had brought her little happiness, and much pain. True, there was Joseph, but had circumstances not been what they were, she would never have married him. By rights, she should be married to Sam. How different her life would have been if she had followed her first plan to spend a short time in Siam and then to return home and marry her first fiancé, James. There would have been no guilt, no Sam, and no Joseph in her life. But then, there would have been no baby Joe, either—and she could not wish for that.

She sat up and reached for the glass of boiled water beside her bed, but as the first strong contraction gripped her, the glass slipped from her hands and fell to the floor, smashing on the polished wood.

Joseph bolted upright. "Elizabeth! What's happened? Are you all right?"

"I think you'd best send Simon for the doctor. The baby's coming."

∞∞∞

Twelve hours later, as he again waited in the hallway, Joseph was reminded of that last time, when Joe was born. Then, as now, Elizabeth's moans had abruptly ceased. Back then, he had heard the baby's first cry. Now, though, he heard nothing. Perhaps his wife was still in labour, or perhaps she had fainted. He prayed that hers would not be the fate of so many other women in childbirth.

Dr Newhaven, looking tired and pale, emerged from the room soon after the silence, drying his hands on a towel. Joseph rushed toward the open door, but the doctor stepped out, closing it behind him.

"Mrs Shaw is in a satisfactory condition," the doctor informed Joseph before he could form the question. "A fortnight or so's rest will see her substantially recovered physically."

"Praise God. And the baby?" Joseph's voice trailed off as he saw the look of deep regret on the doctor's face.

"I'm sorry, Mr Shaw. The baby was stillborn. There was nothing to be done. A little girl, perfectly formed. We cannot tell what could have gone wrong, but it happened at least a week ago."

Joseph hung his head in grief at the loss of his child, his perfect daughter, another innocent life that had been taken from him. He knew, though, that he had to be brave for Elizabeth.

When he entered the bedchamber, Elizabeth was propped up in bed, her face blank and so pale, her eyes closed. She opened them and looked dully at him as he sat beside her on the bed. "I'm sorry," she whispered helplessly. "So sorry."

He could not bear to look at the little blanket-wrapped bundle in the crib. But he tried to be strong, for Elizabeth's sake, even though he felt like weeping forever. He held her cold, dry hands in his.

"Hush, my darling. You must never, ever blame yourself. The doctor said it couldn't be helped, that there was nothing anyone could have done."

"No, it's my fault. My mother was the same. That's why I was her only child. The doctor said I probably inherited the weakness from her."

"Then there must be no more pregnancies."

"No, Joseph, no! I want to give you children, more than anything."

"I would rather have you than ten children. I won't put your life in danger, nor subject you to further grief. Besides, we have one perfect child. He is enough."

"But Joseph, he's not your..." She caught herself before her words could be more hurtful.

Joseph put a finger to her lips. "I could never love a child more than I love Joe. He is ours—yours and mine. That's all that matters. The three of us, together."

"There is such goodness in you, Joseph," she whispered through fresh tears.

"Let's be happy with what God has given us already. With Joe. The three of us together."

As he sat quietly with Elizabeth, Joseph vowed never again to put her in this predicament. He had been celibate for many years previous to his marriage, and could be again. For her sake, because he loved her so.

∞∞∞

On a breezy, cool-season day in December that year, Anchalee gave birth to her first child, after an intense six-hour labour. The baby was a seven-pound girl with chubby cheeks and a thatch of dark hair on top of her head. They called her Kesri, after her maternal grandmother.

Chapter 26

She twisted nervously at a handkerchief as the carriage trundled along New Road toward Edward's residence, where they were to celebrate Christmas midday dinner. It was an occasion she could not make an excuse to be absent from—and besides, she owed it to Joe, now two-and-a-half, to give him a joyful day surrounded by his family. It was the first Christmas he was old enough to really participate in.

Since the wedding in February, she had seen little of Sam or Anchalee, or even of her father. Edward's health had deteriorated since then, and he had been receiving visitors and a diminishing number of clients only at home, instead of going out himself as he often used to. Strange, after having such high hopes for his work just a few years before, he had seemed to lose all interest. Elizabeth supposed it must be his health problems. For a time, the cough had seemed to improve, but after the wedding, it had returned, worse than ever, though he insisted it was really nothing to worry about. The climate didn't suit him, he said.

Then there was Charlotte, whom Elizabeth and Joseph had named and buried on the same day. Since then, the birth two weeks ago of Anchalee and Sam's daughter had brought back to Elizabeth the pain of her losses. Thank God for Joe. Elizabeth had not seen her niece yet: today would be the first time. She had previously excused herself with a cold, saying she did not want to pass it on to Anchalee or baby Kesri.

Christmas, however, she could not avoid. They were compelled to attend a family day with all the trimmings. As they progressed along New Road though, the driver suddenly pulled the coach over, leapt down, and crouched by the side of the road. Joseph looked out the window, craning his neck to see the road ahead. Every other Siamese within sight had done the same as the driver. It could mean only one thing.

"It's the King!" Joseph cried excitedly. He opened the door and helped Elizabeth out, then picked up Joe as they stood respectfully to watch the scene, able to do so because it was commonly understood that European foreigners would not be expected to kneel before the King.

The King's barouche, drawn by six horses, was approaching. Behind was a procession of horsemen, followed by the carriages of His Majesty's favoured wives and children. It was unusual for the monarch to ride out in his carriage so early in the day, Joseph thought. Like many wealthy Siamese, he rarely ventured out until late in the afternoon, when the heat of the day was beginning to dissipate. Joseph surmised that this early jaunt was indeed because it was Christmas; that His Majesty—being a superb diplomat and statesman—wished to acknowledge the day for the benefit of his foreign friends. Indeed, high-ranking members of the diplomatic community were invited to dine at the Palace later that day.

As the King passed, Elizabeth and Joseph bowed their heads, noticing that within the four-seater carriage with him were several of his elder sons. It took a full fifteen minutes for the royal procession to pass, and only when he was sure it had, did the driver jump back into his seat. "My King," he said proudly as they set off again.

Anchalee bustled them inside to the front room, where

she had pinned up Christmas decorations found in an old box in the cupboards under the stairs. Elizabeth vaguely remembered the streamers and baubles from Melbourne, and thought they must have come on the ship with herself and her mother all those years ago: extraordinary items to have brought to Siam, she mused.

Edward sat in a chair near the window and did not stand to greet them. Elizabeth was shocked to see how thin he had become and how grey his skin looked. He was 57, but looked at least 10 years older. His voice, however, was just the same, and he smiled brightly when he saw his grandson. Kesri was asleep in her crib at the back of the house, watched over by the maids as they prepared Christmas dinner to Anchalee's directions. Truth be told, Anchalee had no real interest in Christmas, but she did it for her father—secretly, she wondered if this would be his last.

Joe rushed to his grandfather, clambered on to his knee, and Edward began telling him a jolly tale about the pirate Long John Silver, from Mr Stevenson's new novel. In his fine ship with its black rippling flags, Joe rode the waves, a parrot upon his shoulder. All too soon though, the merriment stopped when Edward began to cough. The fit was so bad that Elizabeth had to lift Joe off him.

Anchalee hurried back into the room with a glass of whisky, into which hot water had been added. The coughing subsided then, and he put away his handkerchief—careful not to allow his children to see it was spotted with blood.

"Have you called the doctor about that cough?" Elizabeth said, deeply worried. "It's not getting any better."

"Nothing wrong with me," he replied gruffly. "Just can't seem to shake this cold." But he did seem to improve after the whisky, colour returning to his face.

Sam stepped into the room then, and if Elizabeth had expected any tension between them, it did not arise. He shook Joseph's hand and knelt to say hello to Joe. She almost gasped when she saw the two of them close together. The likeness was alarming, and she was certain it was obvious to everyone in the room that they were father and son. They both had the same dark wavy hair, dark brown eyes and olive skin, and the identical cheeky grin. Of course, Edward was the only one present who she knew for certain was not aware of the truth. Anchalee and Sam, she more than suspected, had already confirmed in their own minds what was so evident. But she worried mostly that her father would notice—and that the shock of the truth, if he were to discover it, would send his health into further decline.

Sam stood and poured champagne that had been cooling on ice specially brought in from Singapore. He seemed perfectly content, polite but almost detached, and she could scarcely believe he had once been her lover and was the father of her son.

As they chatted and sipped the champagne that had been served in delicately engraved crystal coupes, she realised she was staring at him. When he returned her gaze, she felt the colour creep up her face, but—for a moment of madness— still could not avert her eyes from his. She knew him well, and with that look—the way his eyes met hers and the slight tilt of his head—she knew he had not forgotten a thing. It unnerved her, to say the least, and she forced herself to look away, knowing that he must have seen the longing in her eyes. There could be no secrets between them, no matter how hard she tried to conceal her feelings. When he looked away from her, it was to stare momentarily at Joe, and she was convinced then that he knew the truth. Indeed, anyone who half suspected it need only look at the boy and then the man for their suspicions to be confirmed.

The maid entered, announcing in Siamese that dinner was served. To her discomfort, Elizabeth found she was seated opposite Sam. She didn't know how she could bear it, yet to have asked to be moved would only have been conspicuous. She ate almost nothing of the first course, a hearty vegetable soup, and remained mostly silent during the conversation.

When everyone had finished and even Joe's bowl was clean, she had still taken only a few mouthfuls, and had then set down her spoon.

"You've barely eaten a thing, Elizabeth. Are you unwell?" Edward asked. He looked much brighter than he had done when they arrived.

"No, not at all. It's delicious." She made an effort to swallow two more spoons of the heavy soup.

"I'm teaching Noi to cook more English food," Anchalee said. "The chilli doesn't seem to agree with Father these days."

"Nonsense!" Edward protested. "She mollycoddles me."

Elizabeth smiled fondly, grateful he had broken the tension. She was glad of something to take her mind off the man sitting opposite her. The main course was a feast of roast pork, corned beef, duck, and a huge baked and stuffed fish on a silver platter. The room buzzed with conversation, and Elizabeth ate only because she didn't wish to draw attention to herself again. Yet, she hardly tasted the food. Flamed pudding and custard followed, and they then withdrew to the parlour for coffee, fresh fruit, and port. The tropics were not suited to the consumption of stodgy English food, but no one could deny that it had been a magnificent dinner. It would have been almost a sacrilege not to have celebrated Christmas with a traditional meal. The men loosened their collars and rolled up their sleeves. Young Joe had eaten too many chocolates and had expended so much energy opening his many presents that he had fallen asleep in the window seat, his thumb in his mouth.

As they were sipping coffee, Edward was suddenly stricken by another coughing attack. His face reddened, and he didn't seem able to catch his breath. It had worsened over the previous few weeks and the frequency of the attacks had increased. There was an overwhelming atmosphere of unease in the room. Anchalee held a glass of port to his lips. She hardly dared face up to what it meant. Again, he attempted to dismiss it and grabbed a napkin to cough into. But when the spasm subsided, he seemed almost to collapse, dropping into his chair in exhaustion, the napkin slipping to the floor in front of him. Elizabeth went to pick it up and gasped. Silently, she held it out to Anchalee. All were quiet, except for Joe, who had woken up and, sensing something deeply wrong, had begun to sniffle.

Elizabeth broke the silence. "Father, why didn't you tell us about this?"

"I'll be fine ... in just a minute." There were specks of blood on his chin.

"I had no idea it was this bad," Anchalee said.

"Didn't want to worry you," Edward said, almost in a whisper. "Doctor says nothing can be done. Just have to hope for the best. Should go back home to England, or perhaps to France for the weather, he said. But this is my home. I don't want to leave."

He seemed to recover then, and beamed a bright smile. "Why all the long faces? I have had an interesting life. No one lasts forever, but I plan to be around for some time yet, don't you worry. Anyway, it's Christmas—let's try to enjoy the day."

Insisting he was fine, and that they not hover over him, he took Joe on his lap and his grandson soon settled happily once more.

Elizabeth poured more coffee and tried to convince herself that miracles happened and that a recovery was possible. Deep down, though, she knew she was fooling herself. It was obviously consumption, and sooner or later it would claim him as it had so many others.

It must have been a particularly bad day for him, because he said he would not go with the rest of the family to the afternoon Christmas service. He was emphatic that they all go on without him, that he would be fine at home with the staff. However, Elizabeth was equally determined that she would stay behind with him.

The house was quiet after the others had gone out to the carriage, and she sat talking to her father for some time until he decided to take a nap. She helped him up to his room, closed the drapes, and told him she would be back to check on him in half an hour.

In the parlour, she too decided that an afternoon nap would be expedient. She lay back on the chaise longue, but just as she was drifting off, the sound of the door opening disturbed her.

"It's all right, Noi, you can clear the dishes away later," she mumbled, her eyes still closed.

"I don't think I'll be doing that," a male voice replied.

Her eyes sprung open. Sam was leaning in the doorway, his eyes upon her.

She sat up abruptly, wide awake now. "I thought you'd gone to church. Did you forget something?"

"Those who know me well understand the only time I visit a church is for a wedding or a funeral. I told the others I preferred a long walk to work off that Christmas dinner."

Self-consciously, she smoothed her skirts and wished she had had time to push her hair back into place—then immediately berated herself for such thoughts. What did it matter what he thought of her?

"Um—oh," she stammered. "Well, what did Anchalee have to say about that?"

"She accepts I'm not religious. Neither is she, to tell you the truth, at least in the Christian way of understanding it. She knows that I'd get restless during the service and probably end up walking out. She doesn't want to be embarrassed in front of the congregation by such a heathen. Anyway, she only goes herself to please your father."

"Quite," Elizabeth replied, trying to sound haughty. There was an awkward pause.

"The boy's growing fast," he said suddenly. "Why did you name him Joe?"

She had not anticipated this. "After his father, of course."

"Shouldn't the boy's name be Sam, then?"

"What?" she exclaimed. "Whatever makes you say that?"

"Elizabeth, admit it, just to me. He's my son. He's the image of me, anyone can see that. This story of him being born early is nonsense."

"How can you say such a thing? It's simply not true." She was desperate now, panicking.

"It's Joseph's side of the family—a Maori ancestor actually," she said, lying and unable to look at him. "That's why Joe is dark. And I believe *my* great-grandmother had jet-black hair and olive skin. Perhaps Spanish, we think."

He stepped toward her, almost begging her with his eyes to tell him the truth. Then he said gently, "Let's have no more of this pretence. You don't need to keep up appearances when you're with me. You and I both know the truth."

She felt tears pricking her eyelids. "Sam, for pity's sake, can't you see what you're doing? The hurt you could cause? He's Joseph's son. Joseph is the only father he knows. To admit anything else would be immeasurably cruel. It would help no one. Let the past remain in the past. You're married now." She felt the back of her throat constrict with a sob.

She buried her head in her hands. Unexpectantly, suddenly he was kneeling beside her, taking her hands in his. With a start, she realised there were tears in his eyes.

"If I had known. If you had only told me. I would have stood by you, would have m—."

"Don't!" she interrupted before he could say it. "What's done is done. We cannot change it now. Don't you see that? I do love my husband, I swear to you I do. There's no better man on earth. And you're married to my half-sister. You and I must remain apart—forever."

"But we're not apart. I am your brother-in-law. Can't we at least be honest with each other? I don't want to take Joe from you, or to cause harm to anyone over this. I know Joseph is a good father to Joe, and I accept it. I'll be happy just to watch him grow up—even though he will know me only as his uncle. But please, Elizabeth, admit to me now, once and for-ever, that Joe is my son. Then I promise I'll never mention it to you again, if that's the way you want it."

His voice was earnest, and she gave up. "Very well ... it's true, Sam. Joe is your son. And Joseph knows it."

"Why didn't you tell me you were expecting, Elizabeth? I can't understand ..."

Should she tell him? That her own sister, now his wife, had designed their estrangement, only so she could wed him herself? But what service would it do anyone to tell? It could not change anything between them. And words once spoken could not be rescinded. They were both married: there were innocent children to think of, and her father, in his illness, did not need to suffer the stress of a family crisis. She would have to tell him only half the truth.

"Before I could tell you, you'd gone, and there was no way to contact you—you know that. The shame of bearing an illegitimate child was too much. I couldn't bear the thought of my child labelled a bastard, and of myself a fallen woman forever with no hope of marriage. I confided in Joseph, and when he made his proposal it was as much a shock to me as it must have been to you when you returned and discovered it." She paused to retrieve a handkerchief from her sleeve and wipe the tears from her eyes. "But I could do nothing else. There was no other way. I had to accept. He saved me and my—our—child."

"I understand. But you know, the most ironic thing of all is that I'd decided that when I returned, I would ask you to marry me. I wrote to you, but the letter was lost." He sat be-side her. "Can we forgive each other, Elizabeth?"

"Forgive? There's nothing to forgive. We're both to blame. We're victims of circumstance—and our own stupid-ity." She wanted to add, *and Anchalee's meddling.*

She paused. "But just ... just knowing that you ... that you would have ... It's a comfort, that's all. I'm sure we can be good relatives, even friends."

"You in your marriage and I in mine?"

"That's the way it must be, Sam," she whispered. "I think you should go on your walk now."

He took her hands one last time, and held them tightly in his own. Then all at once, he stood and left the room, without saying anything further. She walked to the window as the front door closed softly, and watched him walking away until he was out of sight.

Chapter 27

It was a lengthy document, written in Siamese on paper that had thinned and yellowed with time. His wife's maiden name was written on the envelope in childish script, and at first, he thought it likely to be an old letter from a girlhood friend, or some such. Had he seen it elsewhere, he would probably have dismissed it, would not even have bothered to discover its contents. However, he had not found it where one might expect to, such as in the box where she kept her other correspondence tied with ribbons. It had been so deliberately hidden, in a place where he would normally never think to look —for anything—that he was sure it was something important, something she wanted to keep from him.

But why? He knew just about everything there was to know about her—or so he assumed. She had been a young girl in her father's house when he had first met her, and that had continued to be so until they were married. What secrets could she possibly have, except the usual childhood ones? She had always had a vivid, if immature and girlish, imagination, and had probably been influenced by the romantic novels she read. But to the best of his knowledge, she did not keep a journal, not being much interested in writing herself.

Lately, however, he had noticed a change in her. She had become fiercely protective of their daughter, Kesri, and spent hours talking to her in Siamese and telling her nursery rhymes the child could not possibly comprehend. She also spent hours at the little Buddhist shrine she had insisted on setting up in her dressing room. Edward would have been disappointed if he knew, for he had done his best to ensure she was brought up as a Christian.

Edward, though, was now confined almost exclusively to his own room, and since Anchalee ran her own household, she could, as she had said to Sam many times, do as she pleased for the first time in her life. When not with Kesri, she was often lighting incense and paying respect to the Buddha. Sam hardly considered himself a Christian, and he didn't care one way or the other what religion his wife followed, but he was concerned at the amount of time she spent alone.

One day, he'd come home much earlier than expected from the United Club, where he had been to meet Louis Leonowens, who was to tell him of his latest adventures. Leonowens had left the King's employ amicably to become a Borneo Company agent at Raheng and Paknampho. Although there was now a fortnightly mail service between Chiengmai and Bangkok, via Moulmein, and an unreliable telegraph service between the two via Raheng, Leonowens liked to travel back to the capital periodically to conduct important business in person. He had returned briefly in late 1884 to apply to his boyhood friend and former employer, King Rama V, for permission to log a teak forest—the Mee Tuen—that he had come across above Raheng. Permission was granted, and Leonowens became the first foreigner to lease a forest in Siam. Others followed soon after.

But Leonowens had arrived at the United Club that day excited and impatient. "I'm to be granted an audience this afternoon, Taylor," he said, slapping his friend on the back. "So, I must be away very shortly. Can't miss an appointment with His Majesty, can I! Come and visit us in Raheng."

Oh well, Sam thought wryly to himself after Leonowens had departed, he had been brushed aside only for the King, after all. Sam ate lunch alone that day, finished his whisky, and went home to surprise Anchalee, thinking he might be able to interest her in an afternoon tryst. Anchalee had, he pondered thankfully, a most unladylike appetite for physical pleasure, and he flattered himself that he had taught her everything she knew. He had not found it necessary, even once, to seek erotic encounters elsewhere. That, at least, had remained constant, even after the birth of Kesri, and it was still something of a surprise to him that he had managed to stay faithful to her.

He let himself into the house quietly, knowing the servants would all be asleep at that time in the afternoon. If he was lucky, Anchalee, too, would be napping in bed. She always slept naked, and he loosened his collar in anticipation as he climbed the stairs.

As he moved up the hall, however, he heard her voice, low and muffled. He thought she must be talking to their daughter, but when he looked in on the nursery, the baby was already fast asleep, tucked into her crib, with a maid asleep on the mat beside it.

So, who was Anchalee talking to? He pushed open the door to their bedroom and saw that her dressing room door was closed. She continued talking behind it, and he could just make out some of her words. "I won't fail you," he heard, "... for what she's done ... I promise."

It crossed his mind that perhaps she was having an affair, that behind the door was another man with his wife. But the words he heard were incongruous. There was nothing for it but to put his eye to the keyhole.

He was relieved to see no one else in the room, but frowned when he saw what she was doing. She was on her knees before the shrine, with a thick envelope clutched to her chest, and, uncharacteristically, she appeared to be crying.

She stood, lifted the Buddha image, placed the envelope in the hollow of its stand, then replaced the idol carefully. She then knelt on the floor again, brought her hands to her forehead and lowered her head to the ground three times before the shrine.

He left the room quickly and went downstairs.

Twenty minutes later, she came across him in the living room, reading a newspaper and smoking a cigarette. She helped herself to one from his silver case and lit it.

"Your father wouldn't approve of your smoking," he said.

"In case you hadn't noticed, I'm no longer Daddy's little girl," she replied, sitting on his knee and blowing smoke into his face.

She wore only a thin silk sarong, and one side had dropped open, revealing her breast, heavy with milk. He circled her nipple with a finger and it responded instantly. She placed the cigarette carefully in the ashtray and stood up then, allowing the garment to fall in ripples to her feet. She was magnificent, he thought, and the slight rounding of her belly—the result of her recently attained motherhood—served only to increase the desire in him. She turned and walked from the room, and he paused briefly, knowing the game well, wondering where he would find her. She rarely favoured their bed for love-making and would often tease him by hiding, heightening his anticipation.

A few minutes later, he found her—it was never very difficult—spread across a trunk in the boxing room under the stairs, lying on her stomach, with her long hair sweeping the floor. She was pretending to read a book. As he entered the room, she glanced sideways at him.

"Did you want something, Samuel?"

He did not answer, but undid his flies, not even bothering to take off the trousers.

He hadn't forgotten that other matter, but it would have to wait.

∞∞∞

A week later, unable to restrain himself any longer, Sam

confronted her with what he had discovered, retaining the document from the Buddha in her dressing room one day when she was out. She stood on the opposite side of the bedroom to him, her fists clenched in rage, while he held up the incriminating sheaf of papers. They could not raise their voices too much, because Edward and the servants would hear.

"And what gave you the right to go through my personal papers and to steal my property—the only thing I have left of my mother?" she hissed at him. "You bastard—I hate you!"

"Well, you certainly didn't marry me because you loved me, did you, Anchalee?"

"What would you know about love?"

"Not as much as you know about hate and vengeance, it would seem."

"You don't know what you're talking about."

"This is all the evidence I need." He waved the pages at her.

"How do you know what's in it? It's in Siamese, a language you're hopelessly inept at."

That barb hurt, but she was right. "I had it translated. Your mother's dying wish—that you should repay Elizabeth for some imagined wrong—it's the ravings of a madwoman!"

"How dare you speak of my mother that way? Elizabeth ruined her—Elizabeth killed her."

"So, you married me, hoping she'd be consumed with jealousy."

"That's right. And you're Joe's father, aren't you?"

Sam looked startled. "How would you come to that conclusion? I believe Joe's birth certificate names Joseph Shaw —Elizabeth's *husband*—as the father."

"That means nothing," she countered. "I know what I see. I'm not as ignorant as you seem to think. You're the father of that child, and anyone who has eyes can see it plainly. I know, Joseph knows—everyone knows. Everyone except my father, and I'm sure the shock would kill him if he did. Perhaps that would make Elizabeth happy—to have killed both my parents. I'll bet she just wishes I'd drop dead as well, so she can have you. You're not fussy after all, are you?"

He stepped up to her, grabbing her tightly by the arm. "You little bitch. Don't you think you can make a fool out of me, because you never will. I'll always have the last word."

"Let go, you're hurting me," she said through clenched teeth.

He relaxed his grip slightly, but still held her. "Not until you listen to me. I didn't find that letter by rifling through your belongings. I have better things to do. I came across it by accident."

"By *accident*? Where I put it? And it has *my* name on the envelope in English, so dullards like yourself can read it. That alone should have told you not to open someone else's private mail."

"I saw you put it there, when you were praying—or whatever it is you do in there."

She jerked away from him. "Have you been spying on me, you disgusting voyeur? Can't you leave me alone for one moment?"

"It's time you starting showing me some respect. I'm your husband, or had you forgotten?"

"How could I forget," she said scathingly, "when you prove the fact to me so often? Anyway, it's none of your business. This is between Elizabeth and me. Or do you still care for her more than you dare admit? I've seen the way you look at her, like a starving vulture, even though you are well *serviced* at home."

"And that's none of *your* business. In any case, your plan hasn't worked out the way you'd hoped. Elizabeth is happy—she loves Joseph, and he's a better husband to her than I could ever have been."

Her eyes narrowed with spite. "Yes, but wait until she discovers the truth about why she isn't married to you."

"What do you mean?"

"Her marrying Joseph was a result of my plan, too." She

wanted to hurt him and she allowed a moment of silence to pass as she went to sit on the edge of the chair nearest the doorway. She was stealing herself to run, should he become violent with anger. This was her moment to triumph.

"I forged a letter from her to Joseph, asking him to think of some way to make you leave so she didn't suffer the embarrassment of having to put you off herself, as an unsuitable match."

"You did *what*?"

"You heard me." She had never seen him this wild. His eyes were menacing, and she had no idea how he would react. "Joseph sent you to Chiengmai to get rid of you. And she thought she'd been abandoned—pregnant and unwed. It was so much fun to watch her squirm! Until Joseph became the good Samaritan and married her himself. That, I didn't plan."

Did you know she was pregnant?" His voice was low and threatening.

She stood next to the door, her head held high, a scathing look on her face. "Yes."

"You disgust me. You're not fit to be related to someone like Elizabeth. And to think she loves you, trusts you ..."

"So, you see, it's me who is having the last word now."

"I wouldn't count on that," he retorted. "You've punished Elizabeth, but she's at least in a loving marriage. On the other hand, you, *Mrs Taylor*, are destined for a long and loveless marriage that you'll regret from now to forever."

"Nonsense, I'll divorce you."

No, you won't, not without my consent—which I'll never give."

"A Siamese court will grant me one, with or without your consent."

"I'm afraid not," he said, more calmly than he felt. "You like to think you are Siamese, Anchalee, but in the eyes of the law, you're an American subject now that you're married to me. And before that, you were a British subject, by your father's line, which is the only one that counts. Siamese laws don't apply to you. They never have. Does the truth hurt?"

He threw her mother's letter to the floor and, still clutching the translation, he left the room, brushing past her and leaving her feeling as if there were rocks in her stomach.

She sat there, stunned. What hurt most was the realisation that she would not have divorced him, even if it were possible. She was doubly bitter because she had come to care for him. She had tried so hard to be what he wanted, to keep him in her arms. But she knew he would never feel for her as he did for Elizabeth.

As she sat expressionless, staring at the yellowed pages strewn across the floor, she pondered her future. He would remain her husband, if that was what he had to do to punish her, but it would be a marriage in name only, for she vowed never to sleep with him again. He would find out how strong her own loathing could be. She resolved to drive him into Elizabeth's arms again. And what would transpire when Joseph discovered his wife was having an affair with her brother-in-law, the real father of her child?

She went to the nursery, where Kesri was sleeping soundly. She touched the baby's tiny hand and gently stroked her soft, downy cheek. At least one good thing had come of their union.

∞∞∞

A week later, they were invited to the Shaws' house for Saturday afternoon tea and croquet on the lawn. For the sake of appearances, they agree to behave as if everything were normal. Sam had decided it would do no service to Elizabeth to burden her with her sister's betrayal. He warned Anchalee that he would be watching her closely, and would not allow her to do anything to further hurt Elizabeth.

The sisters sat in the shade, Anchalee holding Kesri, and

Elizabeth trying to keep Joe in her sight. There were snakes in the long grass at the edge of the property, and he had not yet acquired the sense to avoid them. Elizabeth had once found him poking at one with a stick, and it was fortunate, on that occasion, that the serpent was not of a venomous species: Siamese cobras were common, and whenever Joe was playing in the garden, Elizabeth lived in constant fear of him being bitten, though the gardeners were vigilant in attempting to keep the property clear of them.

"The mosquitoes are so dreadful this year," she said to Anchalee as she scratched again at her ankle. Both had been bitten a number of times already. "They're actually biting right through my stockings. I can remember my mother sitting with a large paper bag tied round her legs. Perhaps we should revive that practice."

Anchalee was unusually quiet today, and she made no reply. Elizabeth suspected she and Sam had had a disagreement.

"Anchalee, is something wrong?" she ventured.

Elizabeth had finally been able to make peace with herself over the fact that Anchalee had married Sam. Talking to him at Christmas had actually been a relief and she had decided the best thing to do was to try to re-establish her relationship with Anchalee.

But her younger sister looked distracted and disinterested.

"Anchalee?"

"No, nothing at all," she answered.

"You seem preoccupied."

Anchalee smiled then, but the expression was not one of warmth. "Being a mother is tiring," she offered. "I didn't realise quite how exhausting it would be."

"Don't worry. It's not so unusual to feel an emptiness. Men simply can't understand why we would feel that way. You're so fortunate to have such a beautiful girl. And before long, I am sure you'll find you're expecting again."

Anchalee nodded, but did not smile. It wasn't likely she would bear Sam another child, she thought bitterly, when they were no longer even sharing the same room. Then a thought crossed her mind. Perhaps Elizabeth would have another child to him when their affair began. For she was sure it was only a matter of time. She could see it in their eyes when they looked at each other. She took heart at the idea, and Elizabeth mistook her smile for one of a brighter mood.

She decided to hurry things along a little. "You see, dear Elizabeth, my husband does not care for me, overly."

Elizabeth's mouth dropped open. "You must not say such things! I'm sure you are mistaken."

Anchalee shrugged. "No. I should never have married him." She looked directly at her sister. "The feeling is mutual, you know. He does what he likes, wherever he likes, if you get my meaning, and I simply don't care."

Edward was dying, he knew it, but he was not ready. He had always imagined himself in old, old age, reflecting on a long and eventful life, entertaining his grandchildren, or perhaps even great-grandchildren, with stories of old Siam. But he had never thought he would be a victim of this decrepit, premature infirmity at a time when he should still be full of vitality.

He felt pathetic in his slippers, unable even to smoke his pipe any longer. Although he appeared a sickly old grandfather, in his mind's eye he was still the adventurous young photographer with a host of experiences still to live. But time was escaping him. As his condition worsened, he had much time for contemplation, and at least all was prepared and his affairs were in order. He had seen to that, with Mr Harbeck's help.

His daughters believed he wasn't really conscious of much that went on around him any more. But he had learned more about his family in the previous few months than he had known for years when he was fit and active. Somehow, his senses seemed to have sharpened, and he had become more aware of the gestures, expression and feelings behind their words.

He supposed he had been a shallow man throughout his life, and would be remembered as such. Until recently, he had never felt the need to analyse his life or any of his actions or their consequences. But now that all he could do was think, he saw things more clearly.

He saw, for example, a streak of vindictiveness in his younger daughter, where before he had seen only girlish spirit. He saw a sense of loss in his elder daughter; and he saw his grandson, Joe, growing into the image of his father, Sam.

Oh yes, he knew Sam was Joe's father. That would surprise them. It was one of the first things he had realised in his new hyper-sensitive state. When one had more time to observe and ponder than anything else, one often came to the truth.

Such matters did not overly concern him, however. It was for them and their future descendants to resolve. Not to mention, he thought wryly, the sins of their father. For he had sinned greatly, he knew.

It was not in his nature to regret, but now that he could see his end, he wanted to confess. He wanted absolution, wanted to leave this earth in the knowledge that he had declared his wrong-doings. If only to ease his conscience, a death-bed peace would be a fine thing indeed.

Chapter 28

It had begun. She could see it in their secretive glances whenever the two families were together. It was apparent in the way his fingers lingered when he passed her a drink. What was most surprising was the suddenness of the affair. It had started at the consulate ball, only a few nights after they had spent the afternoon in the Shaws' garden complaining of mosquitoes and snakes, the day also that Anchalee had confessed to Elizabeth that she and Sam no longer cared for each other. She had made an excuse not to attend the ball, encouraging Sam to go alone, knowing Elizabeth would be present.

When Elizabeth had greeted him at the ball, she had been nervous at first. He'd asked her to dance while Joseph was busy talking to friends across the room, and before she could reply, he had whisked her away.

His arms encircled her for the first time in more than three years. "You're as beautiful as ever," he whispered.

She did look wonderful. The fitted pink satin gown accentuated her figure, which at twenty-five had filled out attractively. Her hair was put up softly and coiled round the top of her head, and she wore a double choker of pearls, and long white gloves.

As they danced and he drew her closer, she thought of

how much had happened since they had first danced together. It seemed like an eternity ago. For a few minutes, she felt as she had back then: young, thrilled by his attention, excited about what could happen. Then she was jolted back to the present. Joseph wasn't far away and it would be improper of her to dance with another man more than once. She pulled away a little from Sam's embrace, but he drew her back and asked if he could see her alone outside the ballroom, naming an alcove in the hallway.

"I don't think I should answer that," she said, extracting herself from him and fleeing to the safety of Joseph. A few minutes later, however, she excused herself and walked out of the ballroom and down the long corridor toward the ladies' restroom. Only, she did not turn into it. Instead, she continued along the passage until she reached the curtained-off alcove. She stepped in and closed the curtain, her heart beating strongly, her breathing shallow, her hands trembling. What on earth was she doing?

A few seconds later, the curtains parted quickly, then closed again behind him. Without a word, he took her in his arms, and his kiss was deep and longing. She did not pull away. He moved behind her, and—as he kissed her neck—his hands roamed from her waist to caress her breasts.

He wished he were touching her bare skin instead of the tight satin, but he could feel the warmth of her body through it as she arched her back against him. Much as he wanted to, it would be impossible to undress her there in that small space. Instead, he gently guided her down on to the cushioned seat, kneeling between her legs as he raised her skirts and kissed her smooth, milky-white thighs.

I can't let this happen, she repeated to herself, but her thoughts were soon lost, no longer any pretence of refusal or resistance, as she felt him stroke her gently, intimately. She relaxed against the cushions and forgot everything but this moment and him.

Later, when she returned to Joseph, he noticed a faint

sheen on her forehead. She lied, so easily, when he expressed concern at her absence, asking if she were unwell.

"Sorry, I ran into Caroline Hooper in the ladies' room, and you know how she can talk," she gushed. "I simply couldn't get away!"

It was true, she had seen Mrs Hooper in the ladies' cloakroom a few moments ago, although she had not actually spoken with the woman for longer than two minutes.

At that instant, Sam passed by, and on his arm was a beautiful and very young woman, the unsullied daughter of a naval captain.

"Actually, Joseph, if you don't mind, perhaps I *am* a little tired," she said abruptly. "I think I should like to go home, after all."

∞∞∞

Anchalee knew none of these details. She knew only that sometime between February and the current month, April, the two had become lovers again. But as much as she wanted now to create a crevasse between the families—one that would last their entire lives—she would do nothing more while Edward was still alive. He had always been good to her, and she loved him dearly. She wanted him to be at peace when he died—for he *was* dying, and they all knew it.

The consumption had deepened in the four months since Christmas. The coughing fits were more frequent and the blood soaking his pillows and handkerchiefs more voluminous. He was confined to bed most of the time, although once or twice a week, she sat him by his window so he could look down at the garden he had always enjoyed so much. His hair had turned white and his speech was slow. He now looked twenty years older than he was, but he never complained, and one day by the window, he said to her, "I've had a good life,

Anchalee. I've known love and happiness. I only wish your mother were here today. I regret ...' The remainder of what he wanted to say was lost in a spasm that sent him back to his bed. When it subsided, he was too exhausted to talk again.

April was the hottest month of the year, and the oppressive heat further depleted his strength. His appetite had all but disappeared, and he would take only weak chicken broth or a few spoons of rice.

One morning, Anchalee simply found him dead in his bed, propped up against the pillows, his mouth open as if frozen in mid-sentence. He looked quite peaceful and composed. Beside him was his writing compendium, on which rested a page with the beginning of a letter in his spidery hand. It began, "My dear family, do not judge me harshly for ..." and broke off. He had either paused for thought, or at that moment had left them forever, dying with regret on his mind. She imagined he meant to say something about her mother and perhaps about Elizabeth's, also. She tore up the page and threw it away. Later, she would find the pen he had used, which had dropped to the floor beside the bed.

She sat in the chair beside his bed for more than an hour, staring at the walls. Until she alerted them all, it was as if he were not really dead, but merely sleeping. Most of the time, when she was a child—not so long ago in years—it had been just Edward and herself, until Elizabeth had returned. Now, excepting their children, Elizabeth was the only living blood relative she knew. Edward had been her last link with her mother, even though he never spoke of her. Anchalee was still only seventeen, but she felt much older. And with the death of her father, she knew that her youth was well and truly behind her.

The funeral was held a few days later. Joseph gave a special reading and Sam attended church for the first time since he had married Anchalee fourteen months before. They stood apart in sorrow, neither of them a comfort to the other. Elizabeth clung to Joseph's hand when he returned from the pulpit.

Then there was Edward's will, which his solicitor wanted to read that same afternoon. Elizabeth would rather have waited. It seemed so final, and there was, after all, nothing complicated about it: the house, his archives, and some personal effects. He seemed to have had no other assets, apart from the photography business, which had dwindled away to virtually nothing, anyway. Nevertheless, Anchalee had agreed that Mr Harbeck would speak to them after the wake.

They journeyed back to the house after the funeral. As she sat on the sofa in the parlour, sipping a cup of tea and only half listening to the subdued conversation around her, Elizabeth caught the eye of Sam across the room. He glanced toward the door and she knew what he wanted her to do. They had joked about getting away during a family get-together, and now he was acting on it. Despite her grief, she felt the blood rush through her veins at the thought of him. She also felt a surge of guilt. Could she do this on her father's funeral day? But she was desperate for him: desperate to escape from this morbid gathering.

He had already left the room, confident she would follow to meet him in the old studio, which her father had not used for more than six months before his death, and which had become one of their rendezvous favourites. She told Joseph she needed to get some fresh air, and when he offered to go with her, she insisted hastily that she preferred to be alone. He understood completely, he said.

Anchalee watched from across the crowded room as first her husband, then her sister, slipped out toward the back of the house. Did her sister have no shame? Could she defile even her own father's funeral with her infidelity?

Sam waited for her in the darkroom off the studio, having let himself in with the spare key they kept hidden under a rock in the garden. He locked the door behind her. Twenty minutes later—they dared not exceed that limit—Sam returned to the house, his absence hardly noticed, he thought, while Elizabeth sat in the garden, looking out toward the river.

As always, after she had been with him, she felt utter remorse, and agonised over how long she could continue deceiving Joseph. She had prayed for the will to resist Sam, to tell him it must stop, but each time he touched her, her resolve vanished. She knew it was unforgivable, but she could not help herself—even as she felt herself sinking lower and lower into a well of lies and deceit. Not to mention the danger of the natural consequences of physical intimacy: they had not been very careful, and she vowed to at least change that.

She did not, however, feel any remorse at all in regard to Anchalee. Although she had tried to let the past be, when their affair had started again she had been reminded just what she had lost because of her sister. She had even tried to raise the subject with Sam, but he had placed a finger over her lips, his other hand caressing her back, and she had lost herself once more in their passion.

Joseph came across her sitting alone on a two-seater cast-iron bench. He sat beside her and took her hand. She said his name as if she were about to tell him something, and he turned to her. But no sooner had she spoken than she stopped and told him it was no matter.

Sometimes she wanted to confess to him, but she could never find the strength to utter the words. She knew she meant everything to him, and it would surely ruin him if he were ever to discover her adultery. How would she even begin? Had she been about to tell him just then? She wasn't certain exactly what she had meant to say. She knew only that after today's encounter, she felt more shame and regret than ever before. Somehow, she had to end it with Sam. Joseph was too good a man to deserve the trauma she would bring on him if he discovered the affair.

Anchalee called through the open window that lunch was served, and Joseph stood and brushed his trousers with the back of his hands. They were covered in leaves and twigs from the seat: the garden had become overgrown and neglected during Edward's last weeks, when it was important to maintain a hush in the house so as not to disturb him if he were sleeping.

Joseph offered his arm to his lovely wife, his heart breaking for her grief at the loss of her father, and she walked inside with him, accepting condolences from the many people who had gathered to mourn Edward's passing.

The guests departed soon after lunch, and Elizabeth, Anchalee, Sam, and Joseph waited for the solicitor in the dining room. At two o'clock precisely, Mr Harbeck arrived. He expressed his regrets at Edward's death, put on his gold-rimmed spectacles, and began to read from the document before him.

The first part of the will was straightforward. It bequeathed the house and contents, except Elizabeth's mother's belongings, to Anchalee. Elizabeth was to take anything of Charlotte's she wanted, and there was a sum of cash allocated to her. Then there were several small bequests to friends and trusted employees. Nothing unexpected there.

Mr Harbeck continued reading. "I should like to bequeath the remainder of my estate, which consists largely of moneys in cash, to be equally divided between my grandchildren, Joseph Edward Shaw and Kesri Taylor, and held in trust until each attains the age of twenty-one, or upon marriage, whichever is the earlier. In the unfortunate event that either grandchild should pass away before reaching his or her majority, the money is to be donated to a charitable organisation nominated by his or her mother—or guardian, as the case may be."

Mr Harbeck removed his glasses and looked up from the paper. "Are there any questions so far?"

Anchalee spoke up. "Yes, Mr Harbeck. How much money

is to be in trust for the grandchildren? I can't imagine my father's cash reserves amounted to much."

"On the contrary, Mrs Taylor, Mr Fairburn was a very wealthy man. Particularly since he preferred to live on the earnings from his photographic business, rather than deplete his inheritance."

There were astonished looks round the table. "His inheritance?" Anchalee continued. "His father died years ago, and his mother last year. I didn't think they left much, except the mansion in England. Any money left has to be spent on its upkeep—and his brothers refuse to sell the family seat."

"Not his parents, Mrs Taylor. In the 1860s, he inherited a very large sum of money from his grandparents, who bequeathed the bulk of their substantial estate not to their children, but to their grandchildren—as he himself has done. I believe he was in Australia at that time and made a trip home to England to settle those financial affairs."

"I remember him going to England!" Elizabeth exclaimed. "Now it makes sense, why he left and why he was gone for so long."

"Quite," Mr Harbeck said, clearing his throat. "And the money remained untouched by him. As you all know, I'm sure, he was not an extravagant man. It seems he preferred to work for a living and to forget that he was, in fact, independently wealthy."

"So exactly how much do the trust funds contain for his grandchildren, Mr Harbeck?" Anchalee pressed.

The solicitor cleared his throat once more, embarrassed. He disliked surprising clients, even with good news. "The capital would amount to approximately £300,000, Madam."

There was a collective gasp.

"That means Joe and Kesri will each inherit £150,000 pounds," Elizabeth remarked, hardly able to believe the sum.

"No, Mrs Shaw," Mr Harbeck said, even more embarrassed. "I meant £300,000 *each*. And it doesn't end there."

There was stunned silence.

"In addition, further interest accrued—over the next twenty ears and eight months in Miss Taylor's case, and eighteen years and two months in Master Shaw's case—will substantially add to the capital; in fact, will exceed it."

He went on as they remained dumbfounded. "There *is* one provision, however. In order to make claim on the funds, each beneficiary will be required to present himself or herself at the London offices of Harbeck & Sons in person at the appropriate time, which is on or after their twenty-first birthday. Mr Fairburn had stipulated that an international transfer of funds from England would not be possible."

There were questioning looks from the family members. Was there a catch?

"That is the only provision," Mr Harbeck announced in reply to their unvoiced concern. "Mr Fairburn, I believe, was keen for his grandchildren to know something of their heritage, for them to visit England, even if only once during their lives."

Thinking the reading was at an end, they began to talk excitedly among themselves. Mr Harbeck cleared his throat once more, and they looked at him again, almost fearfully. What now?

"There is one final bequest, and I'm afraid it's a ... a secret clause."

"A what?" Sam asked.

"Yes, it's for Mrs Elizabeth Shaw to hear only, and I apologise that I shall have to ask the rest of you to leave the room."

Again, there was a shocked silence, but eventually the others slowly pushed back their chairs and did as Mr Harbeck had instructed.

Mr Harbeck closed the door behind them, sat in front of his papers once more, and peered at Elizabeth over his half-moon reading glasses. "I expect you think this rather unusual, Mrs Shaw," he said quietly.

"To say the least, Mr Harbeck. I'm extremely anxious to know what this is about."

"Yes, of course. But I'm afraid I'm not at liberty to divulge very much to you today."

"Whatever can you mean, Mr Harbeck?"

"Well, in fact, this clause has attached to it a short letter to you from your father, which perhaps you should read yourself." He handed her a sealed envelope that had been attached to the back of the will. She opened it shakily, and withdrew two pages dated six months previously, October 31st, 1885.

My dear Elizabeth,

As I write this letter, I know I shall die soon. Although at this point you are aware of my illness, the gravity of it I must keep from you as long as possible, given your present condition ...

She paused and took a deep breath. Since he had written this final letter, this grandchild had also been lost. How disappointed he must have been. First his wife, and then his daughter had failed. She was relieved only that he never knew the depths to which she had sunk subsequently. She read on.

The fact that you are now holding this letter in your hands means that I have indeed passed on. Do no grieve for me, my child, for I have had a full life, and my children and grandchildren have brought me more joy than I deserve.

Elizabeth, I must assure you that I have never forgotten your dear mother. She was my first, and, despite everything, my only true love. Nor have I forgotten how my selfish actions forced her to leave us, forever. I have always felt that in so doing, and then in sending you away from me, I deprived you of something precious that could never be replaced. Although I know your grandmother did her best, I realise that I denied you your own mother's true and abiding love.

Elizabeth, my dear, this is not the only thing to have haunted me in my last days. Recently, I have had time enough to reflect on the mistakes I made in my life, and I must tell you now of the reasons why I left Australia for England so abruptly, and—as it transpired —permanently, in 1867. Indeed, it is also the reason why I needed to be so far from Australia, and—as a consequence—why Siam is now your home.

You might remember that the main reason I returned to England was to oversee some financial matters, which you now know to be my considerable inheritance from my grandparents. I was, naturally, eager to ensure that my brothers did not appropriate my share, as the will stipulated I must accept the funds in person within one year of the reading of the will, or the bequest was forfeited to them. Another reason, I have to confess to you, was to escape, at least for a while, from an increasingly difficult marriage to your mother, one which had become unbearably full of guilt and disappointment.

But there is one other reason, Elizabeth, which you shall discover for yourself in due course, that compelled me to leave you and your mother in Melbourne for so long. it has been kept all these years, since 1867, in a bank vault (but not in my father's and brother's bank, you understand) in England. I am the only person who knows what is inside.

This particular item of great monetary value has personified all my wrongs and all my evils. By locking it up, I believed I could put it out of mind. But not so. And because it has represented such evil to me, such ugliness in myself, I have prayed all these years that one day I could do something to atone; that the evil might eventually be turned to good. I have arranged for Mr Harbeck to wire his head office in London on my death and to request his package be sent to you, accompanied by a paid guard.

I am sure that you, my first daughter, will know what to do with my last bequest. I ask only that you keep this matter a secret until after it arrives—then I leave it to you to inform whomever you see fit, and to do something honourable with this legacy to bury its evil forever. All will be revealed soon.

Your loving father,

Edward Fairburn

She turned the pages over, wanting—needing—more. But there was nothing.

"Mr Harbeck, you must tell me immediately what this is about. It has frightened me half to death. Whatever can it be?"

"I'm so sorry, Mrs Shaw: I know virtually nothing. And what little I do know, I've sworn under oath to keep confidential in perpetuity. Mr Fairburn wanted to do this in his own way. I'm afraid you'll have to wait until the package arrives. It's being shipped, with its guard, I believe, as we speak."

He stood, shuffled the papers in his folder, and put them into a well-worn brown leather briefcase with "Harbeck & Sons, 1820" embossed in a corner in small gold letters. "I shall be in touch soon. Good day to you, Mrs Fairburn."

After seeing the solicitor out, she went, ashen-faced, to join the others in the drawing room.

"Well?" Anchalee asked, agitated. "What's the big secret?"

"A ... a family matter," she stuttered.

"I'm family, of course."

"No, to do with my mother and myself. Just a letter, really. Nothing of interest to anyone else at this point."

Her reply was so obscure and her manner so withdrawn that no one urged her to divulge more. She vowed to herself that she would tell no one until she knew for herself what the package contained and what its consequences could be.

Chapter 29

Anchalee could see no reason to delay much longer. While her father had been alive, and before his will had been read, she feared that perhaps he could have disinherited her, or even Kesri, if he discovered the truth. Not that she had harboured the least idea of the fortune her father had owned. *That* had been a genuine surprise to everyone. But now that Edward was gone, and Kesri's inheritance was assured, containing more money than Anchalee could even have dreamt for her daughter, it was time to act.

Still, one thing disturbed her. She liked Joseph a great deal. He had always been kind to her—and, indeed, to her mother—and she regretted having to hurt him. She justified it by forcing herself to believe it was her duty to tell him what was going on now between the illicit lovers. He had a right to know, she told herself.

She went to see him three weeks after the funeral, on a day she knew he would be alone. It was a Thursday afternoon, when Elizabeth was always out helping at the Library Association, which had been established by a group of American women in Bangkok in 1869 and which was the city's expatriate population's major source of English-language books.

The look of astonishment, of disbelief, then of utter despair on his face was something she would remember for the rest of her life. For a moment, she had wavered when he asked her in a barely audible voice to repeat what she had told him. Her words had sent him reeling, and—for an instant—she considered telling him she had been mistaken, that she had not meant what she had said.

"Joseph, I'm sorry, but I do believe that Sam and Elizabeth are conducting an improper friendship—an affair, to use another term."

"But how? When? I cannot believe it!"

"I didn't want to either, Joseph. But I can't deny the truth any longer, nor have I the right to keep it from you."

Slowly, as if suffering from some infirmity, he sank into a chair in the front room where they were talking. He spoke quietly, defeated. "Are you absolutely sure of this, Anchalee? It would be a dreadful mistake to make."

"I've made no mistake, Joseph. Mark my words. I ask only that you confront Elizabeth with this. Then you'll see."

"But how could this happen? I ... well, I trusted her. Trusted her completely to—." He stopped in mid-sentence, his voice breaking.

"I'm sure you don't wish to know the sordid details, but they've been meeting secretly."

Joseph held up a restraining hand and shook his head slowly. "You're right, Anchalee, I don't want to know the details. But tell me one thing. How do you know this for certain?"

"My husband kindly told me himself," she lied.

"Why would he do that?"

Her eyes filled with melodramatic tears. "We had a dreadful quarrel, Joseph. I'd suspected him of having an affair for some time, but I was quite prepared to forgive him, especially if he promised me it meant nothing. I'm a mother now, and I cannot ... attend to him as much as I used to. Forgive me for speaking so frankly. Perhaps he felt lonely.

"Joseph, I could have turned a blind eye to some ridiculous interlude with a servant, or some married woman I didn't know," she continued. "But my own sister! He seemed almost proud of himself. He even said—and I don't want to believe this, perhaps he was just angry—he even said he'd married me to get to Elizabeth! Can you imagine? All are harmed by his actions." She dabbed at her eyes with a handkerchief, and he did not see that those eyes were perfectly dry. "There's no question of divorce, of course. I won't countenance that. But I thought it my Christian duty to inform you."

He almost wished she hadn't. "So, what now?" he said in a small voice. "What shall we do?"

"I'll leave that to you. But it must not continue."

"Of course not."

"I'm truly sorry to be the bearer of such hurtful news. Would you like me to sit with you for a while? Order some tea, perhaps?" She did feel a stab of conscience seeing his pain.

"No, no thank you. I think I'd like to be alone. This has been a terrible shock."

As she departed, Joseph sat momentarily with his head in his hands. Had he made a mistake in marrying Elizabeth? He had done his utmost to please her, and obviously it was not enough. He could never compete with the brooding good looks and excitement of a Sam Taylor.

Suddenly, he flared with anger. Damn the man to hell! As he shook his fist in frustration, he accidentally knocked over the fragile glass vase on his desk, filled with stems of purple orchids. It shattered in a thousand pieces on the hard-wood floor, the orchids lying limply among the glinting shards. He knelt among them and sobbed.

Anchalee heard the smashing glass as she was closing the front gate behind her. She imagined him to be so angry, he was throwing things at the wall. Now Elizabeth was for it! Her work was done.

∞∞∞

Elizabeth decided not to consult the family physician Dr Newhaven, who had advised her never to have another child. He was bound to ask awkward questions and to want to speak with her husband. And as she well knew, it was not possible that Joseph could be the father.

Instead, she saw Dr Daniels, an American who was new in Bangkok and not acquainted with her family. She needed to be discreet. In the happy event of a false alarm, word was less likely to circulate that she had even suspected she had been pregnant.

"Congratulations, Mrs Shaw. All your symptoms tell me that you are indeed expecting a child," the doctor informed her brightly.

Internally, fear gripped her like a collar of ice, and if she had been standing, she felt she would have fallen to the floor. Externally, though, she had to remain calm for appearance's sake. "Is there any mistake?" she managed to ask. Yet having been pregnant before, she knew there was not. The nausea of this morning was suddenly back.

"Unlikely, though possible," he replied. "But your own experiences are the best guide. Now, any previous complications? You say you have one son already."

But she was miles away and didn't hear him. It was too late even to cajole Joseph into marital relations and to pass off an early-born child as his, she was thinking.

"Mrs Shaw? Are you ill?"

She gathered her wits and tried to present an appearance of normality. "Oh no, doctor, I'm as well as can be expected. A little overcome by excitement, I think. What was it you were saying?"

"I was asking if you had had any complications in your previous confinement?"

"Oh … no, no. Everything was perfectly normal," she lied. If she started telling him about her previous pregnancies and the disastrous results, he would want to know who the attending physician was so they could compare notes.

"Good. Well at a best guess, I think you can expect your child to be born around November, Mrs Shaw."

She thanked the doctor, saying wearily that she would return for an appointment in due course, while already searching desperately for lies and excuses. The irony was that she and Sam had already ended their affair. She realised, however, that she must have conceived as soon as it had begun.

After the funeral, they had met only once more in the old studio.

"It isn't right, Sam," she had told him. "I *cannot* live with myself. To give in to these … these desires is a sin against God."

At first, he had tried to convince her to continue their liaison, but his efforts were, in reality, half-hearted. He, too, was realising the futility of it, not to mention the potential volatility. "You're right, of course. I didn't think we could go on like this—not really. It's too intense, too dangerous."

"Sam, we are not free to indulge ourselves. It can lead nowhere, except to ruin. And Joseph …"

"Yes, Joseph," he had interrupted, gesturing impatiently. "I understand completely."

And he had walked away.

In the three weeks since that meeting, she'd felt as if she were spinning like a top. And in those weeks of dizziness and confusion that followed, she had begun to suspect the truth—but still denied to herself that it could be real. She had even blamed her lack of monthly cycles on the grief caused by her father's death. She had never been particularly regular, anyway.

But now, the worst was confirmed. What were her choices? Tell Sam and abscond with him to their own island paradise somewhere where no one would know their past? Would he abandon his own wife and daughter to go with her when it was most likely the child would die before it was born, and a possibility that she would, too? The notion of illegally terminating the pregnancy was out of the question, the thought of it almost more frightening than that of admitting the truth to Joseph.

With a dread greater than any she had experienced before, she realised there was no other solution. She must tell her husband and face the consequences. He was a gentle, good man, who at least would not act violently toward her. She had no fear of that. But he would be crushed by her betrayal and he would surely never love or trust her again.

Their marriage would be ruined, for she was sure he would never forgive her. How could he? She could barely comprehend her own stupidity in blinding her to the likely result of their affair.

All too soon, her carriage drew up at the house, and reluctantly she walked up the path. In another few minutes, her life would change forever.

Perhaps she could delay telling him. Another day? An hour? A few minutes more before the axe fell? Then she realised that delay would gain her nothing.

Joseph opened the door, and she was so mired in her own misery that she did not see the look of torment on his face. If she had, she would have realised immediately that he knew. He followed her into the front room and she turned to him, without taking off her hat or gloves. There were already tears in her eyes as she prepared to say what had to be said.

"Joseph, I have something to ..." But the words died in her throat as he told her bluntly to sit down, before she could even begin.

She did as he asked, and when she looked up at his face, she saw something she had never seen there before: desolation, darkness, and above all, desperation; he had the look of one who had been betrayed by the person he loved most.

"My God, you know, don't you?" she whispered.

He nodded, not meeting her eyes, but looking past her. "Anchalee came this afternoon. She knows, too. He's admitted it, and it was she who told me."

"Joseph, I swear to you it's over," she cried, realising he could be speaking only of the affair itself. The worst remained to be said, and her tears began. "I beg you to believe me. I love you, I love you!"

She slipped from the sofa and grasped his trouser legs with both hands. He disengaged himself and stepped away, leaving her on the floor.

"How could you do this to me—to us, Elizabeth?"

Tears continued to course down her face, and she lay on the floor and beat it with her fists. "I don't know, I don't know!" she cried. "I ask God to strike me down, to punish me, for there is barely any greater sin than what I have done."

Joseph knew he could not crack. He still wanted to take her in his arms and comfort her, but he also knew that he must not do that at this moment. The tragedy of it all was the worst. He had saved her from that devil's arms, only to see her fall back into them once more. Was it not his failure, too, for not anticipating the danger?

"Get up, Elizabeth," he said.

She struggled to the sofa, trying to control her grief, though her body still convulsed with sobs. Her face was ashen, and she was consumed with fear. But now was not the time for further cowardice.

"There's more than you know, Joseph," she whispered. "More than anyone else knows …"

"I've already told Anchalee that I have no wish to know the sordid details."

"You must know this one," she insisted weakly, and

forced herself to continue. She would tell him the worst, but in that instant decided she would not reveal the fact that they were married only because of a letter forged by Anchalee. She could not do that to him.

She felt as if her lips were almost fastened together as she fought to say the words she needed to.

"I am expecting his child." And she hung her head in shame.

Joseph's legs seemed to crumble beneath him and he sank slowly into an armchair, his head buried in his open palms. His cry of 'No!' was little more than a strangled groan. Now she would be fighting for her life.

When he spoke again, it was mechanical. He felt numb and drained of emotion. "Elizabeth, you could die. Are you certain of this?"

She spoke rapidly through her tears. "Yes. I've just come from the doctor's surgery—a new doctor, for discretion. He—Sam—doesn't know."

"When will the child arrive, if it lives?"

"Late in the year. But Joseph ... I'll leave, of course. I'll not shame you with this. It's God's punishment and I must suffer it alone with the unborn child, even if we both die. You must want well rid of me now. I'll pack my things. I can go back to England. I'll take Joe with me."

He shook his head, confused. "I cannot contemplate this so quickly. But I cannot accept what has happened, either. I shall pray for the strength to find forgiveness. Only God can be our judge, after all."

He looked at her incomprehensibly, with a sudden burst of emotion. "Why? Why in God's name have you done this?" She snapped her head up at his rare use of the Lord's name to curse.

"Joseph, I cannot explain myself. I knew it was wrong, of course I did. I knew what I was doing ... yet I was somehow blind to it at the same time."

"Can you even begin to imagine the hurt and repercussions of your actions for years—even decades—to come? Forever? The shame I feel, the failure? Yes, it's my failure, too." He seemed now almost to be speaking to himself, desperately trying to understand what had happened, and she dared not interrupt him.

"In the last few hours, I've asked myself why I married you. I told myself at first that I was doing it for you. There were those who did not approve of the school teacher marrying his former pupil. But a long time ago, I promised your mother I would watch over you. I told myself that marrying you was a Christian act to save a young woman's reputation; to save her from ruin and rescue her unborn child, also. Oh yes, I know— I am no hero, not really. Part of me was thrilled to be marrying such a young and beautiful bride. And now I am paying the price of my pride.

"There is more. I see now that I didn't do it for you at all. I did it for myself, because of the guilt within me, and because I wanted a life like other men. I believed that because I had saved you from disaster, it would ensure your loyalty. Now I know I was wrong to expect that. My own pride in myself has been my ultimate undoing."

She saw now how completely her actions had destroyed his faith in human nature and any esteem he had for himself as a truly good man. "What will happen to us now, Joseph?" she ventured.

He looked at her with empty eyes. "I don't know. I must pray for guidance. I think we must spend some time apart."

She stood, her body trembling with trepidation. "I shall pack my suitcase at once."

"No. You have nowhere to go. A woman and child alone —a hotel is unsuitable. People will talk, and that's the last thing I want." He shrugged, too broken to talk any more.

She watched as he walked slowly from the room. A short time later, she heard the front door close. He was gone, and she would not blame him if he never returned.

∞∞∞

Joseph walked along New Road to the riverbank in Yannawa district where the Protestant chapel stood, and where he knew he would find Reverend McFarland. It was the same church in which Joseph had consoled a pregnant Elizabeth three-and-a-half years before. He carried a small leather bag containing a change of clothes, his Bible, and little else.

Farang in Bangkok seldom walked along the road, as they would arrive at their destination covered in dust or splashed with mud from numerous puddles, depending on the season. There were potholes everywhere and so many vehicles traversed the street erratically—victorias, trishaws, rickshaws, food carts—that it made strolling uncomfortable and inconvenient.

Joseph did not care, and he waved away the bemused rickshaw-pullers who continually stopped beside him, calling out cheerfully, "*Pai nai?*"—where are you going? In fact, as he walked, Joseph had already decided where he was going, and it was way farther than any rickshaw-puller could take him.

Reverend McFarland had been urging Joseph to visit the American mission station at Petchaburi for some time. "Quiet and peaceful," he had said of his old home of several years, and it seemed to Joseph as good a place as any to seek solace from his torment.

The reverend gentleman could see that Joseph was under some sort of strain, but asked him no questions when he insisted he wanted to leave for Petchaburi immediately. Reverend McFarland simply made the arrangements, and even offered to take over the younger man's classes at King's College while he was away. The reverend was also headmaster of the college which had been established in 1878 at Nantha Uthayan Garden, Suan Anan district, Klong Mon, for sons of the Siamese nobility.

In Petchaburi, the newly-arrived Reverend W. G. McClure and his wife would be grateful for Joseph's company, Reverend McFarland assured him. "Perhaps you'll like it well enough to stay a while, and to set up your family there," he added hopefully.

It was simple enough to recruit able young missionaries for Bangkok, but it was quite another matter to find those willing to travel beyond and take up the Church's work in jungle outposts. Many missionaries did not endure long in such places. They would arrive, full of enthusiasm and idealism, only to leave—or even to die—within two years, once the difficulty and discomforts of the life took their toll. To make matters worse, conversions among the Siamese were rare.

∞∞∞

Petchaburi was not terribly isolated, and the mission had high hopes for it. The town was 100 miles southwest of Bangkok and was becoming increasingly popular as a resort —frequented by foreigners as well as Siamese—where it was possible to revive one's spirit and delight in the fresh air and more sedate pace of life. The King himself had a palace there, where he and his court spent part of every hot season.

On the journey, Joseph was the only passenger in the roomy houseboat, which was just as well, because he didn't think he would be pleasant company for anyone at that time. The six oarsmen rowed throughout the night, and to his surprise, Joseph slept well. He arose in the morning to eat a few mouthfuls of plain steamed rice, refusing the crew's offer of chicken curry and fish sauce, not because he couldn't stomach the spicy Siamese food—his constitution had become remarkably resilient over the years—but because he had no appetite. He would not force himself to eat more: fasting might even enable him to think more clearly, he hoped.

Moving downstream, his anguish would occasionally recede as he gazed appreciatively at the serenity of life along the river. They passed men in small fishing boats, children frolicking in the river, mothers attending to their laundry, and it all seemed so uncomplicated to him, though he knew that in reality, it probably wasn't.

A large white bird flew with the boat, flapping from tree to tree with a raucous "ark, ark" each time it took off. As far as he could see beyond the river were rice paddies, the bright green seeming supernaturally verdant, and every now and then, a small thatched hut on stilts.

On reaching Petchaburi in the early evening of the second day, Joseph was amazed to find it a sizeable town of 20,000, with a number of double-storey brick houses, a leafy main thoroughfare, a substantial market, and numerous glittering temples. The sparkling royal palace, built by the late King Mongkut, stood on a hill overlooking the town.

The only permanent foreign residents were two missionary families, and Reverend McClure was pleased indeed to welcome Joseph and to show him the church.

"We could do with a fine teacher such as yourself, Mr Shaw," he said. "And the company of your family would be a very welcome addition to our community."

On the third morning, Joseph awoke renewed, feeling as if at least some of the burden had been lifted from his shoulders. He knew now what he must do. It was time to return to Bangkok, but only briefly to make the arrangements. If only Petchaburi were even farther from the capital, he thought to himself as the houseboat drew away and his new friends waved goodbye from the landing.

∞∞∞

They sat like strangers, stiff and formal, in the front room when he arrived home. She had received no correspondence at all from him since he had left the week before, and she had been afraid she might never hear from him again.

It seemed now that he was no longer a defeated, sunken man. He held his head high, and he spoke with a strong, unwavering voice:

"For more than three years now, you've been the centre of my life, Elizabeth. You, and then Joe to complete our family. It wasn't difficult for me to accept that you'd been with another man before I married you. As you know, our situations were quite similar, and I couldn't condemn you for making a mistake, as I, too, had transgressed. And you and I had not the slightest hint of an understanding before that time. I believed you'd learnt the same terrible lesson I had.

"I don't consider myself a harsh or unforgiving man. It's not in my nature. But this ... this has tried me beyond all else."

She nodded. "You're right, Joseph. And I cannot ask you again to ..."

He held up a hand. "Let me continue. I don't wish to cast you out, Elizabeth. You are my wife and I'll see us through this, despite everything. Together, we must pray for forgiveness; for your life, and that of the innocent child. That will be enough. If the child lives, I shall accept it, as I accepted Joe. After all that has happened, I find I cannot stop caring for you. I ... I could not go on without you."

She was astonished. "It's more than I deserve," she said, and began to weep with relief. "But how can it work, Joseph? We're bound to see them again, even if infrequently."

"We are not," he replied simply, adding nothing else as he left the room to make the arrangements.

He had a proposal for Reverend McFarland.

∞∞∞

Joseph was more than surprised to receive a message from Sam Taylor asking to meet him at the United Club. He had no desire to see the man again, but reluctantly, he agreed. It would be as good a time as any to lay down the new rules. He was not fond of the United Club and went there only occasionally to peruse the foreign newspapers on the long tables in the reading room upstairs.

Joseph arrived first, sat at a small wooden table by the door and ordered a lemonade from the bar. He didn't stand when Sam entered, nor did he return his greeting, but merely nodded to the chair opposite. Sam understood Joseph's bitterness.

A bar attendant brought Joseph's lemonade and took Sam's order of a gin and tonic. Joseph suddenly looked directly into Sam's eyes. "I know everything. Everything, including the fact that you are Joe's father." When Sam did not comment, he continued. "You seduced Elizabeth first when she was an innocent girl, and again when she was a married woman."

"Now hold on," Sam interjected. "It takes two, Joseph. I never forced Elizabeth to do anything she didn't want to, then or now. I intended to marry her back then. I didn't know she was expecting, and when I returned, she'd married you. I've never been more surprised by anything in my life."

"I'm not saying she wasn't partly to blame," Joseph continued. "But you were older, wiser to the ways of the world. And now, well I suppose this isn't the first time you've had to deal with an angry husband. But she's your own wife's *sister*, man. Have you no shame?" He cleared his throat and seemed to change tack. "I'm not here to discuss the past though. What was your reason for this meeting, anyway?"

"To tell you—actually, to show you—something I'm certain you should be aware of. It's been kept secret for too long." He paused for a second. "You understand, this time Elizabeth and I had agreed already to end our ... to stop seeing each other, permanently."

"Easy to say. Did you know that, once more, my wife is with child by you?"

Sam's head snapped up sharply. "What?"

"Do you realise that another pregnancy could kill Elizabeth, and that even if she lives, the child will probably die?"

"No, she never told me. I knew she'd had some problems, but I never knew it was that serious." His voice was subdued.

Joseph, in contrast, was tense and becoming angrier. "Now do you see what you've done? Your dalliance comes at a high price, as such things always do."

"Elizabeth is—was—no dalliance for me," Sam responded, bristling. "I told you, I wanted to marry her. I loved her, for God's sake."

"Keep your blasphemous tongue to yourself!" Joseph felt his temper rising, but managed to restrain himself enough to keep his voice down. "I'd hoped you intended to own up to your transgressions like a man, and to discuss this civilly."

"I'm nothing if not civil."

The man was infuriating. Damn him! Even now there seemed to be a mocking irony in his voice. He had no conscience whatsoever. "Elizabeth wasn't so fond of you after she became pregnant with Joe. It was she who asked me to send you away. She wrote to me, saying she no longer cared for your attention, and she begged me to intervene."

Sam leaned on the table toward Joseph, and took a long swig of his drink. "Well now, it seems that you don't know everything."

"What do you mean?"

"This brings us to the secret I spoke of before. That letter you speak of was forged by Anchalee. Elizabeth wrote no such letter. It was Anchalee who wanted me out of Elizabeth's way."

"What?" Joseph slapped the table, so that several people at the bar turned to look. He brought his voice down again almost to a whisper. "This is outrageous. It doesn't make sense. How can you say such a thing?"

"Because it's the truth. Confront Anchalee with it if you don't believe me. It was *she* who brought you the letter, was it not?"

"Well, yes. But that doesn't mean … Anyway, what earthly reason would she have for such deception?"

"Oh, there's much more to Anchalee than you know, Joseph. Much more." He leaned back in his chair. "Anchalee's not a meek little girl. Despite her youth, she's a woman with a generation of hate behind her, and she's carrying out a vendetta against Elizabeth as revenge for something that happened many years ago."

Joseph had never heard anything so extraordinary. Then he remembered their wedding night and how vague Elizabeth had seemed, asking to see the letter, reading it as if she had never before seen it. Which of course, she hadn't. She must have realised what had happened, yet still had not told him. Was he the only one who didn't know, then? He sat silently and waited for what Sam had to say next.

"Do you know about the letter her mother wrote her?"

"Yes. I gave it to her. Kesri gave it to me for safe-keeping just before she died."

"And do you know the contents of the letter?"

"No, of course not. It was personal correspondence. Nothing to do with me."

Sam took a sheaf of papers from his coat pocket and put them on the table in front of Joseph.

"Then I suggest you read this English translation of that letter and see for yourself how it concerns you—or rather, Elizabeth. I'll give you some time. I think you'll need it when you discover the truth." He took his drink and walked out to the garden, where he lit a cigarette and looked over to the tennis games on the club's courts. He was greatly disturbed at the revelation of Elizabeth's pregnancy.

Joseph did not feel comfortable about reading a letter addressed to someone else. He knew, though, that he could not ignore the missive. He was desperate to know what it contained, and what Sam really meant. He had always thought of Anchalee as an uncomplicated, if somewhat spirited, girl—although it had shocked him when she had announced her engagement to Sam.

Joseph took up the pages and began to read.

January 10th, Buddhist Era 2412 (1870)
My dearest daughter,

I had always hoped to see you again, to return to you when you were older and could make up your own mind about me. I would love to have seen you become a beautiful young woman, as I am sure you now are. Unfortunately, I have learnt recently that this life for me will soon end.

Do not feel sorry for me, Anchalee, for you know that I shall be reborn to a better life. My only regret is that I cannot see you again. That is why I have written this letter, on this, your first birthday, because I cannot tell you myself what you need to know, and what, I guarantee, no one else can, or will, tell you.

Perhaps you do not even know my name, or anything about me. Perhaps they never speak of me. You will know, I suppose, only as much as your father has chosen to tell you, which may be nothing. But I trust Joseph Shaw to keep his word to me and to give you this letter unopened. I beg you not to reveal its contents to anyone else, but to do what you feel necessary.

Even if your father has told you everything he remembers about me, there are things he did not know. Many things. I will explain everything about myself in this letter, as honestly as I can, so that you really know who your mother was.

At the time of writing this, I believe I am nearly twenty years of age, and my husband (without benefit of any Christian cere-

mony), Edward Fairburn, has forbidden me to see you again. That is the penalty I must pay for something I did which, in your father's eyes, was a crime, but in mine was an act of love for you. You will discover what it was soon enough. But first, let me start long before I knew your father.

I was probably born in February, BE 2392 (Christian era 1850). I have never known the exact date, as records were not well kept in those days and my parents could not read or write. They were slaves of a wealthy Krung Thep (Bangkok) family, and so the date of my birth may be in their records, I do not know. In recent years, I have celebrated my birthday on February 1st, as the foreigners I associate with find it perplexing that I neither know nor care about my date of birth.

I too was born into slavery, but unlike my parents, was determined to escape that wretched existence. I would rather have died than spend my life at the beck and call of someone else.

When I was about twelve, I began to notice that men looked at me in a way they had not a year earlier. I was maturing early and had almost a woman's figure. I was a little taller than most other girls my age, and had fuller breasts, and my skin was smooth and unmarked by the smallpox scars that disfigured so many. Among the men who noticed me was the master's nineteen-year-old son. He was already married with three wives and a number of children, but still I felt his eyes upon me whenever he visited his father's house, which was often, as his own house was within the same compound.

I knew his intentions could not be honourable, because he would not be permitted to marry a slave. However, I also had an idea that perhaps this man could help me in some way. And so, I began to tease him, but making sure no one else noticed. As I poured water for him, I would lean over a little further than normal so that my breasts would brush against him. I did not really understand what I was doing, but neither did I dislike the feeling of his skin on mine. I smiled at him shyly but quickly lowered my eyes as soon as he noticed.

One day, as I was washing clothes in the klong, I was sud-

denly grabbed from behind and pulled into the bushes on the bank. A hand was clamped against my mouth, and I thought I must surely be murdered. But then I was permitted to turn around, and I saw that it was him. He was laughing, and I pretended to be amused, too. What happened next was my first experience with a man, and I closed my eyes tightly and did not cry out when the pain came.

When he was finished, he said he would send for me to visit him at his house. He asked if I would like him to request his father to give me to him. He did not mention marriage, of course, and I knew that I would remain just a slave, officially without rights. But I decided that while he was infatuated with me, I had some power. I also knew his first wife was very jealous. I had seen her looking at me sometimes when she noticed her husband's interest in me, and I knew she did not like it. She did not mind how many wives or slave girls or concubines he had, as long as none were as beautiful as her —and in fact, his other two wives were quite plain, because she had chosen them herself. But I was more beautiful than her and was three years younger, so she viewed me as a threat.

I told him I did not want to displease his first wife, and that perhaps he and I could meet secretly. I agreed to sleep with him whenever he required, and he agreed to pay me for my services. His slave would come to me with his summons, day or night, and I never complained. The son was not a bad man, although he expected so much of me, and I worked hard to earn my money. In fact, we became like friends, gradually, and he told me he believed slaves should be given a fair chance of earning their freedom. He enjoyed my company for about three years, during which time I bore him two sons, both of whom died of cholera a year apart when they were but infants.

When I was fifteen and obviously growing too old for his tastes, a new slave girl came to the house. She was thirteen and he fell for her immediately. He told me my services were no longer required, but I did not mind because now I had enough money to buy my freedom from the master. Like my sons, my parents had also died of cholera—the previous year—so I was free to go where I pleased, and had no responsibilities. But I had no way of earning a *living, except to beg or to become a concubine, and I did not want to do either. I was still beautiful, and my figure was firm and youthful, even though I had borne two children. I dreamed of becoming the first wife of a wealthy man, but I knew that as a former slave who had already had children, the best I could hope for was to become a minor wife while I was still young and desirable.*

Then another opportunity presented itself. In the slum where I lived, on the river near the port, I heard talk of the white-skinned farang, who were all said to be fabulously wealthy, with so much money they could buy whatever they liked. I had seen some of these strange creatures walking in the markets. They were always revoltingly dripping with sweat, even the women, and they talked so loudly in their ugly languages.

Some of the women in the slum said the farang men loved the Siamese women, and some had even married them. Strangely, farang men generally had only one wife, who had access to all her husband's riches and the respect of her position as his life partner. They had concubines, of course, but they were usually kept hidden elsewhere and did not command any honour or respect. This sounded bizarre to me, and I did wonder if being the wife of a farang would be too exhausting, not having any other wives around to share the burden that men make for us in many ways. However, on balance, I considered the benefits would outweigh the concerns, so I was undeterred.

I decided that the only way I could make a better life for myself was to get to know these foreigners. They were ugly, it was true, but I would rather have married an ugly farang who was wealthy than a handsome Thai man who either had nothing, or who would make me number five wife or somesuch. I decided the best way to meet these men was to learn more about them and their languages. In those days, only the King and a few noblemen were reputed to be able to converse with them. I was sure it would not be so easy for me, but I had heard that ex-slaves were sometimes taken in and educated by the farang missionaries who misguidedly thought they might be able to convert us to their most preposterous religion called Christianity.

One day, I got into my little boat—it was practically the only thing I owned, and it was so old and worn that it was likely to sink at any time—and rowed upstream until I reached the American mission. I hid my boat under the landing and arrived on their door-step, explaining that I had used all my money to buy myself out of slavery, that I had nowhere else to go, and that a bad man was after me, and if he caught me, he would force me to be his concubine. Oh, and I was not yet even 16.

The missionaries always tried to save young people such as me, because they imagined their charity would buy our devotion to their religion. It did not. Even the Siamese who accepted baptism would most likely realise their stupidity and soon embrace Buddhism once more.

The missionaries and their habits were strange to me indeed. Some could not marry, while others could. It was very confusing. Also, there was some entity called God, who somehow was everyone's father, but was also his own son and a ghost, all at the same time. Anyway, they were generally kind to me and I stayed with them for eighteen months, trying very hard to learn English. I even learnt to read and write it. But more importantly, and unexpectedly, it not being part of my plan, I learnt to read and write Siamese. I discovered I had a natural ability to learn fast.

I worked as a servant at the mission when there were visitors, as a way of repaying my board in kind. I even hoped that I might marry one of the young missionary gentlemen, but I soon discovered they were interested only in marrying Christian women, and I simply could not bring myself to convert to their religion. It was too strange, and I could not accept it or even pretend that I did. I met Joseph Shaw visiting the mission, although I think he hardly remembers me from that time.

With this training at the mission, I now had the option of being able to be employed as a live-in domestic servant, which might be a better life than being a beggar or a concubine, but not much. I would remain a servant for my entire life, at the beck and call of others, never being paid enough to break away and become independent, or do anything meaningful. So, I did something that

I think few, if any, Siamese women had done before: I hired my-self out as a temporary servant to foreign households when they needed extra help for their dinner parties and soirees. Usually, they borrowed friends' servants for their functions, and the servants themselves did not benefit. But with my new scheme, I was my own mistress, and the harder I worked, the more money I made.

I was in great demand when the foreigners realised I could understand English. I knew how to cook proficiently and could re-member most of the strange recipes for their bland dishes without the need for translation. I worked many nights at balls and dinner parties, and also afternoons at wives' lunches, teas and card games. I still lived in my hovel in the slum, but I saved the money they paid me and hoped it would not be long until I found a man who would keep me in style.

Months passed, and although I knew I was still as attractive as ever, and always took care of my appearance, no one seemed to really see me. I began to loathe serving them. Then, one night at the British Consulate, I saw Edward, your father, and ensured he no-ticed me. We spent the night together, like husband and wife, and a few weeks later, when he had rented a house, I went to live with him. I thought he had fallen in love with me.

The house was like a palace to me. It was the first time I had ever slept in a European-style bed, and the first time I had not had to work from dawn to dusk. I cooked and cleaned for Edward, but in the evenings, we dined together. He promised that soon he would hire a maid, so that I would no longer have to work at all.

Then his wife, Charlotte, arrived from Australia with their daughter, Elizabeth, and my new life changed. I had always known about Charlotte, and accepted that she would be the first wife. I was not upset, but when this woman arrived, she treated me like a slave, ordering me about from morning to night. Worst of all, I was not to retain my own room upstairs as I had thought, but was sent out to live in the servants' quarters and had to pretend to be the maid.

Edward seemed to be ashamed of me and had not told Char-lotte what I really was to him. He sometimes came to my room at night, but he left as soon as he had satisfied himself, and I slept alone on a bedroll on the hard floor. The daughter, Elizabeth, was treated like a princess, and she also gave me orders—she, who should have been made to treat me with the respect I deserved as her father's wife and therefore her stepmother. I could have accepted that from a son of the house—after all, it is customary that mothers obey their sons and their husband's sons by other women —but not from this snooty child-woman who knew nothing, yet imagined herself my better.

When I realised I was pregnant with Edward's child, I was very excited. I thought the news must surely please him so much that I would be restored to my former place. After all, Charlotte cruelly withheld herself from him and refused to have another child. But his reaction was the opposite to what I had expected. He told me I must pack my things and leave. He would provide money for me and for the child, but I was never to live in his house again. So, I was pregnant without a husband—even though he did provide for me quite well, and I had a small but comfortable home on the river. But I was so lonely. When the baby arrived—you, my darling Anchalee—my few friends laughed at your long nose and green eyes. But I did not care what they said, and I thought you were beautiful. I loved you from the moment I first held you, and I was determined that your life would be better than mine, that you would have everything that I had not, and that you would want for nothing. Somehow, I had to get us both back to Edward's house.

He visited us regularly, but I told him nothing of my hopes. His new maid, Porntip, was a friend of mine from my mission days, and I knew she would help me. He still had not told Charlotte about me, or you, and so I decided it was time she knew. I asked Porntip to bring Charlotte to visit me. She did so, and I told Charlotte that Edward was the father of my child. She was so shocked she nearly fainted, and then she demanded Porntip take her home. Shortly after, she went away to England, and I was overjoyed when we were summoned to live with Edward again. My happiness would have been complete, had it not been for Elizabeth, who did not go with her mother. Elizabeth was spoilt and badly behaved. She never accepted me, but I realised, only when it was too late, just how devious she was. Charlotte must have told her to spy on me, and she continued this even after the news came that her mother had died at sea.

I had not wished such suffering on Charlotte, but I was not sad to know she was never coming back. Meanwhile, Elizabeth was jealous of the affection her father had for me, and I knew she wanted me gone. Even though she was only a child, she already had a sly and secretive nature.

One day, she was spying on me, hidden behind the curtains in the front room, and she saw me take a small piece of silver from the cabinet. She noticed me take another piece shortly after, and she decided to tell her father I was stealing from him.

You may wonder yourself, my love, what I was doing. The truth is that I was in need of money that Edward could not know about. I was pregnant again, and it terrified me that he would be angry, as he was the first time. I was also worried that when I had lost my attractiveness in pregnancy, he would take another wife, and that my place, and yours, would be lost. All my experience so far told me men wanted young, perfect women, and that they became bored when babies came along. But more than not wanting to be usurped myself, I wanted you to have everything I had never had. I did not want you to have to share with many brothers and sisters. After all, his reaction to my first pregnancy had been awful, so I did not want to displease him again and risk your future. I could not let this happen. I decided to get rid of the baby. Please do not think me a terrible person: I did it for you.

I knew of a farang doctor who had a secret surgery in China-town where he performed such operations. But it was expensive, and the doctor expected to be paid first. I took the silver pieces to a pawn shop in Chinatown, and I swear I would have recovered them as soon as I was able.

Meanwhile, Elizabeth told Joseph Shaw what she had seen, and they both went to Edward. I do not blame Mr Joseph for that —there was nothing else he could do, really. Edward then had his assistant follow me, and he discovered what I had done. He said he would never forgive me, that he no longer cared for me, that I disgusted him and must leave him forever. I was terrified for you, my child, as all my fine plans had come to nothing. Then Edward surprised me by insisting he would keep you, and saying he would bring you up as his daughter should be, and that you would want for nothing as long as I stayed away. I had no choice. I had to agree. And so, I went. The fancy clothes I wore sometimes while I was Edward's wife were of no use to me now, but I kept them, as well as a small silver locket he had given me when we first met. I want you to have the locket, and I have instructed Mr Joseph to give it to you with this letter.

As I write these words, I wonder how you will look when you are grown and are reading this. I have discovered that I have a fatal disease. A farang missionary doctor who was kind enough to treat me, explained to me that it is called consumption and that I have only a year or two left to live. I know now that I shall never again see my little daughter, that I shall not see you grow up, marry, have children of your own. I will die a broken woman. But, my dear Anchalee, I shall live on through you. It is you who must make my struggles and my death worth something.

Elizabeth must pay for her treachery, for her cruelty to me, and for depriving you of your mother. Only you can decide how she must be punished. But the one who caused so much unhappiness should not be allowed to find happiness herself. For the sake of your poor mother, who will be long dead by the time you read this, I ask you to remember what has happened. Never forget that your half-sister, Elizabeth, is the cause of our lifelong separation.

When Sam returned from the bar, he found Joseph staring out the window.

"So, you see, Joseph, at the time you married Elizabeth, she was still in love with me." He regretted the words as soon as he'd uttered them, but there it was. "Still, that's not the point," he continued. "We were discussing Anchalee. She was determined to avenge her mother, so she set out to marry me, to hurt Elizabeth by flaunting the man who had once been Elizabeth's lover and whom she knew Elizabeth still loved.

"Anchalee had realised I was Joe's father—from the beginning—and having married me, she then decided that if she brought Elizabeth and me into constant contact, there was a good chance the old flame would be rekindled. It was, as you now know, and Anchalee picked her time to tell you, thinking you'd surely separate from Elizabeth, but knowing also that she'd never agree to let me go, so we would have to remain trapped in a loveless marriage. Anchalee's plan was simple, Joseph—that Elizabeth should lose everything and end up alone, as Kesri had."

He stopped to light another cigarette. "She's a devious and evil little bitch, my wife. It's insane, this ridiculous vendetta over something that probably never happened in the way her mother explains it. The accusations in that letter, to my mind, have no basis. At the very least, Anchalee's mother misunderstood the situation. Elizabeth was only eight or nine years old at the time! How could a child that age be so cunning and vindictive? Having read that letter, and knowing Anchalee as I do now, as far as I'm concerned, it's a case of like mother, like daughter: wilful, jealous and destructive beyond belief."

Sam took another sip of his drink, put his cigarette to his lips, and sank back into his chair. "But anyway, she realised early on that this revenge scheme of hers had failed ... because Elizabeth has come to truly love you, Joseph."

At this, Joseph looked startled, and Sam continued: "You've made her more content than I ever could have. It's to your credit that you've decided to stay with Elizabeth. In similar circumstances, I can't say as I'd do the same." He paused. "And the child ...?"

"Will be brought up as my own, of course. It is not the child's sin and he or she must not be punished for it."

"Of course," Sam said, almost bitterly. "I know the hurt I've caused, Joseph, and it's not like me to seek sympathy—nor do I deserve any—but I have lost in this, also."

"How, exactly?" Joseph asked.

"I have a wife who despises me, while the woman I love, and our son and our unborn child, belong to another man. I suppose you'd tell me it's God's punishment for my sins."

"Something like that," Joseph replied. For a moment, he felt almost sorry for the man, but then he came to his senses.

"So where do we go from here?" Sam asked.

Joseph was still shocked by the revelations, and needed time to ponder them. But he believed, more than ever, that his plan was the only solution.

He looked directly at Sam. "I think, under the circumstances, that our two families must be parted indefinitely. We must all pray for the courage to forgive each other, but there's no possibility of a relationship between us in future. We're better off completely separated—forever."

Sam hesitated, but then nodded. "It's the only way, I agree. Elizabeth's adamant she wants to save her marriage to you, Joseph." He sighed, then shrugged. "But how will we do it? Bangkok's a small place for foreigners. It would be difficult to avoid each other, unless we become hermits."

"I've thought of that, and I have a solution."

∞∞∞

"Why didn't you tell me?"

"I wanted to spare you."

"Spare me? *Spare* me? Elizabeth, if only you had told me the letter was not your doing. If only you had trusted me..."

"Joseph, it was our wedding night."

"All the more reason to be honest—to confide in me. I'd not have thought badly of you."

"I thought it was too late; the damage had been done, her plan accomplished, or so I thought. What purpose could it have served?"

"I could have helped, could have done something," he

said. "And who knows, all this might have been avoided. Our marriage could even have been annulled, if that was what you wanted."

"I still cannot believe it of her. That she planned everything, using you as some sort of pawn," she said.

Despite his distress at her affair, Joseph was sorry for her. "If it weren't for her interference, you would have married Sam Taylor."

"Then I do have something to thank Anchalee for," she told him. "I've found true love and goodness in you, Joseph, that I could never have had with him. I know that now."

He looked into her eyes, and was sure that somehow, they could go on together. "We'll not see them again. There is no other way."

Her eyes filled with tears, but she nodded in agreement. She still could not believe the extent of Anchalee's treachery.

She could not help herself—she had to address the matter with her sister.

18th May, 1886

Dear Anchalee,

I can hardly comprehend what Joseph has told me, but he is not a man to stray from the truth, and so I must believe him. I did not come to see you personally because I was not sure you would listen to me, but please, I implore you, read this letter in its entirety before discarding it.

Anchalee, what your mother wrote about me in her letter simply is not true, and you must, above all, believe me when I tell you that I never meant to do her harm. I am not, by any means, saying that she was lying. I am sure Kesri believed she was telling you the truth. But I am afraid that she misinterpreted my actions.

I give you my word that I never intended to spy on Kesri.

What I saw that day was purely by accident, because I was already in the room, reading behind the curtains, when your mother entered. I intended to reveal my presence, but then I saw her take the silver and was dumbfounded. Really, I didn't know what to do. She was sure to be very angry with me if she discovered me there. We hardly knew each other, and I was often in fear of her moods. I admit I did not trust her, but I was a child, Anchalee; I had no conception of wickedness.

After my mother died, I confess that I did believe that Kesri was partly responsible. In my child's mind, I reasoned that if my mother had not had to return to England, she would not have died on that ship. I know now that it is likely she contracted the disease before she departed, and that she most probably would have died anyway, but a child cannot comprehend these things.

My mother loved Father so much, and she suffered terribly for that love of him. There were so many miscarriages and great pain, yet she did not "withhold herself" from him just to be nasty, as the letter alleges. The doctors had told her there should be no more children. She and Father were both afraid for her life. Then he met Kesri, who was so willing, so young and so beautiful.

You must understand that my mother Charlotte's values were those of an English Christian lady. She was deeply shocked when she discovered Father's relationship with your mother, and when he refused to give up Kesri, she could not bear such a betrayal, as she saw it. She conceded bitterly, but gracefully. She would never have been able to marry again, because she would not have considered divorce, and would have lived the rest of her life alone, even though she had a husband and daughter across the seas.

We both lost our mothers, Anchalee; both died tragically, long before their time. We cannot change these facts.

It might come as a surprise to you that I know you forged the letter that made Joseph send Sam away, therefore ensuring we did not marry. I saw the letter on my wedding night and realised immediately what you had done. I thought, when your engagement was announced, that your only plan had been to win Sam for yourself. That, in itself, was bad enough, but I had no idea that there was so much more behind your actions.

    You have done me great wrong and great harm, Anchalee, but how can I blame you when I myself am not blameless? I am so ashamed of what I have done that sometimes I wish the earth would swallow me whole. I shall never forgive myself. This will be the last time I shall write to you. I hope you find peace in your life. It is the best either of us can hope for.

Your sister,

Elizabeth Ann Shaw

Anchalee folded the letter and felt a hollowness she had never experienced before. There was no satisfaction and no feeling of success. Yet, when she thought of Elizabeth carrying Sam's child, she was cold with jealousy at their intimacy. For despite herself, she had come to realise that she cared more for him than she had ever imagined she would. Now, with the prospect of losing him because of his disgust at her actions, she found that she wanted him more than ever. She looked out the window with tears in her eyes. "I've fallen in love with him after all," she cried aloud, "and he'll never love me as he loves her."

    After seeing the consequences of what she had wrought, she could no longer hate Elizabeth. But the gulf between them was too wide now to bridge: too much unhappiness, too much deceit, too many betrayals. They would be strangers from now on and forever, and that was the way it had to be.

Chapter 30

2nd June, 1886

Dear Mr Shaw,

This letter is to formally confirm your appointment to the Presbyterian Mission station at Chiengmai, Northern Siam. As discussed and agreed, you will leave Bangkok as soon as Mrs Shaw is able to travel—most probably in late November or early December.

The journey, as you know, is unpredictable, and can take up to three months or longer. However, we presume at that time of year, it will take only about two months, by river and elephant. Dr and Mrs McGilvary will expect you early in the New Year.

May I personally commend you, Mr Shaw, for your brave gesture in volunteering to take up residence in our most remote station. Your skills as a teacher will be of immense benefit to the community, to be sure. Let me also reiterate how much we here in Bangkok shall miss your gentle manner with our students, not to mention your excellent Bible readings in church each Sunday. God speed.

Yours faithfully,

Rev. S. G. McFarland,
Principal,
King's College,
Bangkok

Elizabeth had not objected to the move to Chiengmai, believing it to be for the best, and as her penance. Joseph did not intend it as a penance, however. It was simply the only way, in his mind, for them to survive as a family.

He had, at first, wanted to leave immediately, but he understood the journey would be even more perilous for a woman with Elizabeth's dangerous condition—that he might very well be sending her to her death. It was safest to remain in Bangkok for the five months or so until the birth. He would attend to business while Elizabeth stayed home with Joe, resting and preparing herself for the ordeal to come. In August, they sent some of their furniture on ahead of them, so it would be ready for their arrival in the house in Chiengmai that the church had acquired for them.

Joseph had decided to go up north no matter what happened—even if, God forbid, Elizabeth should pass away in childbirth, as he feared she might. If that dreadful possibility did eventuate, he determined that he would still go with Joe, and would try to raise the boy with love enough for two parents. He knew with certainty that he would never marry again, because he could never stop loving Elizabeth, despite everything.

Until this latest episode, he could easily forget that Joe was not his natural son. The reminder served to make him strive even harder to love the boy as his own, never to hold the identity of his real father against him. But he could already see something in the boy's eyes at times that unsettled him. It was a dogged determination, a stubborn streak that, he realised, came straight from Sam Taylor.

Joseph wasn't afraid of the journey to Chiengmai, although its perils were well known in Bangkok: jungle fever, tiger attacks, poisonous snakes and rampaging elephants, plus bandits and river pirates who thought nothing of slaughtering an entire family for a mere gold watch. He believed that God's will would be done, and if they were meant to come through the journey unscathed, they would. Besides, he had been more interested in the work of the Chiengmai mission station since the McGilvarys had opened it in 1867. He had met Dr McGilvary twice in Bangkok—in 1873 and 1881—and had been intrigued by the man's experiences, and inspired by his courage. But Joseph had not thought it fair, after he married Elizabeth, to isolate her from Bangkok and her family, especially since she had been away at school in England for so long. He had kept his interest to himself.

At least they would not have to endure what the pioneering McGilvarys had experienced when they first journeyed north. He remembered Dr McGilvary telling him about conditions in Chiengmai when he had first arrived with his wife, Sophia, and their two children, in 1867. Because of a misunderstanding with the chief of Chiengmai, after a four-month journey from Bangkok they arrived to find that the land and timber that had been promised for a house was not to be provided at all. They were forced to camp in a public sala for a year, their every move watched by intrigued locals who had never seen Europeans before.

"But let me assure you," Dr McGilvary had told Joseph when he had visited mission headquarters in Bangkok a few years previously, "that they were very much more afraid of us than we were of them. They at first believed us to be evil spirits, I suppose, and when we could speak the local language passably, we heard mothers warn their children to stay away, otherwise they might be eaten by us!

"Eventually, though, they came to accept our presence, especially when they saw how our medicines could help them. Some even seemed to enjoy our Bible readings. Our first converts came from that time, and I do recall that year fondly, despite its hardships."

After nearly a year, the McGilvarys finally received building material for a house. However, it was mainly bamboo, and for more than three years, they and their fellow missionaries—the Wilsons who had arrived in February, 1868—had to live in fragile dwellings that provided little protection from the elements.

These days, of course, they resided comfortably in fine teak houses, and Joseph was assured that a similar residence would be provided for his own family. The Edict of Religious Toleration, issued in 1878 by the new Siamese resident high commissioner, Phya Thep Worachun, on behalf of the King of Siam, had guaranteed that Christians would be permitted to practise their religion, including observance of the Sabbath, without harassment or persecution.

First, though, there was the impending birth to get through. Joseph found himself wishing, early on, that she might lose the child naturally before half-term. It would certainly be less of a threat to her own health. He had severely admonished himself for such thoughts, and had prayed for the poor child's soul—but still, the thought persisted. Life would be so much more tolerable without the reminder every day of her infidelity. He could forgive, but he could hardly forget. Horrific visions sometimes came to him of her in that other man's arms, and he tried, but failed, to blank them out.

He toiled harder than ever, taking on extra work in the city's slums, teaching the children there to read. He had been an avid pupil himself of the Siamese language, and his diligence over the years had reaped rewards. He spoke the language fluently and could read and write it more than tolerably. It was most valuable in his slum work, where English was of no interest to impoverished children who would have no contact with wealthy foreigners. It was better they became literate in their own language.

King Chulalongkorn had visited Europe and was impressed with the standards of education there. He had made great efforts to modernise it in Siam. A Department of Education had been established by 1880, and primary schools in Bangkok had many thousands of pupils.

The poorer children, though, could not hope to be able to attend. By the age of five or six, most were required to work to supplement their parents' incomes. Not that things were much different in the slums of London, Joseph thought. And at least here, no one froze to death. As it was the world over, the lot of poor children was in stark contrast to that of the lavishly dressed sons of noblemen—with their retinues of servants—whom he was more accustomed to teaching.

He had been surprised to find the slum children to be quick and willing learners. He would spread a blanket on the dusty ground, and the children would crowd around. There were never enough pencils or paper to go around, but those who missed out were content to use their fingers to trace the Siamese characters in the dust. They loved listening to the stories he told from books he borrowed from the school—some of which were translated from Bible stories and foreign folktales—and even their parents would crowd closer to listen when they had time.

In mid-October, when Elizabeth was swollen and almost immobile, she was surprised one day to receive a heavy wooden box all the way from England. In the tumult that had swept through the family after Edward's death, she had almost forgotten her father's last, secret, bequest. Anxiety once again overwhelmed her.

It was about the size of a large hat box, but extremely heavy, and it sat on her drawing room floor, where she had asked the delivery man to leave it and the maid to cut it open at the top. It was beside the chaise longue she was supposed to be resting on, and if she closed her eyes, she could pretend the box wasn't there. Eventually, though, curiosity got the better of her.

Tentatively, she lifted the lid. Inside was a well-wrapped package and an envelope. She decided to open the envelope first.

∞∞∞

For the third time in their marriage, Joseph longed for her screams to end. She had gone into labour three weeks early, and this time was no easier than the others.

Once again, her pain ceased abruptly—only on this occasion, the silence was followed by a tiny wail.

"Thank the lord!" Joseph cried in relief, but he soon began to wonder why he heard no more sounds from anyone, and why it was taking the doctor so long to emerge. He paced the floor, praying she would live.

When Dr Newhaven finally came out of the room thirty minutes later, he anticipated the question Joseph dare not ask.

"Your wife will recover, most probably," the doctor told him, and Joseph let out a long sigh. "She has lost blood, of course, but the baby was small ..."

"Was?" Joseph said desperately. "But I heard its cries! It's alive, surely!"

"I'm so sorry. I did everything I could to save her. She cried once, then she simply stopped breathing."

The doctor, who was also a family friend, took off his glasses and rubbed his tired eyes with the back of his hand. He put a supportive hand on Joseph's shoulder and said again, "I'm so sorry."

Entering the room, Joseph saw how Elizabeth lay there, her eyes open but seemingly unseeing. Beside her, in the little crib Joseph had made, was a tiny bundle covered with a clean white linen pillow case.

"I have been punished enough," she said. Gently, he took her hand. Yes, she had been, but he had no words to express such sorrow.

∞∞∞∞

As she awoke from a fitful sleep, she tried to sit up, craning her neck so she could see into the little crib by the window. It was empty, and the netting, the lace cover, and the white pillow were gone. She knew her daughter had died, but she had wanted some time with her, to say goodbye. She was panicking now. Where was her dead child? Then she heard raised voices from somewhere in the house, voices that sounded angry. Slowly and painfully, she struggled to get out of bed. The voices became clearer as she approached the drawing room.

"In the name of goodness, man, do you not think you've done enough harm?"—Joseph's voice.

"I must see her. I cannot live with myself otherwise," another voice slurred. "Do you have no compassion?" She instantly recognised that other voice.

"How do you of all people dare to speak of compassion?"

"For God's sake, it's *my* child who has died."

For Joseph, it was as if he'd been stabbed. The smell of stale whisky on Sam's breath permeated the room, and made him even more repugnant in Joseph's eyes.

"How dare you come into my house like this, you drunken wretch! You disgust me. You're not fit to be a father, much less a husband. You've destroyed her life, Taylor, and with it mine, and perhaps even that of our son."

"*Your* son?"

"Yes, *my* son. You may have sired him, you devil, but I'm his father. Now get out!"

Sam took a step toward Joseph, his hands at his sides, open palmed, entreating: "Just one minute with her. Let me at least tell her how sorry I am ..."

Elizabeth came to the doorway just as Sam stumbled backward and slumped to the ground.

"Joseph, what's going on!" she said, horrified. "What have you done?"

For the first time in his life, Joseph had hit another human being. All the anger, the frustration and the degradation Sam had brought out in him had swelled within him until it burst and erupted like a poisoned pustule. And Sam, who had already been swaying in his inebriation, had fallen like a fly.

Joseph stared at the unconscious man, and then at his wife in her white nightgown, silhouetted in the doorway.

"My God, Joseph, you've killed him!"

But he had not. In another instant, Sam came to and began to laugh as he rose unsteadily to his feet—a guttural, bitter laugh that Joseph and Elizabeth would forever remember. Feeling the first rush of blood from his broken nose, Sam pulled a handkerchief from his pocket and held it to his face.

He turned as he stumbled out—his laugh ceasing and his mouth twisted with pain: "Well done, Joseph. I was wondering when you'd do that."

10ᵗʰ November, 1886

Dear Sam,

I do not know how to start this letter, only, I suppose, to say goodbye. Joseph regrets yesterday's events and is ashamed of himself for his violence—but not for his sentiments. You should never have come. My only hope is that you can now leave the past be, and that you can continue life with your own family, as we shall also have to do.

You know that in a short time we will be leaving for the mission at Chiengmai. I know you have travelled there several times yourself and have a great fondness for the north, but I beg of you, I implore you, not to return. Please do not tempt fate by showing your face in that place. It can only make things worse.

I heard what you said to Joseph about the child, and I confess I had not even considered your paternal feelings. I should have known better, for despite your seemingly insensitive exterior, I know you can be hurt like any other. That is why I am writing to you, without Joseph's knowledge, concerning Joe. Joseph is right when he says that he is, and will be, the only father Joe will know, but that cannot negate the fact that you are his true father, and I know it would be more than cruel for you never to know anything of his life. Yet I cannot permit you to seek information from us, nor can you see him as he grows up.

I am offering a compromise. It is that I shall write to you once at the close of each year, in which I shall inform you of his progress. The letter will be disguised on the envelope as being from a business associate of yours in Chiengmai, named Mr Dian Cecht. The irony will not be lost on you when I tell you he is the Irish god of healing. You see, a British education has been of some benefit to me!

I ask of you one more thing. Please destroy this letter when you have read it, for it can only do harm if discovered. Correspondence from Mr Cecht will be such that it will appear inconsequential, but you shall understand clearly its meaning. These missives you may keep or destroy as you see fit. That is all, Sam. Please do not try to contact me or even to reply to Mr Cecht's correspondence. It is for the best.

Elizabeth Ann Shaw (Mrs)

Part 3

February 1904—May 1905

Chapter 31

Modern Bangkok
By Samuel Taylor
Photography by Kesri Taylor and Edward Fairburn

Prologue

Foreigners were still calling Bangkok "the Venice of the East" when I first arrived in the 1870s. Now, in 1904, the daily life of the city is concentrated as much on its roads as on its river. But it is still the stately Maenam Chao Phya, the "River of Kings", that gives Siam's capital city its character, its charm and its wit. And it is still this river that provides access to the rest of the country, for there are still few roads beyond Bangkok.

In thirty years, Bangkok has transformed from a medieval settlement hundreds of years in development behind the great cities of the United States and England, to one that is preparing to join the modern world of the twentieth century. There are roads and railways, electric tramways and lights, telephones and a telegraph service, a reliable postal service, daily steamers to Singapore and Hong Kong, and one of the East's finest race-courses. There are three banks, several fine hotels run by Europeans, a French hospital, a British nursing home, and plenty of European, British and American doctors.

The city's official population is around 500,000, including 800 or 900 Europeans and Americans, or "farang", as the Siamese call them. Only a decade ago, the postal roll gave the city's population as 169,000, with only 300 westerners. Besides the official inhabitants, there are many thousands more locals who live in makeshift slums and who are not, therefore, counted in any census.

The foreigners who come here have changed in nature since the early days of modernization when I first arrived. Then, there were many, like myself, who were hungry for adventure, eager to experience a different culture and keen to see things few other western men had seen. Now, they are mainly businessmen and diplomats, with an ulterior motive for being here. Of course, the missionaries are still here, and although they tried hard through much of the last century to persuade the Siamese to convert to Christianity, only a few have given up Buddhism. The converts are, anyway, mostly Chinese rather than true Siamese. I note that through all its changes, upheavals, advancements, and opening to the outside world, Bangkok is still as Oriental, as essentially Siamese, as it always was.

Samuel Taylor, Bangkok, 1904

Before Sam could go on to read over the first chapter of the final draft of his new book, he was interrupted by a knock at his office door. Kesri entered with a pile of photographs—some taken as far back as 1868—which she put on the desk in front of her father.

"Here's the last of Grandfather's Bangkok prints."

"Thank you. How's your own work going?"

"I'm still developing my latest photographs today. But they should be ready for you by tomorrow morning."

She smiled across at him, and he marvelled again at this beautiful, delightful daughter.

Her long black hair fell past her shoulders and framed her golden-skinned face. She was slim, and much taller than the average Siamese woman—or Siamese man, for that matter—with the long legs of her father and the narrow waist of her mother. Her large eyes tilted up at the outer corners as her mother's had, but the most fascinating thing about them was that they appeared to change colour, from a mysterious and intense jade green to a clear honeyed hazel, depending on the light and even her mood. She had inherited much of her mother's beauty, but where Anchalee had been brittle out of necessity, her daughter had been shielded from hurt and distress as much as Sam could manage. There was a sweetness and innocence about Kesri that by circumstance had been denied Anchalee.

"What are you thinking of?" she asked her father, seeing a shadow passing his face.

"I was thinking about your mother, actually, and how much like her—yet unlike her—you are."

"It doesn't seem a year already, does it? I still come home expecting her to be here, dressing for a ball or making sure the table's set correctly for a dinner party."

"She certainly loved the social occasions. She always did, from the time I first met her. She was only about thirteen then."

Kesri sat on the edge of his desk, eager for more. She loved hearing his reminiscences of the early days.

"And was she really allowed to go to a ball at that age? How did she persuade Grandfather to allow it?"

"Your mother had a way of getting what she wanted. When she set her heart on going to a ball, she wouldn't take no for an answer from Edward."

"She must have been very mature for her age."

"Yes, she was, you're right. And I'm glad to see you're not your mother's daughter in that respect."

"It's funny, you know, I always think of her as happy and … well, laughing and dressed up for parties, wearing her sparkling jewellery and her beautiful gowns. I can't seem to remember her being really sick for very long at all. Then suddenly, she was gone." Her voice wavered slightly.

"She didn't want to admit it, even to herself, that consumption had got a hold on her too. It killed her mother and her father. She nursed Grandfather until he died, so she knew exactly what was in store for her. She needed enormous strength just to keep going as long as she did."

He saw Kesri's eyes fill with tears. "She wouldn't want us to be sad, sweetheart," he said gently.

She managed a weak smile and changed the subject. "By the way, there's a letter for you. Mr Cecht has written from the north." She retrieved an envelope from the bottom of the pile of prints and handed it to him. "I haven't seen that name for quite some time. Strange, isn't it? I always remember it, even though he hardly ever writes. And he has never come to the house, has he? Surely he must visit Bangkok from time to time?"

"Not to my knowledge. He prefers to stay away from the city. Business upcountry."

"Well, I'll be getting on with that developing."

He waited until she had closed the door behind her before tearing open the envelope. He had not heard from Elizabeth since December, and he hoped for more news than usual, especially now that her sister Anchalee was gone and thus could no longer be hurt by a re-establishment of contact. There was an efficient post service now, both within the country and overseas, so it was unlikely that letters would have gone missing. In fact, the fortnightly service to Chiengmai had come as early as October, 1885, but it had been a long and difficult journey back then, with intrepid postmen having to trek through the jungle at its end to reach the northern city.

With the beginning of rail construction in 1891, the mail service had improved each year. The first line, between Bangkok and Paknam, had operated from 1893; Korat had been reached in the northeast, and a line was progressing steadily north to Chiengmai. Sam loved facts and figures such as these, and he went to much effort to research and record them in his travel writing. In recent years, however, his adventurous spirit had waned slightly and his journeys had become less frequent.

Nevertheless, he had found a way to continue writing in the same spirit, and at the same time release his creative and emotional feelings without having to travel, by becoming an adventure novelist. His books, featuring the fictional character Thomas Yearby and his travels throughout Asia and the Pacific, drew upon all his own experiences, and already extended to 10 volumes. Each new book was eagerly awaited by a British and North American public hungry for travellers' tales.

He was disappointed to find inside the envelope only one thin sheet with a single paragraph of writing.

1ˢᵗ February, 1904

Dear Mr Taylor,

Just a note to inform you that our esteemed colleague, Mr J., will be in Bangkok on his way to us in late February. He intends, against our advisement, to spend some time in the capital before proceeding to us. He is, nevertheless, well informed as to whom to avoid in the city, and it is our fervent hope that he will not have to contend with any unwelcome advances from certain unsolicited influences.

I remain, sir, a colleague with your own best interests in mind,

D. Cecht, esq.

He sighed in disappointment. Was she really so afraid of his influence after so many years? What did she imagine he would do? And what, he asked himself, would he do if indeed he came face to face with the son he didn't know—in fact, might not even recognise? Would he even want to meet this son who had not grown up as his son? Sam had Kesri, and she was the joy of his life. To his surprise, he had discovered over the years that parenthood suited him, and that he was a good father. In truth, though, he was curious. Joe was a man now, and he would like to see for himself how he'd grown. But he had to admit also that he no longer really thought of him as a son, and that if ever they were to meet, he had no idea what he would say.

Elizabeth had been true to her word and had kept him informed over the years, but now that Joe was an adult—it would be official on his 21ˢᵗ birthday that June—he supposed she might not write again. In his mind, she was still the young woman of their youth, and he hardly ever thought of the fact that she was now 43 and a mature woman who had lived nearly two decades since they had last seen each other.

He went to put the letter in the bottom drawer of his desk with the others and was compelled to pick up the pile and leaf through them. Certain ones stood out from the others; they were the ones that marked milestones in the boy's life. But there was never any word of *herself*. She never gave him any inkling of how she felt, how she coped, if she was happy, or if she ever thought of him at all beyond what she regarded as her duty to inform him of their son's progress.

December 1ˢᵗ, 1890

Dear Mr Taylor,

You may be interested to hear that my young charge, Master J., is soon to be sent to England to ensure he has a broad and liberal education. At his impressionable age, my associate and I feel this is for the best, although we shall of course miss his engaging countenance.

We believe Harrow to be a most suitable public boarding school and shall monitor his progress with eager anticipation. We are hoping Master J. may continue up to Oxford or Cambridge, with a view perhaps to joining our company at some later date. We feel it will be of immense benefit to the young man to grow up around suitable cousins and family connections at home, as certain possible future influences in our adopted homeland continue to be a concern to us.

Our work continues in the north, but we do not seem to

make many sales, so to speak. Still, persistence is all. I trust your family is well. Regards and best wishes for Christmas.

Yours,

D. Cecht

∞∞∞

December 1st, 1895

Dear Mr Taylor,

By the time you read this missive, I shall be on my way to England, for the first time in 13 years. My mother passed away recently, and I am returning to settle the estate and also to see our young friend, who has been there for five years and is pining for Siam.

He is at an age when he believes he knows better than his elders, but we maintain that England is the best place for him until he attains his majority and can decide his own path. He is a bright student, though rather a dreamer, becoming easily bored or distracted, never satisfied with remaining in one place, or so his school reports inform us. He is, I should say, quite like his father in these respects, and I believe you have made that gentleman's acquaintance on one or two occasions some time ago.

Please forgive me, sir, for not informing you earlier of my arrival in Bangkok and imminent departure from the port. You may have assumed that in such an event, we could conceivably have met for some small conversation. However, with my grief at my mother's death being current, and recalling the other business that has occurred historically, you will appreciate my detachment.

Yours,

D. Cecht

∞∞∞

December 1ˢᵗ, 1901

Dear Mr Taylor,

I should like to inform you of Master J.'s graduation from Harrow and acceptance to Oxford University for the coming academic year (and so, we shall thenceforth name him "Mr J."). We have persuaded him to read classics, which we feel a suitable degree for a young gentleman. He may then continue in the study of some profession, perhaps in theology, we dare to hope, in that he may enter the Church in due course. Thankfully, he shows, as yet, no hankering for an early marriage.

Yours faithfully,

D. Cecht

∞∞∞

March 15ᵗʰ, 1903

Dear Mr Taylor,

Please accept my sincere condolences on the passing of your wife. I am so dreadfully sorry. I should have liked to have met her again.

Your friend,

Elizabeth

Sam smiled at this last one, despite its sad subject matter. In her obvious distress at Anchalee's death, she had neglected her *nom de plume*. He perhaps should not have kept the letter, but he had been touched, because it was the first time since they parted that she had revealed something of herself to him.

That brief note of condolence was the only letter he had received between the 1901 correspondence and the one that day. He supposed she had read of her sister's death in the

Bangkok Times when it had arrived in Chiengmai several weeks after the obituary was published. It must have been a terrible way to learn of such news. He had wanted to write to her himself, but she had forbidden him ever to contact her, and he had decided, finally, that he could not risk breaking the frail line of communication he still had with her. He wondered, if she had been in Bangkok, would she have attended the funeral?

Thoughts of Anchalee crowded in then. After the turmoil that had torn the two families apart, she had seemed to settle down. She forgot her quest for revenge against her sister, and Elizabeth's name was not mentioned in their house for a long time. Although Sam and Anchalee continued to share the same house, they led separate lives and slept in separate bedrooms for the next three years. She approached him more than once, but he always rejected her advances, still angry with her for what she had done to Elizabeth—and angry with himself for his part in the events. He found temporary solace in brief, discreet affairs with married women—to which she turned a blind eye—and over those years, his anger gradually dissipated, until it was finally as good as gone. Companionship between them sprang from the simple need to bring up their daughter.

Then, one night in 1890, she simply moved back into his bedroom, without explanation or discussion. He did not ask her to leave. From that day, they lived as a normal married couple, and found their relationship was intact and stable, after all, though she did impress upon him her rule that there should be no more children. Kesri was enough to worry about, she told him, and they were careful.

Sam still indulged in the occasional passionate, short affair from time to time, but as the old century drew to a close, he seemed to lose heart for these romantic entanglements. He came to realise that he was always searching for something that did not exist—another Elizabeth—and that it was better to concentrate on finding happiness where he could, in his own home.

The last four years were the best. They grew close and became true friends, despite the dreadful first years of their marriage. One night, as they lay in bed together, she revealed how she had fallen in love with him even as she plotted against Elizabeth.

"I couldn't see my love for you because I was blinded by my ridiculous obsession. And by the time I realised, it was almost too late. It took a long time to make things right."

He held her close then, and for the first time, felt the deep and abiding love that he knew a husband should have for a wife.

She must have known then that she was sick, because the signs became unmistakeable a short time later. He had found her, only to lose her to a cruel, painful death. When she died, he truly grieved for her and for the years they had wasted. The house seemed empty without her.

But there was still Kesri to think of. The shy girl of the year before was blossoming into a lovely young woman who was also becoming a talented photographer. She had been interested in the art ever since she had found the key to her grandfather's locked studio at the back of the house. His old cameras were far too heavy and complicated for her to use, having been superseded many times by more advanced inventions, but they fascinated her.

Sam was delighted at her interest, and he visited Mr J. Antonio's Charoen Krung Photographic Studio on New Road, opposite the Banque de l'Indochine, to purchase a new box camera, complete with accessories, a supply of film, and a book about photographic techniques and developing. He presented them to her on her sixteenth birthday.

Kesri quickly mastered the mechanics and in no time was experimenting with artistic interpretations of her own, and visiting Mr Antonio's shop herself to discuss what she had learnt. Her prints were so accomplished that Sam was using some in his new book on Siam, along with historic pictures taken by Edward. He thought it was probably the first book to feature photographs by a grandfather and his granddaughter in the same volume.

She had no recollection of her grandfather, of course—she'd been a baby when he'd died—but she felt she knew him through viewing his pioneering work, which she greatly admired. Some of the images he had captured in the early days in Siam would be used in books and shown in museums for years to come. There were boxes and boxes of them, many unpublished, and she planned eventually to catalogue and preserve them all. She had even found one of the current King's father, King Maha Mongkut, taken in 1868, according to the inscription on the back, at Hua Wan, where he had journeyed with a large entourage to view an eclipse of the sun. It was one of the last ever photographs taken of him before he died, and as such was probably quite valuable.

∞∞∞

Sam picked up the prints and leafed through them. Kesri had a good eye for what would reproduce well and had picked only the most suitable images. As he began to ponder which ones to include and which to omit, she knocked and came in again, another print in her hand.

"Forget one, did you?"

"No. This wouldn't be suitable for the book, but I just wondered who it was. She's very beautiful."

She held out the fading print and, as he took it, he immediately recognised its subject.

Sam gazed at the picture of the young Elizabeth; the poised 21-year-old he remembered so vividly. It was how she had looked when he first saw her: head held high, but with a look of wide-eyed naivety in her eyes.

"Do you recognise her?" Kesri prompted.

"Yes. It's your Aunt Elizabeth."

"Ah, the one we mustn't speak of." She wondered yet again why he had been reluctant to tell her anything. "What really happened, Father? Why won't you tell me?"

Sam sighed. "Like I've said before, it's a complicated story, and I'm not sure it should concern you."

"But they're my relatives—why can't I meet them? They must come to Bangkok once in a while. And I'd love to go up north to visit them. It would be an adventure for me. Think of the photographic possibilities! What could have been so bad?"

He made a show of busying himself with his papers, and spoke as if it were of little consequence. "It was something between your mother and Aunt Elizabeth. As I said, nothing that concerns you."

"But it's been so long. it must have happened when I was a baby, because I don't remember ever seeing Aunt Elizabeth, Uncle Joseph, or cousin Joe. And Mother's no longer with us. If it doesn't concern me, why should I not see them? Don't you think the feud has gone on long enough?"

"There's no feud, Kesri. Things are just better left this way. There's a lot you don't know, but you're right, it all happened a long time ago. Believe me though, it's better left unspoken now."

"But what if I meet them socially? By accident? I'm bound to one day. Like at the King's garden parties? Who knows when they could be there? People would think me most odd if I pretended not to know my own family. And the strange truth is, I really wouldn't know them if I fell over them. Everyone knows everyone else in Bangkok society, and they'd all be talking behind my back if that were to happen. Father, it would be so embarrassing."

It had occurred so long ago that in reality only a few long-term expatriates would remember. People came and went, and had long ago stopped speculating over this particular rift. There were new and more exciting scandals every few months, and something that had happened a generation ago was of little interest to the gossips.

Sam considered what she said, and he understood that fundamentally, she made good points. He understood also her desire to be accepted, aware that she felt part of neither one world nor another—and at her age, this was a very confusing thing.

He didn't think Elizabeth or Joseph would ever spend much time socialising in Bangkok. Young Joe, however, would soon be arriving, and he might have other ideas.

"Well, yes, that's true," he agreed at last. "In such an eventuality, you must be polite, of course. Then there will be no cause for gossip. But you're not to seek them out or become involved with them, Kesri—in the unlikely event that you do meet any of them."

"Involved? As I said, Father, I doubt I'd even recognise them. Please, just agree that I may introduce myself, if I do find myself near them at some time."

She should be studying law, he reckoned, for like a good barrister, she had left him with no argument.

"I supposed there'd be no real harm in that—for social appearances. But I'm not at all keen on the idea. And don't expect them to encourage any contact, either."

She kissed him on the cheek and skipped out. "I'm going for a fitting for my dress," she called as she left. "You do remember? For the party next week."

He sat for a long time after she had gone, staring at the photograph of the girl who had been not much older when he first met her than his daughter was now.

He wondered how Elizabeth had aged, how she looked now. He tried to fill in the lines of maturity that the years and the tropical sun would have added, but it was impossible. He could think of her only as a radiant young woman.

He lit his cheroot and went to the window, looking down on the well-kept garden and wondering if he would ever see or speak to her in person again. Anchalee had thought he would. On her deathbed, her last words as she faded were of her sister. "Tell Elizabeth ... that ... that she ... was right. Tell her our mothers ..."

But she was gone before she could finish the sentence, and Sam still agonised over what she had meant to say.

Later that day, at Mrs Smythe's Tailoring Shop—now run by her Siamese daughter-in-law—Kesri tried on the white high-necked dress and looked with satisfaction at her reflection in the three-sided mirror. She hoped her father wouldn't be angry.

The garden party had a Victorian revival theme, and guests were invited to dress in the costumes of late last century. She had found this beautiful old dress of her mother's and decided it was made for the occasion. It needed loosening slightly, but was otherwise perfect on her. Some of the guests who were recent arrivals to Siam would have to have new costumes made, but Kesri was proud to be wearing an original.

Mother must have been very young indeed when she wore it, perhaps about the time she attended that first ball, Kesri thought. It must have trailed on the ground, too, because it was just the right length for herself—reaching to the tips of her toes—and Mother had been shorter.

She had also found a matching pink and white-trimmed parasol in the trunk but had not been able to recover the hat that would have completed the ensemble. Instead, Mrs Smythe's daughter-in-law had made her a new Victorian-style bonnet that framed her face prettily with white silk roses and tiny bows.

∞∞∞

On the Saturday of the party, Kesri dressed carefully, asking her maid to put up her long dark hair under the bonnet. She wished she had curls, or at least some wave to her hair, like her friend, Janie. But her hair was perfectly straight and required a lot of coaxing with pins to stay in place. It was the bane of her life, for although she had inherited the straight hair of the Siamese, it was not thick and strong like theirs, but fine and brittle, making it difficult to style. Still, she and Noi eventually managed, and as she stood back to admire herself in her full-length mirror, she smiled.

"I do look like I belong in the last century, don't I?" she remarked in Siamese. Anchalee had been determined that her daughter spoke both English and Siamese fluently.

"You do, Miss Kesri. Your father will be proud to escort you." Noi was much more comfortable with Kesri than she had been with Anchalee. Noi had been a girl when she first came to work for the Fairburns in 1879. She was middle-aged now, and Kesri treated her with kindness and respect—almost like an older friend—encouraging her to voice her opinions and never requiring her to bow down or kneel on the floor before her in the old way. Noi loved her for it, but did, in turn, make sure she was always properly respectful toward Kesri. Indeed, it was not difficult for Noi to keep her head lower than Kesri's, for the young mistress of the house was a good six inches taller than the maid.

"Do you remember Mother wearing this dress?" Kesri asked hopefully. "It must have been for an important occasion."

Noi pretended to busy herself by adjusting the neckline. How could she tell Kesri that this dress had never belonged to Anchalee? She didn't want to lie, yet was unable to tell the truth. "I'm sorry, Miss Kesri. I can't seem to remember your mother wearing it at all. But I'm getting old and forgetful."

"Nonsense, Noi. You look younger every day." She swirled away then, down the stairs and into the parlour, where Sam was waiting. He had shaken out one of his old morning suits for the event, and the coat, waistcoat and striped trousers were only slightly tighter than they had been twenty years before.

"Well, Father, here I am," she announced.

When he saw her, he was almost dumbstruck. She was

lovely in the white gown, but it was not pride in her that rendered him speechless. It was something about the dress that made him feel uneasy, something that stirred his memory like a whirlpool. Where had he seen a dress like this before?

"I did it to surprise you, Father." She twirled once more before him. "Don't you recognise it? It's an old dress of Mother's. it hardly needed any alterations, either. Isn't it perfect?"

A long-faded, once cherished image was forming in his mind. But he was sure that image was not of Anchalee. "Where did you find this gown?" he asked.

"In a trunk in the studio. The lid had so much dust on it, I don't think it had been opened for 20 years."

Then it became clear. The young woman in the white dress, in a boat on the river, with her father and young sister. It was Elizabeth, the first time he had seen her. The dress was the very one she had worn that day, he was sure now. It must have been left here, forgotten, when Elizabeth married Joseph and moved from the house all those years ago.

Kesri stopped twirling, concerned at the distant look in her father's eyes. "What's wrong, Father? Don't you like it?"

He was sorry for her disappointment—it wasn't her fault. "Of course, yes, it's fine. It just ... brought back memories, that's all."

"You're angry I didn't ask permission..."

"No, not at all. You look wonderful. But we'd best be on our way now. You don't want to keep all those young men waiting, do you?"

Chapter 32

She watched him, pretending not to, and tried to move closer to his circle. She was determined to discover who he was and how she could meet him without appearing to have shown too much interest.

At one point, as she stood nearby talking to her friend Janie, he happened to look in her direction—and their eyes met. She couldn't look away as he half-smiled, then, realising they did not know each other, raised an eyebrow. She turned away quickly then, her cheeks burning, knowing he had caught her out. He looked 20 or more, and handsome in a way that her father must have been when he was that age.

The garden party, in the grounds of Vimanmek Palace, the King's magnificent new Dusit Park teak mansion, was held to take advantage of the last days of the cool season, when temperatures were still pleasant. During the hot season, most foreigners found the heat and humidity too draining to spend much time outdoors.

Every foreigner in town seemed to have been invited. The King was so generous and hospitable, he would simply have his minions inform the various foreign embassies that there would be a party, and the guest list would be left to their discretion. Consequently, the gatherings were always an interesting mix of Siamese noblemen and army officers, foreign consular staff, Danes from the Siamese navy, travellers, doctors, government advisers, missionaries, school headmasters, judges, industrialists, plus the occasional entrepreneur or teak trader in town for business or relaxation.

The King, the First Queen, and several of their children circulated magnanimously, with little of the usual formality, and His Majesty himself was liable to wave companionably to a foreign friend and even to stroll over for a chat.

The minions were always unnerved by—or even distraught at—the lack of protocol, not knowing whether to follow their monarch closely, or to keep their distance. The royal umbrella-bearer had a most difficult task keeping up with his sovereign, and his anguish was clearly evident whenever the rays of the sun were inadvertently permitted to fall upon the royal visage. His Majesty, however, was gracious, and chose to overlook such shortcomings.

Queen Saowapa, although standing under five feet tall, was a commanding presence, and many of the guests were as eager to speak with her as they were with the King himself. She had married him in 1878 when she was just 16, and had borne him nine children, the last in 1893. Two years later, she was elevated to the status of First Queen, when her eldest son, Prince Vajiravudh, was pronounced heir to the throne. When she was young, she had been known as a great beauty, and although she was still attractive, it was her aura of authority these days that most attracted people to her.

It was well known that she had the ear of the King, and in fact, it was due to her intervention that the women of the Court were now permitted to mix with the foreigners at social functions. Before her time, the ladies of the Court had been mostly excluded, although a few old-timers still remembered the days of King Mongkut and the eclipse at Hua Wan, when some of his consorts had participated in the festivities.

Nowadays, the courtesans were present at many of the royal excursions, including picnics upcountry, trips to the palace at Bang Pa-In, and sailing on the royal yacht. The King had even appointed Queen Saowapa as regent while he was away in Europe in 1897, the first time a woman had held such a post in Siam.

Kesri, however, was unconcerned with the royal wanderings. She didn't even notice when His Majesty joined her father and his group some way off, and she found herself drifting from the conversation with Janie.

"Kesri! Are you listening to me at all?" Janie nudged her. "Or are you too busy making eyes at Romeo over there?"

"What? I don't know what you mean, Janie." She was mortified that she had been so obvious.

"Of course you do," Janie said, giggling. "And don't look now, but he's coming our way."

"He's what?"

"Bye." Janie walked away, grinning. "I'll be getting some punch."

"Janie, wait. You can't ..."

But she was gone. An instant later, the young man was standing before Kesri. His eyes were a startling shade of green, not the brown she had expected.

He held out his hand. "I don't believe we've been introduced. I'm Joseph Shaw. Everyone calls me Joe."

She came down to earth with a thud. "Oh dear," she exclaimed unintentionally, and took a step back as she let go of his hand. "I'm your cousin, Kesri Taylor."

He was silent for a moment as the news sank in. Then, "Well, we meet at last."

She began to relax. "I am only amazed we haven't met before now. You live in Chiengmai, I know, but you must have visited Bangkok from time to time."

"Oh, I can explain that," he replied. "I've not even been in Siam for years. I was sent to boarding school in England when I was very young. Then I went up to Oxford to start my degree—I was reading classics. Spent a year there, but got a bit tired of it. Just didn't seem practical, I suppose. So, I'm taking a year off to decide what I want to do. Mother wasn't very pleased, needless to say."

"And what about your father, Uncle Joseph?"

"Oh, Father's a good old stick. Said it was up to me, and whatever made me happy was fine by him. But I know that really, he's hoping I'll go back next year." He leaned closer and said conspiratorially, "Actually, if truth be told, I think he'd rather like me to become a man of the cloth. Or if not, a missionary teacher, like him." He grinned with a mischievous glint in his eyes, and she saw there was no chance of that.

"So, what will you do? Will you go back to England?"

"I expect so. I'd like to be a barrister, eventually, I think. Something useful. Perhaps even come back here one day to help establish a law school."

Janie arrived back with the punch, but seeing the two so obviously enjoying their conversation, she went off to talk to some other friends, thinking how unlike Kesri it was to show much interest in a boy. She was usually too involved in her photography, but she hadn't brought her camera today, at her father's insistence she socialise instead.

"And what about you, Kesri?" Joe asked. "I've heard very little about you from my parents, as you can imagine."

"Yes. Well, actually, there's not much to tell. I was educated here, mostly by private tutor, which was very tedious, and now I help my father with his books."

"Really? Are you a writer, then?"

"No, I'm taking photographs for him."

"Talented as well as beautiful," he said, making her blush. "Wasn't our grandfather Edward a photographer?"

"Yes, I use his old studio. All his photographs are still there. I wish you could see them."

"Not much chance of a family reunion in the near future, I'm afraid."

"Do you know what went on all those years ago? I'm dying to find out."

"No, my parents wouldn't tell me anything except that it was something between my mother and yours," he said.

"It must have been something awful to divide the family for this long. But surely it's nothing that could matter now."

"Yes, I agree. But some of these family feuds go on so

long, everyone forgets what the argument was about, and they simply hate each other. Like the Montagues and the Capulets."

"Janie was just saying that ... oh, it doesn't matter," She said, embarrassed. "Anyway, *Romeo and Juliet* is my favourite play."

He smiled in agreement. "Kesri, let's agree we'll end this feud. That you and I won't continue it, at least."

"Excellent idea! Let the Montagues and the Capulets be friends once more."

"Sealed with a kiss," he said, and before she could stop him, he had taken her hand and raised it to his lips.

Instead of pulling away, she looked at him, noticing again how green his eyes were.

"I'm sorry. You must think me rather rude," he said, at last releasing her hand.

"No ... it's just that you have my mother's eyes."

"No, I have *my* mother's eyes."

"Oh, of course—they must come from our grandfather's line, I suppose. I found a photo of your mother when she was very young, but of course, we cannot tell the colour from a photo. She is very beautiful."

"Yes," he agreed, 'but I've heard from certain parties— not my parents, you understand—that *your* mother was the true beauty of the family."

"She was beautiful, even when she was very ill, to the end."

"I'm sorry to hear she passed away."

"It was so unfair. She was young—only 34. Can you imagine?"

"I vaguely remember going to your house. The person I remember most, strangely enough, is your father. I don't know why, but I've a clear picture of his face in my mind."

"He hasn't changed much. A little grey at the temples, a few more lines on his face. I've always thought he was the most handsome man in the world."

Joe feigned disappointment. "Are you sure?"

"Well, perhaps there are some who could equal him," she teased. "And speaking of my father, he's here somewhere. If I see him, I'll have to leave you. He won't want to be introduced, I shouldn't think. And, while we're on the subject of parents, are you not supposed to be on your way to Chiengmai, to see yours?"

"I should be. But I've decided to take a slightly longer spell in Bangkok than anticipated. It seems odd that I was born here, yet I barely know it."

There was a pause. He took a chance before it was lost forever: "Kesri, is there any way I can see you again? I mean, alone? I realise it would have to be without my parents or your father knowing. I'm sorry, I don't mean to be forward, but we might never have another chance to get to know each other."

She was taken aback, and suddenly nervous. But equally, she realised she wanted to see him again, more than anything.

"I don't know. If only it were possible, but I can't think of a way."

"Think hard, Kesri, please. I'm determined this thing between our parents won't stop us from being friends. It's ridiculous."

"I'm determined, too, but I really don't know how." Suddenly, her eyes brightened. "I *do* know: you could come to my studio."

"Your studio? But it's in your father's house, isn't it? I'd never get past the front door."

"You wouldn't have to. There's a back entrance from the soi behind the house. No one would see you, and no one disturbs me there, especially if I have a sign on the door when I'm in the darkroom. I could show you Grandfather's photographs."

Joe thought for a moment, then nodded. "Why not? Let's live dangerously!"

"Come on Wednesday afternoon," she said boldly. "Father's usually out then, anyway. Here's how to get there ..."

Meanwhile, Sam was looking across the lawn, through the crowds, to where Kesri was talking to a young man. He could not see who the boy was, as his back was toward Sam, but he could see Kesri laughing and chatting comfortably, as if she had met him before.

They had been talking for some time and Sam wanted to excuse himself and wander over to her for an introduction. However, that would be impossible under the circumstances, because the King was still in his circle, and it would be unthinkable to excuse himself and leave.

A few minutes later, he noticed Kesri and the boy parting anyway. She smiled, and the young man took her hand briefly before walking away to another group. Meanwhile, the King took his leave of Sam's group and moved on.

Kesri breathed a sigh of relief that Joe had already gone when she spotted her father striding towards her. When he asked who her friend was, she was evasive. "Spying on me, Father?"

"Of course. I become very protective when I see my daughter so obviously interested in a young man. Someone special?"

"Not at all, I just met him, actually." She changed the subject quickly, trying desperately to prevent her face glowing bright red. "Hey, I bet I could beat you at croquet."

"You? A mere slip of a girl, beat the champion of Bangkok himself? We'll see about that, young lady."

From a safe distance, Joe watched them walk away together, arm in arm. Sam was tall and well built, and Joe certainly did not fancy getting on the wrong side of his uncle.

He had never met anyone like Kesri before who he had so immediately taken to. The girls he had met in England were either upper-class but impoverished snobs looking to catch a wealthy *and* titled heir, thus not interested in him, or bluestockings interested only in his mind. His few intimate encounters had been only fleetingly satisfying and he had lost interest quickly.

Kesri was different. He warmed to her personality even more than he did her physicality—which was strange, because she was an exceptionally beautiful young woman. He yearned to converse with her again, now that he had finally met her.

∞∞∞

It was two o'clock on Wednesday afternoon, and she had been pacing the studio floor since noon. They hadn't agreed an exact time since he was uncertain when he would finish a meeting regarding a shipment of supplies for the mission.

She had thought of nothing but him since the garden party. He had promised he would come, but what if he'd changed his mind, decided it was not worth the risk after all? She felt so strange, so different. Nothing like this had happened to her before. It was not just that she was attracted to him. There was something else; something she could not fathom. Was this love at first sight? How ironic that he was the very person her father would want her to stay away from most.

There was a light, hesitant tap on the door, and she rushed to open it, her heart pounding. She hurried him in, closing the door behind them. They looked at each other as they stood apart, awkward now to find themselves completely alone. Anything could happen, and no one would know.

Joe was consumed by worry that Sam would walk in and find them. "He'd be livid if he found us alone here. I'd have to explain myself, and then what?"

"Tell him you're a client come to see about some portraits."

"You have clients?"

"Well, I might soon. You can be my first. Anyway, I've locked the door. No one can just walk in."

The curtains were drawn and candles burned on the old wooden table. She busied herself pouring lime juice and setting out a plate of scones with jam, and the tension soon disappeared as they sat on the sofa together and looked through the old photographs. They laughed and talked like old friends, and it was as if they knew each other through and through.

When it was time for him to leave—because Sam would return home soon—they were strangers no more. As they said goodbye, he took her hands in his, and she didn't want him to let go.

∞∞∞

He visited as often as he could after that, sneaking furtively from the back soi like a fugitive, even when she assured him her father was out—and, in any case, would probably not even recognise him for who he was. Still, Joe was not entirely convinced and fretted constantly that they would be discovered.

Of course, she couldn't resist taking photographs of him, and he would help her develop them in the darkroom. He could have taken advantage of her on those occasions, but was always a perfect gentleman.

Kesri didn't know it, but Noi had seen Joe heading along the back path toward the studio on a number of occasions, also noticing that he did not emerge for hours. She saw the change in Kesri's eyes, but she was loyal to her mistress and told no one of the liaisons.

∞∞∞

Sam, too, recognised the signs. It was obvious his daughter was in love. But with whom? He always accompanied her to dances and other social functions, and she had not seemed attached to any one particular young man more than another. At first, he had thought it might be the young man at the garden party—but he had not appeared again, so it could not be him. She had her share of admirers, but it seemed to him she made little effort to encourage any of them. The rest of the time she spent alone in her studio.

It had crossed his mind that it might be her girlish imagination, and that her feelings had not been expressed, let alone reciprocated, that she merely dreamed of someone she had met or observed. But her behaviour and the look in her eyes were not those of a girl with an obsession over distance. He knew women well enough, and her demeanour suggested she was confident and sure in her love.

He could ask her directly, of course—and perhaps she was waiting for him to do just that. If she were really in love, and if the young man were suitable, he would have no objections. She would be 19 in December, a time when most young women were thinking of marriage—and Anchalee had been only 16 when they married, though he understood times had changed. He decided he would ask Kesri gently, at an opportune moment, if there was anything she would like to tell him.

Chiengmai, 1904

If he climbed the stairs too quickly, Joseph would find himself breathless by the time he reached the first landing. Sometimes, there was a tightness in his chest, as if a vice were crushing him. He had told no one about it and went on with his daily tasks as best he could.

He was 62 now, had lived in the tropics for more than 40 of those years and had been fortunate never to have had any of the serious diseases—consumption, malaria, cholera—that had killed so many of his friends. Several missionaries had drowned, while others had become chronically ill and had to be invalided home. Many were separated from their families for long periods as exhausted wives took their children and returned home, some never to see their husbands again.

He considered himself lucky that he and his family had so far remained fit and healthy. Elizabeth and he had been careful never again to put her in danger of becoming pregnant, and—in truth—Joseph these days was simply not energetic enough for regular intimate relations with his wife. She did not seem to mind.

He could no longer accompany the great Reverend McGilvary on his upcountry tours, despite the fact that the reverend was a good 14 years Joseph's senior. The old man was a legend in the north, famous for his jungle treks on a gigantic elephant, which gained him access to villages where Europeans had never before been seen. Joseph had accompanied him and his equally adventurous daughter, Cornelia, on an 81-day tour in 1890 to Lampang and Phrae, southeast of Chiengmai, where the reverend had baptised a Siamese convert; then they had continued up to Nan, on to remote Chieng Kong, as far north as Chiengsen, and then down to Chiengrai, where he had established a new church. McGilvary was popular wherever he went, and his procession of elephants was both feared and admired, serving to scare away bandits who might have robbed or even killed them if they had not been so awestruck.

Joseph had not joined the 1891 trip to Burma, which the reverend had planned to continue on to Muang Sing in Laos. That section of the expedition had been cancelled, however, when Joseph's replacement, Mr Phraner, had become seriously ill. There were also reports of bandits in the jungles ahead, so they had turned back.

Neither was Joseph able to travel with McGilvary on his five-month tour to Yunnan, China, in 1893, because he had been needed at the mission in Chiengmai. But he had taken his place on the 1897 trip to Muang Sing, during which the reverend—as usual—busied himself distributing scriptures, speaking to the people in their own language about the word of God.

From 1898, his seventieth year, McGilvary ended his extensive mission tours when the French government refused him permission to carry out further work in Laos. He was greatly disappointed, but he continued to visit villages around northern Thailand, often with Joseph his willing companion.

Joseph liked nothing better than to sit at night round a campfire on the banks of the Ping or Kok rivers and listen to the old man's stories. But it was not all reminiscing. McGilvary was still full of energy and had many plans for the future.

Never before considering himself an adventurer, Joseph was amazed to find himself not at all anxious or afraid during these journeys. He believed that if fever, or a tiger, or robbers were meant to take him, they would—wherever he might be. He also felt that God had too much work for him still to do to allow him to be taken this way.

But 18 months previously, he had returned from a week-long village tour exhausted as he had never been before. "I don't know what it could be," he told Elizabeth. "I don't feel terribly ill, yet I don't feel completely well, either. And this aching in my legs, constantly."

She took his hands in hers. "Joseph, it's nothing, I'm sure. Just that ... well, you're getting old, dear. You're not 40 any longer, or even 50. You can't live like a young man forever."

"But Reverend McGilvary ..."

"Is a walking marvel," she finished for him. "You don't need to try to keep up with him. We all age at different speeds, Joseph, and to tell you the truth, I *have* thought you looked tired lately. You need a rest from all this. Perhaps we should make a trip home, to see Joe. You've never been on furlough, not in all these years."

"Home? Elizabeth, I've never been to England in my life. It's hardly my home. And New Zealand was too long ago. No, the only home I have is Siam. Anyway, I'm needed here. You go again if you want to, my dear."

Now, in April 1904, he felt all of his years and more. He simply did not want to make a great effort to go anywhere, particularly during the hot season, which seemed to be more stifling than ever. He was happy in Chiengmai, as he had been from the moment they had arrived. He felt it had marked yet another chance in his life to start anew—the third chance, to be precise—away from the ugliness of what had happened in Bangkok. He still taught at the missionary school and helped with the Church's many administrative duties. He didn't plan to retire for at least three or four years yet.

Elizabeth didn't give up, and again broached the idea of visiting England. He finally agreed, though the idea held little appeal for him. She had endured much over the years though, had given him all the best years of her youth, and had been devoted to working for the mission's charities at a time when many young women of her class would have enjoyed a rich and idle social life. Now, he felt she deserved more comfort. Once he had retired, too, he knew it would sadden him to be sitting, useless, in a rocking chair in Chiengmai, while younger missionaries took over the job he loved.

There was nothing for him now in New Zealand, so there was no question of his wanting to return there. His parents had long since died, still bitter at their only child's youthful error. They left nothing to him, but donated all their worldly goods to the Church. Not that he had wanted or expected to inherit any money. But it would have been nice to have received a few family mementoes, or even a piece of the beautiful wooden furniture—made of the 35,000-year-old native kauri timber—that he remembered from his childhood.

But there had been nothing. Just a terse note from their solicitor to inform him that his mother and father had passed away, barely three weeks apart, of natural causes. The letter did not even say where they had been buried or who had attended their funerals.

Chapter 33

For two weeks, their entire time together, he had been a gentleman in every respect, making no attempt even to kiss her on the lips, just a chaste peck on the cheek now and again. Perhaps that was why, despite her growing love for him, his words still came as something of a shock.

"Marry you? I don't know what to say! We can't possibly. The family—."

"Hush," he said, taking her into his arms. He kissed her eyelids and the tip of her nose. "Don't you love me as much as I love you?"

"Yes, of course I do. I've loved you from the moment I first saw you. I feel as though we were made for each other. We belong together. You seem to know everything about me, everything I think and feel."

"Then marry me."

"Father would never agree."

"How do you know?"

"Because I know the way he feels about your parents. Because he's told me I mustn't have anything to do with you. He's hardly going to let me marry you."

"From what you've said, though, he's a reasonable man. If you explained to him that you love me, that we're not interested in the feud, that we intend to put an end to it, whether they like it or not, I'm sure he'd agree. Once we're 21, they can't prevent us anyway."

"But I'm not 21 for nearly three years."

"No, but I am. Or will be in three months. I'll be an adult, and they'll have to listen to me."

"I don't know if I could bear it if Father wouldn't give his approval. I don't want to go against him. He's always been so wonderful to me."

He smoothed her long straight hair and wiped a tear from her cheek. "I know. Don't cry, sweetheart. He'll surely listen to you. And after you've explained everything, you'll have his blessing for certain."

"But what about your parents? What will they say?"

"Well, I *would* like their blessing, too, I admit it. But Father's stubborn. Although he talks of forgiveness, I don't think he always practises what he preaches. Mother does have some influence, though. Perhaps I should tell her first and let her speak to him."

"Are you sure we're not too young? And, also, we are first cousins—there are some who would think that a little too close."

"Nonsense, our dear late Queen Victoria, after all, married Prince Albert, who was her first cousin."

"Well, what about Oxford?"

"Come with me to England. With my inheritance, we'll have no financial concerns—whether or not our parents agree."

"And my inheritance equals yours, luckily. Thank goodness for Grandfather."

"It doesn't matter anyway. I'd still want to marry you even if we were paupers, even if we were cut off without a penny and our parents disowned us. Don't you see? You're the most important person in my life now. Oxford, my career, even my parents don't come before you. I love you, Kesri."

He kissed her then in a different way, and she responded as his hand moved to her breast. She felt a ripple of warmth along her spine, and she gave herself up to its pleasures as she sank into his embrace. When she made no protest, he raised her skirt and caressed her thighs through her silk stockings. Then his fingers moved along the fabric until he reached the skin where a stocking ended, and together they sank to the floor.

∞∞∞∞

The pictures of Joe were her first formally-posed portraits, and she had pinned them up round the room, trying to choose the best one to be enlarged and framed. He wanted to present the picture to his mother on his return to Chiengmai and thereby open conversation about the photographer.

As she stood back from one of the images, there was a knock at the studio door. Although she wasn't expecting him, she assumed he had decided to come anyway, and she skipped over to answer the knock. As she swung the door open though, she was caught completely by surprise. "Oh ... Father! I wasn't expecting you."

"I can see that, but you look as if you were expecting someone." He smiled and moved past her into the studio before she could make an excuse to keep him out.

"And here he is, no doubt." He walked from print to print, looking closely, as Kesri held her breath. The young man looked familiar somehow, though Sam was sure he did not know him.

"So, this is the young man, eh?"

"This is who, Father?" When he remained silent, she found herself gabbling. "I'm not sure what you mean. He's just a client who wants a portrait for his mother, that's all. They've turned out quite well, don't you think?"

Sam laughed. "You're not a good liar, my dear. You don't have to keep this a secret from me. He looks like a respectable young man. Why don't you tell me about him?"

He looked closely at one of the shots. Again, he was sure he had seen the young man before, but could not recall where. And he wondered, once more, how he could have missed the developing relationship between them—and where, in fact, it had been taking place. He looked at another portrait—the only one in which the boy was smiling—and felt as if he should know his name.

She poured him a glass of lemonade, nervously considering what to say or do. After a few moments' thought, she accepted that she could not keep it from him any longer.

"Why don't you sit down, Father, and we'll talk."

He sipped his drink, waiting for her to begin.

"You're right," she said. "He is someone I care deeply about. We met only a few weeks ago, but we feel as if we've known each other all our lives. And in a way, we have."

"Are you in love with him, my dear?"

She looked down, embarrassed. "Yes, Father, I—think so."

"And does he feel the same?"

"He does. He's told me many times. In fact, he's ... he's asked me to marry him and I have said yes."

"Kesri, then why haven't I met him? Why hasn't he come to the house and discussed this with me? I don't even know who he is." He paused, waiting for an answer; none was forthcoming. "Who is he, Kesri? Why are you so reluctant to tell me?"

She looked at her hands in her lap, not at him.

"Because I'm ... I mean, he's ..."

Suddenly, he feared the worst. "You're not in trouble, are you, Kesri? Please tell me you're not ..."

"No! No, Father, nothing like that." She prayed that she wasn't.

"I'm relieved to hear it. Now, tell me his name, Kesri."

"I'm afraid to," she admitted. "You won't like him, and you won't give your consent."

"Kesri, I don't even know him. How can I dislike him, and how can I agree or disagree with your decision if I've never met him?"

"The truth is, you have met him, long ago. But you won't

agree to our marriage, I know. It's because ... because of his family."

"Are they good people?"

She nodded.

"Then I'm sure I won't disapprove of them." A thought occurred to him. "You know, it doesn't matter if they're not both European, if that's what you're worried about. Kesri, think of your own mother, and think of my own mother, too—and myself. I am not and could not be prejudiced."

"They're British, as it happens."

"Then what's the problem? Who is he?"

"He's ... he's ..." —she swallowed hard, then said it— "my cousin, Joe Shaw." She bit her lip nervously and looked across at him.

His face was suddenly ashen. He looked as if his life had flashed before him in the split second before death seems certain. And in a real way, it had. Of course. He recognised the face in the photograph because it was very like himself. His daughter wanted to marry his son—her own half-brother. Neither had any idea, of course, so could not imagine the consequences. It would be incest—if it wasn't already. It was horrific to even contemplate.

"I knew you'd be angry," she said in a small voice. "I knew you wouldn't understand."

When he spoke, it was as if he were pleading. "You can't be serious, Kesri. Tell me you're not serious." Never in his worst nightmares had he imagined this happening.

"Father, I *am* serious, and I'm so sorry to have deceived you. But really, it will be all right, you'll see."

"Deceived me?" he said quietly, still reeling from what she had said, but unable to tell her the true reason for his horror. With a shock, he realised Joe Shaw as the young man from the garden party in whom she had been so interested.

"Kesri, you know how I feel about them. How could you do this to me? How could you do this to yourself? Besides, you are too closely related."

"First cousins marry all the time, Father. There's nothing shameful in that. And Joe and I have decided that this family feud is stupid. We won't continue it. It must stop. It all happened so long ago. How can you continue it for so long?"

"There's a lot you don't know, Kesri, and there's so much I cannot tell you."

"But it doesn't make any sense." She choked back her tears. "It's not fair that Joe and I are punished for something that happened 20 years ago between Mother and Aunt Elizabeth."

"It didn't concern only them, Kesri. It involved all of us. You must believe me. You can't marry Joe. You cannot and you *will not*. It's impossible, and that's my final word on the matter."

Tears of frustration ran down her cheeks. "I thought I'd make you understand. I thought you'd listen to reason, that you'd want me to be happy. Can't you at least try to see that I love Joe, and he loves me. That's all that matters. We ..."

"No!" he roared, leaping to his feet. "I forbid you to see him again, do you hear? You'll not see him or speak to him, and you have no hope in hell of marrying him, ever. Have I made myself clear?" He was desperate now.

"No!" she returned defiantly, also jumping to her feet. "I'll never give him up, never, do you hear? I love him, I love him."

He grabbed her by the wrists before she could flee from the studio. "Kesri, don't force my hand on this. If you don't agree to end this now, I'll send you to a finishing school in Europe, and while you're gone, I'll arrange your marriage to some suitable man, and your inheritance will become his property. If you don't do as I say, I will have you committed to a lunatic asylum."

He had never imagined himself talking this way to her —intimidating her in the most monstrous way—and he hated himself for it. He loved her, but this was a situation of utter despair for him. He had to prevent his daughter from marrying her own half-brother without giving away the shameful secret.

Indeed, he had never before spoken to her in such a way, nor had she imagined that he could. She was horrified. "Father, you wouldn't do that, surely? How could you threaten me like that? How could you?"

"I've never been more serious in my life. Mark my words, Kesri. This is no idle threat. It is a promise of the consequences if you do not give him up immediately."

She pulled away and looked at him with disdain, but also with deep hurt. "You really would, wouldn't you? You'd ruin my life, just to continue this ridiculous family argument that has nothing to do with either Joe or me." She turned and hurried for the door. "I'll never forgive you for this. Never!" she said, as she rushed away up to the main house. "And I *will* marry him, you'll see."

He took several deep breaths and tried to calm himself, tried to prevent himself from ripping the portraits to shreds. But then he found himself staring at the photographs, unable to tear himself away from images of the son he had never known, with his own dark wavy hair, his own expression reflected back at him. But there was something else there, too: a compassion about the mouth, and the way he held his head. That was from his mother, Sam thought, and then he wondered if she ever thought of him, and if she had the least idea what their son had unwittingly become entangled in. Was it possible that Joe had already written to her of his intention, that the letter that would break her heart was right this minute being transported up north?

Kesri was right about the feud continuing too long, but what else could he tell her? The truth would be devastating. Even now, he realised, it was better for him to suffer the torment of his daughter despising him, than to have her despising herself—scarred for life—if she knew the truth. If he could just prevent her seeing Joe again, he was sure she would eventually recover from the heartbreak. She was young; time would heal, and she would forget him.

At least she wasn't pregnant, she had assured him—and from her reply to his query, Joe had presumably not made physical advances. That is, if she were telling the truth. He could hardly bare to think of the possible consequences if the worst had happened. But she was not a liar, he was sure. He still trusted his daughter at her word, even after her deception.

He should not have. For in her room, where she had thrown herself on to her bed, Kesri was already planning their next meeting, and how she could continue to see Joe without her father's knowledge. They would just have to find a safer meeting place, now he knew what Joe looked like.

She wished her father had had a telephone installed so she could have called Joe at the mission house where he was staying. The first telephones had appeared in Bangkok 18 years previously, and it was becoming commonplace to have one, particularly among the foreign community. Sam, however, maintained that the irregular service was worse than useless, especially during the wet season, and that if one had a telephone, one would come to rely on it—but in Bangkok, it was liable to be out of order more often than not, he said. As she had no way of contacting Joe easily, she would have to let him visit one more time and hope they were not observed.

∞∞∞

She hurriedly let him in and locked the door when he arrived at the studio the next day. "Did anyone follow you?" she inquired nervously.

"Follow me? No, of course not. Why?"

"Oh, Joe, Father knows. I had to tell him. He saw the photographs and he's forbidden me to see you again."

"My God, do you think he's watching you?"

"That wouldn't be his style. He said he still trusts me to do the right thing. Joe, he says he's going to send me away to Europe if I don't stop seeing you, to some cloistered school, and then he'll marry me off to someone of his choice. He's serious. He doesn't make idle threats."

"I take it he wasn't impressed when he discovered who I was."

"He wouldn't listen to me at all, or even discuss it. He wasn't interested in how I felt. I thought he was going to hit me. I love you, Joe, you know that." There were tears in her eyes, and she sank on to the sofa. "But I don't know what we can do."

He sat beside her and put his arm round her. "Don't worry. We'll elope."

"*Elope!*" She couldn't believe it. Surely that would be impossible.

"I've got a plan. You know it's my birthday in June, and to claim my inheritance I have to appear at the London solicitors in person? You too, when you claim yours. Well, I can be perfectly plain to my parents about leaving for England. I'll tell them I'm going back to university as well, so I'll have to leave very soon. I just won't tell them I'm taking you with me. I shall have to go to Chiengmai first to see them, of course. But it won't be for long."

"Joe, I can't see how it would work, and—well, it wouldn't be right."

"Kesri, just listen. We'll marry as soon as we reach England. Or, there might even be a reverend on board the ship to marry us. We could say we've been living together and you're expecting my child. Whether on board ship or on shore in England, someone will marry us, rather than see you become a ruined woman with an illegitimate child. Even though you are under 21, thus technically need your father's permission, I think we would be able to get around it. I know we could. Then you will be Mrs Shaw, and there will be nothing they can do about it. Trust me, Kesri!"

She could think of a number of holes in his plan, but even greater than those was the thought of leaving her home in disgrace, leaving her father, and sailing for a land she had never seen before. Siam was all she knew.

Chapter 34

In Chiengmai, Joseph Shaw was working at home that day and found himself alone in the house except for Simon, the servant who was still with him after all these years. Elizabeth had gone to play bridge with friends, a rare afternoon off from her good works and one of her few pleasurable indulgences. Simon looked in on Joseph to say he was going out on an errand but that Kob would be home if he needed anything. Kob was Simon's wife of 10 years, who was employed in the house as a maid. She was busy in their own quarters—the bamboo residence Joseph had built at the back of the house—attending to their five children.

Joseph stretched his arms in front of him and looked out the windows to the lush, tranquil garden beyond. There were banana palms, heavy with fruit that Kob would deep-fry with lime juice and sesame seeds as a treat for the children. There were also hedges on which mauve flowers climbed, and there were banks of low bushes with bright orange blooms.

He decided on a nap before Elizabeth returned at five o'clock, and stood warily from his desk, then went into the hallway to climb the stairs. He really was feeling unusually tired and had to pause for breath halfway up. Perhaps he'd ask Dr McGilvary for a tonic, he thought, and then decided it could wait until tomorrow. He hadn't the energy even to summon Kob.

Just as he neared the top, he suddenly clutched his chest.

The pain was more gripping than usual, and as the tightness increased, he gasped for breath. He grabbed at the banister in an effort to support himself on the final step, but missed his footing, and—with everything seeming to occur so slowly— realised he was going to fall. His arm did not respond when he lunged to catch hold of the banister, and then he hit the hard wooden stairs, rolling over and over, down and down— for what seemed an eternity—to, finally, blessed blackness.

$$\infty\infty\infty$$

When Elizabeth returned home two hours later, it was to find Simon, Kob and their children huddled together on the porch, all silently waiting for her. She hurried up to the house, immediately aware that something was very wrong.

"Whatever's happened, Simon?" she called in alarm.

"Madame, the Master is sick, very sick. Doctor with him now. So sorry."

She rushed inside, calling for Joseph. Dr McKean, an American who lived nearby, appeared at the top of the stairs.

"Doctor, what's happened? Where's my husband? Has there been an accident?"

His expression told her it was serious. "You'd best come into the front room, Mrs Shaw."

She sat on the old chesterfield with a great sense of foreboding, as the doctor removed his glasses and sat beside her.

"Mrs Shaw, I'm very sorry to have to tell you that Mr Shaw passed away this afternoon. It was his heart, I think. It just suddenly gave out. He didn't suffer for long, Mrs Shaw, I'm certain. Simon found him at the bottom of the stairs. He must have fallen during the attack."

She looked at him with glazed eyes, shocked. "There was … there was nothing you could do?"

"He was already gone when Simon found him. When the

heart gives up, we're helpless. I'm so sorry again, Mrs Shaw. He was a good man. What can I do to assist you with arrangements?"

"Is he ... is Joseph upstairs?" Her voice was quiet and calm.

He nodded. "Simon helped me carry him there. We thought it appropriate that he lie in his own bed."

"Yes, it's what he would have wanted," she said dully. "I'd like to see him now. I'll go up alone. Thank you."

When she entered the room, she at first thought the doctor had been mistaken. Surely Joseph, lying on the bed so serenely, was only asleep? She leaned over him, touched his cheek, and kissed his lips. But he was already cold. He had been much older than her, and she had always known he would probably die before her. But in her mind, he was still relatively young, and she had never really imagined herself a widow so soon.

And there was young Joe. How would she tell him? He had written to say he had arrived in Bangkok, that he would come to Chiengmai soon, but that he wanted to return to England. That would leave her alone, and the thought terrified her.

She looked again at the peaceful face of her dear husband, and the past came once again to haunt her.

"Oh Joseph, I wronged you so much. I hurt you and caused you great suffering," she cried. "But you always forgave me and loved me, despite everything."

She took off her hat and shoes then, and climbed up on the bed to lie beside him one last time before they buried him in the warm earth of his adopted homeland.

It was unpleasantly hot, with neither a breath of wind

nor a cloud in the sky on the day of the funeral. During the service, most of the more than 100 mourners managed to find shelter under the trees, but Elizabeth stood stoical in the blazing sun, watching as the coffin was lowered into the ground. She stepped up to the graveside, letting the single white orchid she had picked from the garden he had loved so much, slide from her fingers. Then Mrs McGilvary led her away and into the waiting carriage.

∞∞∞

She had sent a telegraph to Joe at the mission in Bangkok the day after Joseph's death, and Joe had left early the next morning, though he knew he would miss the funeral. In the searing heat of the season, a body had to be interred almost immediately. Although travel had improved markedly within Siam, it would still take Joe two weeks to reach Chiengmai.

Kesri received a hastily-scribbled note from a courier with instructions to deliver it to her hands only. It said simply, "My darling, something awful has happened that may see our plans postponed. I received a telegraph to say my father has died suddenly, and my mother, of course, is distraught. I must leave for Chiengmai at once, and she may need me for some time. Nothing else has changed. I love you. Wait for me. All my love, Joe."

Tears came to her eyes as she read the news. She wanted to be there to comfort him, to hold him. The note read almost matter-of-factly, but she knew how much he loved and respected his father, how much he had looked up to him. He, too, would be devastated.

∞∞∞

"I shall stay with you, Mother, as long as you need me," he promised as they embraced. "I can postpone the trip to England for the moment."

She smiled gratefully. He had always been a wonderful son, and he was there for her now, never disappointing her. She was proud of him.

"I've decided to go back to Bangkok to live," she told him. "There's nothing for me here now in the long term. In due course, I think I might even retire to England. But I will spend some time in Bangkok while I adjust to being alone."

Even the prospect of seeing Sam again—perhaps unintentionally, perhaps not—did not concern her now. She was tired of hiding from her past.

Joe agreed with her. "Mother, that's a wonderful idea. It's best for you. And you won't be alone. I'll be there as long as necessary."

"Nonsense, dear. You have your own life to lead. Don't forestall on my account."

∞∞∞∞

Kesri had to wait for the obituary to appear in the newspaper before she could discuss Joseph's death with her father, which she did over breakfast.

"Yes, I heard yesterday," he said, without looking up from the letter from his publisher that he was reading.

"You knew and you didn't tell me?"

"It doesn't concern you," he said coldly, and made no further comment. He certainly did not tell her that he had received a telegraph from Elizabeth herself.

If only you knew just how much it does concern me, she thought. But they would not be leaving for England as soon as they'd planned. She had already started to pack a trunk in her studio, but would now have to unpack it, in case it was discovered. Then an idea occurred to her: Joe had said his father was the one most likely to oppose their marriage. Now that he had passed away, perhaps there would not be such strong objection from his mother. Perhaps Joe could at least solicit approval from Aunt Elizabeth against her father's stubborn refusal.

∞∞∞

Meanwhile, in Chiengmai, Joe had arrived at the same conclusion. He decided to tell his mother about Kesri, hoping that when they returned to Bangkok, maybe she could do something to convince Sam to see reason.

Elizabeth's reaction, however, was as vehement as Kesri had described Uncle Sam's. She went deathly pale and buried her head in her hands. "Oh Joe, this is my worst nightmare. I must have misheard you. Please, tell me I did."

His face fell, and he was shocked at her reaction. "No, Mother, you're not mistaken. I love her dearly and I intend to marry her. I know about the family feud, and I don't care. We don't care."

She clasped her hands together in her lap so tightly, her nails dug into her palms. "You know nothing about what really happened," she said.

"Then tell me. It was nearly 20 years ago, Mother. For goodness' sake, it can't be that bad."

"I cannot tell you what happened ... not now. But believe me when I say that you cannot marry Kesri."

"Please, Mother, hear me out. Why must Kesri and I be punished because of something that happened so long ago? I thought you'd understand."

Again, her head fell into her hands in despair. "Oh, Joe, I understand only too well. Now listen to me: you do not, cannot love her as a husband loves a wife. You must be mistaken."

"No, mother! I know that I love her in this way. Please, when we return to Bangkok, will you at least go to see Uncle Sam to talk about this with him, see what can be done? Tell him how much I love Kesri and how happy I shall make her—if only he'll give me the chance. Will you talk to him?"

Slowly, she raised her head again to look directly into his eyes. "Yes, I must talk to Sam. This has gone far enough. I have no other choice." *You cannot ever marry her*, Elizabeth re-affirmed to herself, *but how do I tell you why?*

∞∞∞

When they arrived in Bangkok, Elizabeth wasted no time. After settling in at the Oriental Hotel and freshening up after the long journey, she went directly to his house, having sent a message in advance. Sam informed Kesri that she was not to converse with her aunt on the matter of Joe, but that she might greet her when she arrived.

Kesri had been looking nervously out of the front room window for over an hour, and when she finally saw Elizabeth walking up the path, she recognised her immediately from the photograph. She was older, of course, but the refined beauty that had set her apart in youth was still striking. Indeed, hers was the kind of mature loveliness that improved gracefully with age.

Kesri opened the door and trembled slightly as she spoke to her for the first time. "Aunt Elizabeth! Please come in."

Elizabeth—almost in panic herself at the prospect of meeting Sam again after so long—had never thought of herself as an aunt. She had, after all, never been addressed as such, either in writing or in person, all these years. The young woman before her had much of her mother's looks, but there was also a softness about her features, a sweet prettiness that was something apart from Anchalee.

Despite the fact that she had come to ensure her son would never see Kesri romantically again—and that this would surely break the girl's heart—she smiled warmly and genuinely at her niece. She took her hand as she entered, and they embraced briefly. "Kesri, it's wonderful to see you after all these years. You know though that I've come to see your father. Please tell him I'm here."

"Where is Joe?" she asked.

"He's taking care of some business at the mission for his father, before he returns to England."

She wanted to ensure the two of them were kept apart and had asked Joe to settle some of Joseph's affairs. She was certain this work would keep him busy until his departure in a few days.

Kesri showed Elizabeth into the parlour, and went up to Sam's study, tapping on the door before entering the room. "Father, she's here."

His face was a calm surface that concealed a maelstrom of emotions. "All right, then. Would you show her up here, please? And have Noi bring us some tea."

"Yes, Father." She almost ran from the room.

He waited apprehensively. It was almost 18 years since they had spoken, and now she was here. What would he say to her? Then he reminded himself that they had business to attend to. The business of their son and their daughter ...

All too soon, there was another tap on the door, and there she was before him. At first glance, she looked almost the same as she had when he last saw her. But then he noticed the lines etched round her mouth, the circles under eyes, and the wan cheeks that had once been rosy. He went toward her, stopping an arm's length away.

She saw he was not much changed. He was as handsome as ever, his dark hair still thick and wavy, greying only a little at the temples. But the young adventurer with the fire in his eyes had mellowed. At 53, he looked comfortable, settled, and satisfied, as if he no longer cared to burn up the world's trails with his energy.

There was a long silence between them until she spoke first. "I had to come, Sam."

"I was sorry to hear of Joseph's death," he replied quickly.

"Thank you. And Anchalee, too. I wanted so much to come to her funeral."

"Yes, I know. But please, sit down." He indicated the leather sofa by the window. "It's been a long time, Elizabeth. Are you back in Bangkok permanently?"

"I'm not sure. I've moved from Chiengmai permanently, of that I'm certain. There is no reason for me to stay, now that Joseph has gone. I'm at the Oriental until I can find a suitable house. Joe's at the mission house, settling the last of his father's affairs. But I needed to see you immediately, Sam. I think you will know what it is about."

He raised a finger to his lips then as he nodded toward the door. "The walls have ears, I suspect," he said. She caught his drift immediately and nodded. From this moment on, they talked in lowered voices. He sighed deeply. "Yes, I do know what it is about. Joe and Kesri."

"Sam, this is a catastrophe, as you must realise. They really believe they are in love and will marry, and they're adamant no one will stand in their way."

"No, not any more. Kesri gave me her word she would never see him again."

"Don't be so sure. From what Joe tells me, nothing has altered their feelings or their plans."

He was shocked that Kesri would disobey him, and he realised now that their attachment was more serious than he had thought.

"Have you told Joe it isn't possible?"

"Of course."

"But have you told him *why*?" He leaned forward earnestly from his chair opposite her.

"No, I couldn't. It would break him to discover so close to Joseph's death that he was not really his father."

"I couldn't tell Kesri, either."

"But we must tell them now, Sam. We must."

"Why? If we can keep them apart and just forbid the marriage, that should be enough."

"Sam, I'm afraid they'll do something rash. I'm worried they're going to elope. After all, in the eyes of the law and on their birth certificates, they are merely first cousins. Marriage would be legal. Oh Sam, we can't afford to take the chance that they might do this. Has it occurred to you that our daughter could become pregnant with her own half-brother's child?"

"I asked her. There's been no … intimate contact. I have to believe her."

"That may be, but if they did run away, we couldn't apprehend them soon enough to stop it. It would be too late."

He thought for a moment, then looked up at her again, utterly defeated. "You're right, Elizabeth, there's no other way. They must be told. Today."

Elizabeth was still afraid of what it would do to Joe to discover in the same breath that not only was the woman he loved his half-sister, but that the man he had known as his father all his life was, in reality, his step-father and no blood relation. She wished Joseph were still alive to guide her. Then again, she was glad he would not have to witness Joe's reaction to the truth, if it came to that.

"We should probably have told them long ago," Sam said. "After all, as Kesri herself says, it's not that unusual for cousins to fall in love and marry."

"But we didn't realise they even knew each other."

"I know, but we were fooling ourselves to believe they wouldn't meet at some time. The foreign community is small; it's difficult to avoid people, even if you want to. Eventually, Joe was bound to spend some time in Bangkok and to move in the same social circles."

"You're right. But it's too late for regrets now."

She stood and walked to the window. "It is good to see you again, Sam, despite these circumstances." She looked at him directly. "I didn't think I ever would. Not like this."

He walked toward her then and she didn't pull away when he took both her hands in his. "The people we could have hurt by continuing even the vaguest of friendships are gone now, sadly. Let's help each other through this crisis. And then—."

"And then?" she asked, realising with a jolt that he still had power over her, and that through it all, even though she had despised him at times and tried to push him from her memory, she still cared for him.

"Then, we can be friends, I hope." He released her hands.

She lowered her eyes. "I hope so, too."

"This will be a terrible shock to Joe, won't it? To find out that Joseph wasn't his father?"

Elizabeth looked up again, tears pricking her eyelids. "Oh Sam, you don't know how much Joe loved and respected him. Joseph was wonderful when Joe was small, and he never once referred or even alluded to the fact that Joe wasn't his son. They were father and son in every way that was important. It may ruin him to discover it was a lie. In one day, he'll lose the woman he wants to marry, and his own identity. Not to mention what he will think of me."

"Wait, Elizabeth. There is another way. A way by which Joe wouldn't have to be told the truth. If you're agreeable, I think it might work."

He motioned to her to sit again, and she did so, desperate to hear anything that might lessen the pain she was about to inflict on her only child.

Chapter 35

Kesri, of course, had put her ear to the keyhole as soon as Elizabeth had entered the study and closed the door behind her. Infuriatingly though, she had been able to hear nothing of their conversation. The teak door was thick and solid, and they had kept their voices low, as if they had known she would be eavesdropping just outside. After a few minutes, she gave up and went back to her own room.

She was back again at her father's call. When she entered the study, she found him and Aunt Elizabeth sitting on the sofa together. Any hopes she had entertained of them relenting faded completely as she noted her father's grim expression.

"Sit down, Kesri. There's something we must discuss with you. Something that will change the way you feel about Joe."

Puzzled, she did as he asked and sat on the chair opposite them. "Nothing will change the way I feel," she said resolutely. "I love him and he loves me. It's as simple as that. As simple as two strangers falling in love."

"Falling in love is rarely simple, Kesri," he said.

"Why? Why can't you accept what has happened and put your silly old feud to rest?"

Sam glanced at Elizabeth. She nodded almost imperceptibly.

"I think I can say that there is no feud between your aunt and me. There never was, as you will see shortly."

Kesri looked from one to the other, now even more perplexed. "But I don't understand. Then why…"

Elizabeth stood and smoothed down her skirt. "I think this is best discussed between the two of you, in private. I wanted to be here today, Kesri, to tell you that you must believe everything your father says, and you must do exactly as he directs. In this, we are united. He will tell you some things that will hurt you, but they're things you must know—for they concern your future, and of course Joe's future. They also concern the past." She paused. "I shall go now. I can see myself out." She motioned for Sam to remain seated as she left. "And please, Sam—Kesri—if there's anything I can do to help—." Her voice cracked, and she turned and walked from the room, closing the door softly behind her.

"Father, has something terrible happened to Joe?" she said, looking suddenly alarmed.

"No, Kesri. Joe's fine. But now we must talk about this love you think you feel for him—this desire you think you have to marry him."

She was becoming impatient with him. "It's not just something I imagine I have. It's something I know I have, something real. I feel deeply for Joe and nothing you say will change that. Not even if he were a murderer, or anything else." She was red with anger now, frustrated with his seeming inability to treat her as an adult. But she was also very afraid of what he would tell her. Not certain she could face it yet, she got up defiantly to leave the room.

"I've had enough of your orders and threats. I will marry him, and I don't care what you say."

Before he could stop her, she had fled. She closed her bedroom door behind her, and sat on the bed, shaking with fury. What could she do to make him understand? She had never known him to be so stubborn, especially where she was concerned. She thought again of dear Joe and yearned for him. He had been away so long, it seemed, and she needed to be with him.

She remembered the last time they were together. It had seemed such a natural thing to happen, and she felt no guilt. When she recalled his intimate touches on every part of her body, she shivered still. Her only thought as he had entered her for the first time was that this was the man she would spend her life with—and she would not have even cared if they had conceived a child then. As events were transpiring, she wished they had, so there could be no further objections. She longed to feel him within her again, the two of them locked in an embrace that felt as if it would never end.

But now there was an impatient rapping on her door and—without waiting for her to invite him—Sam opened the door and stood there, a look of deep distress on his face. "Kesri, you must listen to me," he began.

She hated to defy and hurt him in this way, but she would not relent. "It's no use, Father. My mind's made up, with or without your blessing. I don't care what you have to say."

"Would you care if I told you Joe was your brother?"

She faltered, instantly frozen, a look of astonishment, horror, and disbelief on her face. "My what?" she finally whispered.

She stood and moved toward him, staring at him as if he were speaking a foreign tongue. Fear had completely overwhelmed her, and she was shaking as she asked in panic, "What do you mean, my brother? What do you mean exactly?"

He took her by the shoulders then, guiding her back to the side of the bed and sitting beside her.

"Kesri, the reason I've been absolutely opposed to this relationship between you and Joe—so abhorred by it—is not because I dislike Joe or his parents. It's because such a relationship between you is impossible. You see, a long time ago, your Aunt Elizabeth and I were ... very close. Intimate. It was before I knew your mother well ..."

Her face was drained of colour, her eyes wild and disbelieving.

"Kesri, your aunt and I were in love, and I was planning

414

to marry her. But I was young and impetuous, and I was called away at short notice for an expedition to the north. When I returned, she was already married to Joseph. They had a baby son who everyone said had been born prematurely. I was suspicious at the time, and when the child was still very young, I realised the truth. Elizabeth had been expecting my child when she married Joseph. You see, she believed I'd deserted her. I had not—it was all a dreadful mistake. Actually, there was more to it than that, but we needn't go into that now.

"Anyway, Joseph nobly agreed to marry her and bring up the child as his own, to protect her reputation. It was the most selfless act I've ever known a person to perform."

Kesri was very still, and when she spoke, her voice was almost inaudible and seemingly not her own. "And the child. The child was Joe?"

"Yes. The child was Joe. I'm his father, Kesri. And he is your half-brother. He knows nothing of this. He still believes Joseph is—was—his father. I know it would destroy him if he found out the truth now."

"The King is married to several of his half-sisters," she said.

"What's that?"

She looked toward him, but her eyes were unfocused. "King Chulalongkorn has married some of his half-sisters. The Siamese kings always have, because there aren't enough women of high enough station for them to marry." She was calm, trying to make it right.

Sam knew she was in shock, though what she said was true, and he reminded himself that she was, after all, part-Siamese herself. Despite the fact that she had been raised, for the greater part, as a westerner, there could be no doubt that the country of her birth, its culture and customs—quite distinctive from his own—had influenced her to a great degree.

"Dear Kesri, I understand this situation has worked well for royalty in this country. But, whether you like it or not, you are considered American, as I am. And Joe is considered

British. Under the rules, it would not be allowed. And in our cultures, it is considered an aberration. You would be outcasts forever."

She broke down then, knowing he was right. "Why in God's name did you not tell me this before? Oh Father, I know, I know. I didn't mean I would consider it now. I know I cannot marry my own brother."

"I should have told you, but I had no idea this would happen."

"Does Joe know yet? Oh, it will break him in so many ways."

"That's another thing I want to talk to you about, Kesri. You must know that if Joe ever discovered the truth of this, it would be ... Kesri, he must never know. You must do as I say, and what Elizabeth also asks, for Joe's sake."

He explained the plan to her, and she nodded silently. Yes, she would do it. After he left at her request, she lay on the bed, face down, weeping uncontrollably. Her father would never know the depth of her torment, how far their relationship had gone, and her sorrow at learning the truth.

As Sam walked down the hallway back to his study, he heard her cries of anguish. He resolved to send her away from Bangkok at the earliest moment—hopefully that same day, so Joe had no opportunity to see her before he left.

May 15ᵗʰ, 1904

My dearest Joe,

You will probably have begun to realise by now that I will not be meeting you today. I have decided against eloping with you. I have searched my soul to find my true feelings, and I know now without a doubt that I cannot marry you, not now nor at any time in the future. I am afraid I have come to realise that I sim-

ply do not love you in that way. I love you as a wonderful person, as someone I respect and admire, as a dear cousin, but not as I should love a husband. To go through with our plans would be to live a lie, and I cannot do that to you.

I know how much this letter will hurt you, how you will not want to believe it, how you will want to come running to me to try to change my mind. Please do not, if you truly care for me. My mind is set, and for you to try to contact me at this time would only bring us both more pain. In any case, by the time you read this, I will be away from Bangkok. I cannot tell you where, and it would be futile for you to try to find me. I am truly sorry for the hurt I have caused you.

Please, Joe, go to England and do all you had planned, only it must be without me. Do not look back, and do not wish for something that cannot be. Look to the new life you shall have, the happiness you shall surely find. I should like to think that at some time in the future, we could become friends, as cousins should be. I give you my word that this is wholly my own decision, that these are my true feelings, and have nothing to do with my father's influence.

Your affectionate cousin,

Kesri Taylor

She sealed the letter and gave it to her father. When the time came, he would send it to where she had promised to meet Joe, telling the messenger, "It's for Mr Joe Shaw only. Deliver it into his hands and no one else's."

It was the hardest thing she had ever done. It would leave him distraught, but she hoped it was forceful enough to convince him to continue the journey to England alone. Nevertheless, now that it was done, she felt as if a weight had been lifted from her. She thought she had truly been in love with Joe. She thought she had truly felt passion for him. But those feelings had been taken from her so suddenly that she was now wondering if they had ever been real.

What they had done together filled her with dread and

distress. The memories haunted her, and she constantly tried to stifle them. She was lucky though: when she imagined what would have happened had she conceived a child, she almost writhed in agony—and yes, relief to know definitely that they hadn't.

Now that she knew the truth about Joe, it surprised her to find that her heart did not ache for lost love. Rather, she grieved for the pain he would feel. She agreed that he should be spared the awful truth.

She missed his company already, and she knew with certainty that she would not develop romantic feelings for anyone else in the near future. It just seemed so tragic when she reflected on what romantic love had done to Aunt Elizabeth, to Uncle Joseph, to her own father, and now to herself and Joe. It was not worth it. Better to find some other purpose in life, she thought, some useful occupation or goal that brought reward to the soul, and not a romance that ended in shreds and destroyed those involved.

∞∞∞

Only the day after they had arrived in Bangkok, and despite being preoccupied keeping Joe busy with trivial matters, Elizabeth managed to find a house on Sapatoum Road near the Belgian community. She had learnt to speak French quite well as a girl and had often met French missionaries in the north. She always enjoyed the chance to speak the language whenever she could, so she was hoping to get along with the Belgians, though of course they were at pains to point out that they were not "French", as such.

The house was a modest two-storey wooden building, with slatted windows and a verandah that had been added by the previous occupants, a Belgian legal adviser to the Siamese Ministry of Justice, and his wife.

Over the years, Elizabeth had acquired an impressive collection of northern Siamese artefacts, including lacquered pots etched with gold leaf, lengths of silk in brilliant colours and patterns, and exquisitely-painted paper umbrellas. She had always made wonderful decorative use of her treasures, so that within a few days, the house was starting to look like a home. Their servants had once again moved with them, Simon happy to be back in Bangkok and Kob excited to live in the city and to give their children more opportunities for education and future employment.

Joe wondered if his mother really would return to England one day. He was amazed at her strength of character, at the way she had seemed to rally after Joseph's death. She was still somewhat quiet and withdrawn, but that was to be expected.

He was also surprised that she had raised the question of Kesri only once since her meeting with Sam, but he guessed she had other things on her mind. Unfortunately, as she had told him, that talk with his uncle had not resulted in either of them changing their minds, so Joe had simply made no comment and continued with the original plan to elope. She would be disappointed in him, but he was sure she would get over it, especially when grandchildren came along.

He had not seen Kesri, but they had made their plans before he'd left for Chiengmai, consolidated with further messages since. In a few short days, they would be on their way to England. His mother, believing that he must hurry back to continue his education, had assured him she would be fine by herself and did not need him to stay on. Soon, he reassured himself, Kesri would be his bride and would lie beside him every night. She might even be pregnant by the time they reached England.

Little did he know that his messages sent to her since his return to Bangkok had been intercepted by Sam. Indeed, that they would never have reached her anyway, since she was at Bang Pa-In with family friends.

Elizabeth bustled into Joe's room one afternoon, tutting disapprovingly when she saw the way Joe was packing his trunk. She waved him away. "Joe, you should have let Kob do this. You're absolutely hopeless. Where's your mind at these days? You can't pack like that. Anything breakable will be smashed to bits and your clothes will be completely crushed. Go and get Kob, will you? She and I will do this sensibly between us."

∞∞∞

Joe waited at the docks, ready to board a boat that would take them out to the ship. He had said goodbye to his mother at home, telling her it would be easier on both of them if she did not come to see him off. Surprisingly, she had not objected.

Kesri was late, but he was not yet concerned. Perhaps she was having trouble getting away, or perhaps her father was late leaving home for his club. They had plenty of time. It couldn't have been her luggage causing the problem. She had agreed to pack only one small bag instead of a trunk, to avoid arousing the suspicions of the servants when she left. In Singapore, he would buy her enough to make do for the journey, and when they reached England, an entire trousseau if she liked. Money would not be a problem. He ran a hand over his jacket pocket once more, feeling within the narrow gold band he had bought for her that would seal their marriage in effect, if not in law.

An hour later, she had still not arrived. Time was getting short, with the boat waiting to leave. He paced the dock with increasing anxiety. The last passengers were boarding the steamer and if she did not arrive within minutes, it would leave without them.

Then a boy raced up to him and thrust a letter into his

hands. "Mr Joe?" he said, and when Joe nodded, he quickly disappeared again. With a great sense of foreboding, Joe ripped open the missive and read it, all the while the boatman urging him to hurry.

He scanned the letter quickly, unable to believe it. Was it some kind of joke? Perhaps she was hiding and, in a moment, would appear, giggling and hugging him. But it could not possibly be a hoax, it would be too cruel.

As he read the letter a second time—slowly so that each word stabbed at him—he began to grasp its truth. It was her handwriting, not a forgery. She was not coming, and his heart seemed to sink to his stomach. His shoulders sagged and there was a great constriction to his throat and chest, as if the life were being squeezed out of him.

The boatman called again, and Joe was torn in two. He could not make her marry him against her will; he could not force her to love him. She was very young—had he overestimated her feelings? Had he seen in her a maturity that simply wasn't there? He guessed that she had finally been unable to disobey her father, even though she claimed the opposite.

The boatman was now in a frenzy. He jumped from the boat and tugged at Joe's sleeve, begging him to jump aboard. Joe looked one last time toward the temples of the city. Then he turned and looked down the Chao Phya River, to where the steamer was lying midstream. In another instant, he had leapt into the waiting boat, and a short time later he was on the ship, where he went straight to his cabin and locked the door.

He could not see Siam as he left, and through his tears he could barely face up to the truth that Kesri was forever lost to him.

Chapter 36

Sam showed Elizabeth into the front room. "I haven't seen you in nearly two months—since Christmas," he said. "Why don't you visit more often?"

She smiled and shrugged. "I'm much busier with Joe gone than I ever expected to be." She took off her gloves and hat—a large-brimmed affair of the type that had become so fashionable lately—and set them beside her on the sofa. Sam poured her a sherry and they chatted about various acquaintances.

"And how is Kesri?" Elizabeth asked. "I understand she's become very involved with charity work."

"It's a full-time occupation for her these days. It's not pleasant work for a young girl, though. But she says she's happy to feel useful, and I'm glad for her. Time enough yet to find a husband."

"Is there no young man in her life?"

"None," he replied. "Oh, plenty ask after her, but she's not interested in any of them, it would seem."

"She will be, when she's ready. She's still only 19, after all—hardly an old maid. People are getting married much later these days. Don't worry about her. Let her make the most of her freedom while she has it."

"You're right, I shouldn't worry. And how's Joe? Is he doing well at Oxford?"

"Yes, marvellously well. Actually, he's the reason I've come to see you."

"Oh?" He noticed her eyes were sparkling with happiness.

THE SISTERS OF SIAM

"I've received a letter from him, in which he gives me the happy news that he's engaged to be married."

"That's wonderful. So, he really is over the ... disappointment of last year."

"He assures me he's very much in love with a Miss Victoria Crossley. A lady *graduate*, no less!"

"Interesting. What is her field?"

"She intends to become a doctor. You see what I mean, Sam—we women are catching up with you men. Look at Kesri and her photography."

He smiled. "And when is the wedding?"

"In August, before university starts for the year. And that's what I wanted to talk to you about particularly. Joe has asked if perhaps you would like to accompany me to the wedding."

She took a sheet of writing paper from her bag and unfolded it. "As he says, '*Uncle Sam is my closest male relative, and it would be an honour if he would consent to escort you to England for the happy event.*'"

She looked concerned then, pre-empting his questions. "He doesn't know anything, of course, Sam. All he knows is that Kesri changed her mind. It seems as if he's forgiven us for our opposition to what we considered an unsuitable marriage ..." Her voice trailed off as she awaited his answer.

He needed to think for only a moment. "Very well, I accept. I'll look forward to travelling for the first time to England. There might even be a travel story in it for me, you never know."

To be present at Joe's wedding, even though Joe would never know their true relationship, would be the closest he could come to acting as his real father. The irony of him being considered a sort of surrogate father was not lost on Sam, either.

"It really seems as if this will all work out for the best," she said. "At least, I hope so."

"I hope so, too. But there's something else I'd like to see

happen to complete the circle."

"And what's that?"

"I'll tell you on the ship."

She did not mention it then, but she too had decided it was time to lay to rest the final ghost from the past. Their conversation had convinced her. It would be the act that would finally free her from the mistakes of the past, the end of her guilt, pain and regret.

∞∞∞

Indian Ocean, May 1905

She had not felt so relaxed and worry-free in years—perhaps ever. The new super-liners were the last word in luxury. The vessel's interior was fitted with highly-polished dark mahogany panelling, delicate white and gold trim on walls and ceilings, and electric lamps throughout. A magnificent stained-glass dome rose over 30 feet through the ship's two decks. There was a stylish drawing room with walls of carved satinwood and cedar, and an elaborate mantelpiece over the fireplace. Her luxuriously-appointed suite, next to Sam's, consisted of a sitting room and bedroom, and the whole gave the impression of an exclusive, very expensive hotel—which, of course, it was.

She felt that she and Sam had, for the first time in their lives, developed a comfortable friendship. She discovered a sensitive, caring side to him that she had forgotten. In turn, he discovered a quick intelligence about her that he had not thought important in their early days when they were lovers. They dined together each night, walked on the promenade deck, then said goodnight with a gentle handshake, before retiring to their respective cabins. She owed it to Joseph's memory, she continually reminded herself, to forget what had passed between herself and Sam so long ago.

This was not always possible. One evening, after a wonderful meal, at which Sam had been at his most charming and they had lingered for an extra glass of wine, she found herself unable to sleep. Eventually, she did, but it was only to dream of him. They were on a house-boat together on the Chao Phya River, drifting, oblivious to where they went. Then the lights of London twinkled ahead of them and he turned to her and smiled, his eyes crinkling at the corners. He reached for her and she floated into his arms, and he began to remove her clothing, piece by piece, on the open deck of the boat.

She awoke, trembling and shivering, even though there was also a slick of perspiration on her brow. After more than two decades, she still wanted him, still yearned for his body beside hers. She realised that, throughout her marriage, she had always held some of herself back. That was the part that belonged to him, and him alone. She deeply regretted the affair—it had not been right in any way—but her feelings for him, she now discovered, had never changed.

The next night, she dressed with even more care than usual, in a low-necked, white silk dress. She smiled to herself as she thought how shocked her grandmother would have been to see her now. "Never be a slave to fashion," the old lady had said. "Never drop a neckline purely because everyone else does. It won't suit you."

It might not have suited her then, but it did now, and she felt she had earned the right to dress as she pleased. She had become her own woman and the light of confidence shone from her eyes. Her hair was pinned up softly, and she wore elbow-length white gloves on her slender arms. Her face was still smooth, with only a few lines, and the dark circles and weariness of the last year had vanished. In the dim lighting, she could have passed for 30.

When he met her in the lobby, his gaze swept over her and lingered below her bare shoulders. She felt flushed and excited, almost like she had that first time so many years ago. When dinner was over, they danced again, his warm hand on

her back, his breath brushing her neck as he held her close—
and the years spun away.

She allowed herself to imagine them once more as the
innocent girl and the young adventurer, opposites captivated
by each other and unable to let go. But she allowed her waking
thoughts to go no further. They were no longer those people
and she was wiser now. There had been so many hard lessons,
so much left unsaid, and so much pain over those years. And
yet, he was still the man she wanted after all that time.

Instead of leading her back to the table, he steered
her toward the door and out to the deck, where the breeze
was blowing gently, and where couples were strolling, some
with champagne glasses in hand. She breathed deeply as they
walked in silence. Toward the bow, he stopped and leaned on
the rail, looking out into the blackness, as if deep in thought.
She leaned against the rail, too, facing inward to the ship. He
moved closer, first winding his fingers through hers, then pulling her gently toward him. She went willingly, her arms circ-
ling his neck now, and they kissed gently for the first time in so
many years.

Soon, she pushed him away a little and looked round,
flustered. "Sam, stop. What will people think?"

"I don't care," he answered, then took her hand and led
her along in the direction of their cabins. She offered no resistance.

Inside, he opened the door of her suite, and she was at
first disappointed when he took her hand and raised it to his
lips—thinking he would only say goodnight as usual. But then
he stepped into the room with her, closed the door, and kept
her hand, brushing with his lips the soft, sensitive skin between each finger.

They kissed once more, deeply this time, removing
each other's clothes until they lay scattered on the floor
around them. She stood naked with her legs apart—not timid,
but revelling in his admiration—as he knelt below her, his
tongue tracing its way over her stomach. He moved down be-

tween her thighs, and she cried out in pleasure, running her fingers wildly through his hair. He stood then, turned her away from him, wrapped one of his legs around her to steady her, and was soon within her. When he withdrew and turned her to face him once more, they both sank to the floor, continuing their quest among the rustling white silk of her fallen dress.

∞∞∞

Hours later—after they had fallen into her bed and slept —they lay awake in each other's arms with only the distant sound of the waves crashing against the side of the ship to break the silence. When, finally, Sam spoke, what he said surprised her.

"I may be moving house when we get back to Bangkok," he said.

"Really? Why is that?" It seemed such a strange subject to bring up there and then, she thought.

"Well the house was Edward's, as you know, and was left to Anchalee and me. But there are so many memories there. Too much history. I want to make a fresh start when I marry again."

There was an awful sinking feeling inside her. She should have realised. "So, you're thinking of remarrying?" She felt self-conscious now and moved away from him, wrapping the sheet more tightly about her.

He made no attempt to stop her. "As soon as possible, yes."

"I'm sorry, I had no idea. I would never have asked you to come if I'd known." And would never have given herself to him again if she had, she thought.

"Elizabeth, you and I have known each other a long time. We've been through so much and I once caused you so much anguish. More than once, actually. I owed it to you to come to England."

Was that why he had agreed? Because he thought himself in her debt?

"So that's what you meant when you said there was one more thing that would make your happiness complete—that you wanted to marry again?"

"That's right. But I didn't think you'd even remember I'd said it."

"Had you met her then?"

He seemed to find that amusing and grinned slyly in the way that had always both repelled and attracted her at the same time. "Yes, I'd met her then. I'd known her for years, in fact."

"Do you mind if I ask you who she is?"

"I'll tell you on one provision."

"And what's that?"

"That from now, we share a bed every night for the rest of the passage."

Was that all he saw her as? Someone to satisfy his physical needs while he was away from the woman he was to marry? After all this time, did he still think of her only as a mistress to toy with? She sighed deeply, not angry, but disappointed.

"I'm surprised you could ask me that, Sam, given what you've just told me. You know I won't agree."

He didn't object as she left the bed and began to dress, and he watched and waited until she was finished.

"Are you against sleeping with your future husband, then?"

She turned quickly back to him. "What do you mean?"

He was smiling broadly now. "Haven't you guessed?"

"Guessed what?"

"It's you. She's you."

"Who's me? I don't understand."

He got up, reached for his silk robe and strode up to her. He pulled her gently to him, facing her with his hands on her shoulders. "It's you, Elizabeth. You're the one I want to marry.

I've fallen in love with you all over again. Or perhaps I never stopped loving you. And this time, I don't want to lose you."

She said nothing, so amazed was she by his revelation.

"We're both free now," he continued. "Free to do what we should have done all those years ago. Only now we can, without hurting anyone. It might be a little tricky with Joe and Kesri at some stage, I admit, but—well they're adults now. Say yes, Elizabeth, just say yes."

She looked into his eyes, and found herself speechless. Seeing her faltering, he realised he could not expect her immediate answer. "You'll need time, I know. But I love you, and we belong together. Please think about it, Elizabeth. We could have many good years together."

Later, in her bed alone, she could not sleep, despite her fatigue. She did love him, undoubtedly, but it was the freedom she had that was stopping her from deciding in his favour. Marriage was no longer what she wanted or needed from him, she realised. She had been taken care of by others all her life. Now that poor Joseph was gone, she was completely herself. She had no man to look after her now—but did she need one? With Joe away, she had proven to herself that she could survive alone.

What had happened tonight was different. It was something she felt had to be done. It was desire, yes—but it was also a way of closing one chapter and moving on to the next. She was not even sure of what she would do yet, but it would be a decision she alone would make.

Explaining it to him the next day was much harder. She knew he would do his utmost to convince her otherwise, but she was prepared.

Nevertheless, when she told him, to her surprise he

quickly came to terms with her decision, though he did make a final plea: "I'd give you every freedom, Elizabeth. I'd never try to possess you, and you could do as you liked."

"Yes, but don't you see? That's just it. I don't want even to be in the position where someone else can choose to 'give' me my freedom—or not. I want to be in charge of my own destiny. I've finally become independent, Sam, and I like it. What happened between us last night ... just happened. I don't regret it. Please say you don't, either."

"Of course I don't."

"But it cannot, and will not, ever happen again. I love you, Sam—I can say that with honesty. But I'm no longer *in* love with you. I've gone beyond that. Now I know we can be real friends, not lovers, not husband and wife, and this time, it is right, and good."

He took her outstretched hand and together they looked out from the deck across the vast ocean, and he knew their love affair was over. But in its place was the greatest friendship he had known, and that was enough. He felt old and wise and fulfilled.

"Well, let's go to a wedding anyway—just for the hell of it," he said, grinning. "Our son's wedding."

Epilogue

The young woman lifted the dying child so he could sip weakly from a glass of water she offered him.

"You must see he gets enough fluids," Kesri told the boy's mother, who she noticed was several years younger than herself. "Try not to use river water. But if you have to, make sure you boil it properly first. Fifteen minutes, at least."

The mother shrugged with hopelessness. "There's no other water until the wet season. We used our stored rainwater months ago. There's barely any wood for a fire and we can't afford to buy any."

It was a familiar story, and Kesri felt powerless to help the thousands of people who died from cholera because they had to drink the filthy water from the klongs and river. She gently laid the child on the dirt floor of the lean-to shelter and covered him with the rags that were all his mother could provide. At least it was not cold, and no one froze to death here, she thought. But the boy would die soon, anyway—probably that night.

She excused herself quickly and left, so the boy's mother would not see the tears in her eyes. Once outside, she breathed deeply and tried to compose herself. In a few more minutes, she would have to visit another fetid shack, then another after that, and so it would go on. She would see similar tragedies in all and would be powerless to help any of them. All she could do was try to make the dying a little more comfortable and hold the hands of the grieving.

"It doesn't get any easier, does it?" an older woman emerging from another bamboo-and-thatch hut said kindly. She came over to Kesri and put a consolatory arm round the young woman.

Fanny Knox was the daughter of Sir Thomas Knox, who had been the British Consul in Bangkok in the 1860s and 1870s, and his high-born Siamese wife, Prang Yen. Unbeknown to Kesri, he was the same man her grandfather had met all those years ago when Edward first came to Siam.

∞∞∞

Fanny's story was legendary in both expatriate and Siamese circles in Bangkok, but had probably been embellished in its telling over the decades. Fanny herself preferred to talk only of the present and her work in helping the city's poor and ill.

As the story went, in 1875, aged 19, Fanny had returned to Siam from her schooling in Europe and soon fell in love with a Siamese nobleman, Phra Pricha, a widower 14 years her senior. He was a member of the wealthy and influential Amatayakun family and was a personal friend of King Chulalongkorn. Such was his wealth, that when he had discovered gold in his province, he had not retained the profits for himself, but had presented them to the state.

At the same time, however, Sri Sriyawongse, the then powerful chief minister who had been regent until King Chulalongkorn reached maturity, decided Fanny should marry his grandson, Nai Dee. The match was politically important for Sri Sriyawongse and Knox agreed the union would be fortuitous. Fanny, however, had other ideas. Without her parents' blessing or attendance, she married Phra Pricha at his house in Bangkok and the newlyweds then travelled to his upcountry estate in Prachin.

Meanwhile, Sri Sriyawongse, his plans thwarted, was determined the two should not be allowed to live contentedly. Within weeks of the wedding, Pricha was summoned to Bangkok, where he was arrested and charged with—among other things—insulting the King by marrying without his permission, mismanaging his estate, embezzling state money, and mistreating and murdering workers in the gold mine. He was found guilty of the crimes and—amid debate over the fairness of his trial and the verdict—was eventually publicly executed at Prachin.

Fanny escaped to Europe with her and Pricha's baby son, and with his two children from his previous marriage. She could easily have remarried, having many admirers, and spent her time in quiet retreat in England, but instead, Fanny embarked upon a wild and unmanageable plan to help the French in Cambodia annex Siam and so, she reasoned, abolish what she saw as a corrupt system that gave men such as Sri Sriyawongse such power.

However, Fanny mellowed with age, and after Sri Sriyawongse died in 1883, she returned to Bangkok and rented a small house off New Road. King Chulalongkorn even granted her an annuity, and she decided to devote the remainder of her life to helping the poor and powerless in Siam.

Kesri had heard her father tell Fanny's story, although she did not dare talk to Fanny herself about it. Indeed, Sam had known Fanny since she was young, because her sister, Caroline, had married his old friend Louis Leonowens, who in fact had initially wanted to marry Fanny himself. Sadly, Caroline had died in 1893 when she was only 35, and Louis had remarried in 1899 to a young Australian woman named Reta. Sam still saw Louis and Reta from time to time, although they had just been on a long trip to England and Canada.

∞∞∞

They walked silently to their next patient until Fanny noticed that Kesri still looked disturbed. "Still thinking about that poor child?"

"Actually, I was thinking of you," Kesri replied. "How do you do it, Fanny? Day after day, year after year. Doesn't it make you feel despondent? It's so hopeless."

"It's not hopeless at all," Fanny retorted rather too firmly, before continuing more softly. "Even if we can bring only comfort and a shoulder to cry on, that's something. I believe we're bringing real help to people who need it."

"I'm sorry," Kesri said. "Of course we are. And I love the work, I really do. I'm just having a bad day."

"Why don't you go home early? Forget about all this for a few hours. I can see you've got other things on your mind."

"You make me feel guilty for admitting I have. Compared to these poor people, my problems are slight."

"Do you want to talk about anything, my dear? I'm a good listener."

"There's nothing to say, really. It's just that it's a year ago today that—." She couldn't continue. Her eyes filled with tears, and she had to look away.

Now Fanny understood. "Did he break your heart, dear?"

"Actually, I think I broke his. I didn't want to, but it was simply impossible for us to be together. My feelings were changed when I was told about something that happened before I was born—something that neither of us could have known about. It meant we could never be together, never be married."

"Our lives very rarely go the way we plan," Fanny said gently. "But you'll see, good will come of this if you let it. Perhaps it already has. If I'm right, it was this experience that sent you to me, wasn't it?"

Kesri nodded. "My father suggested it, and I'm glad he did. I have some purpose now."

∞∞∞

When she arrived home, she found a package waiting for her in the parlour. It was so heavy that at first, she thought it might be a shipment of her father's new novel. Then she saw that it had not come from overseas, but just from somewhere else in Bangkok. Perhaps he had left it as a surprise for her while he was away. He had been gone only four days, but already she missed him.

He had asked her to go to England with him—not, of course, to attend the wedding, that would have been too awkward, he knew. But he felt she would enjoy the sights of London, and might even want to travel on to Paris. She turned him down, however, preferring to continue her work, and telling him she would go to England when she had to, in another 18 months or so, but not before. Besides, she did not care to be reminded of her half-brother and what he had meant to her.

Today, however, she had not been able to put him out of her mind, given that it was a year to the day since he had left. The distress over what she had had to do was still raw, and it would be a long time yet before she would recover her spirit.

Sam had not been happy at her insistence on staying in the house with only the servants. He had suggested she stay with Louis and Reta, or some other older couple, but she had been adamant, and eventually, he had acceded. He felt he could not deny her much, after what she had been through, and he could trust her not to use his absence for further romantic interludes. In fact, he was positive nothing of that kind would occur for a while to come, if her mood and demeanour were any indication. That was not surprising—she had had a great shock. She seemed to have regained her good humour though, and there was always Fanny Knox, with whom he had already had a quiet word, to keep an eye on her.

Kesri cut open the package, and inside found an envelope and a square, wrapped box. The envelope contained a letter from Elizabeth, of all people.

May 10ᵗʰ, 1905

My dear Kesri,

You will be surprised indeed to receive this delivery from me, and the mystery of it will be revealed to you shortly in this letter. The package itself, which I am sure you are anxious to open, contains a legacy from your grandfather, Edward Fairburn, originally bestowed upon me when he passed away. Its provenance is explained in the contents of another envelope within.

As he requested in his will, I have always kept the contents of this package a secret; no one knows of it, including your father. To be honest, I have never known what to do with it, but your grandfather said in his letter regarding it that I would know what to do when the time was right. I think that time has come, Kesri, and I believe you are the right person to have it.

As you will discover, the legacy does not have a noble history. Far from it. What you will find in this package was gained as the result of a gross error of judgement by my father. It was a sin he fully acknowledged and regretted at his death, but did not feel able to admit to or atone for in his lifetime. I have even made discreet enquiries in Australia via a private detective, but he could discover no information of the other party concerned, so presumably there are no other heirs or claimants.

Anyway, my dear, please read the enclosed material carefully, try to forgive your grandfather and use this treasure wisely, so that out of such recklessness, some good may come.

Your loving Aunt,
Elizabeth

She unwrapped the package and a large tin box emerged, about 18 inches square, and the same in depth. She levered open the lid—it was too heavy for her to lift out of the surrounding package—and peered inside.

The huge gold nugget, partly covered in quartz as it had emerged from the ground, was positively the last thing she had ever expected to see, and the brilliance of it overwhelmed her. She had seen pictures of similar nuggets in books, and had once seen a real gold nugget at an exhibition, but never anything like this. She ran her finger along the rough surface.

The second envelope lay on top of the huge nugget, and it had already been opened—by Elizabeth, of course, she realised.

Eager to understand—and imagining that her aunt most have felt exactly as she did now when she first saw the nugget—she reached inside the envelope and withdrew a letter and a very old newspaper article. She unfolded the clipping and saw it was a page torn from *The Argus* of Melbourne, dated Monday, October 8, 1866, making it nearly 50 years old. One of the articles had been circled in ink.

BARMAID DIES IN BALLAARAT FIRE.
ALLEGED GOLD NUGGET MISSING.

(FROM OUR OWN REPORTER.)

BALLAARAT, Saturday.
A young woman perished in a domestic blaze in Bridge Street on October 6 last, the house well alight and its sole occupant deceased by the time the volunteer fire brigade arrived. The woman was: Celia Mary Marsden, 26, employed as a barmaid at the Grand Royal Hotel.

Miss Marsden, a Sydneysider who had been in Ballaarat for five years, was believed to have found gold recently on her claim, in the form of a nugget reportedly weighing some 35 lbs. gross. The gold was not found in the house after the fire, and friends and colleagues of Miss Marsden are claim-

ing it to have been the motive for thievery. As they allege, the culprits, on having been discovered by Miss Marsden, then set the house alight before making their escape with the loot. An inspection of the bedroom whence the conflagration originated, however, has revealed it was possibly the result of a smouldering cigar, the smoking of which is most generally reserved as a masculine pursuit. Presumably, Miss Marsden ...

She did not want to read on for the moment. Had Grandfather been a thief—or worse? She turned to the old letter.

To whom it may concern,

> *That you are reading this letter means that I have passed away. At the time I first lodged this treasure with my London solicitors, Harbeck & Harbeck, the year was 1867 and I was a young man expecting a long life ahead of me. But now, as I write this, it is late 1885, and I know that I shall soon die.*

> *My solicitors, as directed by my will, have been ordered to dispatch this package soon after my death to my daughter, Mrs Elizabeth Shaw, even though I feel almost certain she will not wish to retain this bequest, but will, as I have suggested in a separate letter to her, pass it on to someone, who will use it for some good purpose. You are that person.*

> *From the moment I acquired it, this gold has been as heavy a burden upon me as if I were wearing it around my neck like a millstone. The accompanying newspaper article will tell you that it is associated with an event which I now bitterly regret. However, I beg that you do not judge me until you have read this, my own explanation of that unfortunate time. My hope is that you will conclude that, while reprehensible, there was nothing malicious in my actions.*

> *The gold nugget, discovered by myself on a claim I worked with one Celia Marsden—the woman mentioned in the article— actually weighs twenty-eight pounds and four ounces (not thirty-*

five, as reported), of which I am assured that, after separation, around twenty-three pounds of pure gold will be retrieved, the remainder being quartz.

While it is worth only a small fortune when compared with that which I have bequeathed my heirs from other sources, it is most important to me that it is used in such a way as to do some good to replace the evil of its acquisition. The events I will describe happened long ago, long before I came to see the true path my life should take and before ever I listened to, and heeded, God's word. You must now forgive me for having to speak so frankly in the following explanation, but it must be done.

In the newspaper item accompanying this letter, you will read that the young woman in question, Miss Marsden, died in a suspicious fire, and that it was widely believed that the person who stole the gold nugget was responsible for her death. I confess, here and now, that I was the intruder who broke into her house that night, but must state absolutely that I was not responsible for the fire. I also regret to say that Miss Marsden was more to me than a business acquaintance, the circumstances of which will be explained in due course.

At that time, I was at the Ballaarat goldfields working as a photographer. I also prospected occasionally, although I must say that I was never serious in that endeavour, since my photography provided me with a comfortable income. For me, prospecting was more of an adventurous diversion, at which I never expected any success. It was on one of these diversionary occasions, however, that Miss Marsden and I discovered this gold together. Needless to say, we were both astounded at our good fortune, and we entered into a verbal agreement, as I shall explain, about what we would do as a result of the find. She did not honour that agreement and I went to her house that night merely to retrieve what I saw, at the time, as rightfully mine.

I, a young man with a troubled marriage, was besotted with Miss Marsden, falling for her artfully practised charms like a fool. I was blinded to her true nature, and although I had heard rumours that she was an opportunist, a prostitute in all but name, I did not care to listen. To me, she was exciting, vibrant, carefree and yes, dangerous, while my own wife forever consumed me with guilt for my causing her the pain and disappointment of numerous pregnancies, in which all but one of our children miscarried or died soon after birth. Our beautiful daughter, Elizabeth, survived, and I should have been content with that. To my greater shame now, I was not, and when I met Miss Marsden, I could not help myself.

I did not realise it then, and in retrospect I am wiser: Celia Marsden actually despised men and would exploit them for whatever she could gain. Still, as I confessed earlier, when I first met her, at the Grand Royal Hotel, Ballaarat, I was infatuated with her, and we immediately formed a liaison. She told me she wanted to try her hand on the tailings at the Sovereign Hill goldfields, and even though I did not think it appropriate for a woman to become a digger, she was adamant, so I purchased our equipment and we staked a claim. Any day she had free from her work as a barmaid at the hotel, she would be there, working the claim as hard as any man. I had fooled myself into thinking I was in love with her and that eventually, we would run off together—even though for me this would mean deserting my wife and child.

With hindsight, I know it could never have worked and would have led to my complete destruction. I have asked myself time and time again, would I really have gone with her? Or would I have seen sense? I knew very well that if I went through with this outrageous and nonsensical plan, my family in England would disown me and would likely work out a way to disinherit me. I would then be left without a penny and would have to rely on my own resources. I was doing well with my photography and earning enough to keep Charlotte and Elizabeth. But whereas Charlotte was a frugal woman who did not covet fancy clothes and jewels, I knew Celia Marsden would require much more to keep her happy.

Anyway, that is by the by. One day, when I was with Miss Marsden on our claim, we did indeed find gold in the form of the sizeable nugget you now see before you. It was strangely isolated, with little other gold around it in the section we had dug, and I prised it out with a pickaxe while she was above, rinsing tailings in a pan and finding only flecks of gold dust. For a mad minute, I considered not telling her, somehow hiding my find and smuggling it out. But it was rather too heavy for that, and I would have had to bury it again until I found myself alone there. Instead, I quietly announced the find to Miss Marsden, telling her not to breathe a word of it to anyone. I truly believed the find was a portent that would enable me to start anew with her. I trusted her, and gave her the nugget for safekeeping.

Almost immediately, however, she began to behave differently toward me. I had heard stories about her other gentleman callers, but she had always maintained they were just acquaintances, which I suppose, in a way, was more accurate, for she cared deeply for none of them. I had wanted to keep our find a secret, so we could leave safely with it, but she could not prevent herself from telling a few "close friends". I soon heard, from other parties, that she intended to move on, alone, and start afresh somewhere else, perhaps to open her own establishment in Sydney. Her plans very obviously did not include me, and eventually she pretended not to know me, refusing to answer her door when I called. She also had me banned from the hotel as a nuisance.

I was furious, but mostly, I suppose, it was my self-esteem that was broken. I had been useful to her, but was now discarded, and she already had a new fancy man to replace me. I felt extremely foolish and more than a little stupid for having contemplated losing my inheritance and my family for her. It was then that I decided to steal back the nugget late one evening while she was in her usual drunken stupor.

On the night in question, the fire must have started to smoulder before I even reached the house, because, as I was removing the gold from her room, the flames suddenly flared. I assume the fire had begun as a result of her falling asleep while smoking a cigarette or cigar, which she delighted in specifically because it was considered unladylike. I beg you to believe me when I say that, although I tried, I could do nothing at all to help her. It was too late for anyone to save her, and I had to escape quickly to save myself. It is true that it was a cowardly act that I did not rush to alert the fire brigade, nor did I ever own up to having taken the gold nugget. After all, I had found it; she had merely been there at the time.

Miss Marsden had no family or dependents that I knew of, and likely would not have left a will at her young age. Thus, I knew that if I did confess, the gold would have been confiscated by the government who had already robbed the poor diggers blind with their licence fees, before the brave Eureka stockade stand in Ballaarat during the 'fifties. In addition, I would surely have been charged with theft at least, and perhaps with murder if they did not believe my story. That was and is a hanging offence, of course.

A detective did visit me at my lodgings in Ballaarat, referred by some rogue from the hotel who had been acquainted with Miss Marsden but usurped by me, and so had a grudge to bear. Luckily, I was able to persuade the detective that I, an English gentleman, had no reason for an attachment to such a common woman, and that I knew her only slightly as the hotel barmaid. A small gratuity helped the detective believe my story. Fortunately, the claim had been registered in her name only.

Although I was determined to keep the gold for myself, it was clear to me that I could never sell it in my lifetime, not only because of the increasing guilt and remorse I felt with its association, but also for the practical reason that I lived in fear of some connection being made if I ever attempted to do so. It was most propitious that I had to return to England about the same time, and so I took the nugget with me in my luggage and deposited it with my solicitors there in a locked box, which they deposited in a bank, never to know the contents.

All the rest of my life I have regretted such a grave error of judgement as taking up with that woman. However, now that I am an old man, staring at death, I have decided that some good must come of this cursed find. I ask only that it be used to finance some project of charity, preferably in Siam, my adopted homeland, where there are many who could benefit.

Edward Benjamin Fairburn

She ran a finger over the nugget once more. It was dazzling, like a golden honeycomb caught in the sunlight. Now that she knew the whole story, she did not think so badly of her grandfather. It had all happened so long ago, nearly half a century.

She knew just what to do with the gold.

January, 1906

There was already a long queue of women waiting outside when she arrived to open the doors. Many carried sick babies, others were ill themselves, and still others were simply curious. Local women in the vicinity of New Road—and from much farther afield—had quickly learnt that you went there to see Khun Kesri if you had nowhere else to turn, if you needed to see a doctor but could not afford to pay, if your children needed vaccinations, or if you were being bulled or abused by your husband or anyone else. She had persuaded several respected Western doctors to work as volunteers at the centre, plus graduates and interns from the Medical School and College in Bangkok that had been established by King Chulalongkorn.

Kesri taught the women about the dangers of consuming contaminated water and food. She taught the girls how to sew, speak English, and to read and write Siamese. Fanny Knox was always willing to give advice, and at the beginning, Kesri would have been lost without her. She had offered Fanny the role of director of the centre, but the older woman had declined, explaining that she preferred to work independently with the young people of Bangkok, particularly the students who would one day become its policy-makers. At 20, Kesri often felt overawed by her own venture, but she also felt strongly that this was her vocation. As she saw it, the sins of the fathers—and indeed, her own sins—were truly being redeemed.

∞∞∞

The carriage stopped outside the house and a woman got out. She stood for a while, observing the mothers and children waiting outside and the activity all around the building. Moments later, her niece appeared at the door and rushed down the pathway to greet her. They embraced, then walked back up the path to the house. Beside the front door, on the wall, was a small brass nameplate. It said *Ban Si Thong*, The Golden House. Kesri waited expectantly for her aunt's reaction. Elizabeth simply smiled, nodded, and took Kesri's hand. The two women went inside together: there was much work to be done.

Afterword

English spellings translating Thai place names and people's names varied widely in the 19th and 20th centuries. In most cases, this novel uses the spelling that was more popularly used in English-language travel writing of the time. All the main characters and the plot in the novel are fictional. However, the storyline is placed in the context of actual events, and many of the peripheral characters are based on real people. Extensive research was conducted for historical accuracy, but some poetic licence was taken to suit the plot. Any errors in interpretation of historical research are the fault of the author.

Acknowledgements

I would like to thank the following for their contributions:

My husband, Gordon Dann, for constant support and encouragement.

My mother, Dr Sheila Eastgate, for first telling me I could be a writer and for being my most enthusiastic reader.

My late father, Dr Harold Eastgate, for information about 19th-century weaponry.

The Siam Society in Bangkok, whose library provided access to extensive historical material used to research this book.

My former colleague in Bangkok, Howard Richardson, for encouraging me to seek a publisher for the first edition, when this book was a manuscript sitting in a drawer.

The writer, Janet McLeod Trotter, author of the India Tea and Raj Hotel series and many other books, for wise advice on producing the second edition of this book, including generously sharing her knowledge of the digital publishing industry.

About The Author

Caron Eastgate Dann

Living in Thailand in the 1990s led Caron to an interest in travel books and guides written about it since the 13th century. In particular, she was fascinated by Thailand as a country that was never colonised, unlike others in the region. Her interest in historical literature provided the research for this novel, originally published as The Occidentals.
Caron later graduated with a PhD from Monash University, Australia, examining representations of Thailand in Western literature, published as Imagining Siam: A travellers' literary guide to Thailand.

Born in Dunedin, New Zealand, Caron was also brought up in the UK and the US, immigrating to Australia as an adult.

She worked as a print-media journalist for more than 20 years, before changing careers to become an academic teaching communications and media studies in Melbourne.

Printed in Great Britain
by Amazon

87470844R00261